An American Nurse in Paris

An American Nurse in Paris

Novels of the Great War

John F Andrews

46 North Publications, LLC

Map of France, May, 1918

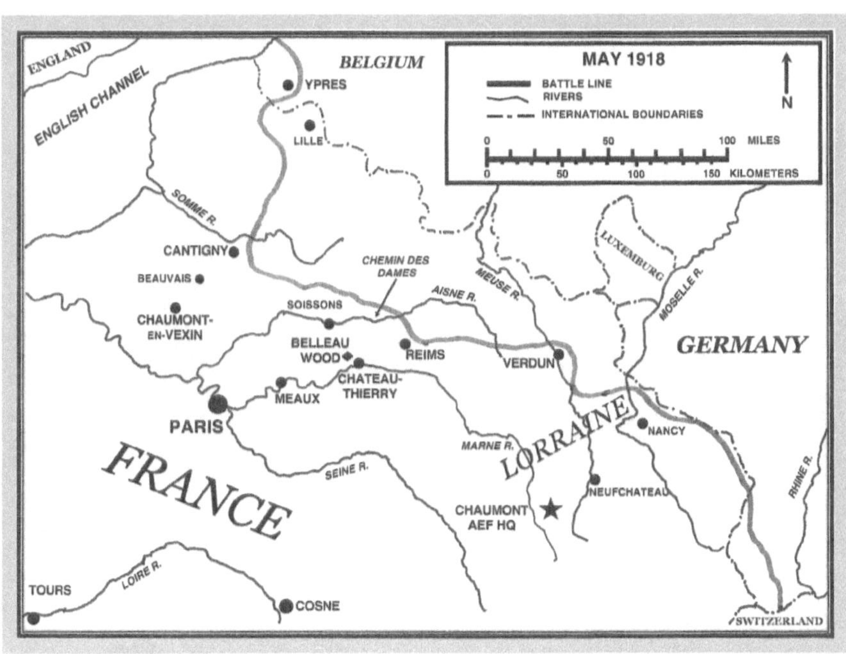

Map of the region of France where the novel takes place

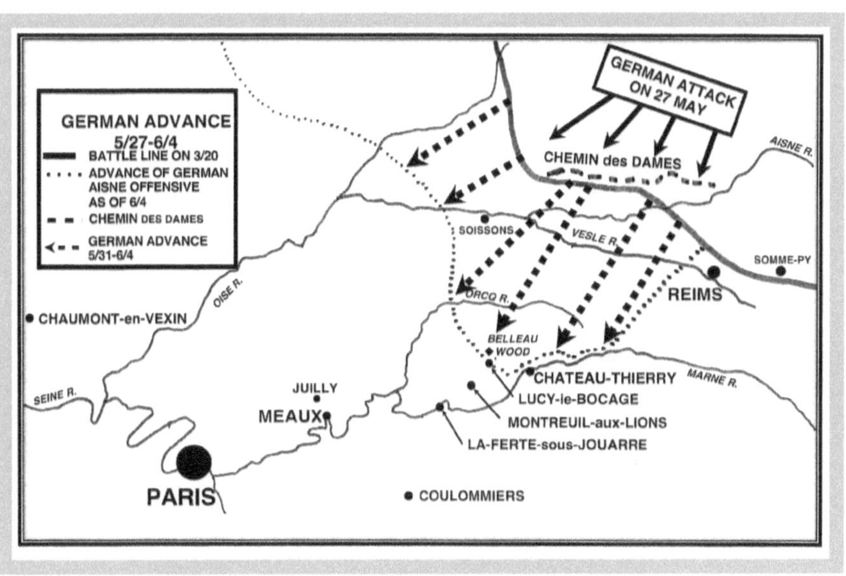

This novel is dedicated to the nurses and doctors who cared for the wounded marines and soldiers from the Battle of Belleau Wood and to the doughboys who put their lives on the line when victory seemed distant and the most they could hope for was to survive.

Chapter One
Alice Simmons

Paris, France, Friday May 24, 1918

They don't need to paint a target on me. I wear a skirt. The only one in the American press corps in France.

This straight-backed wooden chair has tormented me since my arrival at twelve thirty for my meeting at one. It's three thirty.

My bladder is making me regret the extra cup of coffee I had for lunch.

I still my restless right leg. This waiting room is a cubbyhole—hot, humid, and redolent with fumes from the chinless, chain-smoking private sitting behind a metal desk. Germany will have nothing to fear if all the clerks type with one index finger like this fool.

Snick . . .

This is so typical of things since I arrived in Paris. Six male journalists have come and gone since I sat down in this accursed chair. One gave me the familiar smile usually reserved for fashion columnists—the only reporting job most of them think women are suited for. The others ignored me as they passed through. All of them went straight in.

Everything I've done since I arrived in Paris boils down to this one meeting. I was scheduled to meet Colonel McCabe. When I arrived, the one-finger-typing private told me McCabe is out of town. My meeting is now with Major Richard Martel, whom I've never met. They don't *invite* me to the routine briefings he gives the other reporters.

This won't make me give up. I've come too far to quit.

So, this is it—I'll be off to report on the war if this meeting goes well. If not, I might as well hop on the next ship and head back to the States.

Pure professionalism dictated my attire for the day—tan blouse under a dark brown jacket and a summer-weight woolen skirt. The hemline is longer than the mid-calf ones many of the women in Paris wear. I decided to not play an intimidation game with my height, so on went the tan flats. Hell, I'm taller than half the men here and eye to eye with most of the rest. No makeup, of course, and hair in a modest bun —tight ones make the angles of my face look too severe.

I push my glasses up. Damn things—been with me since I was a kid. The good thing is that they make my oddball eye color less obvious. I call them hazel, but there are bits of green and blue. It's as if my parents' genes couldn't make up their minds and compromised on . . . whatever color you want to call them. Today they're hazel. Tomorrow? Maybe greenish.

Someone with less self-respect would doll herself up with makeup, mascara, a little perfume here, and, perhaps, one button less. A touch of elegance? I'd only be kidding myself if I tried. In high school, the home-coming queen wished me a successful career as a librarian as I sat, reading, in a corner by myself during prom. That's who Alice Simmons is— who I am. I don't mind it. Much.

Truth is—it gets lonely. I can only count two close friends in this world. One is in an office a floor below me—Ira Cunningham. The other, his daughter Trudy, is on her way here to work as a nurse. I've got to see Ira after I'm done here. If I'm ever done. If Major Martel will even see me.

"Private?" I ask.

"Lady, you blind or what? Can'tcha see I'm workin'? Count yaself lucky Major Martel'll see you at all." He slaps the carriage return with a ding.

The back door opens. A reporter I don't recognize emerges wearing an expression like he's just eaten an unpeeled lemon. The phone rings on the clerk's desk. He speaks quietly, with a sidelong glance toward me. "Yessir, she's still here." He hangs up. "Simon. Front and center. Major Martel'll see ya. Got two minutes. Make it snappy."

"It's Simmons. Miss Alice Simmons."

The clerk leads me down the hallway and knocks on a closed door.

"Come," says a resonant baritone. The clerk stands in the doorway, leaving just enough room for me to shimmy through sideways. The door clicks behind me. A dribble of sweat trickles down my right side.

Major Martel could have starred in the movies. The term "matinee idol" had been just a whisper before the war, but he fits. Mid-to-late thirties? Brilliantined black hair swept back, wisps of gray at the temples, brooding brows over coal-black eyes, with a pencil mustache above a chiseled chin. I'm not sure about his cologne, but it's not cheap. A partially smoked cigar rests in his cut crystal ashtray. A small silver bifold picture frame lies closed next to a Montblanc fountain pen set. My father has the same set.

Major Martel's eyes flash over me. The quick assessment of an experienced army officer or something else? I pull the lapels of my coat closer before thinking. He spreads his hands, palms up. "Alice, I'm so sorry to make you wait. This is a very busy afternoon. What can I do for you, sweetheart?" Martel's accent flows like Louisiana molasses.

An apology?

Sweetheart?

He doesn't motion me to sit. "I came to request a pass to permit me to report outside Paris. I've written all the stories I can find here. I'm a medical reporter. As far as I know, the only reporter with a medical background here. I trained as a nurse while getting my journalism degree and offer a unique perspective to the folks back home. And I speak fluent French. My problem is that the French won't let me in their Paris hospitals, and all of ours are outside the city. Now, I'm not asking to go anywhere near the fighting, just to the base hospitals, to report on the human side of the medical effort here."

Martel frowns and rubs his hands. No wedding band, but a large golden class ring adorns his right. "Our French *amis* will never approve a *laissez-passer* for a non-accredited reporter."

"Sir, reporters who arrived after me have been going to those places without accreditation. I've served my time here in Paris, been responsible. All my articles comply with your censorship rules. The French have relaxed their earlier restrictions, according to the others." I smile, straightening my shoulders an inch. For all the bad things I've heard about the man, he seems to be listening to me. The flattering glint in his eyes is astonishing. Men don't look at me this way. It's unsettling, and something else—alluring? He's also the most handsome man I've ever met.

"Alice, I regret to inform you that there is simply no opportunity for you to work outside Paris. To go farther afield would be excessively hazardous for a gentle lady like yourself. Current circumstances and the French leave me no choice but to deny your request. Now, mind you, this isn't from me—it comes from on high." He gazes up toward the ceiling as if he gets his orders from God.

"Sir, if I may, I'd like to explain my proposal further—"

"As you can see . . . I'm a very busy man. But I'd like to hear more—under less formal circumstances . . ." The glint reappears.

My ears are on fire. Is he asking for a date? Is this a genuine offer, or just a come-on? Does he care about me, or is he just looking for *female companionship*? "I'm not sure I understand."

"Well, it's fairly simple, my dear. I'm usually free in the evenings around suppertime. Perhaps . . ." His gaze drifts down to my chest and lingers as though weighing my breasts.

I push the glasses up. "Major, I . . . I . . ." I'm dumbstruck. His eyes trickle down to the space between my legs, as though seeing through my skirt. I shift an inch to my left.

A frown gathers on Martel's face, and his eyes cloud. "Alice, I'm sorry, but if there's nothing else, I must get back to my other duties."

"If only you'll reconsider . . ."

"Consider this, Alice." Martel stands and walks around me. I hear the door open. Martel stands beside the doorframe. He cups my left shoulder. "I'm much more . . . attentive . . . after work hours. Your cause may not be lost." A friendly smile grows on his face. A warning rattles underneath my schoolgirl blush.

Chapter Two
Alice Simmons

My heart hammers and blood hums through my limbs on the way to the ladies' room. I close the door and lean against the wall, breathless. He refused my request, but his idea of further discussion leaves me wondering. He was flattering, but a little . . . invasive. And he was so familiar, using my first name—not in a denigrating way, but a friendly one. My mentor and friend, Ira Cunningham, works under Martel and doesn't like him. He's always danced around the reasons for his opinion. Ira's office is the next stop after this. We have to talk.

Ira's office is room 223—I hope he hasn't left for the day. I pop my head in the door and smile at Ira's clerk, Stan.

"Major Cunningham's busy, Miss Simmons." Stan looks up from his typewriter at a small wooden desk next to a closed inner door. His smile is that of a friend.

"I can wait if he isn't going to be tied up too long . . ."

"Talking to a reporter. Take a load off."

The padded cloth seat is a welcome relief. Stan's a good egg. He must have taken the advanced army typing course—he uses both index fingers on his Royal. The anteroom is well ventilated through the transom above the door—with the aroma of the fresh coffee steaming in the brown mug next to Stan's typewriter. I pull out my notebook to look over the scribbles from my morning interview with an industrialist's wife. What sort of vanilla drivel will pass the censors tomorrow? *Paris, May 24, 1918. While the flower of French youth march toward the battlefield, their mothers, sisters, and sweethearts toil in smoky factories, stores, and government offices to keep the home fires burning. With chins raised and smiles on their faces . . .*

Thoughts of Martel keep intruding while I struggle to concentrate. No man has ever treated me with such deference, other than Ira. Courtesy was the last thing I expected, having never gotten it from the army before. But then, the way his eyes seemed to play with me, and his offer to meet . . . after work.

I touch the locket Grand-Mère Elise gave me in my distress when I was ten. Nervous habit. "Remember, *mon lapin*—you are swift like the wind. And strong. Let this remind you," Grand-Mère had said. I smile. *Mon lapin*—"my rabbit"—her nickname for me. I was a fast runner, then.

The inner door opens, breaking my reverie. Ira Cunningham pokes his head out and starts to say something to Stan. A smile grows on his face. "Alice. Come in. There's someone I want you to meet." Ira has an uncanny way of making me feel expected.

He's been "Mr. Cunningham" to me since he came into my life when I was twelve, when he and his family moved into the house next to ours in Minneapolis. It seems awkward to call him Major. Now, at twenty-four, I'm privileged to use his first name when we're alone, though it feels a bit like calling my parents by their first names. He stands two inches taller than my five-ten, with short graying brown hair rimming his bald head and a tight mustache. He looks like the newspaper editor he was before the war—serious eyes, jowls that tighten under pressure, and a few pounds too many from all the time he spends at the desk he describes as his "command."

Ira motions me into his office with a flourish of his hand like a royal invitation. A middle-aged man in a brown two-piece suit with a fedora balanced on his knee sits in a guest chair. A battered leather portfolio leans against a chair leg. The man rises and stands eye-to-eye with me as he extends his right hand. "Howard Enright, *Detroit News*."

"Alice is my protégé, Howard," Ira says. "*Wisconsin State Journal*'s rising star. I like to think I taught her everything she knows, but I'm pretty sure she surpassed me a while ago."

"Been here long?" Howard asks.

"Five months." I take a seat.

"Must know your way around by now."

"I spent several summers here when I was a kid, and then a semester in college." At the time it had felt more like exile—a way to get me out of my parents' sight when my very presence seemed to repel them. Grandmother and Paris were my saviors.

"Getting much work?"

I huff and roll my eyes. "I've interviewed every matron who hasn't fled the city."

"While a war rages just out of earshot." Howard shakes his head.

He has a medium build with broadish shoulders, trim, not paunchy like Ira. I'm bursting to tell Ira about the meeting, but not in front of a stranger.

"Better shove off," Howard says. "Why don't you both join Emily and me at the New York Bar Saturday evening. Pete and Mary Sloan'll be there. Say, about nine?"

"I can't, sorry," Ira says. "Alice, if you ignore Howard and his bombastic friend, you'll find their wives delightful."

"If you say so. I'll be there," I say. Howard leaves, closing the door with a soft click on his way out.

Ira's chair squeals as he leans back. "Trudy'll arrive tomorrow or the next day."

"Where's she going to work?" I haven't seen my best friend in over six months.

"American Red Cross Military Hospital One in Neuilly-sur-Seine."

"Penny for your thoughts?" I know that look. Something's eating him.

"Feeling a little guilty, truth be told."

"Go on." I pull a handkerchief from my purse and polish my glasses.

"I got you into this."

"You didn't make me come here."

He loosens his tie. "I played my part in convincing you to be a journalist instead of a nurse."

I twirl my glasses by one earpiece. "If I'd done that, I'd be with Trudy, working as a nurse, about to arrive." Ira's face is painted with worry. He's been more of a father than mine, more of a friend than my mother.

"If I knew you'd have to deal with Martel and our esteemed fellow journalists, I would have told you to join the Nurse Corps, like Trudy."

"If you were me, would you have listened when you were my age?"

Ira shrugs, then gives me a sheepish grin. "Hell, I was only five years older than you are now when the coppers came gunning for me. The first time." His mouth twitches.

"Sometimes you have to take on city hall, no matter the consequences."

"No." Ira's face pales, his mouth tight. "Consequences matter. If I learned anything in St. Paul, it was that." He pauses to take a deep breath. "Sometimes you have to take a different angle."

"How did that go?"

"O'Connor's still St. Paul's police chief." Ira stands. "And my family and I are alive."

That was unfair of me. Ira had rooted out the corruption surrounding the St. Paul chief of police. He had reported on the bribes Chief O'Connor took to look the other way when wanted criminals holed up in St. Paul. Ira nearly died for the effort more than once. His courage had changed nothing. But he had been courageous, nevertheless.

"How'd things go with Martel?"

I slip my glasses on and stand. "Let's talk over a drink. I need the sage advice you usually only offer after I ply you with scotch. Maybe two."

Chapter Three
Alice Simmons

Ira leads the way out of the building. Neither of us speak as we walk north three blocks, then take a right toward our favorite bar. I'm still digesting my encounter with Martel. There's something about Ira's eyes that belies his otherwise composed demeanor. He's probably replaying an old memory too.

A horse-drawn carriage clatters by, the aroma of the black mare's sweat strong in the breeze. A taxi pulls up to the curb to let out an elderly couple—the only taxi in sight in a city that was jammed with them the last time I was here. Paris isn't a ghost town, but it seems ghostlike in comparison with its pre-war glory. A woman wearing a tattered brown skirt and blue shirtwaist hurries by, her eyes meeting mine for a moment, forlorn and frightened. The few others on the sidewalk wear muted clothing, a far cry from the colorful Paris of my youth.

The bar is a comforting refuge filled with cigarette smoke, murmurs, quiet friendships, and confidences. The dark wooden bar on the right side of the narrow space has been polished by a half-century of elbows. The few bottles behind it are orderly and clean. Wartime sparse. Patrons sit at tables and a few in the booths that line the opposite wall. We settle into the back booth, Ira facing toward the front door, something he's done as long as I've known him. *Never turn your back on the door,* he warned me years ago. It saved his life in St. Paul.

The owner, Jean-Luc Talbot, drifts over and wipes our table. "Mademoiselle Alice. The usual?"

"*Oui, merci.* Same for this doddering soldier."

"Thanks a lot," Ira mutters.

"Anytime." I smile through my tension, hoping the Famous Grouse will help.

Jean-Luc brings tumblers of scotch—two fingers, neat. Ira taps the rim of my extended glass, and I take a long, slow swig. The burn feels wonderful all the way down. I take another sip and then set the glass down. Of all the things Ira has taught me, sipping scotch is one of the best. Famous Grouse. Nothing haughty or exotic. Solid.

"Tell me, I'm dying to hear," Ira says.

"Well . . ." I take a sip. "He's not what you led me to expect. He apologized for making me wait. Courteous, suave, friendly. Never said a bad word. Used my first name from the get-go. Not in that deprecating way the other reporters use." I tell him the rest. Ira's face reddens at the end of my account. "I'm a bit flattered by his offer to meet outside work." Ira's expression tells me I struck a nerve. His judgement about others has always been on target, but I hope he's wrong this once. "I got the feeling I might have a chance to get through to him in a . . . less official setting."

Ira's face hardens. "Don't be misled by his use of your first name. He does that to all the other reporters too." Ira downs the rest of his scotch. "Watch out. Don't take him up on his proposition." He looks me straight in the eyes. "He gets around. He may be a deacon at his church at home, a family man, but his reputation is anything but holy here. He'll just use you."

I stare into my glass. It's hard to imagine a man that handsome being attracted to me. But Ira has it in for Martel. He would have chafed under the command of anyone other than the editor or owner of a major newspaper. The irony is that the man who replaced Martel in the artillery, Robert McCormick, owns and publishes the *Chicago Tribune.* He's the only army officer in France Ira would work for without grousing. So I have to leaven Ira's opinion.

"You notice the photographs on his desk?"

"No."

"Small silver bifold picture frame next to his ashtray. Come on, I know you never miss a detail like that."

"It was folded, lying flat."

"He has it up, facing the guest, when I'm in the room. Picture of his wife and two children standing in front of a church. As if saying, *lookee here, y'all, ah'm a family man.* She's quite attractive, by the way. Belle-of-the-ball type pretty, his wife. He probably didn't want his marital status to influence the only female reporter on this side of the Atlantic. Don't suppose he had his wedding ring on."

My face is hot with a blush. "No."

"The man's a predator."

"That's not my impression. He's so . . . considerate. Well, other than the three-hour wait." I take a sip. "Problem is—I'm dead in the water without his approval."

"Looks are deceiving in this case." Ira takes a deep breath. "You're an adult. Make your own mind up. I'm just saying—he's not one of the good guys. So he won't let you out of town?"

The scotch trembles as I drain the glass while stilling a shaking foot. "No."

"Remember what I said about finding another way? Howard Enright's wife, Emily, will be Trudy's boss. One of the senior nurses at the hospital in Neuilly. Something you might consider." Ira narrows his eyes.

"I don't want to give up reporting."

"Not saying you have to." Ira points at his glass when Jean-Luc walks over with a refill for me. "Can I offer a bit of advice without getting a fat lip?"

I've never punched anyone, neither friend nor foe. Well, there was this one boy in fifth grade, but . . .

"You're as good a journalist as any of the men here. Better than most. The whole point of you going to nursing school was to give you a better angle on medical and science reporting, right? To make you so unique that gender wouldn't matter."

"Well, in part. I have a little secret I never told you. Promise you won't tell my folks."

Ira mimics closing a zipper over his lips.

"The other reason I did nursing was to keep the money flowing. My trust fund didn't kick in until I was twenty-two. That and the fact Trudy and I could do it together. It made Mom and Dad happy, for a change—their remaining daughter following in their medical footsteps."

"Your dad would have preferred you go to medical school."

"I want to be a reporter, not a doctor. Your wife convinced me to get the nursing degree."

Ira raises his left eyebrow.

"One time she, Trudy, and I were out for lunch. Ethyl understood my dream to be a journalist. She told me how much hostility I would run into as a woman—and she was right. She urged me to study nursing so I'd have something practical to fall back on. I may have aced the curriculum, but I have no intention of working as a nurse—I'm a journalist."

Ira smiles. "So back to my point, young lady. What better way to get the inside scoop on the medical side of the war than under a nurse's cap? Here's the silver lining: Martel's not in that chain of command. American nurses are in our base hospitals outside of Paris. Who knows? As our part of the war ignites, you might get closer to the front than you like."

"Nurses pull long hours. I might not have time to write."

"I'm not saying the idea is perfect. Talk to Emily Enright. She's a gem. Mind you, she's like my wife—high expectations and no tolerance for mediocrity. Think about it."

"But how will I get my stories out? I'm sure Martel will blackball me if I don't accept his *proposition*."

"Let's worry about that later."

"I'll consider it. What about you? Will you still be here to back me up?"

"Now it's my turn to say mum's the word."

I make the sign of the zipper over my mouth. This is more holy between us than the sign of the cross is at the Vatican.

"Requested a transfer. To somewhere else inside Intelligence. Supervising press censors is killing my journalistic soul. And you know how I feel about Martel. With Trudy coming, though, I don't want to be too far away."

"I'll be glad to see her."

"Me too, sort of," Ira says.

"Sort of?"

"Glad to see her. But there's a war on. I'm worried."

Chapter Four

Major Ira Cunningham, US Army Reserve

Saturday, May 25

The aroma from the café two doors down wafts through my office window. An early morning shower scrubbed the stench of horse manure from the street. The sun beams across my desk, and I pull out my handkerchief to wipe off the skein of dust. My stomach reminds me of the time. Most of the coffee in Paris is what they call *ersatz*—the pleasant European euphemism for phony crap—but the java at that little joint comes from Brazil, courtesy of another major in the building with the right connections in supply. Same with the pastries. Real flour without the usual French sawdust. Time to mosey over to the source of my temptation now that I've finished the morning dispatches. I read the final redacted versions of two press reports my censors submitted earlier. Pure tripe—but that's what my career has withered down to. The business with Alice kept me up last night, worrying. Sure, she's not my daughter, but she is as dear to me as Trudy, truth be told.

I tell Stan I'll be back in thirty and walk down the two flights and out the front door. The Germans may not have reached Paris yet, but if I didn't know better, the drab clothing and dour faces would have fooled me. They're a lot like the people I saw while visiting Berlin before the war. In fact, the Germans were more colorful than those I pass. I wend my way into the café, order three eclairs—two in a bag for later—and a coffee. I take a seat at one of the window tables and watch the traffic between crosshatched window tape. Businesses have paper-taped their windows to limit the risk of flying glass shrapnel if a German bomb hits their buildings. Instead of just slapping the tape on like merchants would have at home, they created intricate patterns like lacework. Parisians. I admire their defiance and panache.

The coffee is strong this morning, as though the chef knows I need it. I'd really like to add a shot of something to it, but the army frowns on that and I know Martel would love to fire my ass back to the States. So I linger, enjoying the morning. The rest of the day looms ahead under a cloud.

My chest tightens as I reenter the headquarters lobby. Neck hairs come alive with each step like antennae receiving a wireless signal. Major Dick Martel is a problem that can only be solved with a transfer. Mine or his. I know he wants out, but word is that the artillery doesn't want him back. My request will probably be approved, but with the army you never know until the ink is dry. I doff my hat and run my hand over my head. Where's it gone—the time, the hair? At least the pastry's only put on a little paunch. Pershing is on a mission to root out the fat and unfit among his officers. I'll cut back and walk more. Tomorrow.

Stan looks up when I enter the office. "Sir, Major Martel wants to see you in his office about the daily reports."

"Dandy." That isn't what I want to say, but I can't put Stan in the middle. "I'll be indisposed for a few minutes." I lay an eclair on Stan's desk. "Here's your cut."

"Thanks, sir. If he calls, you're on the phone with a colonel."

I close my door and open the bag. Martel can wait. The man is proof that there are more horses' asses in the army than there are equines. I take my time eating, wishing I'd brought a second coffee. Alice's naiveté gnaws at me. How can she be so gullible? To be taken in by Martel—it's disgusting, in two ways. One is the obvious. The other is Alice's maddening sense of being the ugly duckling. Her parents were never very supportive, regardless of how well she did in school or anywhere else. She was a tomboy when I first met her, all arms and legs, elbows and knees. She thought all that made her plain and unattractive. She should look in the mirror with objective eyes.

After the last bite, I grab a stack of files and make my way to Martel's office. Typewriters clatter and doors creak as I pass harried staffers in the main hallway. My shoes click on the terrazzo floor as a janitor works a mop. I walk into Martel's waiting room. The clerk smokes a cigarette while practicing his version of Chinese water torture on his typewriter one . . . letter . . . at . . . a . . . time. "Major Martel ordered me to report." The notion that Martel can order anything beyond beignets is a disgusting thought.

The clerk looks up. "Major's expecting you, sir."

I roll my neck and straighten my tie before knocking on the doorframe.

"Come."

"I have those reports for you, Major," I say.

"How're my censors doing?"

Martel's voice irks me. It might be Yankee prejudice, but I envision him calmly ordering a lynching with his mellifluous Southern cadence. His eyes are discordant. Soft as snow at moments. Hard as a Klansman burning a cross the next. How much is act and how much genuine? And what does he mean by *my censors*? I do all the supervisory work. They answer to me. "Quite well. The men before them made a word salad out of coherent writing. These boys passed freshman English, so at least it doesn't come out chopped to pieces."

"And our so-called esteemed Paris-based correspondents?" Martel sneers.

I continue to stand in the hope of making this short. "Frosty over the censorship. No journalist worth their salt wants anyone to change their final product."

"Which is where you come in, am I right? They'll mind you a tad less." Martel snorts. "They're lucky they were allowed off the boats, so far as I'm concerned. Bane of my very existence."

"Since Washington loosened the rules, we've had a migration of reporters, some better than others. I don't get to interact with them as much as you. Regarding my work, sir, there's a big difference between being a newspaper editor and what I'm doing here." The thought chokes me.

"What do you want? To be their . . . welcoming committee? Give them all hugs and pats on the back?" Martel scowls.

I look at the photographs on the desk as I compose my response. A small silver bifold frame shows the family photo I'd told Alice about on one side and a wedding photo of Martel and a woman I assume is his wife on the other. "It might be a better use of my time, sir. Lieutenant Green is doing a fine job. Needs very little supervision. And I'm a journalist by trade. I know their ways. Can tell good from bad in a few moments."

"Meaning you don't think I am capable of doing that work properly?"

Martel's eyes are shotgun barrels aimed at my face. "No, sir."

Martel breaks the stare. I slide the censored files across the desk. Martel ignores them. "Heavens to Betsy, man, they're even sending over *womenfolk* who think they can do a man's job. Next thing you know, I'll be expected to accredit Communists." He puts a special emphasis on the *u*.

"Sir?" I tilt my head and raise my left eyebrow.

"Hell's bells, man. What's our world coming to? Shoulda seen the fancy tart that marched in here yesterday. She was full of herself, carrying on and on."

Here it comes. Keep my face flat and don't look in his eyes.

"Well, I'll tell you, she was a fine filly, she was, if you catch my meaning. I can see right through her, though. Wears those stupid glasses to look smart. Behind them lurks the brain of a suffragette. A muckraker."

"Sounds bad, sir." I frown. Damn this man. But I want to find out more. It reminds me of the way I baited an alderman in St. Paul one time. "Communist?"

"No doubt whatsoever. Very typical of the type, really. Only thing missing is that she does not appear to be a Jewess." Martel's eyes narrow. "Though some are quite sneaky. Heavens—war's a man's game. Women have no business here. No business a'tall." Martel pulls out and relights the cigar from his ashtray. His face is red. He dabs his forehead with a handkerchief. "I escorted her out—her all high and mighty, chin in the air. Nearly called the guards."

"It sounds like she needs a good editor to sit down and counsel her."

"What she really needs is a man with a crop." Martel's lips curl up at the corners.

"What paper does she work for?" I'll string Martel along a bit longer. Sun Tzu wrote: *know your enemy.*

"Some rag in Wisconsin. The state's brimming over with Krauts, for God's sake. Should be evicted from the Union, far as I'm concerned. Or maybe walled off. We don't need troublemakers like Miss Alice Simons mucking up the war effort. Sending an upstart girl to do a man's work? Sometimes I don't understand civilians. Leastways those from the North."

"No, sir." I pause while Martel takes another pull from his cigar. Transfer. Definitely a transfer, before I go stark raving mad. "Is there anything else you want from me, sir?"

"No. Dismissed."

A new stack of reporters' dispatches fresh from Lieutenant Green lies on the desk when I arrive at my office. I shake my head as I slump into the creaky wooden chair and gaze at the photos next to the pile. One shows a younger me, with a full head of thick brown hair, my arm around Ethyl's shoulders on our honeymoon in the mountains of Vermont. The next photo shows Ethyl and me standing next to Trudy and Alice at their college graduation. Trudy is a cute black-haired peanut next to her best friend. Alice's wavy auburn hair stands out from a face that seems like a failed attempt to imitate a librarian. She's too tall and trim to fade into the crowd. Not pretty like Trudy—striking would be the word, with a straight nose and a strong angular jaw. And while Trudy was always a bit of a flirt, Alice seemed awkward around the boys. She needed the glasses for her nearsightedness, but I think they're a sort of shield. Her emotions have been a battened-down ship as long as I've known her.

The third photo had been taken the same day—Trudy and her fiancé, Bill Stevens. Like Trudy, Bill is headed here, an army private despite his college degree and the offer of a commission. Bill has a sort of noble yeomanry about him, reflecting his upbringing on a farm, a real throwback to an earlier era.

It leaves my chest empty. The soldiers of Bill's Second Division are going into the fight soon. They're slated to go north to back up the First Division's fight near Cantigny, but I hear disturbing rumblings that may send them east.

One thing *is* certain. This war is much worse than the one reported at home, thanks to me and my censors.

The truth terrifies me.

Chapter Five
Alice Simmons

Golden cirrus wisps streak the sky as I make my way past other Americans on Rue Daunou. Before the war, this street would have been filled with Parisians decked out for a night on the town. Tonight, however, the men under sixty wear either American uniforms or the suits of reporters thirstier for a cocktail than a scoop. The women appear to be wives or girlfriends. The crowd gravitates toward two destinations—the Hotel Daunou, with the hottest jazz club in Paris, and the New York Bar across the street. The bartender, Harry MacElhone, possesses an uncanny understanding of his clientele—remembering names and their preferred libations.

I stop a few doors away and watch patrons enter the bar, recognizing several reporters. A clarinet hits a high note deep inside the club across the street. A car passes by, leaving a trail of blue smoke that makes me cough. No rush to go inside. The place will be full of reporters. I've been here a few times for drinks, but the reporters I'd gone with ended up wanting dates rather than the shop talk I had hoped for. What will this one be like? Howard seems okay. And Ira vouches for him. Deep breath, square my shoulders, and make my way toward the bar.

If *Vogue* ever did a spread on the Librarian Look, I'd be a shoo-in. Except maybe my brown calf-length Russian boots with one-inch heels and square toes. I want the added height and threat tonight. The boots are comfortable, solid. A high-necked blouse, a brown cotton skirt, and a light raincoat over my arm complete the look.

Most of the men of the American press corps who can afford it will filter through the New York this evening. An American woman wearing a flowered ensemble that seems out of place glides by, leaving me a wall-flower in her wake. But I've never been a head-turner other than for my height. I've come to terms with that. For the most part.

Voices fill the humid, smoky air. A rattle draws my eye. Harry smiles and gives me a wink while shaking a cocktail. "Miss Alice. Lovely evening," he says in a Scottish brogue. "Grouse, neat?"

"It sure is, Harry. And no—*vin rouge*. Howard Enright here?" Harry pours a martini with a flourish. I figure there are two reasons he knows me—I'm the only female journalist here, and he's a hell of a bartender. His partner, wearing a white shirt with arm garters, stirs a concoction and pours it into a Collins glass.

"Mr. Enright and party are in the lower bar. I'll send your wine down." Ragtime piano plays below me as I descend the narrow, winding staircase. The piano and a small bar are on my right. I pass a table of US Army officers on my left and see Howard and three others at a back table. Women are a distinct minority, most of them decked out, making my plainness seem to shout out its mediocrity.

Howard Enright stands when I approach, followed by the other man, whose back is to me. Howard smiles and shakes my hand. "Miss Simmons. Glad you could come. This is my wife, Emily, and our friends Pete and Mary Sloan. Pete's a reporter for the *Chicago Evening Journal*, recently arrived."

"We beat away a couple of thirsty reporters to save the seat," Emily says as she stands to make room between their chairs, facing the back wall—not the spot Ira would approve of, but my only choice. Emily's in her forties, about four inches shorter than me, with gray eyes, wire-frame glasses, and a straight nose. She looks imposing, but not in a threatening way. Mary Sloan appears to be in her early thirties, a few inches taller than Emily, slender and attractive.

"Please, it's Alice. And thank you."

A waiter delivers my glass of Bordeaux. The others at the table have a variety of cocktails and a bowl of bar nuts.

"That's a lovely locket, Alice," Emily says.

"Thank you." I take off my locket and open it. After a moment I hand it to Emily. "My grandmother gave it to me when I was ten, just after my sister, Justine, died. The photo is of the three of us, taken the year before."

"How did she . . ." Emily hands the locket back.

"An accident." I don't want to talk about this.

"Where do you hail from, Alice?" Pete is an inch shorter than me, a wiry man with a five o'clock shadow on a tanned face with wavy black hair.

"Minneapolis." Thank you, Pete, for changing the subject.

"Go to school there?"

"U of M. The new nursing program and journalism." I go on to tell them about my decision to get a nursing degree and registry even though my goal was always journalism. Several conspiratorial glances pass between Mary and Emily as I rattle on.

"Some of the correspondents have probably been less than welcoming," Emily says. She frowns across the table at Pete. "That last soiree we all went to was like a stag party."

"It's like I'm beating my head against a brick wall." I shrug. "They won't let me out of Paris, and our soldiers are everywhere but here."

"Truth is," Howard says, "that's the case for most of us. Only a handful are fully credentialed. They're the only ones Pershing'll let near the troops. They're not necessarily much better off, since the army insists that they base themselves in Neufchâteau. That's a long way from the action. The army's press section keeps a tight rein on everyone. I'm curious, though. How'd it go with Martel?"

"Not sure," I say. "He is charming, handsome. But Ira warned me about him. I have the impression my only hope for a pass out of town is to let him make a pass at me."

"Friend of mine told me they brought Martel in a few months ago. A genuine ass," Howard says. Emily shoots Howard a sour look.

I take a sip. The friend must be Ira.

Raucous laughter draws my eye to the table of American army officers near the piano. The bartender works on a shaken cocktail as three of the reporters at the bar stare toward the officers. One of the army men slaps the back of another, and then the two clink their beer glasses and down them both.

"Howard and I publicly act like we don't know Ira since he's the head censor," Pete says. "He's mentioned you in conversation. How'd you come to know him?"

"His daughter, Trudy, and I are chums. We went to school together from seventh grade on through college. I consider Mr. Cunningham—uh, Ira—my mentor."

"Still, how'd he become your inspiration?"

"Courage. Intelligence. And his integrity. I sensed those right away when I met him. They moved into our neighborhood after the St. Paul police shot Trudy's dog and left it on their porch with a message. I've never met anyone as brave."

Pete nods. "Taking on Chief O'Connor was . . . well, noble. Maybe not the smartest thing in the world."

"That was the spark," I say. "Mr. Cunningham convinced me to specialize in medical reporting since nobody else does it, at least nobody who knows anything about medicine. Being a girl—that didn't matter as much, at the start. It seemed like a good angle to be the only reporter with an RN. We thought it would open doors, or at least unlock a few."

"That work?" Emily asks.

"In Milwaukee. Not here."

"How'd you pull off Paris?" Pete eats the olive from his empty martini glass.

"My mom's parents are from Allier, east of Bordeaux. We spoke French at home. I spent several summers here as a kid." It seemed like such an adventure then. Now I realize they wanted me out of the house. "When I presented the case to my editor, I told him it would cost the *Journal* nothing more than my base salary to send me here. I'm the only French-speaking reporter he has. The rest speak German—well, it is Milwaukee. He took me up on the offer."

"We need nurses more than journalists," Mary says.

Another sip of wine. I catch the eye of a waiter and ask for a water. I need to keep my head clear.

"Now please don't take this to be patronizing, because that's not how I'm offering this, okay?" Howard says. "You're not beating your head against one wall. There are at least two. The easy one is the press corps. They don't like trailblazers. And even those who support suffrage? Ply them with enough liquor and they'll tell you a woman's place is in the home." Emily touches Howard's sleeve. His face flushes, and he looks around the bar. "The press is like an athletic club. But it pales next to the army. Their wall's a rampart most civilian *men* can't crack. Mary's right. Think about nursing."

Mary and Emily exchange a glance. Mary says, "Emily and I both work at the American Hospital in Neuilly. Emily is the chief surgical nurse, and I run one of the surgical wards. We're desperate for nurses."

"Won't I have to join the army?" I ask.

"Not necessarily. The lines between the Red Cross and the army are . . . complicated. You could come in under the Red Cross banner if your credentials check out."

"Are you registered in Wisconsin?" Emily asks.

"Sure." I hadn't expected to be recruited tonight. It's not what I want—or is it? It would mean giving up my dream. A sip of water quenches my dry throat. "What would I need to do?"

"Do you have your diploma and certificates?" Emily asks.

"I didn't think I'd need them when I came here."

"That'll slow things down. I can cable our Chicago headquarters. They'll check with the Wisconsin board. Think about it. Come by the hospital and we'll see what we can work out."

"When?"

"Monday's not too soon," Emily says.

"Sure. How about mid-morning?"

Emily nods.

Howard and Ira might be right. But isn't that like throwing in the towel, admitting the old boys' club has won? I slip off my glasses and clean the lenses with my handkerchief.

Shattering glass catches my attention. I put my glasses on and turn around. The army officers sound well into their cups. A broken beer glass lies on the floor. A small captain wearing his hat at a cocky angle smooches at me, followed by a leer that showcases brilliant white teeth.

Then the shrimp winks. My face warms, and I break eye contact. Damn him. I take a sip of water, not sure if they're getting louder or if I'm just paying more attention. I shift my eyes to a reporter playing a passable Scott Joplin tune on the piano.

Conversation around the table drifts between journalism and nursing and life stories—mine the shortest and least interesting, by far. It's time for me to take off, but I need to visit the powder room and make a point of not looking at the army officers on the way.

As I leave the restroom, an arm blocks my path. Major Martel, his red eyes struggling to focus, a leer on his face. I hadn't noticed him earlier—did he come in after me? "This is your opportunity to take me up on my offer, Alice." His smooth baritone comes out slurred.

"I don't understand your meaning, sir." My face flushes. I don't want this. But refusing means I go nowhere but home unless Emily hires me. That is suddenly very clear. Why can't they let me do my job, as a reporter? But how can I slide out of this *opportunity* without provoking Martel?

"Let's just say the safe play would be to let me walk you home—to my apartment—for a nightcap." Martel struggles to stand up.

"Major, thank you so much for your very sweet offer. But, with respect, I'm out with friends tonight. Now, if you'll excuse me." I push past him. The others at Martel's table laugh. One whistles in my wake.

Part of me wants another drink, but the prudent part of me wants to get out of here, now. Another glass won't help.

"You look angry," Mary says.

"That man with his back to us, at the table making all the noise? Martel. He could barely stand."

"Yeah, that's him," Howard says. The waiter brings another bottle of mineral water for our table.

We continue to visit for the next quarter hour. "I hope you'll all excuse me, but it's getting late."

"Need a lift? I have my car," Pete says.

"No, I need the air." And Pete's in no condition to drive.

Laughter makes me glance back at the table with the army officers. Martel is staring at me like a hawk eyeing a rabbit.

Chapter Six
Alice Simmons

I glance at Martel's table on my way to the door. The captain winks at me. Martel stares at his half-empty glass. I make my way upstairs, past Harry, and through the front door. Though still muggy, the fresh air is a relief after the smoky bar. The jazz band wails a finale across the street. A car weaves its way past, the driver's face one of inebriated concentration. After a right turn on Rue Daunou, I pass several couples walking arm in arm. A group of four men saunter toward me on the sidewalk. I drape the light coat over my left arm. The marquees are dark, the tape-patterned front windows of the bars and restaurants curtained. Before the war, there would have been a line of taxis along this street. Tonight—none.

Pedestrian traffic thins after I cross Avenue de l'Opera at the end of the block and turn north. I settle into a city walk—not hurried, but not slow either—mulling over today's events. The noise of a stumble and muted chuckles behind me makes me stop and turn. The light spilling out from a closing restaurant door across the street reveals two figures a half block back wearing military hats. I keep walking. The presence of the American army here makes me feel safer.

I reach up and touch my locket amid memories of my college semester in Paris—studying French literature and art history at the

Sorbonne. A respite from biology, chemistry, nursing, and journalism. Aunt Monique took me under her wing. My cousins and I traipsed through the Luxembourg Gardens, took walks along the Seine, and picnicked in parks all around central Paris. At night, the city aglow, we strolled through our neighborhood with no worries about the time or our safety. But now? Most of the Parisian girls have evacuated to families in the west or south, their fathers at war and mothers slaving in factories to make the bullets and bombs to kill the fathers of German girls.

The two soldiers narrow the gap during my reverie. I'm more aware of their footsteps, the street otherwise quiet as I look over the nearby buildings—doors closed, no lights, an alleyway to my right. Then the footsteps rush up behind me. A slurred baritone voice startles me.

"Not so fast, there, sweet thing. Like to have a chat."

Martel. This is not good. I scan the street—I'm on my own. My heart seems to leap, neck tightens.

I take two quick steps to put some distance between us.

A hand grasps my left shoulder and another my hair and spins me into the alley. I turn my head at the last moment. Jesus, that hurts. My cheek grinds into the bricks, my glasses spear into my temple and then break away. I struggle to squeeze my right eye shut. My pulse pounds in my face, my head.

Pain spears my right ear. My vision flashes red, my brain fogs.

Two hands from behind rip open my blouse. I shudder as a hand grabs my right breast. Raspy breathing fills my left ear. Hot beer breath replaces the air between my nose and the bricks, a man's face inches away. He's shorter than me. A wet kiss dribbles down my neck, ending with a nibble.

"I tried," Martel slurs. "Lord knows, I tried. I gave you a wonderful opportunity. We could have done it the easy way. Now, you've left me no choice but the hard one."

A hand snatches up the back of my dress.

I hear screaming.

It's mine.

The hand on my hair pulls back, slams my head forward, and I go numb. After—how long, a moment, a minute?—my head starts to clear.

Blood rushes through my ears. Consciousness fades. Stay awake. Stay awake. But everything seems far away.

Have to think. Figure out how to fight back. I can't seem to connect my thoughts.

I shout for a policeman in French.

A hand smothers my mouth. Not that big. Soft skin. It jerks my jaw upward.

"Yell again, bitch, and the next one'll knock your fucking brain out." A low, tense voice in my left ear. New York accent. My face throbs; blood trickles from my nose. The fog enveloping me begins to clear. My heart races. Sweat trickles along my sides. Things are moving too fast.

Ira told Trudy and me that one trick in an assault is to slow things down. But how?

A hand reaches across my throat. My necklace tightens against the back of my neck.

A sudden snap. My locket's gone.

The hand on my mouth loosens. I gulp air. The other hand still grasps my hair. For a moment, I'm back in Minneapolis with my friend Kim Yeong, in high school. The boys had teased Kim about her owlish glasses, which were a lot like mine. Kim's brothers had taught us a few things—just in case. Not something young ladies learned in the open, but . . .

A belt buckle clinks. A grunt behind me. A hand grasps the waist of my bloomers and tears them down. I concentrate on stepping out of them, right foot, left foot. Martel will think I've surrendered.

My head is clearing.

Time has slowed.

Need both legs free.

I lick the hand gagging me. Make him to think I like what he's doing. Draw them in, then . . .

I ease my mouth open and tilt my head down farther into the hand as if to kiss it again. Hardness on my right buttock—he's about to . . .

There's a subtle shift, like the man gagging me and holding my head is looking back at Martel. Good. He's distracted. I hope.

Slip his thumb into my mouth as if I'm about to suck it.

Then, with everything I have left, I bite like a predator clamping down on her prey. Blood fills my mouth. A howl erupts next to my ear.

The hand on my hair disappears as I shake my head like a wolf breaking a chicken's neck.

The thumb is still attached to the soft hand when I spit it out. He continues to yelp.

I cock my right hand, fist open, and drive the palm down into the short man's face like Kim's brothers taught me. Something pops. The howl becomes a gurgle, and he collapses backward into a garbage can. The lid clatters down the alley.

Next target.

Time crawls.

Martel's slacks dangle at his knees. Just enough light to see his excitement. "I'm going to kill you, you fucking whore."

I kick with all my might.

My Russian boot connects with Martel's crotch. He bends forward with a guttural grunt.

I pull the foot back, shout once, and release a lightning kick to his face that lifts Martel off his feet and into the wall behind him with a sickening thud. He won't be getting up soon.

Where are my glasses?

Time speeds up. Work fast.

I bend down and feel for them but encounter only wetness and a few stones. I snatch up my coat and purse.

No more time.

I sprint along the street, take a right turn, and glance back at the next intersection.

No pursuit.

I turn left on the larger avenue and begin to look for a policeman while slipping on my coat. My clothes are ruined. The world's a blur. My favorite glasses, gone. The adrenaline seems to seep out from every pore, sweat running down my back. A cold shiver wracks me. I stop and lean against a wall.

Thoughts are jumbled. Gotta come up with a plan. Lacking that, I head home.

The memory of Martel's fingers between my legs. At least he didn't get any farther—he didn't touch me with his . . .

Damn them. Hope the captain dies from an infection in his thumb as I spit out his blood. The taste lingers. I'm glad the streetlights are out. I must be a heck of a sight—scraped face, lips bloodied like the muzzle of a lioness after a fresh kill. It won't go over well with police at this time of night. And that makes my mind up.

Finally, my apartment building. I pull a key from my purse, unlock the outside door, and dash the three flights to the flat where I rent a room. The lights hurt my eyes for a moment. The apartment is empty, silent. The landlady works nights in a munitions factory, thank God. I slam the door bolt home and jam the iron doorstop underneath for good measure. My skirt's askew, and I feel naked without my bloomers. Anger erupts at the memory of Martel's fingers. The sound of his rasping breath, the smell of beer as the other man slopped a kiss on my neck. The weasel must have been on his tiptoes to do it. I go to my bedroom and rummage for my spare glasses—the round ones with wire frames.

A dark stain around the square toe of the right boot marks my success as I unlace it and then take off the remains of my shredded skirt. The buttons on my shirt are gone. I run the hot water into the bathtub while I brush my teeth with a big dollop of carbolic tooth powder. The water runs pink with blood. I brush until what comes out is clear.

Then to the kitchen for a clean glass and into my room where I keep a bottle in the bottom of my steamer trunk. Two fingers of Famous Grouse. When warm water finally reaches the tub's tap, I plug the drain and add powdered soap. The first sip of Grouse gags me. The tooth powder may kill bacteria, but it doesn't mix with scotch. A glass of water later, and things are better. I slip out of my brassiere and ease myself into the water, hoping to erase the memory of groping fingers. I scrub my neck with a washcloth—will the bite mark be there tomorrow?

My mind replays in a blur as I close my eyes, sip scotch, and struggle to slow time down. It's funny how that works under stress. The warm, soapy water comforts me. Rational thought settles in when the tumbler's empty and the bathwater cool. I can't go out to find a policeman, not now. The best thing to do is towel off, have another Grouse, and pray for sleep.

After getting into my nightclothes, I return to the living room. My boots lie where I kicked them off. The right one is bloody, so I take it over to the bathroom sink and turn on the cold tap. The water runs red with Martel's blood. I rub soap in, feeling like Lady Macbeth. After that, I down what's left of my glass, hoping the scotch will dull the memory that keeps intruding. The cool air on my bare back, the fingers, groping, the beer breath in my face. I consider another scotch but go to bed instead. No need to add a hangover to my throbbing head.

The memory of the men's fingers returns each time I close my eyes. The hand ripping my locket. I lie on my right side, then roll to the left, blood coursing through my ears, each beat a reminder. Hugging a pillow doesn't help. My heart pounds against my breastbone when I try lying on my stomach. No use. I get up and pace the bedroom and then wander to the kitchen and run water for tea. Recheck the front door, jiggle the knob, turn the lock back and forth. Twice. Am I nuts? Maybe. Talking to myself, rehearsing for the meeting I'll have with the police. But all that does is strengthen the memories. I grab my copy of *The Wonderful Wizard of Oz* off the side table, hoping it and the weak tea will distract me, but I can't concentrate on the words.

I touch my neck where the locket had rested for every waking moment since I was ten. Where is it? In the alleyway, abandoned? Or did Martel steal it? The thought of him having it, possessing it . . .

Chapter Seven
Alice Simmons

Sunday, May 26

A siren wails. Above—the drone of German Gotha bombers. Three thirty in the morning. I don my emergency clothing—loose-fitting dungarees and a shirt that would look right at a lake cottage—and sprint downstairs to huddle with other residents in the cellar. Bombs reverberate through the foundation. I comfort several ladies who shake in fear and for a short time forget my anger. There are no military targets nearby, but that doesn't seem to matter to the Germans. After a half hour, someone says they hear the all-clear siren, and I trudge up the four flights to my untouched apartment. Dawn is a knife edge in the eastern sky and sleep a lost cause.

Another bath. A dull headache throbs, and my forehead is tender when I touch it. A damage assessment in the mirror—bruised right cheek, skin scraped raw, a blood-encrusted right ear, and a shiner on my forehead like a beacon. Makeup won't hide it. The bite mark on my neck. Damn him. At least he didn't break the skin. Swollen upper lip, but the teeth underneath are good. No cracks. The taste of warm human blood—will that memory ever leave? I settle into the welcoming tub, take deep breaths, memories rushing in circles again.

The bar. Who was the other man? Double bars on his uniform. A captain. Shorter than me, not big, and not all that strong for a soldier. Drunk. Well, very drunk. That was my luck, in a way. I don't think I could have fought them both off if they were sober. What did his face look like? Too dark to tell, but I'm sure he was the captain with the radiant white teeth in the bar, so I'll have no trouble picking him out.

Martel. The fingers. Jesus. I didn't do anything to provoke them. Nothing about my dress, appearance, or manners could have led them on.

Stop.

It's not my fault.

They attacked me. Me.

But don't they always say that the woman provokes it?

They say . . . Damn *them*.

I slip on a charcoal outfit as provocative as funeral garb. The boot I washed off last night is still damp, so on go my flats. I put on no makeup and arrange my hair in a comb. My clunky wire-frame glasses need a wash, but the best I can do now is to buff away the streaks. I stuff last night's torn garments, including the boots, into a shopping bag. One last glance in the mirror. I look like hell. So far, so good.

Outside, I stand at the stoop, searching in both directions. I'm going to the alleyway first, hoping the locket is still there—it's precious to me. I walk at a brisk pace, peering behind every half block. Are they stupid enough to attack during daylight? Probably not. They might not be in any shape to rape anyone today. Especially Martel. My boot made a solid impression on his manhood. I rub my neck, then the right ear, still sore. The abrasion on my right cheek itches, and I don't want to touch it and start it bleeding again. Each step closer to the alleyway sends a little shock through my legs, my heart quickening as the distance grows shorter.

Outside the alley, I feign nonchalance while glancing up and down the street. The odor of horse sweat and leather from a nearby carriage and the sound of pedestrians fill the air. I tense when the horse snorts. It clomps a shod hoof and whinnies. The stench of rotting trash with a hint of urine makes my nose tingle. I jump when a taxicab honks, heading away. Okay, now or never—I swallow hard and step into the empty alley. My grime-trampled bloomers lie on the cobblestones. Puddles of dried blood give me no satisfaction. My tortoiseshell glasses lie next to a splash of dried blood. The lenses are intact, but the frame's hopeless. Where's my locket?

I look both ways and then get down on my knees next to the wall they slammed me against. My locket is gone. I examine every nook and cranny, but no locket. A broken front tooth, a bloodied upper incisor, lies next to a segment of my broken silver necklace. I slip the necklace fragment and the tooth into my purse.

An officer with a missing front tooth should not be too hard to identify.

I want to weep, but my eyes are dry and hot, filled with anger, not despair.

Why?

Why do men do this to women?

Why did they do this to me?

Chapter Eight
Alice Simmons

The ninth arrondissement police station is a half mile east of my apartment. The walk helps clear my head. Things are different this morning. My senses are on full alert. Smell is acute—the patisseries and flowers more fragrant, but the auto exhaust more irritating and the horse manure more pungent. I pause at a leather shop and pretend to look in the window, trying to appear casual as I search the area for American army uniforms. There are two enlisted men talking, neither looking my way. I restart at a brisk pace, peering down each alleyway, glancing back like a crook on the lam. I stop outside the police station and take a deep breath, realizing that I've been tromping along, chest tight, hardly breathing.

I've never visited a police station before and have no idea what to expect. It seems like a boa constrictor is wrapped around my chest when the door slams shut behind me. The station is a large, high-ceilinged room filled with cigarette smoke. Wooden chairs line the wall on both sides of the doorway. A railing with a swinging gate separates the waiting room from the inner workings of the station. An officer with thin red stripes on his epaulets wears a bored expression while reading a file at a desk inside the rail. Do I act like a wronged American, or speak French and seem more native? Which will get me further?

The officer raises his eyes with the quick up-and-down appraisal I expect from a cop. I say in French, "Pardon me, monsieur. I'm here to report a crime."

"What sort of crime, mademoiselle?"

"Assault and attempted rape."

"And you are the victim?"

"Yes."

"When did it occur?"

"Last night."

"Why didn't you report it then?"

"The air raid . . ."

The officer seems to consider the matter for a moment. "Please take a seat. One of the investigators will take your report." He motions toward the line of chairs.

I cross my legs, right foot restless, tapping. The victim. I've never been that before and don't like it one bit. Damn Martel and his captain. The officer comes back to his desk, nods at me with a grim expression, and returns to his report after creaking into his chair.

About ten minutes later, a tall officer with a large Gallic nose and two white stripes on his epaulets pushes open the gate and says, "Mademoiselle, please follow me." He holds the gate open for me. I sit in one of the guest chairs in front of his well-used wooden desk. He wears a strong cologne—the brand escapes me, but a cheap one. My ears catch every sound in the room—conversations, a ringing phone, typewriters, footsteps, creaking desk chairs.

"Papers, please, mademoiselle."

I rifle through my purse and pull out my passport and visa and hand them over. The lieutenant inspects the papers and writes on a form. His back straightens when he gets to my press credentials. He casts a grim eye at me and turns back to the form and fills in blanks for the next several minutes. My right foot taps on the floor, and I will it to be still, knowing how irritating that can be to some people. Don't aggravate this man. I swallow and brush a strand of hair from my face, then touch my right ear. The man's cologne only partly covers the strong aroma of humans around us who don't wear deodorant, and their cigarettes. A dozen desks like this one populate the room, half with officers in blue uniforms writing reports, several clattering away at typewriters—a pained grimace on the face of one hunting and pecking with two fingers. Why is it that so many men refuse to learn to type properly? Two officers write while civilians in guest chairs speak in hushed voices. Private offices with wooden doors and glass transoms above line the three walls around the main room. Electric ceiling lights illuminate the room, with smaller lamps on the desks. A phone rings, drawing my eyes back to the officer at the reception desk. Four men and a gaudy woman sit in the chairs along the far wall while the desk officer speaks to them, fielding a complaint about a neighborhood dog.

"What is the nature of your report, mademoiselle?"

"Two men assaulted me. One tried to rape me while the other held me."

"Tried?"

"I fought them off."

"A mademoiselle against two men?"

"They were drunk."

"Do you know these men?"

"One of them, yes. Major Richard Martel. He's an officer with the AEF Intelligence Press Section."

"Stop." The lieutenant holds up his right hand.

My face grows hot, and I take a deep breath. "Why?"

"If your allegation involves American army officers, you must report the incident to their provost marshal. We have no jurisdiction. If you were a French citizen, it might be different, but they have very limited recourse in incidents like this too." The lieutenant's face is expressionless, though he seems less rigid than when he saw my press credentials. He tells me the address of the office I need to go to. "If there is nothing else, you may go. *Bonne chance*, mademoiselle."

I turn left on the sidewalk outside the police station and decide against a cab. The two-mile walk will help settle my nerves. I buy a paper and sit at an outside table of a small café about halfway to the army provost's office. A coffee and a croissant revive me as I read the news. The Gotha raid last night killed six people when it hit a residential neighborhood northeast of mine. A fire burned for several hours and half of a block was demolished.

The coffee tastes like elm bark; the croissant has a hint of maple sawdust.

My hands grow restless, and I reach to my neck where the locket should be. A wisp of wind stirs the memory of the captain's breath, the taste of his blood. My eyes wander—down the street, at the other patrons—on the lookout for Martel. My mind won't leave the alleyway.

It's strange. I always felt at home in Paris. Today, I'm separate, as though I'm looking through a window at dusk. As much as I felt out of my element in the police station, my next stop is the lion's den—the law enforcement end of the US Army. How likely is it they will take the word of a reporter about an unwitnessed assault by two of their own? I don't want to go in with any delusions. This may be worse than a waste of time. But the only other option is to stay silent. No. Not me.

Chapter Nine
Alice Simmons

The American army provost marshal's office is quieter than the police station. The sergeant at the reception desk takes my name and phones a lieutenant. I take a seat and cross my legs, trying to keep my feet still and not look too defensive. It's a quarter after one. I reach up to my neck to touch a locket that isn't there—a tender streak where the captain ripped it off.

The same questions swirl around in my mind. It's as though the thoughts hold me captive. Why me? Is it that I'm a woman doing a man's job? Was it a spur of the moment act, or have they done this before? Now there's a thought. The two of them—they seemed like a team.

A tall, thin first lieutenant walks in, locks eyes with me, and motions me to follow him through a door. He says nothing and leads me into a cramped interview room with a table and four chairs. The aroma of stale cigarettes tinged with vomit assaults my nose. A butt-filled metal ashtray sits on the table.

"I'm Lieutenant Malone."

"My name is Alice Simmons. I'm here to report an assault."

Malone pulls a pen out of his coat pocket and takes notes while I tell him my story. He eyes me when I tell him about my clothes being ripped off, Martel's excitement, and how I fended them off. I feel naked, exposed, vulnerable to his gaze. He's good at keeping his face neutral, but his eyes tell me something else. Each sentence feels like I've got a spade in my hand and I'm digging my own grave.

"Where did the alleged event take place?"

"There is nothing alleged about it. Look at my face. They did this to me. Look at my clothing. Their hands ripped it up." I stand and dump the contents of my shopping bag on the table.

"Do you allege there might be something remaining at the scene? That we need to send investigators to look it over?"

"Do you mean did I leave a dead body?"

"Evidence."

"Here's the evidence. I saved you the time. Here are the clothes I wore and the glasses they broke."

"So you corrupted the crime scene."

"One of them stole a locket of mine. Here is part of the necklace."

He looks at it. "I'll have to keep this."

"I don't want to give it up." I grab the necklace fragment. "And I'm wearing my spare glasses—I have to get these fixed."

"You're not helping yourself here."

"You want more evidence? The captain's missing a front tooth. Like I told you, he has nasty bite mark on his hand—I think it was his right. He was a few inches shorter than me. Maybe five-six or so. New York accent. Major Martel won't be walking upright today, and I'm pretty sure I broke his nose. There can't be that many American captains or majors walking around with those injuries. Their blood is back there. Look in the AEF Paris Press Office building." I stop, thinking, probing my memory, anger coursing with each rapid heartbeat, my hands tingling. The bastard. One of old boys' network.

Alleged.

The word sears through me.

I look into Malone's eyes, searching for a clue, something to indicate that he's a friend of Martel or the captain. He breaks my gaze and jots a note. "Everything I have is here." I point at the pile of clothing.

"Of course, a defense attorney would accuse you of ripping the blouse yourself and making this all up. Besides, the notion of a single girl winning a fight against two American army officers is not credible. Miss, we're warriors, trained to fight. You wouldn't stand a chance."

"Martel was so drunk he could barely stand. The other man was drunk and not very big. They probably didn't expect me to fight back."

Malone huffs. "Anything else, Miss Simmons?"

"What? Look at my face. The captain shoved me into a brick wall. See my forehead? The scrape on my cheek? Look at my ear. And I'm sure you noticed my fat lip. Or do you *allege* I did this myself?"

"Same issue. Good attorney'll say you fell, due to inebriety. Can you prove that's not so?"

"How do you prove a negative, Lieutenant?"

"Hardly my problem, miss. Anything else?"

My heartbeat pulses through my ears; the room is hot, close, the air used up. I feel the fingers, smell the breath. Malone's on their side. "That's the whole story."

"So, it was dark, you didn't get a clear look at their faces, your glasses were broken, so anything you allege will be thrown out by an amateur on the defense. All you know is that they were officers, by their uniforms, and you claim you recognized the voice of one, who you allege is Major Martel."

"Lieutenant, I don't allege anything. I stated the facts. I know Martel's voice, and I got a good enough look to recognize him. There is no mistake."

"Yeah, well, not much to go on. Since you don't have any witnesses to corroborate your side of the story, this is a case of 'she said, he said.' And those don't go very far, to be frank about it. Not a reporter against a major."

"In other words, since he's an officer and I don't have witnesses, forget it. And what if they succeeded and raped me?"

"Makes no difference. Unless the other man comes forth. Sometimes the accessory to a crime feels guilty. Then we can consider doing something."

My every muscle is taut. I want to slap Malone. But that will only get me a seat in a jail cell.

"Well, I guess that's it, huh? Are you going to file a report, investigate Major Martel?"

"No." He closes his notebook. "None of this is substantial enough to risk ruining the career of a well-respected officer or risk my own in so doing. I'll talk with my boss, but I'm sure that's what he'll say as well."

"Then I've wasted my time."

"You can be the judge of that. You've wasted mine."

"Keep your eyes out for an officer with a bandage on his right hand and another with a limp." I stand to leave. "Though I get the feeling you're not going to look, are you? Let me ask you one thing, Lieutenant."

Malone will not look at me.

"What's going to happen to the notes you took? Will they end up in your circular file?"

"Not necessarily. My superior officer will make that decision."

"Please consider this, then. This may not be the first time these two have done something like this. I know you all like to think of yourselves as officers *and* gentlemen. But I hope you've been around the army long enough to know that not all officers are the latter. You will be guilty of negligence if you don't keep a file on this."

"Leave the law to us. I'll show you out."

"Are you going to keep these, or do I take them with me?" I point at the clothes on the table.

"I'll keep them, just in case."

"I need the boots."

"Suit yourself."

I want to say I may need them again and that next time I'll leave the corpses in the alleyway for him to find as evidence, but that won't help my case. I shove the boots into my bag and leave the room. I take a deep breath of fresh air when I get outside the building. The sun doesn't cheer me up. All I see is the alleyway, the captain, Martel's excitement, my face in the mirror. Malone's words. *A well-respected officer. WELL RESPECTED?*

Chapter Ten
Major Ira Cunningham

Monday, May 27

The weekend reports lie on my desk. I leaf through censored dispatches and add a few journalistic touches to make my censors and the reporters look better. The last vestige of my former self still allowed to express itself. My colleagues in the press don't know what's really going on. None have been to the front. The information they receive in press briefings is fashioned to mislead the Germans rather than to give the folks at home accurate war reports. The dance between the press and military intelligence fascinated me at first—how to report events without giving the enemy useful information. But my job turned out to be a clumsy iron fist with no velvet glove. Fascination is now disgust.

At 7:28, I leave my office, get a cup of coffee, and head for the intelligence briefing. I nod at my lieutenants as I sit down and look around the room. "Where's Martel?" I ask Lieutenant Green.

"Called in sick."

A captain walks in, pulls a sheaf of papers from a briefcase, and lays them on the podium. He shuffles through them while smoking a cigarette. Not our usual briefer, Captain Buck. A hush falls over the room as he clears his throat. "All right, here's the latest." My mind wanders to my new assignment while the captain drones on about division dispositions, training, and locations. Trudy's arriving soon. Where is she now? On a ship? A train? It'll be so good to have her here—and Alice needs her friend. She seems so isolated. I can dish out fatherly advice, but she needs a peer, someone she can confide in—in a way I can't offer.

"Questions?"

I sip my coffee, now cold. Did I miss anything important? Maybe the bitter dregs in my cup will help.

A first lieutenant says, "I heard some scuttlebutt about the French government moving to Bordeaux again, like they did with the Battle of the Marne in '14."

"Not moving—moved. None of which can be reported. Redact anything about that if you see it in a press filing. Truth is, a Paris reporter would have to be blind not to notice. The German attack at Chemin des Dames, north of Reims, is serious."

"Where do *we* stand?" I ask. "Are there plans to evacuate Paris?"

"Officially, no. Between us? I packed a bag this weekend. Colonel Nolan warned the French that the Germans would hit Chemin des Dames. I can't tell you how we knew. Suffice it to say, the boss let the French know. It didn't go over well. They seemed to be insulted that we presumed to have intelligence they didn't. So officially, all is well, but we may need to move if the French don't hold."

"How about our civilians?" I ask.

"We need to keep a lid on this. Say nothing. Any other questions?"

The room remains silent. The captain slides the report into his briefcase, snaps it shut, and walks out. After a trip to the coffee room, I return to my office and shut the door. My eyes settle on my family photos while I mull over the briefing. On the broadest level, the German strategy is simple—take Paris and the French will sue for peace. That was their plan when they attacked in 1914, and it almost worked. French capitulation will break the back of the alliance and end the war before the US can mass enough troops to defeat the Kaiser. It's no secret, though my men suppress any mention of that in the press. It seems futile. Reports get out despite censorship. American ingenuity, creativity, and a few well-placed bribes take care of that. The briefer's unspoken answer to the question about civilian evacuation hangs over me. If the Germans reach Paris, what will they do to American civilians like Trudy, Alice, and my friends in the press?

I'm just settling in behind my desk when a knock on the door startles me. "Come."

My clerk, Stan. "Sir, Miss Simmons is here. She seems rather upset."

"Send her in."

Stan eases the door shut after Alice enters. She stands, restless, eyes full of fire and darting from side to side, hands fidgeting, face drawn with fatigue. She looks like she went a couple of rounds in a boxing ring. She wears her old wire-frames instead of her usual tortoiseshell glasses.

"What happened?" I ask.

"I met the Enrights and Sloans at the New York Bar Saturday evening," Alice says. "After I left the bar, Martel and some other officer, a captain, assaulted me. Tried to . . . well . . . take advantage of me."

My face flushes hot, the air in the room still, close. Rape? A vice grips my chest. I stare at the photo of Trudy and Alice, smiling. How can the father of a young woman's best friend ask about such a personal subject? Nothing could have prepared me for this. And how to control my temper? She doesn't need me going off a cliff here. I take a deep breath and slip a sheet of blank paper on my blotter. My first impulse is to find Martel and finish the man off. Okay, I have to calm down and get the facts before I cut his throat. Time to fall back on old journalistic habits—my version of warrior training. I pull a pen from my desk set and focus on the blank sheet of paper as I control my voice. "I'm sorry. Tell me what you . . . feel comfortable talking about. Take your time."

Alice tells me about the assault and doesn't seem to hold anything back. Instead, it's like an ice jam lets loose and the story flows out. It reminds me of some of the conversations I'd had with her before the war, where the line between daughter's friend, mentor, and confidante blurred. I avoid eye contact while she talks, taking notes I will not need, all the while struggling to think about what to do, how to respond. A bucket of guilt pours over me. The only reason I begged off going to the bar was tiredness. The attack wouldn't have happened if I hadn't been selfish. I could have been there.

Should have been there.

My blood boils while she describes meeting Lieutenant Malone at the provost marshal's office. I don't speak until she's done. "Martel wasn't at the briefing today. Neither was Ralph Buck, the captain who usually briefs us. They're drinking buddies."

"What does Buck look like?"

"A New York banker. Maybe five-six, hundred and thirty?" I chance eye contact. "Definite New York accent."

"Really white teeth? Perfect smile?"

"Yeah. Whitest teeth in the building. Got to be him."

"What can I do?"

"Sounds like you did a good job defending yourself. I didn't know you were a pugilist."

"No, just scared as hell. That put a little extra in my kicks."

What I want to do and what I recommend have to be two different things. "I hate to admit it, but I think Malone's right about one thing: it'll probably be your word against that of two officers. You can expect no help from the provost marshal. I'm sure you'll be persona non grata in this building, so watch yourself when you come here."

"I plan to take the back way out."

"Yeah, but you're one of the few women in the building. No crowd for you to blend into. There isn't anything I can do directly to Martel, since he's technically my superior. If my transfer comes in, I might not be in Paris." Alice takes off her spectacles and rubs the lenses on her skirt. The gears must be whirring in her brain. Mine too. "Are you open for a suggestion?" She nods. "Do your interview at the hospital. Think long and hard about using that nursing certificate of yours. That'll keep you away from here and will raise your value to the war effort. That may be helpful."

"Do you mean my reporting career here is dead?"

"No. Just . . . deferred. Look, Alice, it's like what I did after the time O'Connor threatened my family. Sometimes the best thing to do is to make a tactical withdrawal and find another way to prevail. Nursing is that for you. Your ace in the hole. Keep notes, write articles. It's not like there'll be any other reporter working in the hospitals. You may not get things out on a schedule, but I bet Pete and Howard have ways to get stories back to the States without my censors seeing them. I'm not officially advising you to do that, but it is possible."

"Will Martel get away with this?"

"How many rapists are convicted?" I hate to say that as anger flashes in Alice's eyes. "I'll see what I can do, but I can't make any promises." My words seem like a lame excuse. And, while I vow to do whatever it takes to bring Martel to justice, it feels like trying to sail into a raging headwind. The army protects its own.

I should have been there, walked her home that night.

My neck tingles at the memory of two Irish off-duty coppers walking toward me on the trolley, right hands inside folded newspapers . . . "I'll talk with Colonel McCabe, my boss. My transfer is the key. I can do nothing censoring reports, but I might be able to do something about Martel and Buck from the main intelligence office in Chaumont. I just need to figure out whose ear to bend, whose sense of honor to enrage."

Alice stands to leave.

"One more thing," I say. "Trudy'll get here soon—the thirtieth. Sneak through the back and pop in when you can. I'll buy you both lunch, like old times."

After Alice leaves, I go for a walk. I need a plan. Alice likes to fight her own battles. Physically, she won round one. But Martel won't stop, I'm sure of that. I hope I convinced Alice to work with Mary and Emily. Martel can't touch her at a Red Cross hospital. That will give me a chance to work behind the scenes. This will take some imagination and more than a little luck. And luck has no place in a battle plan. I'll need help. But I need to sort out who I can trust.

I return to the office a half hour later and smooth over the usual rough inconsistencies that my censors are blind to. I make the *Chicago Tribune*'s Floyd Gibbons look like a literary genius—again. Front-Page Floyd. Dashing, handsome, talk of the town—hell, talk of the world. And the dispatch going out is better than Floyd wrote. His melodramatic prose is filled with the bravado of a man who wouldn't understand his limits even if they smacked him in the eye.

And what am I? Not dashing, not handsome—a middle-aged reporter gone to seed, pulled off the assignment that got me on the front page by an editor who either cared about me and my family or was on the take. I'm not sure which. Then the job change, like a coward running away. But I had Ethyl and Trudy to think about. Heroes don't get their family killed. I look at Trudy's photo and feel my pulse course through my ears, a slight tremor in my right hand as I initial the final draft of the dispatch before it goes to the telegrapher Floyd bribed to get it out first. He thinks I don't know. Front page, above the crease. All of Floyd's stuff gets on the marquee. Am I jealous? Not really. I was a lot like him fifteen years ago, all full of myself, almost getting shot, putting my family at risk. I shake my head, toss the thing in my out-basket, and pick up the phone.

"I need to speak with Lieutenant Colonel McCabe, G-2 in Chaumont," I say when an operator comes on the line. "Yes, I'll hold."

Ten minutes later, a voice crackles over the wires. "McCabe."

"Cunningham, sir."

"Yes?"

"We need to talk."

Chapter Eleven
Alice Simmons

A gentle shower patters on the roof of the trolley as I mull over my visit with Ira. I hate to admit it, but he's right. There's no question whose side the army will take. None at all. One reporter against the institution of the US Army? Even with Ira's help, it would still be two against the War Department. Like Tennyson's "The Charge of the Light Brigade"—heroic futility. I'd present a less gallant picture going down in flames. I won't drag Ira down with me—I won't ruin his career too. So, like Ira said a few days ago, find another way.

But if that's so, why do I feel like a coward, running away with my tail between my legs? I was the one who stood up to the bullies at school, always on the side of the underdog. I am the one who goes straight at an enemy and beats them. But Ira's right—I may be able to break a tooth or nose of a drunkard, but I can't take on the whole army. There's got to be another way—like Ira said, a way to flank them—not the whole army, just Martel and that captain. In the meantime, I need a new job—one outside of their control.

So I'm on my way to Neuilly-sur-Seine to meet with Emily Enright. Americans just call it Neuilly—pronouncing it *Newly*. I smirk at the thought. My countrymen butcher the words, molding them to mouths and noses immune to Gallic intonations and subtlety. In French, it sounds more like *New-yee*. A distant cousin, now dead, had lived on the Île de la Grande Jatte, at Neuilly's northwest edge. Georges Seurat's painting of a Sunday afternoon there is one of my favorites—I saw it during one of my stays in Paris. That brings my first smile of the day. That time of my life reminds me of the painting—quiet, contemplative. But that could have been as much of an illusion as the tiny dots the painter used to create the work.

Tree-lined avenues and parks give Neuilly a relaxed, urbane air without too much pretension. The well-to-do live here. The French bourgeoisie knows how to tone it down for the sake of good taste. My mother's family fit that mold—they had done well but didn't blow trumpets.

I hop off the trolley and walk the last mile to let my thoughts settle. But they don't, and I frown at the memory of the crunch I felt when my palm hit the captain's face. But then there was his fetid beer breath, the heat, the nibble, the hate.

At least Trudy will be here soon. That'll put my two best friends close. The day she and I graduated from Minnesota was exciting, chaotic. Trudy couldn't keep her eyes off Bill, nor her hand off his elbow. The smirks on the faces of Trudy's and Bill's parents were precious. Grand-Mère Elise was regal, imposing. I imagined Queen Victoria looking up at her, then curtseying. Grand-Mère kissed both cheeks and whispered in French, "You live for two, dream for two. Follow your dream with courage, wherever it leads, my rabbit." Bile rises in my throat at what the dream has become. The memory of Justine. My little sister, barely old enough to have a dream. The shout of the wagon driver. The scream of the horse. Dead. My fault in Father's eyes.

Birds flitter from tree to tree, chirping a serenade to accompany me along Avenue Victor Hugo. I pass a park on the right, see the hospital, and turn left toward the entry. The street sign says *American Red Cross Hospital 1*, but the engraving on the gray stone standard above the door reads *The American Hospital*. My pulse quickens as I walk along the administrative corridor toward the nursing offices. After I identify myself, a clerk shows me to a small waiting room.

Emily Enright wears a navy-blue Army Reserve Nursing Corps uniform with a nursing cap and walks with a bustle and air of authority.

"Alice, I'm glad you came. Let me show you around—" Emily stops and squints. "What happened to your face?"

"Clumsy me. Fell right into a wall." I push my glasses up. "My others broke, so I'm stuck with my spares for now."

"You're feeling all right, though?"

"I look worse than I feel." I can't hold Emily's eyes with the lie—I want to scream the truth, to tell the world what Martel did. But I don't want to ruin my chances for a position at the hospital and don't know how Emily would react if I told her the whole story. Men aren't the only ones who put all the blame on the victim of a rape. Ira had been my confessor. Emily seems like someone I can confide in. Maybe I should trust her. I take in a breath, about to say . . .

Emily turns and walks out of the room. "Well, come on. I'll show you the original hospital, and then we'll go to the Annex. It's four blocks away."

"That seems pretty far away for an annex." I'm sweating from my near outburst of the truth. Better to hold off for now.

"Best we could do. This building only had twenty-four beds when we started. We needed to expand, but the adjacent buildings weren't suitable. The French agreed to let us use a nearby high school for the duration. Its real name is the Lycée Pasteur. Officially, it's called the American Ambulance since most of our current patients are French. Made sense to use their word for hospital, not ours. We just call it the Annex."

We tour the original hospital, the surgical suites, and then the small medical and surgical wards. After that, we go outside and stroll south to the Annex. A wrought-iron fence stands between the sidewalk and a large gravel parking lot fronting a four-story pink-and-gray stone building complex. It looks like it was built around a courtyard, though it's hard to tell from the sidewalk. The name *Lycée Pasteur*, carved on the standard above the main entry, becomes visible as we walk through the parking lot toward the front door. The putter and pop of idling ambulances makes conversation difficult, the air strong with gasoline exhaust and cigarette smoke. A French sergeant shouts orders, directing litter-bearers carrying stretchers laden with wounded men to the waiting ambulances. A dozen men wearing tattered uniforms line up behind a troop truck. They must be convalescent patients, not ready for discharge, but on their feet.

"We're doing a transition right now," Emily says. "The French have been moving their patients to hospitals farther away. We're taking it over. This building brings us up to six hundred beds, and we can expand that up to a thousand with tents in the courtyard."

"These patients don't look ready for discharge."

"The French started moving them out two days ago. They haven't told us anything. The men are being transferred farther west."

"I heard that they evacuated their government to Bordeaux over the past week." Rumors are fodder for reporters.

Emily nods. "Big doings somewhere near Reims. Things seem ominous, but there isn't much I can do other than carry on. I'm worried about Howard and Pete, though. There are rumors the French are teetering and that if the Germans break through, they could be here in the next two weeks. We may be safe—the Germans need nurses. They don't need American reporters."

"Are you expecting many admissions soon?" Familiar hospital odors fill the air as we walk through the building—alcohol, Lysol, and a hint of carbolic acid. Polished parquet floors sparkle in the sunlight. Footsteps echo along the long halls.

"Anyone's guess. The French are very tight-lipped. I think they consider us a security risk, but we're not alone."

I narrow my eyes. "How could we be a security risk?"

"You'll have to ask the French. One of our nurses is married to a US Marine lieutenant colonel. She says the French are so obsessed with security that they often don't tell the officers about a planned attack until the moment the unit steps off."

"That makes no sense."

"Her husband's words aren't so kind, according to his wife. Though I suppose you can't have a security lapse if nobody, including your own people, knows about an attack."

"Where do your nurses live?"

"The top floor is a dormitory. We're using that for some of our staff."

"Is there room for me?"

"Not right away. We have to start you as a nursing aide until your credentials are verified. I'll warn you, some of our senior nurses resent the aides. As a compromise, we don't house them in the dorm—only nurses and other fully credentialed staff. When this place gets busy, you won't want a long walk home."

"How about the pay?"

"Fully qualified nurses make fifty-five dollars per month, including the room and board at the dormitory. Pay for aides is half that. Rents around here are steep. You won't find a nice place on that salary."

"I have a little trust fund that will help."

Emily shows me several wards, introduces me to nurses, and finishes up at the canteen for a cup of coffee. I scan the large cafeteria. "It seems eerie. It's so empty."

Emily looks up from her cup. "Maybe not for long. Like I said, something's up."

"I've had time to think about it over the weekend. I'm ready to sign up." I'll keep Saturday's events to myself for now. Nurses have been terminated for having sex before marriage, and rape is the most brutal version of that. But then, by not telling Emily about it, am I lying or covering it up? Will that come back to haunt me? Better to take that risk than to have another door slam in my face.

"Let's go back to my office. I've got the paperwork for you there."

As we go back through the parking court, I ask, "Could you explain a little more about the army side of this?"

"It's confusing. For you to join the Army Nurse Corps, you'll have to go back to the US, apply, and go through military training. Then you might or might not end up back here. I need you here, now. We'll get you into the Red Cross. Then we can look into the Corps. I should warn you, nurses don't have the rank of officer nor the rating of enlisted personnel. We're in limbo land. Nobody knows whether to salute us or not. At least they pay the Red Cross scale."

"I'm trying to sort out what to do about my reporting job. Would I be able to write an occasional article?"

"You can write all you want. I doubt the army will let you publish them until after the war."

Chapter Twelve
Major Ira Cunningham

Wednesday, May 29

The morning briefing is about to begin. I grab a cup of coffee on the way and spill a dollop on the floor when I enter the conference room. Martel's face is a mess. A large bandage covers his nose. Martel sits in a front-row seat with a seething expression and a posture that says *don't ask*. I stifle a smile, sit across the aisle, and take a surreptitious sidelong glance. Alice really did a job on him. I want to stand up and accuse Martel, to lift the curtain of silence and reveal the man for what he is . . .

Brisk footsteps stop me. Captain Ralph Buck strides past with a bandaged right hand. He raises the cover on the map at the front of the room using his left hand. He looks like he's been hit by a train. A bulging, violaceous bruise on his upper lip tells me everything I need to know. The other officers in the room murmur.

"Let's begin." Buck slaps a pointer at a spot northeast of Paris. "None of the following leaves this room." He frowns. "Several German corps attacked the French Sixth Army . . ."

Every *s* whistles while Buck talks. Instead of showing off his teeth like usual, Buck speaks with tight lips as if to hide his most telling injury.

I wish it had been my hand that mangled Buck's face. But if I had been there, Buck and Martel would have chosen another victim.

Anger and outrage distract me while Buck drones on.

"... broke the back of the French ..."

It's obvious why it would have taken both of them—Buck is as intimidating as a member of the debate team. I've seen plenty of these types—officious prigs that prance around with overblown airs of authority.

"... the German Crown Prince's forces are elite. Seasoned ..."

Alice's handiwork fills me with a sense of fatherly pride amid my personal guilt.

"... at the current rate, they'll reach the outskirts of Paris in a week . . ."

Parental rage churns my gut. I imagine pounding both men's faces to a pulp if they attack Trudy. But I won't resort to violence. It isn't worth it. My time in St. Paul taught me how to deal with crooked cops and the machine politicians that protected them. It forced me to play a subtler game. Well, not a game—the ones who had come gunning for me played for keeps. Where had I read it? *The acme of war is to win without a fight.* Or something like that. My strategy over the years since St. Paul. Deep breath. Keep my emotions in check. Discipline.

"Questions?" Buck's fat lip slurs the word.

I have plenty but hold my tongue.

"Thank you, Captain Buck." Martel stands. "Dismissed." It's almost comical how the blocked nose affects the Louisianan's accent and makes his baritone a sort of shallow whine. Buck pulls the cover over the map and leaves.

I face Martel with an itch to deliver a roundhouse fist to his nose. But . . . Discipline. Violence will not help my cause. "Glad to have you back, sir." The other officers filter out of the room. When we are alone, I ask in the kindest tone I can muster, "If you don't mind my asking, sir, what happened?"

Martel frowns, and his face colors. He doesn't meet my gaze, looking to the right instead. "Attacked by a gang of ruffians after a top-secret meeting on Saturday evening. Buck and I fought for our very lives."

"They catch 'em?"

"No, but I'm sure we sent more than a few to the hospital." Martel's unmarred hands make his lie obvious.

"Any reason they attacked you?"

"They have some sort of connection with that damned reporter I told you about last week—Alice Simmons."

"What sort of connection?" I straighten my fingers from the fists that are beginning to form.

"Some sort of . . . conspiracy, I do believe."

Martel's eyes flash with anger. As if he knows I know Alice and is ready for me to confront him. "A reporter? How?"

"I am surely bewildered about that matter myself. Buck and I were walking home from a secret briefing, minding our own business, when out of an alleyway popped these thugs. Led by that . . . girl. It was dark, so I can't be sure, but I think there were at least ten of 'em." Martel starts walking like a bronco rider after a very bad go as we leave the briefing room. "She comes in? Call security, hear me?"

The story about the secret briefing will fall apart with testimony from the dozens of reporters at the New York Bar that night. Martel is being more creative than I had thought possible. What is the phrase? *Never underestimate your enemy.* The underlying threat worries me. Accusations like these divert attention from the guilty.

I go to my office and put a call in to Lieutenant Colonel McCabe. After a few minutes of static, McCabe's voice comes over the receiver. "Ira, I was going to call. Your request for transfer is approved."

"Thank you, sir." I smile. "In follow-up to our previous conversation, Captain Buck has a bandage on his right hand and a bruised face. I'm not sure about the missing tooth, but his speech sounded like it. Major Martel looks like a raccoon that ran face first into a truck— broken nose and dueling shiners. Hell of a limp, too. Told me Miss Simmons is leading a gang of ruffians. Claims he and Buck were in a top-secret meeting."

"Credible?"

"No. I've known the young lady for more than a decade. Martel is spinning a story, sir. Classic diversionary attack. Both men were in a bar immediately before the assault, quite drunk, according to a couple of witnesses I personally know and at least a dozen more I can reach out to if necessary."

"Well, not your problem after tomorrow. Report to Colonel Nolan in Chaumont on Friday."

McCabe has it wrong—it is my problem.

Chapter Thirteen
Alice Simmons

It takes a half hour to pack my meager possessions into the steamer trunk that serves as my dresser and armoire. The room I rent has as much emotional significance as a hotel room. The choice was one of expediency rather than expectation. My landlady is staying at a cousin's place for a few days. The only noise is the tick of my alarm clock. Four bangs on the apartment door startle me. I finish slipping a pair of socks into the trunk. Two more bangs and a loud voice calls, "Miss Simmons."

"Who is it?"

Two more loud knocks.

"Again, who are you?"

"Provost marshal's officers."

Maybe it's my new paranoid self, but I'm not going to just pull the door wide open to whoever this is. I ease the iron doorstop three inches back, set my left foot on it, then unlock the door. A booted foot tries to shove in the door, but the stop works. "What do you want?"

"Miss Simmons?"

"That's my name. What do you want? I'm not a member of the military." An American sergeant stands at the door, a corporal behind him, both with sidearms.

"We have orders to escort you to the provost marshal's office. Major Burrows wants to talk with you."

Lieutenant Malone's report must have gotten through. Maybe he wasn't as bad as I'd first thought. I nudge the doorstop away and let the two men in. "I'll be happy to come with you. Let me grab my purse."

"We'll have to search it."

"Why?" I feel my face flush.

"Routine, miss. Just . . . hand it over."

The man opens each pocket and picks his way through as if he did this every day. Why do they care? Do they think I carry a gun? He hands it back to me.

The sergeant motions to the door. The other backs into the hallway. Do they think I'll bite? I lock the door and follow the sergeant down the stairs, the corporal behind. On the street, the corporal opens the back door of a staff car while the sergeant gets in the front passenger seat. The back seat smells like last month's cigarettes and a few fetid odors I don't want to know about. The windows are closed, the air close, hot, and muggy. I want to open a window, but the window and door handles are missing. The corporal slides behind the wheel while the sergeant fires up a cigarette.

"Sergeant, could you open a window, please? It's stuffy back here."

The car pulls into traffic. The men keep their windows closed. Neither speaks, nor do they seem to invite any conversation. Fine. I watch Paris go by as we drive to their office.

At least they aren't ignoring my report. Things may be looking up.

The sergeant opens my door when we arrive at the provost marshal's office. He has a firm grip on my right elbow as he navigates me into the building and back to the same small room where I met Lieutenant Malone. The ashtray is empty. A strong odor of Lysol fills my nose. Have they found the captain? He shouldn't have been difficult to spot. And Martel? How had he explained his wounds? I smile and look up when the door opens.

A man in his mid-thirties wearing a well-pressed US Army officer's uniform walks in. He's about six feet tall with short, sandy hair. He sits without looking at me, opens a folder, and lays out two typed pages. They must be Malone's notes.

Without raising his eyes, the man says, "I'm Major Burrows. You are Miss Alice Simmons?"

"Yes, I am. I'm glad to meet you."

"Humph." Burrows reads one of the sheets. "Why's that?"

"I assume you're reading Lieutenant Malone's report. I met with him Sunday and told him about the assault."

"Really?" He still doesn't look up. "Malone didn't file any assault reports involving women this weekend."

My neck tingles. "I gave the lieutenant my report about two army officers assaulting me. Major Martel and a captain. Saturday. Are you his commanding officer?"

Burrows stiffens in his chair. "Yes. As I said, he didn't report anything important to me from the weekend. He's off today."

"He told me he would discuss the matter with you. If this isn't about my report, then why am I here?"

"I have affidavits from Captain Ralph Buck and Major Richard Martel accusing you and a gang of hooligans of assaulting them on the night of Saturday, May 25." Burrows looks up and finally holds my eyes.

My face flashes hot as I clench my fists below the table and try to slow time down. Ira always told me to never answer an accusation quickly. Take your time, take a deep breath. Think before you speak. I straighten my fingers and look into Major Burrows's face. "They accused *me* of assaulting *them*? With a gang?" Burrows nods. I stand, set both palms on the table, and glare into Burrows's eyes. "That's the most *ridiculous* thing I've ever heard. *They* assaulted *me*—tried to . . . force themselves upon me." Somehow, the word *rape* is a like a branding iron. I can't say it. I pace. "Beat *me* up—look at *my* face. Broke my glasses. Ripped *my* clothes off." I know I should act like a demure belle, wronged by fate. No. So much for calm. This is too much. And I'm overreacting, doing exactly what Ira warned me never to do.

"Sit down. Now. If you don't, I'll have you arrested."

"On what charge?" My voice is tight.

"Threatening me." He stands and thrusts a pointed finger toward the chair I had been in. "Sit!"

I sweep my right hand gently around the room. "Threaten you? Me and my gang, here in the room? Are we scaring you?" I glare at him.

"This is pathetic." I stand a safe distance across the table from a man who I'm sure wants to pound me into the floor. Settle down. Ira warned me . . . I gaze at the ceiling, take a deep breath, and sit.

"You're not helping yourself." He lowers his tone and sits back down. "Have any witnesses to back your allegations up?"

"I was alone. That's how rape works, for the most part. Maybe they didn't teach you that in cop school." Ok, calm down now. I take a deep breath, then consciously relax my face. "I reported all this to Lieutenant Malone on Sunday in this room."

"I'll go see if he filed a report." Burrows rises and locks the door behind him.

My mind races. Chaotic fragments of that night come to me—the sound of drunken voices, slurring the edges of words; my blouse ripping; the hot beer breath of the captain—Buck. Martel's fingers.

Shouldn't have blown my stack. What's wrong with me? How could they accuse *me*? This has unglued me. I remember a couple of rape victims I took care of in nursing school. I thought they were emotionally unhinged, weak, psycho. I owe them an apology.

After several long minutes, the door lock clicks and Burrows walks in. "There was no report. Miss, you're in a lot of trouble. Best start telling me the truth. It'll go easier that way."

"I told you the truth." I speak through clenched teeth. "They assaulted me."

"Not according to the testimony of two officers. I have no reason to believe you and every reason to believe them."

"I gave Lieutenant Malone what was left of my clothing."

"Not in evidence. I checked."

"Then you'd better find out where he hid them."

Anger flashes in his eyes. "Lady, don't presume to give me orders."

"Don't presume to give me any either, Major. This whole thing smacks of a cover-up. Unless I'm under arrest, I'm leaving."

Burrows stands, face red, looking like he's ready to slug me. "At this point, the only thing keeping me from arresting you is a jurisdictional dilemma. As much as I want to throw the likes of you in a cell, I can't arrest a civilian." His voice is strained with anger. "Nor can I legally hold you. The Paris police will be the arresting agency." He unlocks the door and walks out.

I storm out of the office and hop on a trolley. My mind races, struggling to absorb the facts, to process them—but I can't make sense of it.

But to accuse me? I didn't start this.

Stop.

Think.

Of course. That's the way it often goes. Though usually, the man accuses the victim of luring him, provoking him. The victims aren't usually accused of leading a band of hooligans. That's a creative twist. But then, how else could Martel and Buck explain their injuries? The idea that a mere girl could do so much damage to two brave and courageous army officers would be an affront to their manhood. Never mind that they were blind drunk.

The French executed Mata Hari last year on evidence as flimsy as this. That may be Martel's plan.

Part of me would like to hop a ship and head home, but I'm sure the French won't let me leave with these new accusations. Paris passes by as I watch through the window. I'm suddenly alone and vulnerable in ways that are completely foreign to me.

My fingers find the necklace fragment in my purse. I was ten, running behind my little sister, Justine. Chasing our dog along Lake Street. Fluffy darted into the street, and Justine followed without looking. Then the awful sound. Childhood's end.

Chapter Fourteen
Alice Simmons

Thursday, May 30 - Memorial Day

My senses sharpen as I walk along the street toward Ira's office building, still on edge after my interrogation by Burrows. I hardly slept last night—pacing softly in my room, trying to not bother the neighbors, muttering to myself like a nutcase, scripting what I'll say if I cross paths with Martel or Buck. I can't expect any help or support from the other correspondents. Some of them will relish my downfall. They'll say things like, "What do you expect . . . ?" or, "She had it coming . . ." or, "That's what happens when women try to do a man's job." And really, if any try to help me, Martel will blackball them.

Ira's office is my safe harbor in the middle of a stormy sea. Maybe Trudy will be there by now, seeing Ira. I need my best friends. Maybe my only friends.

I stride up the front steps and scan the reception area—no Martel. No captain with dressings on his hand. What does his face look like? Ira had told me to come in the back, but that seems cowardly. No. I won't creep around like a criminal. I continue past the reception clerk without my usual nod and smile, take the stairs to the second floor one deliberate step at a time. The humid air is close, constricting, redolent with tobacco smoke and coffee. The clatter of typewriters, murmur of conversations, and ringing of phones seem louder than usual.

Nobody stops me, and I get to Ira's office without being shot. Stan glances down the hallway after I enter, like he expects the police to rush in. He puts his right index finger to his lips and motions me to follow him. He sticks his head out the hallway door and looks in both directions. We slink down the corridor. He uses a key to open a door and ushers me in. "Major Cunningham's talking with his daughter. He wants you here. Martel's keeping an eye on our office. I'll bring Miss Cunningham here, then the two of you will have this room as long as you like. The major said he'd like you and Trudy to join him at the café two doors down in about twenty. Be careful. Martel's on a warpath." He locks the door after he leaves.

The small office has a desk and two chairs coated with a layer of dust. A row of worn thumbtacks line the bottom of a smudged cork bulletin board above the desk. I slump into the swivel chair and lean back with a squeak.

A knock on the door five minutes later is followed by a key scraping into the lock and a click. Stan closes the door as soon as Trudy is in.

"Dad told me to meet you in secret. What's this all about? He wouldn't say." Trudy's smile melts into a concerned frown. She gives me a hug, stands back, and narrows her eyes. "What happened to you?"

"Long story."

"Are you sick?"

"At heart, maybe, but physically okay. Mentally, I won't swear to sanity."

"You look like you got beat up after pulling one of our all-nighters back in nursing school. Where's your locket?"

Trudy's iridescent blue eyes glow against her porcelain complexion. She wears the dark blue serge uniform of the Army Nurse Corps with polished black shoes and a snug fabric belt around her tiny waist. An Army Nurse Corps pin shines on her left collar—a gilded medical caduceus with the white enameled *NC* just below the snake's heads in the center.

I plop into the desk chair, motioning for Trudy to sit. "How was your voyage?"

"Came over on a tub called the SS *Caserta*. They kept me and the girls in the upper decks—officer country—to protect our virtue. Jack Johnson's dad, Ab, was on the boat, so I had good company. He's with Dad now, in his office."

"How is Jack? I haven't seen him since graduation."

"Not sure. His dad told me they'd had a falling out over Jack joining the marines. I think he respects my Bill's decision to enlist in the army more, even though Bill is only a private. Jack's a lieutenant."

"Any word from Bill?"

"No. It's driving me buggy. I send letters, but none come back. He's in France, but they apparently keep moving the Second Division around so much the mail never catches up."

"How about Jack?" I ask.

"Bill told me he was in Virginia, last he heard. Training as a replacement officer."

"I hate to think about why they will need replacement officers." Trudy wasn't the only one who tried to set me up with Jack in college. We hit it off—best of friends. But I was reticent over relationships with men at the time. He's a handsome, rugged Montanan—he can do better than the Librarian. And I'm not ready for more. "When did you arrive?"

"We landed in Brest a few days ago." Trudy chuckles. "You French have a strange way of naming things. Anyway, after that, a long train ride. But really, how are you?"

"Not sure where to begin. Angry, frustrated, and maybe a little afraid."

"What about?"

I tell her about the events of the last week, leaving out nothing. At the end, my hands tremble. I'm drained. "And that's where my locket is. In Martel's possession, I assume."

"Dad know?"

I nod, looking down at the floor.

"That explains his mood. There must be something he can do."

"I fight my own battles." My face is tight. "You know me."

Trudy holds her hands up in surrender. "That's the Alice I know." She puts her hands down. "But if you're planning to take on the US

Army, don't do it by yourself. You have friends. Lean on them. Dad can probably help. Maybe Mr. Johnson too. He's a major, like Dad."

"When I reported it, it seemed like the first action was to circle the wagons and blame me. I'm honestly not sure how to fight that." I need to change the subject. "Where will you be working?"

"I report to Nurse Enright at Red Cross Military Hospital Number One. Know where that is?"

"Yeah. I start on Monday as an aide."

"Aide?" Trudy's eyes widen. "You're one of the best nurses I know."

"Didn't bring my papers. I guess I was so full of my dreams that I didn't have a plan B. Mrs. Enright is waiting for my credentials. Where are you planning to live?"

"At the hospital. There's a dorm. That's what they recommended. You?"

"I found a room a couple of blocks away—"

An explosion knocks the air out of my chest and obliterates my words in midair. A loud crash sounds, my ears ring, and the office fills with dust through the shattered window. We rush to the door. A sneeze catches me amid the dust storm as I open the door. I reach for a handkerchief to put over my face. It doesn't smell like fire—not yet—just plaster and dust.

"What just happened? Did a boiler explode? What?" Trudy shouts.

I peer into a corridor that's suddenly too narrow for all the staff surging by. Panicked reporters dodge past, several with cigarettes stuck to their lips, eyes terrified. An army captain touches my elbow, and I glance at a worried face and uninjured hands. "Better get along, miss. Have to evacuate." He wears medical pins. I follow him through the hall, down the stairs, and out into the street, Trudy at my heels.

Chaos and panic greet us when we reach the sidewalk. The shattered windows of the café where Ira invited us to breakfast hang on strips of tape. Tables and chairs lie upended in the rubble. Trudy dashes toward the café when Ira and Jack's father emerge, looking like snowmen, covered in white dust. Mr. Johnson holds a cloth napkin over his bleeding nose. Ira pulls a chair out of the rubble as Trudy arrives and eases Mr. Johnson into it. Trudy doesn't need my help—she can handle this. I look around, trying to decide what to do. Reporters write furiously in notepads, their cameramen snapping photos, helping nobody, and I realize how useless the press is at a moment like this.

The facade of the building above the café has collapsed across the street, crushing a taxicab, the driver still in it. The sides of the building stand, smoke rising from the cratered center. The rubble is a jumble of glass, stones, and wooden framework fractured like a tornado blew through. And people. Bodies. Shouts. Barked orders. To my left, a man holds a small girl with a red stain spreading across the front of her pink-and-white-striped pinafore. I start in their direction. Shouts to the right draw my eyes to a woman, her right arm a gory mess. A small man wearing an immaculate navy uniform shoves by to tend to the young girl, so I pick my way toward the woman with the ruined arm.

Two army medical officers stumble through the debris alongside me, the captain from the hallway and a colonel. The woman stares at her right arm, whimpering. She mumbles confused French. Her hand is crushed, two fingers hanging by threads. Bright blood spurts from torn arteries. Bone fragments jut through her wrist. The colonel grabs the arm above the elbow while the captain fumbles with his Sam Browne belt. I speak in French to the victim while the captain gets his shoulder strap off. "Don't worry. You won't die. I have two fine doctors here with me to care for you."

The navy surgeon rushes up, shouting at the colonel. "You fool, that's the wrong spot." He shoves the colonel aside and uses both hands to compress above the elbow. Why did he do that? The colonel had good compression on the artery. I work my way behind the woman and wrap the captain's belt around the arm, above the doctor's hands, and tighten it. The captain hands me a window frame remnant. I tighten the tourniquet, glance into the Navy doctor's intense gray eyes, and nod. He wears US Navy medical collar pins and the sleeve stripes of a lieutenant, junior grade. "I think it's tight enough to try loosening your grip, sir."

The surgeon's hands ease off. No bleeding. "Great work. Can you stay with her? There are others . . ."

"Thanks, Lieutenant—what's your name?"

"Beck."

"Thanks, Lieutenant Beck. I've got this." The navy surgeon and the army captain pick their way toward the remains of the café. The adrenaline is flowing, but my hands are steady. An odd feeling settles in. I've felt it before while working in the emergency room at Minneapolis General during training—like being in a hurricane, chaos surrounding me but I'm the calm at the center. Trudy holds a towel over Mr. Johnson's nose, red spreading around her hands. I'd like to help others, but this is my patient now. My job is her care. I'm her nurse.

Martel stands on the building's stoop shouting orders, though I can't understand them. His voice is strangled—it makes me smile for a moment. My boot took away part of his baritone. He locks anger-filled eyes on mine. I focus on my patient and ignore him.

Sirens wail and bells clang as emergency vehicles squeal to a stop near me. The clatter of shod hoofs on pavement and shouts in French grow louder—the fire brigade arrives and unwinds their hose with a loud grinding noise. Two ambulance attendants bring a litter. The colonel and I help settle the woman onto it, and the four of us carry her to the ambulance. The attendants slide the stretcher in, and the colonel says, "Didn't I see you with the press corps earlier?"

"Yes, sir."

"What's your name, if I may ask?"

"Alice Simmons."

"And you're a reporter?"

"Been trying to be."

"You must have some medical experience."

"Yes, sir. I'm also an RN."

"A suggestion, Nurse Simmons, from a doctor who knows his nurses. Quit wasting your time with reporters. The army is desperate for nurses like you. Call me if you need a reference." He hands me a card. I glance at it and then back as Colonel Wadhams stumbles through the detritus toward the café.

The ambulance attendant says in French, "Nurse, are you able to ride with the patient? My assistant is new and has already vomited once after seeing the wound."

I clamber into the back of the ambulance and sit next to the pasty-faced assistant. "Where are your dressings?" I say in French. The assistant stammers a few words and points to a box. I paw through paper-wrapped Red Cross dressing packets. These are like the ones I helped Mother make last year. What would she think if she could see me? I rip open one with a white label, cursing the person who made it—too much glue. I slip the gauze sponges out of their sterile packing and lay them on the wound. "Please, sir, lift the arm so I can get this underneath."

The patient screams when the attendant raises the arm a few inches off the stretcher. I swathe the hand, wrist, and lower arm with a roll of sterile gauze. I'm afraid the sweaty attendant will erupt again and need to distract him. "How long to the hospital?"

"A few minutes. At the most, five."

"Good. Ease the arm down, please."

The ambulance careens through the streets, jerking us around a corner, then to a stop. The driver comes to the back. I help him slide the stretcher out, then grab the other end while the assistant vomits next to the rear wheel. "It's going to be a long day with your friend."

We carry the woman into the receiving area and lay the stretcher on a cart. A doctor walks over, trailed by two nurses. "And what have we here?" he asks the ambulance driver. The driver nods to me.

"Right hand crush injury," I say in French. "She has extensive palmar and digital lacerations, near amputations of the fourth and fifth digits, open wrist fracture with bilateral arterial lacerations. There was severe hemorrhage at the scene with shock. I applied a tourniquet, then four-by-fours to the wrist, an absorbent dressing to the hand, and wrapped it with gauze on the ride here."

"You are perhaps a physician, mademoiselle?"

"No. I'm a nurse."

"A very good one, at that."

"Is there anything else I can do to help, Doctor?"

"We'll take it from here." The physician points toward a man. "Monsieur Girard will not let the orderlies take his dead daughter away. Perhaps some kind words from you will help."

Monsieur Girard clutches his dead little girl—the one in the pinafore that Dr. Beck had gone to before he worked with me. She must have been killed instantly. I ask the orderlies to bring the two to a private room. The poor child's chest has been ripped open by shrapnel. Her name is Anna. Her pretty face, slack where dimples may have been, pale in death, eyes closed—thank God for that. I brush a strand of soft blond hair out of Anna's face.

I put a hand on Monsieur Girard's shoulder and peer into his tear-filled eyes. Mine are dry, and I wish they weren't. I blink hard. Nothing, despite the empty space in my chest as I look down at the little girl. Oh God. So like Justine. Same age. Same hair. I was a river of tears after Justine, until my father let his opinion slip. His accusation was a spear through my heart. Grand-Mère's love was the only thing that got me through it, but I haven't shed a tear since. Haven't been able to, even in a situation like this.

I stay with them, speaking with the father like I wish someone had talked with me after Justine died. I need to stay with him as much as he seems to need me. I may have finished nursing school at the top of my class, but I never connected with any of my patients like this. For the first time since I arrived in Paris, I have a place in the world. And, perhaps, a way to forgive myself.

Chapter Fifteen
Major Ira Cunningham

Ab Johnson is still at the hospital when I arrive back at the office to a scene of quieting chaos. The fire in the building next door is out. Firemen pick through the remains of the building. A few windows in ours are now boarded up, the staff dusting and mopping up. I go to the restroom, take off my uniform and shake out the dust and flour, then rinse Ab's blood off my right sleeve, all the while thanking God Trudy and Alice hadn't joined us for breakfast. The woman sitting at the table next to us died of a broken neck. The only parts of the chef not crushed were his legs. My uniform is still a mess, and I don't have a spare here.

The war is so close, so immediate. Jack's on his way over and Bill's here, though I don't know where. The fate of my daughter's heart is in peril she cannot imagine, and there's not a damned thing I can do about it. Hope for the best. But hope is like an unraveling thread from which we all hang.

I've known Ab's son Jack since the age of three. He was born in Paris when Ab worked at the embassy. I saw him grow up during intermittent visits over the years. Then Jack roomed with Bill at Minnesota. Ethyl and I had the four of them—Trudy, Alice, Bill, and Jack—over for suppers on weekends all through their college years. The best of times. I always hoped Jack and Alice would become more than friends. They seem like a good match, but I have learned that friendship, real friend-ship, can be more durable than romance. And Alice needs friends at a moment like this.

My hands still shake from the explosion still reverberating inside me. I'm glad to be getting out of here, but what about Trudy? She'll be exposed to the massive German cannon everyone calls the Paris Gun that hit us today, imminent invasion, scoundrels like Martel. I want to spirit her away to a tower in southern France with a suit of armor.

A knock on the door startles me. "Sir, Major Martel wants to see you." I follow the clerk, feeling like luck has abandoned me.

Martel looks up from a report. "You're a disgrace to the uniform. Look at you. Dusty, bloody."

"I just came from the hospital. No time to put on a fresh uniform."

"Consider yourself to be on report." Martel's eyes bore into me. "I heard the little bitch was in the building earlier."

On report? Bitch? From the pig I'm looking at. Okay, Ira, simmer. "Who, sir?"

"You know damned well who I mean. Simmons." He smacks his fist on the desk.

"Passed her in the hall."

"I ordered for her to be arrested on sight." Martel's spittle sprays his desk. "I heard she went to your office. You should have reported it to the security detachment. She's dangerous."

"I was distracted, sir. An old friend arrived, and I was taking him out for breakfast." I try a diversion.

"That could have waited."

"Thought didn't occur, sir." I don't ordinarily like to lie. But with Martel? The word *sir* sticks in my craw.

"I'll put you in the stockade if that happens again." Martel grabs a cigar out of a crystal holder, snaps off the tip, taps the end on his desk twice, and raises it to his lips. He motions his head toward his lighter.

It takes me a moment before I understand. This is pure bullshit. I grab the lighter on the desktop, flick it to life, then extend it toward Martel's cigar like a servant. And I'm tempted to raise the flame and set the man's hair on fire. That hair tonic must be flammable. The thought almost makes me smile. I wonder if the slaves Martel's family undoubtedly had thought the same thing as they lit the massa's cigars.

"You have been on the edge of insubordination, Cunningham."

"Sir?"

"Don't deny it, Major." Martel blows smoke in my face, the corners of his lips upturned as he leans back.

I keep my poker face. "You're aware that there are two sides to this story—"

Martel leans forward. "I am taken to understand that your lovely daughter is now in Paris." His gaze bores into my eyes. "It would surely be a tragedy if this swept her up as well, wouldn't it?"

My blood turns to ice. The final confrontation with Chief O'Connor on the steps of city hall flashes through my mind. It's happening again.

"Say no more," Martel says, "and I'll have no reason to inquire after her . . . health. Even a whisper and . . . You take my meaning? Clear out your desk. Be gone by three. Don't presume to show your ugly hide in these parts again. I'll keep an eye on your daughter—make sure nothing . . . amiss . . . occurs. I have it on good authority that she'll be residing in the nurses' dormitory, in a building they call the Annex."

I walk out of the room without saluting Martel. The nightmare of St. Paul roars through my thoughts. What century does Martel think we are in? And that business with the cigar. Nothing but an egotistical show. A statement of power.

Threaten Trudy?

No.

Not this time.

I won't run away.

But isn't that what I'm doing, transferring to Chaumont? Maybe I should cancel my transfer. But I need to be outside Martel's control. I'll talk with Emily Enright about Martel's threat to Trudy.

Withdraw, regroup, and come at him from a different angle.

I ask Stan for a box when I get back to my office. A small one will do. After loading in my photos, pens, and smoking supplies, I pause near the press room and look in. Howard Enright is handing Lieutenant Green a sheet of paper. I linger at the door and catch Howard's eye.

"What's up?" Howard asks, nodding toward the box.

"The finest commanding officer in the AEF is *allowing* me to leave early. I'm thinking the Talbot. Gotta talk with you and Pete about a few things."

"Five?"

"See you there." Howard leaves, and I turn to my favorite censor. "Lieutenant Green, a word?" I usher Green to a corner and in a hushed voice say, "You're on your own. I'm out of here, now."

"Bit abrupt."

"Martel gave me the heave-ho. Can't really say I got the boot since I was leaving anyway. Teed off I didn't arrest Miss Simmons. He's making some ridiculous accusations against her. I think you need to be aware . . ."

"Scuttlebutt suggests Major Martel's story is as fishy as the hold of a Norwegian herring boat."

"Worse. Keep your ear to the ground and stay in touch."

"Will do, sir. And it's been an honor."

I shake Green's extended hand and leave.

After dumping my boxed possessions at my billet, I put the things from the office in my already packed bags. I don't have a ride until Saturday, but I might be able to bum one in the morning with one of the intelligence officers I know. I don't want anything to do with the army tonight, so I change into my one set of civvies.

My lower back has been a Gordian knot since the café explosion. I stop to stretch it several times on my walk. By the time I reach the Talbot, it feels better. The hushed bar soothes me. Howard and Pete are in a back booth, both facing the door, tumblers in front of them.

"Monsieur?" asks Jean-Luc as I pass. He's already placing a tumbler on the bar.

"Usual."

"Le Grouse it is."

Jean-Luc delivers my scotch and makes his way back to the bar, taking an order from another table along the way.

"You have the look of a long day, old friend," Howard says.

I take a sip. "Yeah. Ab dropped in this morning. He and I were blown up while waiting for breakfast."

Pete and Howard stare into my eyes, and even in the dim light, their faces pale. "Well, we weren't blown up as in killed." I go on to describe the events.

"How's Ab?" Howard asks.

"Broken nose. Cuts and bruises. He'll be all right. Fair to say we're both shaken. Never been under fire before, even though we're both majors."

"We almost caught it ourselves later in the morning."

"Where?" I ask. Part of me wants to tell them Alice's story. Not yet. Let them tell theirs. At moments like this I have to remind myself to listen.

"Church of the Madeleine."

"What happened?"

Pete takes a sip of his drink. "Howard's bright idea. Go to a Memorial Day service. Sure. The one with the most brass hats was at l'Église de la Madeleine." He exaggerates his French. "Packed with officers when we got there. Ours and the Frogs. The Kaiser lobbed a big one from the Paris Gun. Fifteen minutes earlier and about thirty feet farther south and we wouldn't be here to regale you with our tale. Cratered the sidewalk on the north side of the joint."

"That's just dandy. Don't know about the two of you, but I got an immediate sense of my own mortality today," I say. "Before this, the war seemed almost abstract. Numbers, dispatches, statistics." My glass shakes as I bring it up for a sip. I cup my tumbler with both hands. Theirs are unsteady too.

"Lot of rumors about the German breakthrough at Chemin-des-Dames," Howard says.

I glance around the bar and speak in a soft voice. "You didn't hear it from me, and they'll never let you send this out. Paris will shortly become an unhealthy place to stay. You might want to look for a story near the coast or perhaps a short fact-finding trip to, say, Spain."

"Shit," Pete says into his drink. "Our wives are here. Not like they can take a vacation right now."

"I wish Trudy was going to one of the base hospitals farther west. I couldn't wait to get out of here. Now I wish my transfer hadn't gone through." I ache to tell them the rest—to ask them to keep an eye on

Trudy. But the nurses' dorm in the hospital seems like a safe place. For now.

"Know what you'll be doing?" Pete asks.

"No. Didn't care before. Anything would be better than working for Martel. I need an assignment that will keep me here, but with a boss who doesn't have his head all the way up to his appendix." I sip my scotch, thinking about my time in St. Paul. All the help in my journalistic circles couldn't have beat Chief O'Connor's gunslingers and the criminals they protected. But here? I have to do something. Okay. I hope I don't regret this. Alice won't like me telling Howard and Pete about the assault. But these are men I trust with my life. Their wives need to know. "I have this one problem . . ."

Chapter Sixteen
Alice Simmons

Monday, June 3

On Friday I found a room to rent from a woman whose husband and sons are in the army. Haughty and nosy. Bourgeois. But it's two blocks from the hospital annex. I don't plan to spend much time there other than to sleep. I purchased a nurse's aide uniform on Saturday along with two Red Cross nurse's uniforms for later in the hope they won't arrest or shoot me before I have a chance to wear them.

On Sunday, Trudy and I spent the afternoon at the Île de la Grande Jatte, a few blocks to the west of the hospital. A picnic lunch and a leisurely bottle of Bordeaux did little to lift her spirits. Trudy's emotions swung like a pendulum between her worries about Bill and her father. Behind those were her concerns about Ab Johnson and Ab's son Jack. I share all of those worries.

My cheeks were drawn and hollow, my eyes bloodshot when I looked in the mirror this morning. I haven't slept a full night since the assault—haunted by nightmares of the alleyway, interrogation, accusations. The scrape on my cheek seemed less obvious, the fat lip looked almost normal, and the shiner on my forehead had yellowed. I wish I could cover the scrapes and bruises, but nurses and aides aren't permitted to wear makeup.

The morning sun promises a hot day as I walk to the nursing offices in the main American Hospital building. I wear the regulation gray nurse's aide uniform with no head cover. Only nurses wear white caps. I go to Emily Enright's office and knock on the doorframe. Emily points me to a chair and takes another minute to finish reading a report. She slips off her reading glasses and lets them dangle by a chain around her neck. She looks me over. "Uniform becomes you. Though I hope we can get you in a nursing uniform soon. Face is a little better."

"How long do you think my clearance will take?" I need to dodge around any more questions about my face.

"Several weeks if all goes well." Emily stands and walks around her desk. "Haven't tripped and fallen into any more walls?" Emily gives me a long look as if to invite me to tell her the real story.

"No, ma'am."

"Anything else I need to know before we start?"

"Uh, no, ma'am." Ira and Trudy are the only ones who know—other than Martel and Captain Buck. I look up and struggle to paint on a smile. I want to tell her the whole story. No. Say nothing. I've had plenty of practice at that.

"Let's go," Emily says with a sigh. We leave the building and walk along the tree-lined streets of Neuilly to the Annex. Emily stops at the front gate to let an ambulance pass. Litter-bearers load men into waiting ambulances lined up along the front of the central building. "Oh, I forgot to tell you, the other day, when you asked about where these patients are going. Don't talk about the disposition of our patients unless it's with me or one of the other nurses, and only if there is no possibility of anyone overhearing you. German spies look for information about the movement of patients and medical supplies." We watch teams of litter-bearers at work for another moment, then head for the front door. "The French tell me they're everywhere—the spies. Could be a cook, in the laundry, a janitor—anyone."

German spies monitoring hospitals. I hadn't heard anything about that before. It makes sense, though.

Emily leads the way into the hospital and motions toward an alcove away from the corridor. She speaks in a hushed voice. "The French still won't tell us a thing. But their medical people are in a dither. The worst-kept secret of the week is the breakthrough northeast of here. Keep a bag packed and ready to go. We may need to evacuate on short notice."

I squint. "It's that bad?"

"Rumors, but told by folks I trust."

"With all the French soldiers moving out, will there be anything left for me to do?"

Emily gives what seems like a forced smile and leads the way up two flights of stairs and into an empty ward. The expanse must have been a ballroom. Cut-glass chandeliers hang from a high ceiling; green wallpaper is topped by ornate crown molding. A nursing station with a counter and an oak desk stands at one end. While the rest of the room is elegant, the nursing station looks like it was cobbled together in a hurry. Curtains billow in the breeze from large open windows at the other end. Ranks of white metal-framed beds line the walls, with a double row, head-to-head, along the center. Small white metal bed stands separate the beds. Towels and bedsheets lie in haphazard piles on the parquet floor. Mounds of soiled linens sit on some of the mattresses. A faint odor of putrefaction and Lysol lingers despite the open windows.

"Good God!" Emily gasps while taking a breath in. "This will never do. I know they were in a hurry, but this is ridiculous."

I take in the chaos. No nurse could have seen this room. The thought of contaminating the floor with soiled bedsheets is shocking. "I'll get a laundry cart."

"After that, find the maintenance men and have them mop that floor with disinfectant. Strip and disinfect the beds and remake them. I want to see a quarter bounce off the sheets. After that, restock the linen closet, then straighten up the supply room and make sure everything is shipshape. All the bedpans, treatment stands, and carts need to shine."

"What would you like me to do after lunch?"

"I like your attitude, Miss Simmons. There will be several other aides to help. Your French will be useful in that regard. Your head nurse is Marion Pickler. Be forewarned, she has been incensed about our use of aides. To call her persnickety would be an understatement."

"I'll do my best, ma'am."

"Now, as an RN, you'll be in an awkward position working as an aide. I feel obligated to let Mrs. Pickler know your background. I have a meeting with her later today. Might be best the staff nurses know too."

"I'd rather you not. I prefer to earn my stripes with the nurses from the ground up."

"You sure?"

"Yes, ma'am."

Emily walks away as I rest my hands on my hips, inspecting the room. A young woman walks in with a broad smile on a pretty face. She's about four inches shorter than me, with light brown hair in a tight bun, wearing an aide's uniform that fails to hide a figure that makes me feel like a homely cornstalk. I smile and introduce myself.

"I'm Betty Harrison. New here?"

"First day," I say.

"I've been at this a few weeks. New to this ward, though. I hear the head nurse is a battle-ax."

"Then we'd better get to work. Mrs. Enright told me to start by stripping and remaking the beds."

"I'll look for a laundry cart."

I get to work. Betty returns with an empty cart and loads the used linens into it, starting with the ones on the floor. "Where are you from, Betty?"

"Cleveland."

Betty's speech is not Cleveland, though. Farther east and probably from money. "How'd you end up here?"

"After college. Finished my lit degree at Vassar in '13. I'm a writer. Heard this was the place to come. Met Gertrude Stein and her crowd."

"What'd you think?"

"Peculiar gang. I didn't fit in. Some of the men wanted my attention but didn't give a hoot about my writing, just . . . some things I wasn't willing to furnish. Others were odd. Good writers—well, better than me, but I'm working on it."

"Hard way to earn a living."

"Money's not a problem. Good thing, since nobody will pick up my work yet. I felt guilty, though, with the war on. Mrs. Vanderbilt convinced me to work here. So here I am." Betty smiles and tips her head back.

"You know the Vanderbilts?" Now the speech and manner make sense.

"Acquaintances of my parents. She's done a great deal to promote this hospital and inspire volunteerism among the American expats here in Paris. Met her?"

"Heavens, they're out of my league." I scan the room. "We better find someone to mop this floor."

I'm comfortable in the academic circle of my parents, but not the world Betty circulates in. The events of the past few days have shaken my confidence. Maybe working as an aide is all I deserve. But . . . darn it, I'm a nurse. The woman with the crushed arm, Dr. Beck, helping the man at the hospital mourn his dead daughter. I made a difference that day.

Betty goes to find the maintenance man while I start scrubbing beds with Lysol. Betty walks like a girl who's been through finishing school— shoulders just so, back straight, head level enough to walk with a ruler on it. She returns and says that Monsieur Barton is on his way with another to start the floor, then helps me wipe bedframes with Lysol.

I stretch my back after finishing the last bed and watch Betty. She has the air of a privileged upbringing, but her hands don't look like they belong to someone who's dined with the Vanderbilts recently. I take my bottle of disinfectant to the linen room and rinse out my sponge in a large porcelain sink. Betty joins me and scrubs her hands in carbolic solution. "I'll show you where the laundry is. How's your French?"

"It will do," I answer in French.

"*Bon*," Betty replies. "Vassar has a good French department."

We wheel two carts with soiled linens to a closet. Betty holds the door to a laundry chute while I dump the linens into it. "We'll wash up when we get downstairs," Betty says.

The laundry is a hothouse in the basement. Older French men and women toil over steaming vats with a strong smell of bleach. We grab clean linens and load them onto carts and head to a dumbwaiter.

Upstairs, we collect the carts and roll them toward the ward. A thin nurse about two inches shorter than me blocks our path. She's in her forties, the years etched in frown lines around her lips, with a pointed chin. Her brown hair, flecked with gray, is pulled back into a severe bun that must hurt. A white nursing cap stands at perfect attention atop her head. The creases on her army nursing uniform look sharp enough to present a laceration hazard. I stifle a smile. She holds up a bony hand and says, "Stop right there. Where do you think you're going with that?"

"Mrs. Enright told us to change the bedsheets in the ward two doors down. We're on our way there, ma'am." I stand straight, shoulders back.

The nurse walks over to Betty's cart. "What kind of ignoramus are you? Do you see how these are folded? This is completely unsatisfactory. Were you raised without a mother, girl?"

"But, ma'am, I just picked up the cart from the laundry. They folded them."

"Don't offer excuses for your incompetence. Identify yourselves."

"Alice Simmons and Betty Harrison, ma'am," I say.

"I am Nurse Pickler. You will address me by that title and none other. Do I make myself clear?" Her Bostonian accent has an edge like snips cutting tin. "I take it you are both nursing aides?"

"Yes, Nurse Pickler. But I'm also . . ." I start.

"I don't care if your last name is Vanderbilt." Nurse Pickler's face reddens, her spine rigid, as if trying to tower over me.

"But . . ." I try to interject, standing taller. Two can play that game.

"Silence, Miss . . . what is your name, again?"

"Simmons, ma'am."

"You have three minutes to fold these properly. I will inspect them before you shelve them. Now *go*, time's a-wasting." She claps her hands twice.

I hustle to the linen room, the wheels of the cart clattering. Pickler shouts, "Simmons, slow down; you'll wake the dead with that racket. Did they teach you nothing in elementary school?"

Betty's cheeks are flushed while we fold sheets. After the larger things are stacked on the counter, we turn to the pillowcases and then the pajamas. Betty's creases are clumsy as she fumbles with shaking hands.

"Here, do it this way." I suppress my anger to help keep Betty on task before Nurse Pickler comes back for round two. "You take the bottoms, and I'll do the tops. Neat creases, sharp folds." I did enough of this in nursing school to be able to do it in my sleep.

Crackling steps approach after we finish the last pair. Nurse Pickler enters the room in a huff. "'Send us experienced nurses,' I told them. 'Not a bevy of giggling debutantes.' You poor little rich girls may think you're doing good. The powers that be overruled our objections, *my* objections, and forced us to accept aides. Well, I can't keep you out of this hospital, but you're not welcome here." She tosses one pair of bottoms from Betty's cart on the floor. "Next time fold them properly before they deign to enter *my* ward. Make up all the beds." She turns on her heel and strides out.

"Thank you, Alice," Betty says. Her eyes are hard, mouth thin, like she's struggling to bottle her hurt and anger.

"You didn't volunteer to take that abuse. Neither did I." I pick up the pajama bottoms. "These were fine. She's just trying to make you cry."

A wicked little smile grows on Betty's face. "I heard one of the girls talk about her. She's a widow."

"I imagine she looked at him one day and he turned to stone." I give Betty a sly grin.

Betty chuckles. "I knew there might be days like this."

I use my own quarter to check the beds after we finish making the last one. An instructor at Minneapolis City Hospital had insisted that quarters bounced "just so" off a properly made bed. Nurse Pickler enters, verbally dressing down two Frenchmen carrying boxes. A man rolling a mop in a bucket makes me look twice. He resembles Claude Monet, one of my favorite painters. On second glance, he isn't.

Nurse Pickler speaks in loud, slow English, as though that can make the French janitor and his helper understand her. After Pickler turns to do her bed inspection, a look passes between the two men that is as old as men and women and makes me smirk. She inspects each bed with a nickel. "This will never do. Which of you hopeless girls did this one?"

"I made this bed." And I want to say, *this isn't boot camp*—but no. Don't rock the boat.

"Did your mother teach you how to make beds? Or, perhaps, your nanny?"

"Mother, originally. Nurse Pickler, with due respect . . ." I'd love to say more.

"Your mother was obviously incompetent."

"My mother . . ."

"Probably functions well among her society friends at bridge club, but she failed to teach her daughter the simple task of making a bed." Nurse Pickler rips the bed apart and throws the linens on the floor. "Send those to the laundry and do it right." Nurse Pickler marches off the ward, head high.

I stand over the pile, hands on hips, and struggle against the burning desire to confront the gorgon. But for now, I'm the lowest lifeform in the hospital—a new nurse's aide. There is no way I will bother Emily Enright with this. I need to figure out a way to deal with the head nurse. I pick up the sheets and lug them to the laundry chute. The man who looks like Monet follows us and holds the door. He returns with us to the ward and takes up his mop, humming a Debussy tune.

"Think she's competent?" Betty asks.

"I expect more from a head nurse."

Betty raises her left eyebrow.

I sigh. "I grew up in a medical household, listening to my parents talk around the supper table about doctors and nurses, good and bad." I sigh. "She doesn't impress me. I expect my head nurse to set high standards, but that bed was perfect. She tried to tear me down just like the bed—to treat me like the sheets. Betty, this isn't how we behave— nurses, I mean. Heavens, if she can't cope with two aides and a Frenchman with a mop, imagine what will happen when the first patient arrives."

"So what do we do in the meantime?"

"We carry on—we do our best and let the chips fall where they may." I gaze at the curtains fluttering in the breeze. "You've been here longer than me. I've been wondering where the other ward nurses are. It's just been you and me today. And Monsieur Monet," I say, nodding toward the mop man.

"He does resemble Claude." Betty chuckles. The way she says that leads me to think she knows the painter. "Oh, I heard the nurses are all in staff meetings. Why?"

"My best friend is a new nurse here. I'm trying to find her."

"Where's she living?"

"In the dorm. I'm thinking of looking for her after our shift."

The Monet man stops and stretches with a groan. He approaches and says in French, "Pardon, mademoiselle. I am Henri Barton. I will be working this ward—unless that . . . woman removes me."

"Do you speak English?" I ask.

"Enough to pretend I don't when that woman shouts," he says in English.

I chuckle and shake his extended hand, and answer in French. "Have you always worked here?"

"*Non*. Before the war, I was a wine broker. My family is from Vienne. We made wine—Cote-Rôtie. Someone had to sell it. You speak our tongue like a native."

"My family's from Allier. Pascal Duval et Freres. My great-grandfather."

"We used your barrels. Very fine." He has a beautiful, wistful smile. "For Pascal's great-granddaughter? If I can ever be of help. Good day." He wanders off, mopping as he moves toward the door, whistling "La Marseillaise."

Mary Sloan bustles in, eyes glued to me. "Alice, I have a little job for you."

Chapter Seventeen
Alice Simmons

What is my *little job*? I rush to catch up with Mary Sloan, who seems intent to get to our destination without explanation. The corridor is packed with older Frenchmen carrying patients on stretchers and pushing wheelchairs toward ambulances outside the front doors. A slender young girl sits on a bench next to the corridor wall, watching the chaos with a frightened expression.

I'm lightheaded.

My face must look like a sheet.

Deep breath. Deep breath.

Oh my God.

Knees weak, I sit next to her, never taking my eyes off what seems like an impossible ghost.

My little sister died. I was there—saw it—was blamed for it. Intellect tells me this is not her. Justine was only two years younger than me, so she'd be twenty-two now, not this pale teenaged waif. Her eyes are the same sort of mixed-up hazelish green as mine—fine blonde hair edging on brown, facial bones almost identical, chapped lips on a haunted face.

"Justine," I say.

"*Non, je m'appelle Geneviève.*"

"She arrived by ambulance a short while ago," Mary says. "A refugee.

The French military ambulances are only supposed to transport troops. Without the ride, she would have had to walk from Meaux. My husband's friend, Ab Johnson, convinced them to take her."

"I know Ab," I say. "His son, Jack, is a close friend."

"Close?" Mary cocks an eyebrow.

My face flushes. "Friend. Not that kind, though everyone was trying to set me up for more."

Mary narrows her eyes as if imagining *more*. "In any case, the girl has pneumonia and needs care."

"Here?"

"No. This is all military. There's no pediatric ward. There is an orphanage a mile or so away that can provide medical care. I need your French skills to help me get her there. Geneviève doesn't speak English, and my French doesn't extend beyond ordering a glass of wine."

Geneviève is a frightened lamb, arms tight across her chest, feet flat on the floor, leaning forward as if ready to bolt. She wears a yellow dress with brown blotches that make me think of blood hastily washed off. Three battered suitcases sit on the floor next to her.

"Ab Johnson came across this girl, her brother, and their dog in Montreuil-aux-Lions," Mary says. "They barely made it out before the front overtook their village. Bouresches. Do you know it?"

"No." Though I've been in any number of little hamlets that I imagine are like her home.

"Their mother was killed in a German strafing run. The bloodstains are her mother's. Here's Ab's letter."

Mary hands me the letter. Mr. Johnson goes on to write that he conned the French to transport her here by ambulance. I speak in French. "I am Alice Simmons, a nursing aide. This is Madame Sloan. The man who sent you is a good friend of ours, Major Johnson. His letter tells us you are sick and have been diagnosed with pneumonia. It says you and your brother escaped just ahead of the Boche and your name is Geneviève Durand. Is that correct?"

"*Oui.* They would not let Marcel and Abby—she's our dog—in the ambulance with me. They're walking here."

"All this way?"

"*Oui*. I'm worried. We've never been in Paris. He doesn't know the way. And they have no maps."

"There is nothing we can do for them until they get here," I say. "Keep your hopes up. I'm sure they'll show up in a few days. We don't take care of children in this hospital. We will get you to a safe place. Are you able to walk?"

"Not far. I start coughing. I can't breathe enough."

"Are you still having fevers?"

"Yes. Two, three a day. And I shake so, before I burn up."

I hold up my hand to get the attention of a French officer who seems to be in command of the ambulances. "*Capitan*, I have this orphaned French child who has pneumonia. She's a refugee from the Château-Thierry sector. We need to get her to the orphanage—you know the one."

"Mademoiselle, my orders are to transport these men to military hospitals."

"This girl can't walk to the orphanage."

"My orders do not allow—"

"What do you suggest?" I struggle to keep my voice even.

"Perhaps a taxi."

Geneviève narrows her eyes as if trying to understand what we're talking about. She comes from the sort of village where taxis are unheard of.

"When is the last time you ate?" I ask Geneviève.

She narrows her eyes as if struggling to remember. "This morning, I think."

"I'm going to stay with you while Madame Sloan gets you some food. There is a restroom down the hall." I motion one of the older men over and ask him to watch Geneviève's things. He seems relieved to be able to sit. I hold on to Geneviève's arm to steady her as I take her to the restroom. All the wheelchairs in sight are occupied by patients.

After the restroom and a wash of her hands and face, I take the young girl back to the bench. Mary Sloan brings a glass of water, a sandwich, and a chocolate bar.

"Geneviève, I'm going to get a taxicab to take you to a place that will care for you."

I walk to the street outside the hospital gates, hail a passing cab, and direct him to park between two ambulances. The driver grumbles—an old man whose hearing must be impaired by all the hair growing out of his ears. I load the suitcases in the trunk and motion Geneviève over. The interior is like an ashtray. Geneviève starts coughing as I slide into the back seat and give the driver the orphanage address.

"Get out!" the man shouts as he rushes from the cab. He stands ten feet away, waving his fist. "I will not catch tuberculosis from this filthy pig of a girl!"

As much as I'd like to slug him, to give him a lecture about the needs of the child—the children of France as a whole—it would be a waste of time with this fool. I help Geneviève out of the cab and over to the hospital's front steps. The cabbie tosses her luggage into the middle of the parking lot like infected trash and speeds away in a cloud of smoke. I shake a fist and shout a few things after him that cause an ambulance driver to catch my eye with a smile and a tip of his hat.

Geneviève waits by the luggage while I march out to the street to flag down another cab. It takes fifteen minutes, but this man looks more friendly, and the cab doesn't stink as I ride in the back toward Geneviève. She looks even more like Justine at the moment and pulls at my heart all the more. I explain to the cabbie that Geneviève has pneumonia and that she's been tested for tuberculosis and that it has been ruled out. Okay, I'm lying, but so it goes. I offer him a mask, but he declines, telling me he spent two years in a tuberculosis sanitarium when he was a teenager. That may explain the lack of cigarette odor in the cab. We load the suitcases and head to the orphanage.

Tears stream down Geneviève's face as we pass well-tended gardens in front of magnificent apartment buildings where people who might describe themselves as *comfortable* live—the bourgeoisie who dominate Neuilly-sur-Seine.

"What's wrong?" I put an arm around her shoulders and hug her close. So like my little sister . . .

"That word, orphanage. It makes me think of Maman and Papa. Dead."

"First, we need to nurse you back to health," I say. "Focus on that before all else."

"Marcel and Abby. Will I ever see them again?"

"I'll keep an eye out for them." I should know better than to make promises I can't guarantee.

The rest of the day is quiet. Betty and I eat supper together in the cafeteria at the end of our shift. After that, I wander the halls until I find a stairwell leading to the dormitory. I walk up and enter a long hallway with rooms opening on both sides and stop at a lounge area, where four young nurses play cards. One looks up and says, "This is the nurses' dorm. Aides aren't allowed here." Hostility drips from her voice.

"I'm looking for a friend, Trudy Cunningham. Do you know her?"

The nurse is in uniform, dark brown hair in a snug bun, a few inches shorter than me. She hurries over to block the doorway. She can't be more than twenty. Her eyes are daggers. "You. Didn't. Hear. Me. Leave." She thrusts a pointing finger near my ear.

Two of the other nurses walk over and stand behind the first. One sneers. The other looks embarrassed.

"I was just—"

Dagger Eyes grips my right elbow. "I don't want to say it again. Out." She shoves me, then points toward the stairs. My face is hot as I walk to the end of the hall and look back. The nurse, hands on her hips, has not moved.

I'm making more enemies than friends so far.

Chapter Eighteen
Alice Simmons

Tuesday, June 4

The ward door bursts open at ten in the morning, and a tidal wave of chaos rolls over us. A procession of older men carry litters with young American soldiers lying in filthy, bloodstained uniforms, boots still on. The ward reeks of sweaty, unwashed men, blood, and barnyard. Their dressings are soiled and bloody. Nurse Pickler stands in the middle of the ward shouting orders. The Frenchmen carrying the wounded don't understand Pickler's commands. One of them asks where to put the patients, in French. Pickler rages. "Of all the insolence. Who allowed these ignorant men to barge into *my* ward?"

The man in charge of the litter-bearers speaks to Nurse Pickler in French.

"Speak. English. You. Ignoramus," Pickler screams, chopping at the air with her right hand.

"Ma'am, he's asking where you wish them to unload the casualties," I say.

Pickler scowls. "Then why doesn't he say so? I want them to start at the far end and work forward. When this ward is full, they will do the same with the next. Is that so difficult for them to understand?"

The man smiles, nods, and touches his beret with his right index finger after I explain what Pickler wants. When Pickler marches away, he sticks out his tongue and several others laugh. The comments in French are not complimentary of Pickler, her future with Frenchmen, men in general, and a few other things that make me blush. Henri Barton wears a wry grin when I catch his eye. He gives me a slight bow, which I return. Well done. I love France.

"Simmons, you and Miss Debutante get cracking." Nurse Pickler claps her hands twice. "Remove these filthy uniforms, wash the patients, and make them presentable for the doctors. Do not *touch* their dressings. *Get to work.*"

I motion the French aides over and lead the way to the workroom. Betty and I fill basins with warm water and set them on top of our wheeled carts along with soap and towels. The French girls stack pajamas and backless hospital gowns on the lower shelves. Two aides hustle off to the kitchens to get samovars of hot coffee and cocoa.

Three nurses, including Trudy, rush in. I catch her eye and smile. Pickler orders them here and there, her voice with an edge like scraping fingernails on a chalkboard. I motion the other aides to the bedside of the first man to be cleaned. "Let me show you how this is done. What's your name, soldier?"

"I'm not a soldier, ma'am. I'm a marine." The man speaks with a lilting Carolina accent.

"Okay. How do we tell the difference? I thought you were all doughboys."

"That term applies to all of us. Uniforms are the same, but most of us marines wear our pins. But it'll be simple, ma'am." He waves his right hand toward the ward. "All these guys is marines. Name's Anderson, ma'am."

"All right, where are your wounds?"

"Right leg. That's all."

"Okay, Anderson, we're going to get you cleaned up. Can you sit?"

I help him out of his soiled shirt, then his undershirt. Dirt crusts his skin, and the stench from his underarms is nauseating. Betty and I work from each side to clean his upper body, starting at the head. A washcloth takes care of his short hair—good thing, since we don't have any shampoo.

"What are you going to do with my uniform, ma'am?"

"Not sure. We didn't know we were getting new patients until you arrived."

"It's just—I'd like my pins. You know, the Eagle, Globe, and Anchor. They're the ones I earned in boot camp. They're special, is all."

A clock ticks in my head as I remove the pins and set them on the white metal bedside stand. I speak to the aides in French, since Betty and I are the only Americans in the team. "It's important to not disturb the wound while we remove his trousers and boots. First take off the puttees—the wrappings over the calves. Then the boots. Be careful not to pull on the wounded leg. Use dressing shears to cut the trousers off."

Betty and I unwrap the puttees. They smell of dung. Then off come the boots, caked with dirt and mud, and finally trousers stiff from sweat and blood. Anderson looks squeamish at having his privates exposed to the young female aides. I remain clinical in my manner—this should help him as I examine his pubic area.

"Wasn't there long enough to get cooties, ma'am, if that's what y'all's looking for." Anderson cracks a grin. "Moved from Vixen to Lucy so fast the cooties couldn't keep up. The boys say they're coming with the cooks and'll be issued with the first hot meal. All's we got was cold rations."

"Vixen?" I've never heard of a town by that name.

"Chowmount in Vixen. Or some such. French twists my tongue, ma'am."

The two French aides snicker. I remain clinical. He must mean Chaumont-en-Vexin, northwest of Paris. But where is this Lucy he talks about? I don't recognize that one.

Betty and I bathe Anderson and slip a backless gown on him when we're finished. "The doctor will need to inspect that leg, so no bottoms until after that."

"Thank you, ma'am."

I turn to the other aides. "Got it?" Heads nod. "Split into teams and get to work."

The night shift arrives at eight, but I work until eleven thirty, never having time to say more than hello to Trudy. At the end, Trudy and the other nurses are gone. I'll catch up with her tomorrow rather than risk more humiliation in the nurses' dorm.

Pickler worries me. The woman is insufferable. How could she have been appointed head nurse? She must have been competent at something, sometime. Pickler seems like the wrong person in the wrong place at the worst time. Unable to cope with chaos. What is it about aides that sets her off so? This won't be easy. It seems like Pickler has already singled me out to be—what? Her challenger, insurgent, renegade? Or maybe it's my willingness to work as an aide even though I'm a fully qualified RN.

The shift was too busy to think about Martel. But the memory of his fingers follows me as I make my way back to the apartment building, looking over my shoulder at each intersection as night overtakes Neuilly.

An open-topped Paris police car stands next to the curb outside the apartment building. When I near, the man in the passenger seat gets out and approaches me. He's in his thirties and walks with a limp. His face is serious. "Mademoiselle Alice Simmons?"

"*Oui.*"

The policeman walks away without another word.

Chapter Nineteen
Alice Simmons

Thursday, June 6

My eyes are blurry from another bad night. Things were hectic yesterday, and I could, maybe should, have stayed longer last night, but I need sleep. I wish I could stay in the dormitory instead of this apartment. Horns and noisy ambulance traffic throughout the night, along with memories of Martel and interrogations, kept me awake. Why can't I let the anger go so I can sleep? It boils up when the lights are out.

A police car with two men sits across the street from the apartment building. Is that for me? I turn left on Boulevard d'Inkermann and walk south toward the Annex. Ambulances stream past like a freight train. A policeman ducks behind a tree about a hundred feet behind me when I scan the street—are there others? Henri Barton is on the other side of the street, walking with the nonchalance of Parisian men his age. I catch his eye, and he nods. He must live nearby. My heart sinks as ambulances buzz past in both directions.

As I reach the hospital gate and look back along the road, the policeman turns and puffs on a cigarette. Damn them. They *are* following me.

Ambulances crowd the parking lot with a new stream of arrivals. The hospital grounds look like an army encampment. Sledgehammers clink on metal stakes as soldiers erect canvas tents on the grass at each end of the lot. I jostle my way among a motley assortment of older French men carrying stretchers as I enter the central building and make my way upstairs to the nursing aides' cloakroom. A quick mirror check shows that the bruises are fading, and my scraped cheek is almost healed. I look at my watch and take a deep breath. I have to find some way to get together with Trudy after work—there is so much to talk about. But where? When? After midnight doesn't make sense.

I enter the linen room and hear Nurse Pickler chiding someone in the ward. Her target of the moment is Henri. He speaks English perfectly well but pretends to not understand, which makes me smile. Better go over and help him in his charade.

"Don't you know the first thing about organizing your men?" Pickler says.

"Ma'am, may I help? Monsieur Barton doesn't speak English, but I can translate for you."

"Simmons, fold and organize bedding. Go." Pickler points an imperious index finger toward the linen room.

"But—"

"If you can't follow my orders, get out of my ward."

My shoulders tighten. I say in French, "I'm sorry, Monsieur Barton. We are not all like her."

Barton's mouth turns up at the corners. "I know."

Pickler glares at me. "Simmons. Get. To. Work."

My neck tingles on my way to the supply room, where I find Betty Harrison organizing bedpans. "How's my favorite debutante today?"

Betty snickers. "Well, you know, she pegged me. I did have a debut. It was expected. Gigantic waste of money. Why, for the cost of that party, we could have equipped several operating rooms here. I'm embarrassed when I look back at things like that."

Pickler's voice rises again, shouting at an orderly at the far end near the windows. She chops at the air with her right hand like a lumberjack after too much coffee. I duck back into the linen room and whisper, "I'm concerned about her inability to handle the French workers. She seems to think that speaking loud and slow is the way to force her orders across the language barrier."

"She won't let me translate," Betty says. "I'm afraid we'll come in one of these mornings and find them all gone."

"So here we are, the bedpan and sheet brigade," I say. We fold clean sheets that came up from the laundry on the night shift. When the linens are shipshape, we walk into the ward. Pickler stands with her hands balled into fists on her hips, scolding an aide who is cleaning up a new arrival. The aide is Marie Moreau, a banker's daughter who doesn't speak English.

"What about this do you not understand?" Pickler asks.

Marie speaks in quick French. "But madame, I do not understand what you want."

I translate as I approach. "Nurse Pickler. With due respect, please tell me what you want Marie to do, and I'll make sure she understands."

"Are those sheets done?"

"And the towels and the bedpans. Ma'am, please. Let Betty and me help with the French. Most of them don't speak enough English to understand your orders."

Another voice speaks. I turn to see Emily Enright. "Nurse Pickler, I *suggest* you take advantage of Miss Simmons's abilities. Let me reiterate what I told you two days ago. Alice speaks French like a native Parisian and *is* an RN. The only reason she's working as an aide right now is that we are still waiting for her credentials."

Pickler's face colors. She folds her arms, fixing me with a hostile glare. "Mrs. Enright, I resent that these two debutantes were forced upon me. Aides have no place on my ward. Any hospital ward. What we need are qualified nurses."

"And Alice is one. You can't use her in that role yet, but she can do more than fold towels. And for what it's worth, she is no debutante."

"University of Minnesota. Bumpkin." Pickler turns her scowl at Emily, who seems to ignore it with a gentle smile.

Emily says, "Miss Harrison is also fluent in French, are you not, dear?"

"*Oui.*" Betty gives Pickler a sweet smile.

"So, I *suggest* that you have them translate for you when you need to communicate with the French, who we are very fortunate to have. Now we have admissions streaming in, so let's get to work." Emily claps her hands twice. She winks at me and strides away. Pickler goes to the nursing station and surveys the room, mouth puckered like a prune.

"Let's get the other aides," I say. "It looks like business is picking up." Emily walks over to Henri, who glances in my direction while they talk. Then Emily points toward Trudy with her head, and Henri nods. Nurse Pickler glares at me from across the room.

The fifty-bed ward held twenty-two patients when we clocked out yesterday evening. It's now full, half of the men still in filthy uniforms. Open windows barely soften the stench of war, wounds, and carbolic disinfectant. An orderly armed with a flyswatter patrols the room. Trudy works on an irrigation treatment on the other side of the ward. I want nothing more than to work with my best friend—we were a great team in nursing school. But I don't want to put Trudy in Pickler's sights.

Betty and I round up the aides and organize them, then get to work removing uniforms and giving sponge baths. We have eight aides and three nurses. Marie and I team up. After we finish with one man, I watch Betty walking to the nursing station with Geneva, marine eyes tracking them. My face warms. I'm not sure if I should be hurt or offended—maybe a little of both. I never get those kinds of stares. Betty's stride exudes pure class. A champagne glass atop her head would not spill as she glides along. Geneva is gorgeous. I look at my chapped hands and push my granny glasses up my nose. This will be a long day for the Librarian.

My next patient's a marine private lying on the bed with a dressing on his right side and another on his left thigh. I have Marie unwrap the man's puttee leggings while I unbutton his tunic. "How long ago did you get here?"

"Couple hours."

"Sorry we made you wait." The man's wound card, held in place on his tunic by a safety pin, reads: *Cherny, Elmer, PVT, USMC 2/5.*

"The witch kept me amused. Reminded me of this nutcase DI from boot camp."

"What is a DI?"

"Oh, sorry, ma'am . . . miss . . . drill instructor. He was a real psycho, like her."

That makes me smirk. "How were you wounded?"

"Arty—uh, I mean, artillery. The Boche sent tons of explosive greeting cards to welcome us to the front. Been continuous. Mailed us gas when they felt the need for a change of pace. My foxhole filled with mustard. Had to get out. Shrapnel did the rest."

"Tell me about your evacuation." I continue to work, using the conversation as a distraction. Besides, I'm curious.

"Guess we don't have much between there and here. Evaced me through a few aid stations. Took all night. Sat on the lawn outside a hospital called Julie or something like that yesterday. Least there were shade trees. All night in the ambulance, pitching around like we was riding a bronc."

How many died in the ambulances? Or even before they got that far? The goal is to operate on men like this within twelve hours. I try to imagine the chaos—panic, confusion, doctors and corpsmen, working without nurses, flooded, overwhelmed.

"The potholes had potholes. I swear to you: them drivers is trained to plant a wheel in every one of 'em. And the dust. Half choked me to death."

"I'm not sure I can ask, but where were you?"

Cherny motions me to come close and speaks softly. "Out northwest of Chatoo-Terry. Got there a couple days ago. Diggin' holes, no food, bad water. Then the waiting. Drove us nuts, not knowing nothing. Lying in those fucking holes—begging your pardon—wondering if there's a shell with your name on it. Helpless. Waiting—that's the worst."

"Let's sit you up and get your coat off. Your name's Elmer Cherny?"

"Yes, ma'am. Dayton, Ohio. Call me Scooter. I'm a fast runner." He drops his gaze to his left leg. "Well, was, I guess. How bad?"

"I'm an aide. Our job is to get you out of this filthy uniform and wash you up. We can't remove the dressings or give you any prognosis on your wounds. That'll be the doctors. They come later."

"Right. Well . . ."

I remove the pins from his tunic collar and lay them on the bedside stand. "No food? I thought Napoleon said something about that . . ."

"You got it, sister—I mean, ma'am. I guess Pershing didn't get that memo. Lots of dry mouths and growling stomachs."

"It must be a huge battle, all the marines coming in."

Marie stands listening, probably understanding nothing. My fingers itch for my notepad. I haven't used it since starting work here. This is a heck of a story. Work comes first—no chance to take notes. *Famished, parched hometown boys pushed to the front, lying in holes waiting to see who lives, who dies. Life and death a roulette wheel, artillery rounds the ball . . .*

"Nah. So far, only one battle. And I didn't get to fire one stinking round."

"Why?"

Scooter motions me closer. "Not sure how much I can say. They didn't tell us. Anyhoo . . . we was in reserve, see? The Second of the Fifth held the line at a place called Les Mares Farm. Shit—'scuse the French, sorry—well, a flock of Krauts—probably a whole regiment, I heard— came at 'em. Our guys mowed them down. Showed 'em that us marines is the best shots in Europe, y'know? Just wished I'd gotten a shot off."

"I'm confused. Second of the Fifth?" I hadn't asked about the jargon before, afraid of looking like a fool. But I'm comfortable talking with Scooter. The nickname fits. He reminds me of a boy from high school.

Scooter leans back and speaks in a normal voice. "Sorry, ma'am."

"You don't need to call me ma'am. I'm only two years older than you. My name is Alice." I turn to Marie and tell her in French to remove the left boot. "So, tell me about this Second and Fifth thing."

"Sorry, ma—" He chuckles and looks away. "Best I start at the top and work down. Took a while to memorize this business, I'm telling you. So there's divisions that are about twenty-eight thousand strong. They number the divisions one, two, and so forth. All the guys here are in the Second Division. There's two brigades to a division, each about ninety-five hundred. The Second Division is half marine, which is us, in the Fourth Brigade of Marines. The army half is the Third Brigade. Not sure where they are in all this mess. Anyhoo, there's two regiments in each brigade. So, to keep the numbers as confusing as possible for the enemy, the Fourth Brigade of Marines has the Fifth and Sixth Regiments. I'm in the Fifth, so that's the second part of that phrase. Each regiment has three battalions, about a thousand guys, numbered one, two, and three, following me? So I'm in the Second Battalion of the Fifth Regiment. We shorten it to 2/5. Our company was in reserve. Oh, sorry . . ." He smiles. "A battalion has four companies of two hundred and fifty. See, it all adds up. Well, I'm sure you figured that one out."

My head swirls with the jargon and numbers. There's no chance to take notes. Instead, I silently repeat what he told me. It will be important if I'm going to write a story about all this. The censors will never let it go through, but maybe it'll see the light of day after the war. "So, you were in reserve? Oh, trousers are next—I'll have to cut off the left pant leg."

Scooter unfastens his belt and unbuttons his fly. He grunts when he raises his pelvis to pull them down. I cut the left trouser leg to the waist with shears and tease the cloth away from the leg, never touching the dressing on Scooter's left thigh. Marie slips the remains of the trouser down the right leg. Beads of sweat glisten on Scooter's pale face. I need to distract him. "Tell me more about all that reserve stuff."

"Lieutenant Colonel Wise—he's our battalion CO, oops, the commanding officer that is—he put three companies on the line and held us in reserve. That's pretty much how we do things. Always keep a reserve 'cause, you know, it's war. Guys get hurt, and if you put everyone on the line, there's nobody to fill in when someone gets his."

"Gets his?"

"When a guy gets hit."

How am I ever going to keep all the terminology straight? "I've heard of Lieutenant Colonel Wise. His wife is a nurse here. I haven't met her yet. Let's get your undershirt off." I tell Marie to start washing Scooter's head and face while I cut off the undershirt above and below a muslin bandage holding the dressing over his right flank. It looks as though he's been dragged by a horse, with blood seeping through the bandage.

"So, lieutenant colonels run the battalions?"

"Colonel Wise—we usually drop the *lieutenant* part of his rank—

does. Majors run most of the battalions. Major Berry runs the 3/5, for example. Good man too. Wise is a pretty senior guy. Good CO. Captains are the skippers of the companies, and second lieutenants run the platoons."

"Ever run into one named Jack Johnson? Friend of mine."

"Nope. Could be in another company. I stay away from officers."

I wipe the grime off of Scooter's chest and abdomen with a soapy washcloth. After I finish the front and Marie is done with his scalp and face, I say, "Let's sit you up and get your back." Marie and I help him sit. "So, you were saying?"

"Krauts poured in arty before their attack. Probably meant to hit the front lines—soften 'em up and all. Shot long and hit us. That's how most of us got ours. The front-line guys were barely nicked, see? It was bad, ma—Miss Alice. Hearing guys scream when they're hit. Not able to do nothing about it. Then, after, looking around for your buddies. Some only bits and legs."

My hands shake while I wash Scooter's back—the image of what he described flashes through my mind. Will I include this in an article? No. I can't put families through that. Even my parents hadn't been able to handle it when Justine died. They had only been able to sob next to my little sister's corpse, lying under a heavy wagon wheel. Father had ripped off his shirt and laid it over Justine's face. His eyes had cut into mine before he took Mother into his arms. A surgeon and a nurse—they'd seen it all before. I shudder. How would the letters from the War Department read? *He died instantly, with no pain* . . . I thought of them as lies before—deceptions. But these fabrications may be the threads that allow families to weave grief into recovery.

"Sorry to scare you, ma—Miss Alice." Scooter nods toward the man in the next bed, who stares at the ceiling, mute. "He was there, foxhole next to me. The guy on the other side of him? Smithereens. Showered us with his . . . parts. The head was in that guy's foxhole. Well, see, the rest of us, we figure we're alive. So what the hell? We kinda help each other out, got each other's backs, you know? Been together since that stinking swamp in South Carolina, the mud in Quantico, then frozen marches last winter. These greenies?" He motions his eyes toward the man next to him. "Nobody knows his name, leastways none of us. That's how it is, see?"

Marie and I finish his back and ease him down. "We'll have to cut those underpants off next."

"Don't worry. No cooties down there, see? Don't mind the stink. Haven't changed them since the twenty-ninth, not that I'm counting."

I cut off the stained olive-drab drawers. "Don't want to invade your privacy, Scooter, but it's our job." My face warms. Why? I've done hundreds of bed baths. But Scooter's about my age, good-looking after getting off the grime and blood, and he's so much like boys I met in school.

"Miss Alice, you never been to boot camp. We all seen each other, us marines."

Marie and I wash Scooter's genitals, which require several soakings to get completely clean. The soiled leg dressing is stiff with blood, pus dripping from the lower margin. The skin is red in a ring two inches around the wound. The tissue beneath the reddened edge crackles. Gas. Oh God, no. The blood rushes from my head, and I steady myself on the foot of the bed. Gas gangrene is usually fatal and always an emergency.

The clatter of cartwheels and clicking heels approaches while we finish.

"You'll change his bedsheets after the doctor is done. Now stand aside," Nurse Pickler orders. "The doctor will be here shortly."

"Nurse Pickler, I'm concerned that Private Cherny may be developing gas gangrene."

Pickler looks at the leg. "Nonsense. Stick to bedpans."

"But touch it, just above. There's gas."

"I don't need to spread infection. My eyes tell me all I need to know. And Captain Jensen will be doing rounds soon enough."

I motion Marie to join me at the foot of the next bed. Trudy rolls her wound cart next to us and gives me a friendly nudge. Nurse Pickler stands sentinel between us and Scooter, her back blocking my view while she bends over, examining the wound.

Trudy and an orderly wash their hands in a basin. "We have to remove your dressings and tidy up your wounds," Trudy says. "We'll start with the leg." She cuts the muslin bandage encircling Scooter's left thigh with her shears. The skin around the wound is crusted with blood and filth. She dunks a four-by-four-inch gauze pad in a bowl of Dakin's solution and dabs the skin around the wound. A jagged four-inch laceration with purplish edges draws my eye. Pus and dark blood ooze out of the cut, releasing a stomach-wrenching odor when Trudy prods the skin next to the wound.

"Simmons. Quit gawking. You and your French tart get to work," Pickler says.

I catch Trudy's eye and mouth, *Gas*. Trudy nods, her eyes showing alarm.

Nurse Pickler leaves for the day at eight sharp. My shift ends at that time, but the day crew and I stay until ten. I catch up with Trudy talking with several other nurses at the nursing station. Scooter is in surgery. But are they in time?

Trudy looks up with fatigued eyes. "Nurse Pickler's punching bag in the flesh." Two other nurses nod. It's the first time any of the nurses other than Trudy acknowledge my membership in the human race.

"I get the impression she doesn't care for me."

"What did you do to get her goat?" asks one of the others.

"Not sure. That I dare to breathe? She started in on me right way. She doesn't like aides. That's all she told me."

"Join us for a late snack?" Trudy asks.

I trail the three nurses to the cafeteria, through the line, and to a corner table.

"So, what's the story on you and Miss Debutante?" asks one of the others with a chuckle.

I give them a short version, leaving out Martel and the cops. "I don't think the fact I'm an RN matters to her. If anything, an RN willing to work as an aide is like gas on her fire, I suppose."

"The farther you trained away from her revered Boston matters," Trudy says. "Fact that we're from Minnesota makes us practically Asian in her world."

"Do any of you know her story?"

One of the nurses says, "I heard she started in peds, then was the head nurse in the urology ward at Mass General. I met someone who knew her back in Boston—said she was a very good nurse but very . . . fastidious. Husband and daughter died in an accident last year. Maybe that has something to do with it."

The conversation continues while we eat, then the other nurses head back to the dormitory wing. "Any word on Bill?" I ask Trudy.

"None. Don't know where he is. Dad's down at army headquarters now, trying to see what he can find out. It's driving me nuts. Every time I see a new patient? Each one, as they come in? I look to see if he's Bill. They're from the kind of unit he's with—the infantry. Each wound—I see Bill."

"Hard not to. That one who goes by Scooter—doesn't he look just like Erik Carlson in Biology?"

Trudy's eyes widen. "Scooter could be his brother. I didn't realize that before."

"Hear anything about Scooter?" I ask. Dr. Jensen had a conniption when he saw the leg and rushed Scooter into surgery. I take no satisfaction in being right but hope they amputate in time to save his life. I think about Bill, and Jack Johnson. All the Bills and Jacks and Scooters and Andersons out there.

I should write their stories.

Chapter Twenty
Major Ira Cunningham

After I find a billet at AEF Headquarters in Chaumont, they tell me that Colonel Nolan, the head of intelligence, is out of town until tomorrow. So, I do what I suppose any good major should do—go from place to place at a brisk pace, salute when necessary, and look busy until I receive further orders. I suck in my gut when passing senior officers, since General Pershing is on the warpath weeding out the unfit and infirm from our ranks. I decide to skip breakfast and lunch for a week or two and hold off on the booze for a bit. All the while, I'm distracted by intrusive thoughts of Martel, what he did to Alice, what he might try to do with Trudy, and how I can take him down.

My journal is my solace at the end of each day—I've started work on an article about Martel and Buck. Not for publication—writing is my best way of thinking through problems. And those two are a problem, not just for Alice and me, but for the AEF. Officers like them give us all a black eye.

On the morning of the fifth, I report to Colonel Dennis Nolan's office. Nolan's clerk, who looks more like a grad student than a spy, shows me into the large corner office. The decor suggests a man who spends little time at his desk—no photos or papers, only a blotter, desk phone, and fountain pen set. The G-2 Intelligence section is a new addition to general staff structure. These sections are usually headed by a general. Nolan, though only a colonel, is the highest ranking officer Pershing could find for the position.

Nolan enters and shuts the door behind him. I snap to attention and salute. The general returns the salute and sits, motioning me to a chair. "Sounds like you couldn't wait to get out of Paris, Major."

"Well, sir . . ."

"I hear you and Martel are not . . . intimate friends."

"No, sir."

"Foisted on me by my counterpart in the artillery. They told me about Martel being on the fast track—promising, proper bearing, effective. From the right sort of family, according to some who think soldiering is somehow inherited. Influential friends back home and, I have to admit, takes a good photograph. Once in Paris, things got worse." He shakes his head. "I thought I licked the problem stationing you there. But here you are."

"Sorry I couldn't help more, sir."

"I'm not shocked."

"May I speak freely, sir?" Nolan gives me a *go-on* roll with his hand. "Major Martel may be an officer, but he's no gentleman. He and Captain Buck assaulted a young woman, a reporter named Alice Simmons. They now allege she is a German spy."

"Any possibility she is?"

"No, sir. I have a conflict of interest I need to confess. I've known her since she was twelve. Family friend. If she's a spy, General Pershing is the Kaiser in disguise. I hope we can debunk this before the French decide to shoot her."

Nolan stares at the ceiling for a moment. If the clerk looks like a lit major, Nolan is the department chair—professorial, with thinning light brown hair, but a military posture. "I hear you're a crime fighter. Took on that crook O'Connor. What was his scam?"

"Not *was*—he still runs it. I exposed the problem but didn't solve it. My editor pulled me from the case, probably to save my life. The O'Connor layover agreement. When a wanted criminal comes to St. Paul, he goes straight to police headquarters, registers, and pays a *tribute*. So long as he doesn't break the law within city limits, the coppers leave him alone and have never heard of him if outside authorities come looking for him. Chief O'Connor is a powerful man with lots of friends. I reported about it. Bad choice, I guess."

"I need *that* reporter working for *me*. Weed out bad apples. A man who isn't afraid to ruffle a few feathers—that still you?"

"The thing that made me back off? I'm ashamed to say it. I feel like a coward. Gunning for me? I could handle that. They shot my daughter's dog. Tossed a message on a rock through her window. She wasn't home at the time."

"What did it say?"

"*The little girl's next.*"

"Taking care of your family is *not* an act of cowardice."

"Feels that way." A dribble of sweat trickles down my spine. "Martel told me, in so many words, to keep my mouth shut or my daughter is next."

"She's here?"

"A nurse. In Paris."

"Which hospital?"

"American Red Cross Military Hospital One."

"Hmm." Nolan leans back in his chair. "Living outside the hospital?"

"No, sir. In a dorm, in the building."

"Her first name?"

"Trudy."

Nolan takes a sheet of paper from his center drawer and jots a note. "Paris could fall in a couple of days if our Second and Third Divisions don't hold. I'm sure the hospital administrators are keeping the staff up to date on that. Closer to home, I need you to clean up your old office. I want Martel in a stockade if he's a criminal. We need proof. I have an idea about how to protect your daughter." He writes two additional sentences on the note, signs, and folds it. "I also hear rumblings about problems in my old department—Sanitary. The pinch points are Paris and Château-Thierry. You have a driver and car. Find the facts and report back to me personally. Show me the man who took on city hall."

Chapter Twenty-One
Alice Simmons

Friday, June 7

My bedroom door crashes open. Two men rush in and grab me by the arms and haul me out of bed. They drag me into the living room, their grip like vices crushing my elbows.

"What are you doing?" I mumble, groggy with sleep.

"Silence!" one policeman shouts and slaps my left cheek.

I blink, confused. Where are my glasses?

Two uniformed policemen tear my room apart. They haul my steamer trunk into the living room and dump the contents onto the floor. One rips the lining of the drawers with a stiletto, then slices and tears out the lining of the sidewalls. Another lugs my typewriter out. I gasp when he tosses it on a table.

"Something to hide, mademoiselle?" asks one while another slides a sheet of paper between the rollers and pecks away with each key. He looks at the first man and shakes his head.

A thud from the bedroom draws my eyes. One man dumps out the contents of a drawer—my undergarments. He sweeps my three books and broken tortoiseshell glasses off the dresser top onto the rug. The other policeman grins at me as he grinds the glasses into the floor with his boot. "Boche," he hisses through tight lips.

"Why are you doing this?" I ask the man restraining my right elbow. Pain sears down my arm when he tightens his grip. The two force me into a wooden chair, one walking away while the other lets go of my elbow and jerks my head back by the hair.

The shouting settles into loud voices and crude remarks about my undergarments. My purse flies out of the bedroom and bounces off a wall, spilling out the short bit of necklace chain. I try to get up from the chair. The man jerks me back by the hair. "Don't tempt me. Spies don't get a trial."

"Spy?" What are they thinking? Who would make such a ridiculous accusation?

Martel.

My spine tingles, neck about to break, and my scalp is on fire from the man's grip on my hair. My pulse pounds from ears to toes, every muscle tight, mind flying over the events of the past few days. The audacity of it—his accusation that I had assaulted him was not enough. Now my "gang" is a spy ring? Is everyone so stupid, so gullible they believe Martel?

"*Oui*, you are a filthy spy."

A sergeant unholsters a revolver and aims it between my eyes.

The muzzle is a black tunnel five inches from my face.

It fills my vision. My heart hammers. My face sears with heat. The man behind me lets go and moves next to the sergeant.

He must not want to be hit by the bullet, or my brains.

The sergeant cocks the revolver. The cylinder turns—dull gray slugs ready to snuff out my life. Finger on the trigger. Twitching.

The muzzle trembles.

A thought, a memory flashes amid my confusion. Ira has told me many times about staring down the barrel of an assassin's pistol in St. Paul. What did Ira do?

Then I remember.

Nothing to lose.

Moments to live.

I pry my eyes away from the cold steel ring, over the front sight, up to the sergeant's eyes. His pupils are saucers. I bore my gaze into them—hold them, as if memorizing his soul so I'll remember him when he joins me in hell. Or if wronged spirits really do walk the earth, I'll find him. That was how Ira faced down his would-be assassin, a St. Paul cop.

What I see are a father's eyes. Not the dead eyes of a killer. They're the eyes of a man who will not pull the trigger. That was what Ira told me he saw at the last moment.

Hope rises in my chest.

"Monsieur," I say in a voice barely above a whisper. "The man who sent you is an American officer who tried to rape me. He is covering his tracks with false accusations against me. *I* am the victim. Will you shoot the victim? Ask yourself, can you live with my blood on your hands? Can your family? Your children?"

He blinks.

The muzzle moves away.

An officer emerges from my bedroom as a lieutenant enters the apartment. "Nothing, sir. She must have hid it somewhere else."

"Hid what?" I ask.

"Silence," the lieutenant snaps. A sneer grows on his face. "The code book. Where is it?"

How can I answer if I'm supposed to be silent? "I have no idea what you're talking about."

"Of course. You're just an innocent Américain, minding her own business. This is a waste of time," the lieutenant says. He turns to the landlady. "You will evict her, now."

"Where will I go?" I ask.

"The gallows if I get my wish," the lieutenant hisses through clenched teeth.

"Throw the whore out," My landlady shouts. She points at two policemen. "All this . . . trash. Out. Into the street." She turns to me, her eyes hot. "Get out, Boche." She spits into my face. A warm dribble creeps down my cheek.

Two policemen stuff my scattered clothes into the broken trunk. I'm still in my nightgown. Where's my uniform? What time is it? My watch, where is it? My mind is as jumbled as my things, trying to make sense of what's happening and what to do.

"Out!" screams the landlady, pointing at the door with a shaking arm.

The landlady is unglued, pacing, shouting, wringing her hands as if wiping off an imaginary stain. I'm not going to dress in front of these people. I snatch up my broken silver chain and slide it into my purse, then go to the bedroom and try to straighten up my trampled uniform. I put on my wire-frame glasses. Things look foggy from the greasy fingerprints smeared on the lenses. I close the door and quickly don my uniform and pat my skirt flat. The door flies open with a policeman shouting that if I do that again he'll throw me out the window. What an ass.

No more fear—now I'm just mad.

I collect the rest of my possessions and carry them to the trunk. The landlady's hysterics continue, but I shut them out and focus on what I need to do. I slow down and take my time to fold my things and put them into the drawers, skirts on hangers. A slap on the back of my head swings me around. The woman clutches a kitchen knife in her tremulous left hand. Screaming—accusing me of everything short of being the Kaiser's mistress. She had seemed so nice when I first met her.

"Shut up," I say. "I'll take my things. Just get out of my way." After the pistol, the crazy woman's knife seems tame. I won't turn my back on her, however.

The sergeant guides the woman away, gripping the hand holding the knife, assuring her I'll be prosecuted to the fullest extent of the law and then hanged as a spy. What a nice man.

I settle the typewriter in its case and then carry it and my small suitcase with my toiletries downstairs and set them under a tree in the small yard. Then I go back upstairs and wrestle my trunk back together. The police have broken the lock. I grip the top handle and pull it down the stairs one crash at a time. I can only hope it leaves a trail of splintered stair treads. Out front, I yank the trunk near my other things.

The cluster of policemen stand in a loose circle, smoking cigarettes. I go up to the nearest smoker. "If anything is missing, I'll file a formal complaint. This is ridiculous."

The men laugh. The lieutenant draws his right index finger across his neck in a slitting motion, then points it at me. "The dead don't complain."

Chapter Twenty-Two
Alice Simmons

Standing by the rubble pile of my things, slowing my breathing, I wonder what I should do, where I can go, and how I'll get my things to wherever that is. God, I wish Ira was here. I could use a cool head to help me think this through.

My eyes settle on a man with a familiar face, sitting on a bench across the street, watching, smoking a cigarette, leaning back, legs crossed. His face is grim. He stands, field strips his cigarette, and walks over.

Henri Barton.

How long has he been there? I hadn't noticed him before.

"What's wrong, Mademoiselle Alice?"

I pace while talking, heart in my throat, voice tight, and tell him the whole story, starting with the New York Bar. If Henri is surprised by my outpouring, he shows nothing, nodding and listening without interruption. One of Henri's coworkers walks toward us, rolling a hand dolly.

Henri motions the other man over. "Luc, our other chores can wait."

One of the smokers stands next to the upended trunk, kicking my clothes. Henri shouts at the man, who fixes him with a hostile glare. Is

Henri crazy? Yelling at the cop like a schoolteacher scolding a truant fifteen-year-old. They'll arrest him.

The lieutenant pushes the others aside. Henri plants a finger square in the middle of the man's chest and shouts, "Gaston, this is Pascal Duval's great-granddaughter. Treat her with respect."

The lieutenant frowns. "Duval? Her name is Simmons."

"Gaston, she's one of the good ones, no matter what they told you. I vouch for her." The lieutenant, Gaston, frowns. Henri lowers his voice barely above a whisper. "Gaston, I am so disappointed in you. You were sent here under false pretenses. Let her go."

Gaston backs off and grinds his cigarette butt into the grass. He walks away and mutters to his men out of earshot. One casts a wide-eyed look toward Henri. The face of the man who pointed the pistol at me goes white, and he sits down.

Henri and Luc help me repack my things and secure the trunk with Henri's belt. The sergeant and Gaston help as well, shocking me. What is this? I grab the three books I brought from home, including my favorite—*The Wonderful Wizard of Oz*. Luc rolls the trunk back to the hospital with the dolly. Henri carries the typewriter, quiet, as if mulling things over. When we enter the loading dock, Henri sends Luc back to his original chores. "I am sorry. Gaston is my nephew. Filled by his own importance."

"Thank you. I was afraid they would arrest you, the way you talked to them."

Henri huffs. "It's an old tale. Young men with guns—action before wisdom."

"Do you have any idea where I can stay? I'm afraid the police will do the same thing no matter where I move next."

"I know a place. It is not nice, but nobody will think to look for you there. Come." He rolls the trunk to a dumbwaiter. The trunk descends as Henri works the ropes. He leads me to the basement, where he rolls the trunk on the dolly. Bare bulbs flicker in the long corridor. The humid smell of bleach makes the place feel close. Henri turns into a narrow side aisle, around two corners, and then stands before a metal door. He looks behind. "Empty storage room. Very safe." He opens the door and rolls the trunk in. The room has limestone walls, moisture staining one seam. The concrete floor is dry, though, and the room isn't moldy. A bare electric light dangles from the middle of the ceiling on a brown cord. "I will get you things—cot, chair, table—later, when I have a chance. Don't worry." Henri bows, hands me the key, and leaves.

The trunk, the typewriter, and my suitcase fill one corner. I look at my watch—I'll be late. Pickler. Oh crap. I rush to the door, closing it with a squeal of metal, click the lock, and jog down the corridor toward the stairs. I struggle to focus on work. But I can't put away the memory of the pistol, the muzzle, the bullets glaring at me.

The halls are filled with new arrivals when I near the ward. Nurse Pickler doesn't deal with mess, dirt, or chaos well. Or late arrivals. I check my watch again. Eight fifteen.

I had told the aides to all be here at seven—each shift arrives an hour early and stays at least an hour afterward. I scan the ward. My aides are working, following the routine Betty and I established for them. Strong body odor, barnyards, sulfur, and a hint of putrefaction sting my nose. I take a deep breath and steel myself—the day is already a disaster, and it's only just begun. Voices fill the room amid a clatter of carts and background moans. A new batch of wounded marines sully Nurse Pickler's pristine bedsheets. And my problems become a molehill compared to the misery surrounding me.

Trudy and the other nurses circulate among the new admissions. Where's Scooter? He hadn't come back to the ward by the time I left— his surgery must have been a long one. What if he died on the table?

"What is this lunacy?" Pickler demands from a very young army lieutenant. "You are bringing men in here who are not only unbathed— they have lice. We never allowed anyone with lice on my ward at Mass General."

"System's flooded, ma'am. No time to delouse 'em. All we can do is haul 'em here." The lieutenant flashes an expression that suggests Pickler is lucky he is unarmed, and leaves.

Pickler looks at her watch. "You're late, Simmons." She glares. "Did you sleep in your uniform? Tidy up and get to work."

"Sorry, ma'am."

"Sorry doesn't cut it. We have new arrivals, and some of them have lice."

I scurry to the linen room to make sure that everything is in proper Pickler order. On the way, I pass Scooter lying in a bed with an amputation tent over the lower half. I catch his eye. He gives me a little wave. I let out a breath of relief. He made it. My fears last evening were false. Thank you, God.

Betty and the aides gather in the linen room with me. Marie tidies my hair, asking what happened. I tell them I can't talk about it now, that we need to get to work. Betty rebuttons my shirt.

We set tubes of NCI cream and shakers of NCI powder on the carts. The combination of naphthalene, creosote, and iodoform controls lice. I scratch my head. That's the problem with lice on a medical ward. Now every itch will be suspicious. The aides gather around me, and I review bathing and NCI application procedures with the admonition to wear gloves and not touch themselves. I send two of the French aides to the laundry to get more linens and pajamas. The great thing about being overwhelmed with work is that I have no time to ponder my own problems.

Betty and I lead the aides into the ward. Pickler shoots me a frown. Marie and I start working on our first new arrival, getting his uniform off, dumping it directly into a laundry cart to avoid contaminating the floor. He doesn't have lice, but I powder his groin and underarms with NCI, just in case. The hair on his head is too short to justify it. We scrub our gloved hands in a basin of soapy water between patients. Aides don't ordinarily rate rubber gloves, which are in short supply, but lice are the exception.

Nurses follow us, checking temperatures, starting charts, inspecting wounds after the patients are deloused. A process that had been awkward four days ago is now like a well-rehearsed ballet. Trudy works on the patients after Marie and I finish cleaning them. She removes the dressings for an initial inspection by Captain Jensen, the ward surgeon. He is demanding, precise, proper. And quite handsome —tall, about thirty, with sandy hair, sky-blue eyes, and a thin, straight nose, an inch or two above six feet. Two nurses assist Jensen on his rounds.

Marie and I continue to clean new arrivals and try to keep spirits up. Marie's smile is the sort that even men in pain return. We start working on the man in the bed next to Scooter. I give Scooter a warm smile, the kind I would give my favorite cousin, and ask how he feels.

"Guess it was worse than I thought, Miss Alice. Bet I'll be hopping around on crutches soon, though. We'll have a race, what say?"

"When did you get back from surgery?"

"Sometime last night. Don't remember things so well. In and out. Gave me a lot of morphine, so it don't hurt so bad right now."

"We have plenty more if you need it. Don't be shy." Scooter's cheeks are flushed. He grins with faraway eyes. Morphine. I touch Scooter's hand. "We'll have that race, you'll see. I bet I'll beat you, though. So watch out."

"That's okay, Miss Alice. Stop by after your shift. Don't want to get ya in hot water."

As I walk away, the image of the revolver muzzle flashes before me, the man destroying my tortoiseshell glasses. Martel's fingers. I shake my head to banish the memories.

A shriek breaks the moment.

On my left a new arrival lies in bed, washed and gowned, blood pulsing from the man's left thigh. The nurse from the dorm—Dagger Eyes—stands, frozen in place, staring at the fountain of blood running down the leg onto the bed and into a growing pool on the floor. Captain Jensen has his hands in another marine's wound. I rush to the bedside. Dagger Eyes is transfixed, hands on the wound, covered in blood. "Get out of my way." I shove Dagger Eyes aside and jam both hands into the crease between the leg and the pelvis to compress the femoral artery. My eyes lock on the wound while I push with all my might.

The bleeding stops.

Take a breath.

Dagger Eyes stands at the foot of the bed, her uniform spattered with blood, gloved hands dripping. Her face is now red with rage, eyes blazing. "Don't ever touch me again."

Trudy pulls Dagger Eyes away. "You're a mess. Wash that blood off and get in a clean uniform before Pickler sees you." Trudy stands across the bed from me. "You okay?"

I look at the young marine's face—ashen, only the whites of his eyes showing. His pulse is rapid, weak. "Yeah. Tourniquet."

Captain Jensen looks up from his work. "You got that?"

"Yes, Captain." I nod. "Shrapnel must have lacerated the femoral artery. It probably migrated when the wound was undressed, sir."

"Be there in a jiffy. Maintain pressure."

Heels click in cadence behind me. Nurse Pickler says, "This is nurse's work. Stand back."

"Beg pardon, ma'am, but I have it."

"You are exceeding your privileges . . ."

"But not my training, ma'am. This patient can't afford to lose more blood. I'll keep my hands where they are until the captain can take over."

Captain Jensen walks over and stands beside me. "Doing okay?" he asks in a quiet, authoritative voice. I look at him and nod. Captain Jensen turns to one of his nurses. "Get me a tourniquet." He looks into my eyes. "Miss . . . ?"

"Simmons. Nurse Cunningham is getting one."

"Miss Simmons, if your hand gets tired, warn me. I don't want big red to erupt again."

Trudy hustles over with a tourniquet. Captain Jensen looks at me. "Good thinking."

"Nurse," Pickler says, "fetch that Frenchman, what's his name, the one with the mop. Clean up the mess you've made here."

"Belay that," Captain Jensen says. "I don't want anything done until I have the tourniquet on and the bleeding controlled." Nurse Pickler's mouth purses. So I'm not the only one who has a problem with Pickler's fixation on cleanliness, it seems. But something Trudy told me before now makes sense. Pickler worked in one of the finest hospitals in America—Massachusetts General. One where patients came to the wards washed and gowned. The pediatrics and urology wards there are worlds apart from the mayhem surrounding us.

"Okay. Miss Simmons, maintain steady pressure. You two—" He looks at the nurses assisting him. "—raise the leg enough for me to slide the tourniquet underneath. You," he says to Trudy, "grab the other end and hand it to me."

The maneuver is done in seconds. The tourniquet encircles the thigh about midway between the groin and the wound. Captain Jensen draws it tight. "Miss Simmons, let off very slowly. If it bleeds, reapply pressure." His grim face relaxes. He looks over at me, holding my eyes for a moment longer that I expect.

I concentrate on the wound as I let off pressure. Blood wells up, and before Jensen can speak, I push in and stop the bleeding. Jensen tightens the tourniquet two more turns. He nods at me. I ease up. This time the tourniquet works.

"Gurney. Now," Captain Jensen says to Pickler. "We need to get this man to the OR. Simmons, let's clean up this leg."

Trudy rolls the dressing cart over and helps Captain Jensen and me clean off the fresh blood with gauze pads, avoiding the entry wound and the shard of metal protruding from it. Next, we use moistened gauze sponges to clean off the rest of the blood. I look at my watch and write the time on a paper tag, then tie it to the tourniquet. Captain Jensen lays a loose gauze sponge on the wound edges. We load the man onto the gurney. "Simmons, come," Captain Jensen says. "We'll wheel him straight to surgery. The rest of you, clean up this mess. We'll be back soon."

"I have qualified nurses to accompany you, Captain." Pickler scowls, arms folded in front of her. "Simmons is only a nurse's aide, and new here at that."

"I need someone I can trust." Captain Jensen points at Trudy. "You're a qualified nurse, right? Let's go."

I glance back. Pickler stands, hands on hips, face red.

Chapter Twenty-Three
Alice Simmons

Captain Jensen pulls the gurney while I push, with Trudy following. I may have just won the first battle, but this might send Pickler from bullying to all-out warfare. A nurse's aide doesn't have a prayer against a head nurse.

"I'm not used to surgeons doing orderly work, Captain," I say.

"You know how the expression goes—if you want something done right . . ." A loose wheel on the gurney clatters as we rush along the hallway toward surgery. We weave between hospital staff and patients on parked gurneys. Litter-bearers carrying new patients dodge out of our way. Jensen's white coat flares like an apparition. "What's wrong with that woman back there, Pickler?" Jensen asks.

"She's my boss; I'll have to take the fifth on that," I say.

"And you're just a new aide?"

"Well, I'm an RN. I'm working as an aide until they confirm my credentials."

"Nobody told me that."

"I'm not here to blow my own horn."

"Let me know if they talk about moving you. You too—what's your name?"

"Trudy Cunningham. Alice and I were classmates at Minnesota."

"Finally! Someone from a sane part of the country. If your head nurse extolls the virtues of Boston medicine one more time, I'll tracheostomize her."

When we arrive in pre-op, Jensen says, "Stay with him. I'll find the charge nurse." He jogs toward an office, returning with a portly nurse who appears to be in her forties. "Check with the ORs and put this man at the top of your list. He needs to go in the moment a team is ready." The nurse hurries off through a set of swinging doors with a sign that says *No Admittance*. Jensen lets out a long breath. "Now we wait. We'll stay with him until I can hand him off." He rolls his neck. "So, how'd you end up here? You didn't come from Minnesota to Paris to be an aide, did you?"

I give him a short version of my story, leaving out the parts about Martel and my near-death encounter this morning.

Jensen glances at the double doors. "I'm from Saint Cloud. Went to U of M. Undergrad and med school. Fair number of Minnesotans here." Jensen narrows his eyes. "Simmons. Related to Dr. William Simmons?"

"He's my father. He—"

"Lectured our classes in surgical microbiology. Rotated on his service." His eyes show a new interest. "Did my surgical training at the university and Minneapolis City."

"Our mothers are nurses at City," I say.

"Now it all makes sense. Your mother's a heck of a nurse. Well . . . so are you," he says, glancing at Trudy. "Ethyl Cunningham?"

Trudy nods.

"Scared the hell out of me. She puts up with nothing. Great nurse."

The double doors to surgery pop open. A man in blood-spattered surgical whites shambles toward us, his face slack with fatigue. A surgical mask dangles from his neck, and a sweat-stained white cap sits on his head. "What've you got, Mark?"

"Thigh wound. Retained shrapnel. Must have migrated when one of our nurses removed the dressing. Had an arterial pumper going until this nurse got good compression on the femoral. We applied a tourniquet."

"Good work." The surgeon turns to his team. "Get him in OR three and gas him. How long's the tourniquet been in place, Mark?"

"About ten minutes. Miss Simmons here put the time tag on it."

"Good. I'm about dead. Gotta get some joe. You game?"

"Nah. Better head back before the Pickle kills someone." Jensen's face reddens. He turns to me. "You didn't hear that."

"Hear what?" I ask.

"You're my favorite aide. How long before they get your credentials?"

"I'm not sure."

Jensen says to the weary surgeon, "She's William Simmons's daughter."

The surgeon whistles. "He wear that bow tie to bed? We always wondered."

Father's colleagues kidded him about his tartan bow ties. I want to defend him, but I have to make friends. "You'll have to ask Mother. He wore it from dawn to dusk. Had a rack of them in his closet."

The surgeon chuckles and limps away.

After we get back on the ward, I join Marie and get back to work. The cleaning, nursing, and surgical assessment process continues for several hours. After a quick lunch in the cafeteria, we stop in the laundry and restock the linen room. Marie and I watch Captain Jensen and two nurses set up Carrel-Dakin wound irrigations on the patients who underwent surgery last night. Dagger Eyes gives me her evil-eyed look while the other nurse works. My face warms, but I don't break eye contact. This is nothing after staring down the barrel of a revolver. Dagger Eyes blinks.

Why is she on Captain Jensen's team? She froze when the hemorrhage started earlier.

Then I'm back in the apartment, my arm shrieking in pain from the vice grip of the policeman. The muzzle again, larger than ever. Then, that night. Martel's fingers.

"Alice?" Marie asks.

"Yes? Sorry. Lost in my own world there."

"What are they doing?" Marie motions toward Captain Jensen and his nurses.

"Carrel-Dakin treatment. To cleanse wounds. You know how the farmers fertilize their fields. Centuries of manure and night soil—these men are covered with it. Bacteria coating the skin grow like wildfire in wounds. Does that make sense?"

"*Oui.*"

"The idea is to get the wounded here as soon as possible and to operate within a day. At the end of the operation, they insert rubber tubes into the deepest nooks and crannies."

"I wondered about all those tubes hanging out from the dressings."

"A French surgeon, Alexis Carrel, pioneered this. He worked with a chemist, Dr. Dakin, who invented the chemical solution we run through the tubes. Dakin's solution is dilute bleach. A little eosin dye is added to make it pink so they don't mistakenly put water or alcohol into the wound. We trickle it through the wound two or three times a day. The bleach kills bacteria, and the irrigation washes out the wound. In a few days, Captain Jensen will remove one of the rubber tubes from each wound and send it to the laboratory for culture. The men will dislike that even more than the irrigations, because each removed tube must be replaced with a new one."

"How do you know all this?"

"My father is a surgeon. His research interest is surgical micro-biology."

"Why are you not a doctor?"

I gaze around the room. Pickler stands at the nursing desk talking on the phone, calm for a change. Captain Jensen starts a wound irrigation. The marine's face pales, dripping sweat, hands clamped on the sides of his mattress. "I didn't plan to do any of this, Marie. I'm a journalist. That is *my* dream." Mine isn't the only shattered dream in this room.

Pickler leaves the ward for a meeting. I go over to Scooter's bed and glance at his vitals board. His temperature of 101 worries me. I fill his empty water glass from a pitcher on a nearby cart and hand it to him.

"Thanks, Miss Alice. Know what?" Scooter's voice seems weaker than earlier. His pupils are pinpoints—from all the morphine he's received. "You're the prettiest girl I ever seen."

"Don't have to look any farther than the nursing desk over there to find a prettier one." I nod toward Trudy, who is talking with Dagger Eyes. "Why, when you get out to the convalescent hospital, they'll fawn all over you."

"No, I mean it. You are. Just thought I ought to say that. Not that I'm looking for a date. Just . . . sometimes you have to say something—case you don't get a chance to, ya know, later. Grandpap taught me that. Kind of a philosopher, he was."

"You're not bad looking yourself, Bub." I peer into his gray eyes.

"You're just saying that," Scooter says. "I look like shit, pardon the French. Won't be much to look at later, neither, peg leg and all. Unless I get an eye patch and a parrot."

I chuckle, and Scooter joins in.

"Don't be silly. You never told me what you want to do after you get home."

"Sales. I'm thinking cars are going to be a commodity after this is all over. Guys coming back, not wanting saddle sores and stink on them, and seeing how the Fords go everywhere here? Gonna sell Fords, is my plan." He stares at the tent covering the lower part of the bed. "Lack of a leg won't hurt me there 'cept on test drives. Won't be able to work a clutch. But then, nobody wants the salesman to drive their new cars anyways. You?"

"I want to work as a reporter. That's what I was doing before this." I wave my hand around the room. I won't bother him with the details of my derailed career.

"Well, you can use my story, if you think it's worth anything. Got my permission and all." He makes an act of scanning the room. "Better get back to work before the witch catches us." He coughs. I squeeze his hand. He holds mine for a moment.

There is something hopeful in Scooter's eyes.

The pallor to his face and sunken cheeks tell a different story I hope will not come to pass.

Chapter Twenty-Four
Alice Simmons

The shift is nearly over. I want nothing more than to sit down to a reasonable meal with a glass of wine and time to think, to absorb what happened this morning. If not a session with my typewriter, I need to jot a few notes before everything blurs. But I have to help the night crew, since they stay past their shift to help us each morning.

Okay, skip the meal. But there's no wine in the cafeteria—one of the detriments of American management. We're such prudes compared to the French, though sobriety on the job is not optional here.

Memories flood in now that the pressure is off. It was so sudden—policemen shouting, jerking me out of bed. The landlady screeching like a harpy. Her knife. That must have been the police's plan—shock out a confession.

The pistol. The trembling finger on the trigger. Gazing into the eyes of the man about to kill me.

I bury my shaking hands in my pockets.

Henri. What a happy accident that he happened by. He dressed down the policemen like he was their commanding officer. But he's a civilian—a wine broker.

For him to be sitting on that bench at that moment strikes me as an odd coincidence. Another thought occurs—the way he field stripped his cigarette makes me wonder if he served in the military. Oh well, empty speculation.

Then there was the hemorrhage patient. I saved that one, but any good nurse would have done the same thing. Captain Jensen had been more than friendly, especially to an aide—but then, he trained under Dad. At least that makes sense. But is there more to the occasional looks he's cast my way?

I scan the room, but see another scene, heat rising in my cheeks. The pistol pointed at my face—the face at the other end is now Martel. Then the alley—his fingers, probing, searching. He is behind this. I shiver. Regroup. Think. Okay. How would Ira handle this? I wish I could talk with him.

My eyes settle on Scooter. His spirits held during the day, always a wan smile when I caught his eye. A foreboding cloud hangs over him. The nurses have been giving him morphine every couple of hours. My previous thanks to God may have been premature.

The ward smells like the mothballed sweaters in my aunt's armoire from all the lice powder we've spread around. Captain Jensen works on a leg wound two beds away. Fatigue etches his face, his movements languid, his nurses nowhere to be seen. He was still working when I left at midnight last night and was here when I arrived this morning. Betty and Marie stand to the side while Captain Jensen rinses his gloved hands in a basin of alcohol. Betty looks done in, so I go over and whisper into her ear. "You and Marie look exhausted. Go ahead and take a break. Bring fresh linens on the way back." Betty taps Marie on the shoulder, and the two leave.

Captain Jensen stands at the foot of a bed, looking over the chart. He motions me over and smiles, his weary eyes showing something beyond professional interest. Is it that thing about my eye color again? I look toward Scooter. One of the nurses lifts a water glass to his lips. Each time I check him, he's worse. My fear for him rises.

"Miss Simmons, I'd like you to observe—get the hang of things. Unless you have other duties right now." He waves two of the night nurses over.

"Thank you, Captain," I say. "I'm off shift, so sure."

The next patient lies with his right leg surrounded by a Thomas traction splint. The steel frame of the splint forms an elongated *U* along each side of the leg—padded half rings at the groin and hip are the endpoints. The short end of the *U* is like a stirrup six inches below the man's grimy combat boot. A latticework of cloth wraps around the boot and loops around the frame below. A wooden stake has been used to wind the cloth between the boot and the stirrup, creating traction to hold the shattered bone fragments of the man's shin apart. He smells like he's been dragged through a horse paddock.

"Let's look you over, Private . . . Stoops." Captain Jensen looks at me. "How did this man end up here and not in one of the enlisted wards?"

The man in the next bed interrupts. "I told them that if they put Hiram anywhere else I'd knock their blocks off."

The speaker wears a patient gown, so I can't tell the man's rank. He has short dark brown hair and brown agate eyes filled with hostility. About the same age as me, a hard man with a square jaw, its muscles quivering. Neither handsome nor ugly. A rough face. Big and muscular. The sort of man who'd make a football lineman run for his life.

"Hiram saved my life. So take good care of him, or else, Doc."

"I'm too tired for this shit," Captain Jensen says. He points to his captain's bars. "*Second Lieutenant* Grant, you may give doctors orders in the field, but here, I outrank you."

Grant's jaw muscles move as if chewing on the information. He sighs. "They wanted to siphon Hiram off at each stop." Grant looks toward Hiram and gives a firm nod. "I owe him; he stays with me."

The man in the next bed is another new arrival. Older, in his forties. I don't know his name. He must be one of the senior officers and has a silent presence—watching, listening. If Grant is a linebacker, this is his head coach. The man radiates authority.

"Let's get on with this." Captain Jensen turns back to Stoops.

Private Hiram Stoops has a lean frame and the feral face of a backwoodsman. His short black hair looks like a fellow marine chopped it off with a dull knife. He has an acne-scarred face, an overbite, and a weak chin. His brown eyes dart between Lieutenant Grant and Captain Jensen before settling on mine with a beseeching expression.

"Miss Simmons, please remove the dressing," Captain Jensen says.

"But . . ." I start.

Captain Jensen makes a show of sweeping his eyes around the ward. "Pickle's not in sight. Time to be a nurse, Nurse."

Hiram's leg is bare except for the dressings and the boot. My throat tightens at the sight of bone fragments under torn flesh as I tease the last gauze pads off the shin. Blood oozes as Captain Jensen pokes and prods. Hiram's face contorts in agony, sweat gathering along his brow. Captain Jensen goes to the cart and rinses his gloved hands in alcohol. "The leg will probably have to come off. The field hospitals are overloaded, so I don't blame them for simply cleaning it up. There's suppuration. I'll schedule you for surgery tonight. We'll send you down for an X-ray to see if there is any chance of saving it, but don't get your hopes up, Private."

"Supper what?" Hiram asks. The lilt in his voice is pure rural Minnesota.

"Suppuration." Captain Jensen looks at me and rolls his eyes. "Pus. Infection."

"Doc, I don't wanna lose my leg, dontchaknow?"

"It's infected. Infected bones don't heal. I'm trying to be honest with you, Private."

Will Hiram have a tent over his bed before sunrise too? I sneak a look at Scooter. His face is flushed. He wipes his brow. I have to get over there—check on him.

"But Doc, how'll I walk then?"

"We have good prosthetic departments back home."

Fear takes over Hiram's eyes. "Peg leg?"

"That's dime novel stuff—Jolly Rogers and pirates. If needed, we'd amputate below the knee, and your stump will fit into a receptacle. The rest is wood, with a mechanical ankle and a part that will fit in a shoe."

"But, Doc, sir, ain't there no way you can save my leg? Running's all I'm good at. Cut off my leg? Well, might as well take off my noggin, too, dontchaknow? I seen a few guys with them legs. All I knows is farming and running. No leg, and I'm useless as a teatless cow." He blushes and glances at me. "Sorry, ma'am." Tears streak Hiram's face, his hands shaking.

"You planning to get an orthopedic man in on the case?" Lieutenant Grant asks.

"When did you get your MD, Lieutenant?"

"Didn't say I had. In Chicago, at Cook County, when we'd bring vics in with things like this, they'd call the orthopedics boys."

"When you get that degree, come back here. We don't have enough orthopods to take care of all the leg fractures during the past two days."

I'm not sure who is surlier—Grant or Jensen. The two glare at each other, then Jensen's frown slackens.

"What did you do at Cook?"

"I'm a cop. Seen legs like this on ambulance runs. Auto wrecks, industrials." He winks at Hiram. "Our docs there fixed 'em up. Didn't amputate much, far as I could tell."

"Yeah, but they brought them in right away, didn't they?"

"Got me there. Hiram was shot in the leg on the sixth. He was carrying me to the aid station—saving me—when a German round hit him. Now I'm making sure you take good care of him."

"That's all I ever try to do, Lieutenant. I'll take good care of him."

"Let's hope you do, Doc."

Chapter Twenty-Five
Alice Simmons

Orderlies bring Hiram back from his X-ray, and about fifteen minutes later, Captain Jensen enters the ward along with another doctor. Two nurses trail them, including Dagger Eyes, who gives me what I now consider her signature glare. Lieutenant Grant raises himself on an elbow, his face grim. Hiram's expression is one of confusion.

"Private Stoops, this is Captain Scully," Captain Jensen says. "He's the orthopedist I'll be working with on your leg."

It's after ten at night as I stifle a yawn. The surgeons will be working through the night again. I blink. Focus. Four hours of sleep last night before the police barged in. A momentary flash of the alleyway where Martel attacked me pops into my head.

Scooter. A nurse strokes his forehead with a washcloth. Hiram—focus on Hiram. Do what's right in front of you. Don't make mistakes. A yawn comes out of nowhere.

Focus. My problems don't amount to a hill of beans compared to Scooter's. Or Hiram's, or those of most of the men in our ward.

Dagger Eyes unwraps the dressing on Hiram's leg, which remains in the Thomas splint, his filthy boot still on. He grimaces while she works.

After he finishes his exam, Scully says, "I understand you're a litter-bearer."

"Yes, sir. I am, dontchaknow."

"He was carrying me off the field when he got his," Grant says.

"Captain Jensen told you about the risks," Scully says. "You need surgery. If we don't do it, you'll die from infection. Problem is, the wound is infected and you may lose the leg anyway."

Hiram's face pales. "You see, sir, this is how it is. I'm not much good for nothing, like Mom always said. I lose the leg? Well, like I told Captain Jensen, you might as well—"

"Captain Jensen told me. I understand. I can't make any promises. I won't cut off your head, however. We don't do that here. No neurosurgeons handy right now. Got it?"

Hiram looks at Grant, then back. "Sure, I guess." He stares down at his leg, his face downtrodden. "Just don't know what I'll ever do."

"Even if we save the leg, your running days are over," Scully says.

"Hiram, we'll work something out," Grant says.

"We'd ordinarily take you to surgery first," Jensen says to Grant, "but Private Stoops may take a while, and we really need to get going. Any questions?"

"Just . . . well, I said my piece," Grant says.

"Give him a quarter grain of morphine," Jensen says to one of the nurses. "I'll head to the OR." Scully leaves while the nurse jabs Hiram with a dose of morphine.

Hiram swallows. "Lieutenant Ben, so, anyways, I'm real worried. Captain Jensen is a real jerk, dontchathink?"

"Hiram, surgeons are that way. My gut says Jensen's okay."

"Private, Captain Jensen will take good care of you and the lieutenant." I like Jensen. He's on my side. But then, does that cloud my judgment? I haven't seen him in the OR, haven't known him for more than a few days. Even though it is one of those things nurses always say to reassure the patient, did I just lie?

Jensen lingers at the nursing station, scribbling on a chart. Scooter looks worse—breathing rapid, face flushed. "Doctor, if it's okay, I'd like you to look at Cherny," I say. "He's worsening."

"You're speaking out of turn," Dagger Eyes says. "That's a nursing job."

Captain Jensen gives the young nurse a tired sigh and leads the way. Sweat beads on Scooter's forehead, and he shakes with a chill. I hold a water glass to his lips. He sips and nods thanks.

"Private, we're going to have to look at that leg." Captain Jensen turns to Dagger Eyes. "Nurse Walker, please remove the dressing while I listen to him." He pulls out his stethoscope.

Dagger Eyes—Walker—removes the pus-soaked dressing, releasing a putrid odor. The stump is a high thigh amputation. Oh no. God, don't let this happen. Scooter's eyes are closed, mouth contorted. He looked so good this morning.

The amputation is so high that to go any farther they would have had to do a hip disarticulation. The skin above is greenish black. Captain Jensen prods the crease between the remaining leg and pelvis and frowns. "Re-dress this, Walker." He wipes the sweat from Scooter's forehead with a gentle hand and whispers, "We'll do what we can, Marine. Stay strong."

I stand next to Captain Jensen as he douses his gloved hands in an alcohol basin, unable to look at the wound. "This is what I was afraid of." He shakes the alcohol off his hands. "Damn. It took him two fucking days to get to me. Goddamned gangrene." His face reddens. "Sorry. Long day."

"He's not going to make it," I whisper.

"No. I'll have the night shift keep him on morphine. Nothing else we can do. This one's in God's hands."

"Do you mind if I stay with him, Captain?"

"That would be the kindest thing any of us can do. Thank you, Miss Simmons. Consider that an order—in case Pickle comes back through."

Scooter's eyes are sunken, his gaze far away as I settle into the chair next to his bed and hold the water to his lips again. He shakes his head. The pupils of his blue eyes are pinpoints from morphine. The skin of his hand is hot and dry, his face red with fever. "Thank you—'case I forget to tell you." His voice is raspy.

After several minutes I wring a washcloth in the basin and wipe his forehead and his cracked lips. He sticks out his tongue, and I moisten it.

His breathing is rapid, and deep despite the morphine—his pulse weak, thready, rate over a hundred and fifty.

You're not alone. I gaze into his eyes and smile.

I'm with you.

I try to push those thoughts into his eyes from mine. I keep my fingers on his wrist, not sure what else to do.

I've sat with dying patients before. But this one is different.

Keep contact.

Don't let this happen.

God, why couldn't they get him here sooner? What was wrong with them? Letting him lie in a field for hours. Sitting on the ground outside that hospital, what did he call it? Julie. Probably not the real name. A whole day with no care. Bacteria, festering. They should have done surgery then. We don't let this happen. Operate within twelve hours. That's the rule. What's wrong with those doctors in Julie? God damn them all and this stupid war.

Scooter's breathing is ragged. He pulls harder. Is his throat swelling? The sheets over his abdomen sink with each breath in. His eyes are far away, not seeing me.

I hold his wrist, lean over, cradle his head in my left arm, and set my forehead on his.

A jagged gasp.

Then nothing.

The pulse slow, weak.

Then none.

Scooter's body lets go.

"No," I whisper.

Chapter Twenty-Six
Alice Simmons

S cooter. I don't want his spirit to go alone. Do spirits look back on the vessel they departed and those surrounding them? How can I know, other than when I die? I look up, toward the ceiling. I'd like to think he's up above, looking down. After all, I was raised to be a good Catholic, confirmed and the whole bit. Okay, I drifted after high school, haven't been to confession since my freshman year in college, not to Mass since I got to Paris and rarely before.

Still, I sit.

Tears would be so appropriate but don't come. Can't come.

All I did was cry after seeing Justine lying dead on Lake Street. Swore I would never weep again, never again experience the depth of despair of that moment. The memory of Geneviève sitting on the stairs of the hospital, looking so much like Justine, flashes before me as I stare at Scooter.

God, I wish Ira were here. He'd know what to say. Or just put an arm around me like my parents haven't done since I was ten. Just his presence would help. Trudy's busy on the other side of the room. I'm not sure I can walk that far. So I sit.

Not a tear since I was ten. None now, and that cleaves my heart almost as much as Scooter's death.

Still, I hold his hand, staring into nothingness, my mind filled only with Scooter and who he was and could have become and Justine and sadness.

The murmurs of the room come back to me in bits and pieces.

A touch on my shoulder. Trudy. "It's time," she says.

I stand and push my glasses up and look at Scooter's eyes, staring at the ceiling, pupils now wide. Another memory flash of Justine—dead on the street, her eyes had seemed like saucers. The pupils—I hadn't realized that before.

Trudy and an orderly slide Scooter onto the bare metal top of a morgue gurney. I follow behind while the other two roll Scooter toward the doors. Like the priest following the cross and his alter boys after celebrating Mass. I become aware of Grant as we leave. His eyes hold mine for a moment, and instead of the hard agates, I see nothing but compassion. The older man in the next bed is also looking at me with kindness. Kindred spirits, not hardened warriors for the moment.

Then we're out the door, rattling down the hallway to an elevator. I want to be there when Hiram comes back from surgery, but there is no way I can stay awake that long. He'll be in the operating room for hours, and then they'll work on Grant. How does Jensen stay on his feet?

We roll Scooter to the basement morgue. After settling my friend in the cool room, I follow Trudy, who lingers as the orderly rolls the gurney down the hallway.

"He was just a boy . . ." I begin.

Trudy puts her arm around me and leads me along the hall. "I know. They all are. What was it about him? You're usually so . . . clinical. What happened?"

"I don't know. Just . . . it's been a long day."

"Heading home, or do you want a bite?"

"I couldn't eat. Can't imagine it. Not after . . ." I stop and press a hand on the wall to hold myself up. It's late and our shifts ended hours ago. I'm too exhausted to go back to the ward.

Trudy puts an arm under my left shoulder. "Home."

"Do you want to see what I call *home* now?" I spit out.

"Sure. How far?"

"We won't need umbrellas if it's raining. Come on." Trudy is beside me as I lead the way along the central hallway and off into the side corridor that goes to my new digs.

"This is creepy," Trudy says, holding my elbow.

The lock grinds as I turn it. The metal door screeches when I pull it open. I flick on the light. "Welcome to Chez Alice." I sweep my hand around a room I expected to look like the one I left in the morning.

But Henri has been here.

A hospital bed with clean, taut sheets sits in a corner, a new steamer trunk, a nicer model than my old one, at the foot of the bed. A table and two ladder-back chairs sit in the middle of the room, my typewriter on the table with a stack of paper next to it and a handwritten note in French. Two bottles of wine and a corkscrew stand next to the paper with one glass. I read the note: *It is humble, but the wine is good. H.*

"'Least there are two chairs," Trudy says and guides me to one, taking the other. Trudy stares at the bottle labels. "Well, I don't give a hoot what you want to do, missy, but I'm cracking this thing. I need one. And so do you. Let's see how good our wine broker's taste is." After filling the glass, she says, "I'm not used to you looking this way. What happened?"

I spill out the events since the morning, just now realizing that I haven't spoken to my friend all day. "This is my new home, for now." We pass the wine glass like a chalice at Mass.

"We'll get you in the dorm."

"Not until my papers come through. I can't ask Mrs. Enright for that big a favor. Especially with Walker and her friends standing guard."

"She's just a spoiled bitch."

"Manners, dear," I chuckle. Then my shoulders slump.

"Not sure what we can do about Pickler. She treats the other nurses and me better, though that seems to be inversely proportional to the distance from Holy Boston. Someone told me Pickler's daughter died in a hospital, after an accident. Her husband died later from the same accident. Hit her hard—well, what could you expect?"

"It all seems futile, you know? I mean . . . look at Scooter. They didn't get him here in time. Now he's lying cold in the morgue. How many others didn't make it this far?"

"Scuttlebutt is—a lot. Couple of the officers told me the evacuation system was chaos. So much for the efficiency of automobile transport. Those new arrivals—Stoops and Grant—were caught up in it. Grant would be one to talk to if you get a chance."

"He seems pretty hard-boiled," I say.

"'Lot like my best friend." Trudy's mouth turns up in a wry grin.

"Who is that older man in the next bed?"

"Their commander. Colonel Catlin."

I grab my purse and set the broken necklace on the table.

"I never told you the story behind the locket."

"Figured you'd tell me when you were ready."

As I look into Trudy's eyes, I realize how silly I was to not tell her sooner. We have no secrets between us, save this one. I couldn't bring myself to tell it—to face the fears, the possibility she would think my reaction was . . . well, overwrought. Deep breath. Now's the time. "The worst day of my life. When everything changed." I take off my glasses, no longer able to face a world of clear, crisp images. Trudy fills the glass. "I was ten. Justine, eight. She loved to race, but I always beat her—well, you know. Longer legs. We were coming back from a store on Lake Street. We lived near Lake Calhoun then. Justine bolted out in front of me, yelling, *Catch me if you can, googoo-eyes*. That's what she called me. I had glasses even then. I chased, and she pealed with laughter, arms pumping, little legs churning, looking back. I shouted for her to watch where she was going, but she was like a terrier after a squirrel." The images are as fresh as yesterday. "We had one, you know, a terrier. Fluffy."

"Never knew you had a dog."

"Yeah, well. Anyway . . . Fluffy ran ahead of Justine, me gaining on them. Fluffy darted into the street and Justine followed, looking back, sticking out her tongue at me."

I gaze at the necklace as I talk.

"The teamster shouted. The nearest horse reared, a terrible scream like I'd never heard from a horse. A yelp from Fluffy. People screaming —Mother, hands on her face. Father shouting. Everyone yelling at me, pointing. Justine, crushed. Mother yanked me back and put her hand over my eyes. But before that, I saw Justine's eyes. Wide open. Pupils huge, like Scooter's. I tried to push my way toward her. To hold her hand. My little sister. I so wanted to go to her. Father shouted that it was all my fault."

"That's terrible."

"All I could do was sob. There. All the way home. For the next week."

"What about Fluffy?"

"Shattered hind leg. Father took her to his laboratory."

My heart pounds in my ears, the hiss of blood and memory coursing with each pulse.

"Father wouldn't talk to me. He didn't acknowledge me. It was like I turned into a ghost. Mother didn't touch me after that. Grand-Mère Elise sat me down. Just the two of us, a week later. She spoke of life and death and courage. It was way over my head at the time. She handed me the locket—heart-shaped with a photo of Justine and me inside. She made me hold it in both hands and said, 'Seal your tears in here. The brave shed no tears.' I never cried again. I can't. Even when I want to. I locked my heart in there."

"I knew you had a sister, but . . ."

"We never talked about it afterward. Father mourned in his way— we saw little of him. I think he tried to do it through saving lives. Mother went back to work at the hospital, and they put a nanny in charge of me. A year later we moved to the house along River Road, the one you knew."

"The perfect family. That's what everyone called you."

"With ice in our veins."

Tears blur my vision. I'm only vaguely aware of my friend moving next to me until her arms embrace me as I sob.

Chapter Twenty-Seven
Alice Simmons

Saturday, June 8

Where am I? It's as dark as the bottom of an inkwell. I sit up. Dank air with a hint of wine. Mouth—cotton. Head throbbing. Nightshirt on. When had I gotten into it? My alarm bell dinging. I feel around for the flashlight Henri set next to my alarm clock on the nightstand and fumble for the button. The dim beam reveals a stone-and-mortar wall, timbered ceiling—my basement room. Safe, but like a crypt.

I get up on unsteady feet and turn on the ceiling light, scrunching my eyes against the pain. Trudy. The wine. Scooter. Justine. A small pitcher of water on the table—thank God. Trudy must have put it there. I down a glass, refill it, and sit at the table, staring at my typewriter. Where's my watch? The alarm clock says six thirty. I touch the typewriter, yearning to feel the keys. No time to write now.

Hiram. How did he do?

Does he still have a leg?

Bill. Trudy's Bill.

I was so brokenhearted about Scooter that I forgot to ask about Bill. Any one of the men in the ward could have been Trudy's Bill. Imagine, rolling Bill's warm corpse into the morgue, dead because his wounds had festered during the time it took to evacuate him. Trudy must have had that on her mind all the while she comforted me. I pray she will not see him on the ward, lying in a bed.

Scooter became the crucible that held all my heartbreak.

Is any of this worth it?

It would be so easy to just chuck it all and leave.

Nobody would blame me, if they even care. Pack up, take a train to St. Nazaire, Brest, Bordeaux. There are plenty of berths on returning ships. They'll probably give me my old job back in Milwaukee, depending on what Martel told them. It would be so easy.

But would the French let me leave with a spy accusation hanging over my head? No, I'm stuck here.

Stop it. I'm not a whiner. Not a complainer.

I'll chart a new course. But in the meantime, I have another day to get through.

Just put one foot in front of the other . . .

I think about Scooter while I dress. My eyes tear up again at the last memory—rolling him into the morgue. It was like I had lost a dear friend, a kindred spirit. And I had only just met him. Then there is Hiram. Will he be next? He seemed like a deer that had found itself in the middle of downtown Minneapolis, at Seventh and Hennepin, frozen with fear, confused by honking cars in every direction. Did Dr. Jensen and Dr. Scully save his leg?

If I skip breakfast and hurry . . .

The orthopedic ward is one floor down from ours. It's a long, narrow room with rows of beds along the walls, all with traction trestles. More legs than arms, and some amputation tents. The odor of rubbing alcohol and chlorine dominates the place—no putrefaction. I ask about Hiram's location at the desk. He lies staring at the ceiling, his right leg in traction, foot sticking out of the dressing.

I smile as I near and clear my throat. Hiram looks over. He's like the neighborhood dog whose ears you can't help but scratch every time you see him. "Hey, Hiram."

"Hay's in the field. That's what my friend Carl always says. You'd like him. Handsome, smart, like you."

"Handsome is a word you use for women who aren't very attractive, Hiram."

Hiram's face flushes. "No, I mean, you're real pretty."

Not really, but thanks anyway. But I'm not here for an argument.

"Were you and Lieutenant Grant friends before the battle?"

"No, ma'am. Guys like me don't mix with officers, mostly. Aside from getting orders, dontchaknow."

"Kinda odd being in a room full of 'em yesterday, then, dontcha-think?" I wink. "Where you from, Hiram?"

"Minnesota. Grew up on our farm outside Osakis."

"I'm from Minneapolis. My friend Trudy too."

"Really? Makes me feel good, knowing someone's from home, sort of."

"Do you have any brothers or sisters?"

"Yah, sure. Abel's the oldest, workin' the farm, you see. Sam's helping him. Ida moved to the big city and works in a store—St. Cloud. Ya heard of it?"

"Sure, Hiram. I've visited there. That's where Captain Jensen's from."

"Well, so, then, I suppose he can't be all bad, 'n so?"

If Hiram thinks St. Cloud is the big city, Minneapolis must be as mythical to him as Oz. "How did you end up in the marines?"

"Well, you see, when we got in the war, my brothers and me thought one of us better go. What with them two runnin' the farm, that was me. Thing is, they's the hunters. Me? Never killed a beast. Not sure I could. But I heard the marines were the best. So I thought I'd give 'em a try. Turns out I'm a lousy shot but a real fast runner, 'n so. Well . . . was." He frowns. "So, they made me a litter-bearer. The fast ones whose hands aren't strong like mine? Runners. Carry the messages between officers, n'so. Don't last long. There's one I'm 'specially worried about, my friend I mentioned. From Edina, know where that is?"

"Sure, Hiram. I know kids from there. What's his last name?" How many others on the ward are Minnesotans?

"Larsen, Carl Larsen—ever meet him?"

"No. I know a few Larsens, but none from Edina."

"Well, you'd like him. Make a good boyfriend for the right gal." Hiram raises his eyebrows.

I chuckle. "You trying to set me up?"

Hiram blushes. "No, miss. Nothing like that, 'n so."

"It sounds like it was bad out there. Where did you get yours?"

"Got our orders and had to march across this wheat field to get to Belleau Wood. Problem was, Germans were expecting us. Well, walkin' or runnin', don't matter if you're in an open wheat field against a thousand machine guns. You're looking at the ones what made it here. Lot of guys died, ya know. Friends."

"You were hit early in the battle?"

"Yes, ma'am. Ben—I mean, Lieutenant Grant—he's a hero. See, I was there. He'd got his and all. Down on the ground, bleeding from three places. Our corpsman takes care of Ben—I mean the lieutenant—and calls us over. Then his sergeant, Levi Comstock, takes a knee next to us, and the lieutenant tells him what to do, cool as a cucumber in a blizzard. Me and my buddy Dan unfold the litter to put Ben—I mean . . ." I roll my hand in a *you have my permission to call him Ben* motion. "Then him and me's running Ben to the aid station. That's when I got mine. Dan and two of our other buddies loaded me up and hauled us off the field."

Hiram stares into space, as if playing events back in his mind. Tears roll down his cheeks. I hold his hand as my eyes well up, thankful for the tears.

"You figger they're going to chop off my leg, don't you, ma'am?"

I gaze around the ward, at the wreckage of the battle, and swallow. "I know they'll do the best they can for you." At least that isn't a lie.

"'N so, if the leg's gone, so am I. I won't know who I am, you see? Like I told you, I ain't good at much. Mom used to say, I ain't the brightest bulb in the lamp. I lose the leg? Nothin' I can do. I ain't good at numbers and all that."

"Did your farm have electricity, Hiram?" Most of central Minnesota does not.

Hiram's face seems puzzled, then a smile grows, and he beams at me. "Well, so I never thought about that. How could I be the dullest bulb in a lamp with no electricity?" He chuckles. "That's a good one."

"Hiram, Captain Scully is a very good orthopedist, one of our best, I hear. He'll do a good job for you." My face warms—there's that nurse assurance about the doctors. I hope Scully is competent. The leg is still there, though, so that's a good start.

"Long's you say he's on the level, eh?"

I lean over, kiss Hiram on the forehead, and give his hand a squeeze as I stand. Nobody seemed to notice my lapse. "Anything else I can do for you?"

"Can you write?" Hiram's face flushes. "Sorry, I guess I should have known, you bein' a nurse and all."

"What would you like me to write?"

"Letter to Ma. Tellin' her I'm alive and all."

"Let me get a piece of paper." I go to the nursing station for a pencil and paper and then hurry back to Hiram. Time is getting short before my shift. I pull Hiram's chart off the end of the bed to write on.

I ask for the address, and Hiram tells me. "What do you want me to write, Hiram?"

"Well, you know we can't say much, like not where I am or where I been, 'n so. My sergeant told me—always start out with *Somewhere in France*. Tell her I'm all right, 'n so. Don't mention the leg. Say the grub's great and that we're giving the Heinies a taste of their own medicine. Tell her to say hi to Sis and my brothers, and that's about it, I suppose, eh?"

I jot a note. A tear wells up in my right eye. I wipe it. My problems pale in comparison to the reality Hiram faces. What happened to Justine was a tragedy. Each bed in the hospital holds another of no less import to the patient or his family. That doesn't diminish Justine's memory. I can't change the past, bring Justine back, make my parents love me again, hug that stupid dog. And I can't bring back Scooter, either. But Hiram is alive, lying in front of me. I can do something for him and the others.

"I told your mom I'm an aide working in a Red Cross canteen, and that you asked me to help you with the letter. Sign here." Hiram writes his name in a crude scrawl—I had expected an *X*. I fold the letter and put it in my pocket. "I'll post this for you."

I rise and walk toward the door. In the hallway I turn right, square my shoulders, and pick up the pace. My heart surges. I fill my chest with a deep breath. This is it.

Be the nurse I never planned to be.

Write their letters to home. Give and get a couple of smiles.

Remember.

Write their stories.

My new mission.

Chapter Twenty-Eight
Alice Simmons

The smell of cigarette smoke hits me when Marie and I roll our laundry cart with fresh sheets into the linen room. I walk into the ward to find a cluster of men in an animated conversation, all smoking cigarettes. Several speak in loud voices—a sure sign of ruptured eardrums from the artillery barrages they've endured. The mood in the room isn't like a surgical ward in a civilian hospital, where a gunshot wound would be viewed as a tragedy and crime. Even if I had not held his hand, Scooter wouldn't have died alone. He died surrounded by his brothers.

The smokers glance around like teenaged boys behind a school. I squint and tilt my head. The ringleader is familiar. A large bandage covers his head and wraps around his left eye. Staccato heels approach—Pickler marches toward the men with a scowl on her face. I make my way over, straightening bedspreads and charts along the way.

This could be fun.

There is a little wicked part of me . . .

"Trouble. Douse 'em," one of the smokers says.

"Look at that floor." Nurse Pickler's words are ice.

"Wouldn't be a problem if you provided ashtrays, nurse . . ." one of the men begins.

"Didn't know we couldn't smoke." The left arm of the speaker, the one with the head dressing, hangs from a sling, his shoulder bandaged. His feet dangle past the end of the bed, his head and shoulders elevated on three pillows. I'll be darned. I know his voice. Floyd Gibbons, the war correspondent from the *Chicago Tribune*. He'd been at the New York Bar that night . . . I shake my head. I was so low on the press totem pole he wouldn't have noticed me, but everyone knows Front-Page Floyd.

"Simmons, clean up this mess." Pickler turns her anger toward me.

"Henri is on his break, ma'am."

"I don't mean him. You. Did your nanny neglect to teach you about the proper application of a broom?" Pickler marches away.

I snicker on my way to grab a broom and dustpan. For once, Pickle's wrath is mostly directed at others. I keep a deadpan face when I walk back toward the truants.

"Sorry to cause a ruckus, miss," Gibbons says as I sweep up the ashes he and the other man had flicked on the floor. "About those ashtrays . . ."

"Nurse Pickler forbids smoking."

"I hear that's not the case in other wards," Gibbons says.

I sweep the butts and ashes into the dustpan and then kneel to sweep underneath each bed. It's hard to concentrate on my work, two feet away from one of the preeminent correspondents in the war. I'm dying to ask him about the front, how he was wounded, a thousand other questions.

"Miss . . . you look familiar. Haven't I seen you before?"

"Yes, sir, Mr. Gibbons. I'm Alice Simmons. I work—worked—at the *Wisconsin State Journal*."

Gibbons gives me a wry grin. "Call me Floyd. Smashing way to get a scoop—posing as an aide." He pauses, then says, "Seems to me—one of the boys said you wanted to report on the hospitals. I have to admit, if I were you? I'd be wearing that uniform too. Fabulous angle. And a hell of a lot safer than my methods." He points to the dressing on his head.

I stand and dump the debris into a wastebasket while debating how much to say. Keep it simple. "Martel shut me down. He's trying to get the French to boot me out of the country. I'm a trained nurse, so I got a job here. There were no other options, really. They're running me ragged. I'm too tired at the end of my shifts to write."

"Rumor is that Martel's nose has something to do with you."

I shrug.

"Do not respond to my last statement. Good work. Smashing." He chuckles and pretends to clap—awkward with his left arm sling. His smile is electric. "Believe me, the boys have a lot of respect for you. Most of us would like to have done that but don't have your guts."

"I'm afraid Martel's revenge is not done with me."

"Really think he'll get the French to give you the boot?"

"I started the day yesterday staring into the muzzle of a French pistol. Something tells me they don't like me. But I didn't know anyone cared. I'm constantly looking over my shoulder, if that answers your question."

Gibbons' face turns serious. "Some of us do. Care, I mean. And notice." He points an unlit cigarette toward the door Nurse Pickler went through. "Head nurse got the grindstone for her battle-ax out there?"

I smile and look over each shoulder. "Pretty much." A newspaper lies on Gibbons's bedside table. The headline reads:

US MARINES SMASH HUNS!
GAIN GLORY IN BRISK FIGHT ON MARNE

CAPTURE MACHINE GUNS, KILL BOCHES,
TAKE PRISONERS!

The byline is Floyd's. "How was it?" I ask.

"See this?" He points at the dressing wrapped around his head. "Underneath this jaunty look, there's no left eye. Look around. These are the ones who made it."

"How did you get the story out?"

"Rather embarrassed about that. Wrote it before the battle and left it with a buddy who filed it after he heard I was killed. It's a fabulous story—if I were writing fiction, that is. Like Sam Clemens said, the rumors of my death were greatly exaggerated. Well, my *last dispatch* was in print before I crawled out of that damned field. I have a little explaining to do to my editor. For now, I'm going to let the dust settle. And this headache."

"I'm glad you made it out alive."

"Don't be a stranger." Gibbons motions me closer. His voice is quiet. "Word is you're the best nurse on the ward. Just thought you should know. And think about it—you have a fabulous angle. Keep writing, for God's sake. I've read your stuff. You're good. Like I said, some of us *do* notice. Don't worry about Martel or the censors. I've got a telegraph operator on, well, I suppose I should call it a retainer. Get your work to me and I'll send it to the *Trib*. Won't put my name on it, either—promise. Think about articles or books after we win this blasted war."

"Thanks," I say. "Better get back before the Pickle returns with her axe." Gibbons and the man in the next bed break out in laughter as I walk away. Someone did notice. My fingers itch to touch the keys.

Two orderlies roll a gurney through the door. I look over to see a drowsy Lieutenant Grant. The orderlies and I slide him onto his bed, then tuck the sheets up around his shoulders. He coughs, mutters a curse, and takes a deep breath. I feel his wrist. The pulse is strong. He opens his eyes and grimaces.

Grant's scowl grows to a weak smile as I hold his hand.

The older man in the next bed clears his throat. What was his name again? Colonel something-or-other.

"Good morning, Colonel," Grant says.

"Welcome back. How are you, Grant?"

"Had better days, sir."

"Haven't we all?" the colonel says.

Grant turns to me. "How's Hiram doing?"

"So far, so good. His leg is still where God meant it to be. I just saw him."

"Are you going to honor me with an introduction, Lieutenant?" the colonel asks.

"Oh. Right, sir . . . um. Colonel Catlin, the young lady is Miss Simmons. I'm afraid I don't know your first name."

I rise and go around the foot of Grant's bed and stand next to Colonel Catlin's. I extend my right hand. "Alice Simmons, sir. I'm one of the aides."

Catlin shakes with his left hand. "Sorry. Bullet paralyzed my right side. Getting a little movement back. Well, there you have it. Miss Simmons . . . I wonder if I could bother you . . . to write to my wife on my behalf."

"I'll be happy to, Colonel." Catlin speaks in short sentences, his breathing a bit fast and shallow. The nurses will attack me if I presume to say anything. With his chest injury, I have to keep an eye on him.

"Colonel Catlin's the CO—commanding officer—of the Sixth Marine Regiment," Grant says. "That's the unit Hiram and I are—were —in."

"You're still in it." Catlin looks at me. "We were all wounded at the same time. In an aid station together . . . little town called Lucy-le-Bocage. Wonder if there's anything left."

That must be the town Anderson told me about—Lucy.

"Not much," Grant says. "Shell hit the aid station after they got you out. We spent the night in a cellar. That doc that took care of us went to pieces—kinda sad, really."

"I remember him," Catlin says. "Odd little fellow. While the rest of us lived on coffee . . . the senior surgeons kept it away from him. Seemed to know his stuff, though. Those custom-made navy blues really stood out." Catlin shifts his gaze past Grant. "I already said a prayer for your friend Stoops. I'll visit him . . . when they let me."

"Thank you, sir," Grant says.

That small, intense navy doctor in a custom uniform can only be one man—Doctor Beck. I can see how he'd ruffle a few feathers. But now I'm concerned about him—a breakdown? "I'd better get back to work before you-know-who sees me."

I find Betty in the linen room. We busy ourselves changing sheets on the beds vacated overnight, including Hiram's. After that, I write a letter for Colonel Catlin, whose first name is Albertus. He has me sign the letter *Al*.

Two hours later, a weary Captain Jensen walks in. Walker and another new nurse accompany him. He motions me over.

"I saw Stoops this morning. He looked pretty good," I say.

"Scully thinks he may be able to salvage it. It's infected, but no gangrene. Not like Cherny. We left about twenty irrigation tubes in place, and he'll be in traction for months. He'll need several more clean-outs in the OR."

Nurse Pickler's heels approach. "Don't you have work to do? I don't recall saying you could take time off."

"Miss Simmons is joining us for rounds. She can help my nurses cleanse wounds. I thought she could discuss what she learned about wound microbiology while working in her father's lab. He's Professor William Simmons. Harvard man, by the way, Nurse Pickler. Ever work with him?"

"Obviously not good enough for them to offer him a position."

Jensen turns his back on Nurse Pickler, who folds her arms across her chest and glares into the back of his head as he walks away.

"Miss Simmons, thank you for joining us," Jensen says, waving his hand toward the others. "Would you care to tell us what you know about the subject of surgical microbiology?"

Walker smirks. She must think Captain Jensen is calling my bluff. I glance around the ward. Trudy returns a chart to the end of her patient's bed and joins us. She gives me a conspiratorial grin. We stand at the bedside of Major Berry, whose arm is ready for a Carrel-Dakin irriga-tion. Captain Jensen adjusts the irrigation system while I lecture on the subject, comparing the microbiology of wounds sustained in France and those in the upper Midwest, the organisms involved, complications, and treatment. My father may not love me, but I did work in his lab a few summers and can rattle off the subject in my sleep.

The nurses stare at me when I finish. Walker's face reddens. Jensen looks impressed. Colonel Catlin clears his throat and asks, "She know what she's talking about, or did she just give you a line?"

"She knows her stuff." Jensen catches my eye and winks. "And she's more succinct than her old man."

Chapter Twenty-Nine
Alice Simmons

Lunch is a quick respite—wilted salad and bread that tastes like sawdust, species unknown. Trudy is passing through the cafeteria line as I leave—we do meals in shifts. Floyd Gibbons is talking with Henri when I go back into the ward. Gibbons meets my eyes and nods in response to something Henri says, as though they're talking about me. No cigarettes. Henri shrugs and glances at me. What are they talking about?

I want to speak with Gibbons again, but no time for that now. Getting in his good graces might help my journalism career. I yearn now to write about the people I've met at the hospital. There are so many stories in this ward. But they will probably never be published with my byline. The world would never have heard of Florence Gibbons if Floyd had been born female. Maybe after the war, using a pen name like Alex Simmons or A. Simmons.

If the French don't shoot me first. The image of the pistol muzzle flashes in my eyes. I take in a sharp breath, and it disappears.

Lieutenant Grant sits on the side of his bed, talking with Colonel Catlin. I make my way to them. Both look up when I approach. There's a glint of interest in Grant's eyes that dissipates after a beat.

Trudy told me about Catlin's injuries. He was standing in plain sight, shouting orders at his marines, when he was shot through the right lung. It is a miracle he's still alive. He bled into the chest, and the doctors have removed fluid twice to reinflate his lung.

The colonel speaks in shorter sentences than earlier this morning. I count his breaths—twenty-eight a minute. His face is pale, neck veins prominent, but his larynx—the Adam's apple—is midline. He must be building up fluid or air around the right lung. Not an emergency yet, but he needs an X-ray, and soon.

"Miss Simmons. Looking lovely as ever," Catlin says.

"I feel bedraggled." I sweep a strand of hair away from my right cheek. "Colonel, you sound short of breath."

"Not to complain . . . but yes."

"Did you have a chest X-ray today?"

"No."

"See Hiram?" Grant asks.

"They barely let me have lunch," I say. "I'll see him after my shift."

"When do you think they'll let me visit him?"

"Not sure. Ask Captain Jensen when he does rounds."

"Let Hiram know I'll stop by when I get clearance."

"Seems you've taken . . . a shine to . . . our young private . . . Miss Simmons," Catlin says.

I shrug at the colonel's smirk. I can't hold Catlin's gaze and glance at Grant. His eyes seem inquisitive. "I know I'm supposed to maintain clinical distance, but there's something about his innocence that makes me want to do more to help him. The least I can do is write letters for him."

"How about another . . . for me? Don't neglect . . . an old colonel."

"Sir, you're not that old."

"Forty-nine's . . . feeling pretty old . . . this afternoon."

"I better get busy before Nurse Pickler arrives." I hustle off to the linen room after scanning the ward—Captain Jensen isn't here. Has he finally gone for a nap? I'm sure Colonel Catlin needs to have the fluid taken out of his chest again, but I can't say that to the other nurses without them jumping down my throat. Trudy'll be at lunch for another half hour. I could talk to her when she gets back, but how long can this wait? It's like the moment I felt the gas under Scooter's skin.

I'm caught in a dilemma—tell Pickler or not? A shroud of guilt has hung over me since I mentioned the gas under Scooter's wound and Pickler's response seemed to delay things, more to spite me than anything else.

Without Captain Jensen, though, I'm stuck.

I do a quick inspection of the linen cabinets, then send Marie and Geneva to the laundry to replenish supplies. Betty rushes in, hair in tangles after taking a walk to get some air instead of lunch. Staccato clicks approach just as I finish helping Betty get her hair back in order. I wonder if our head nurse is a tap dancer after hours. But that would be far too frivolous for the Pickle. The thought makes me smile.

"Something amusing, Miss Sunshine?" Pickler asks.

"Nothing, ma'am. Is Captain Jensen doing afternoon rounds yet?"

"What matter is that to you?"

"It's just that I haven't seen him yet."

"Again, what business do you have with him?"

Okay, here I go. "I think Colonel Catlin's pleural effusion is getting bigger. He needs a chest X-ray."

"Those are nursing concerns." Nurse Pickler moves to the door of the linen room and looks toward Catlin's bed. "He looks fine to me." Her heels snap against the floor. I look to see if they've dented the parquet.

"Betty, let me know the moment Captain Jensen gets here. In the meantime, I'll Pickle-proof the linens." By this point, everyone calls her Pickle behind her back. The French call her *le cornichon* to her face since she doesn't know a word of their tongue. I poke my head out the door to see Pickler listening to the colonel's chest with a stethoscope.

Captain Jensen enters the ward about fifteen minutes later, trailed by Walker and another new nurse I haven't met. Nurse Pickler approaches them. I finish folding a bedspread and tuck it into a cabinet, the corners in perfect alignment with the ones below. I make my way over to Captain Jensen's entourage as Walker rolls a clattering treatment cart.

"We've had four more admissions this morning," Pickler says. "Two second lieutenants, one first lieutenant, and a captain. All from the same battle. They all need surgery according to the sign-out I received. The other patients on the ward are stable. Start with Colonel Catlin. I think he needs a chest X-ray."

Captain Jensen goes over to Catlin's bed. "Colonel, how is your breathing this afternoon?"

"Worse . . . came on gradually . . . started last night . . . worse as . . . the morning wore on. I don't want . . . to be a bother."

Captain Jensen pulls a stethoscope from the pocket of his long white lab coat and listens to the front of Catlin's chest. "Let's help you up." Captain Jensen motions for his two nurses to help the colonel sit up, steadying him by each shoulder. Jensen listens to the back of the chest. "Any pain?"

"Not really pain. Pressure on the right."

"Lightheaded?"

"When I sit up."

"Nurse Pickler, order a stat chest X-ray. Tell me the moment it's processed."

The Pickle's expression is hard to read when she glances at me. It's not hostile, for a change. Maybe one of grudging respect? Catlin says, "Thank you." Lieutenant Grant's face is impassive, but he gives me a quick wink.

I return to the linen room. Marie and Geneva fold pajamas with Betty, all nattering in French while they work, talking about boys. Marie's boyfriend serves in the French Army. She received a letter from him that was so heavily censored she couldn't make head or tail of it. Geneva has not heard from hers in a month. Betty looks up at me and asks in French, "Does Alice have a beau? I imagine they are falling over each other to catch your eye."

Why is everyone so preoccupied with my need for a boyfriend? "I'm too busy for such foolishness." What I see in Geneva's eyes argues against attachments to soldiers. No word in a month? That could mean that the young woman's love is lying dead in no-man's-land, or too busy to respond, or the letter never got through. The same thing that is driving Trudy to distraction. I didn't come to Paris to fall in love only to have an artillery barrage break my heart. The image of a boyfriend dying like Scooter makes me shudder. Trudy and I were trained to be objective, professional, detached. But all around us are boys and young men who could be our brothers, cousins, schoolmates, boyfriends—fiancés.

My heart has been in the box I created at age ten. Scooter came along and slipped a key into the lock and turned it. Hiram opened the box. The danger lies in fully opening my heart. I'm not sure there will be anything left by the end of this war if I do.

Jensen's eyes have shown an interest that's flattering. But I don't want to go down that road either. How long will it be before they ship him to a field hospital or the front? Word is that casualties among surgeons are mounting in the Belleau Wood offensive. I heard stories about a dentist doing corpsman's work only to be killed by an artillery shell; surgeons gassed and out of commission; the rest, out of gas from the long hours and stress. Lieutenant Beck, the navy surgeon I'd met, is shell-shocked according to Grant. How long ago did I help him save the woman with the arm hemorrhage? He'd shoved Colonel Wadhams out of the way. The act had shocked me at the time, but then I did the same thing to Walker when the marine hemorrhaged. It's hard to believe it was little more than a week ago.

And then there is Lieutenant Grant—as hard to crack as a Brazil nut. For all of that, a bit shy. How can a Chicago cop be shy? Maybe . . . awkward is the right word. That's my problem too. Well, one of them. Tall, gangly, gawky—awkward. And these stupid wire-rimmed granny glasses creeping down my nose.

An hour later, the rattle of gurney wheels announces Colonel Catlin's return. A radiology tech carries the colonel's film jacket and snaps an X-ray on the single-pane view box behind the nursing station. Jensen and the two nurses finish setting up an irrigation on Major Berry's arm, and the three walk over to the view box, talking among themselves. I edge behind them to listen.

"As I suspected—large right pleural effusion." Jensen yawns. "I'll draw blood for a hematocrit. In the meantime, get the procedure room ready for a thoracentesis."

"Right away, Captain." Walker marches off after jabbing a resentful glare at me.

"Miss Simmons?" Jensen asks.

"Yes, Doctor?"

"Assist in any thoracentesis procedures?"

"A couple dozen at the university."

"She's not credentialed, Doctor," Nurse Pickler says loudly enough for the whole ward to hear.

Jensen bores his eyes into Pickler. "She'll be there to hand us supplies."

Jensen leaves, and I start toward the linen room. Nurse Pickler clamps a hand around my left arm and yanks me away from the doorway. "I know what you're trying to do. Don't think for a minute you'll get away with it. Exceed your credentials, and I'll hang you out to dry."

A memory of the last time someone grabbed my arm and swung me around like that flashes through my mind. Captain Buck. My arm muscles tense. I open my palm, the way I did that other time, in the alleyway.

Colonel Catlin looks straight into my eyes and shakes his head, as if he knows what I'm thinking. Henri puts his mop aside and saunters toward me. I take a deep breath and focus on Pickler's hot stare. "I'm not sure what you think I'm trying to do other than my job. If Captain Jensen asks me to do something or be somewhere, I will comply. If you like, I'll confirm that with Nurse Enright. Do I make myself clear?"

"You have no standing to speak to me that way. Apologize."

"For what?"

"Impertinence."

"Let go of my arm."

"When you apologize."

I square my shoulders. My jaw tightens. I flex my right hand, remembering the shadow of Martel's face.

Chapter Thirty
Alice Simmons

Lieutenant Grant limps up behind Pickler and twists her claws open. "What's the problem?"

Nurse Pickler's red face pales. "Lieutenant, return to your bed. This is an internal disciplinary issue and none of your concern."

Henri and Luc walk toward us as the orderlies roll Catlin away on a gurney. I use my right hand to massage the skin where fingernails left their marks. "I think we're done here. Thank you for your concern, Lieutenant. Captain Jensen wants me in the treatment room."

"You're skating on thin ice, Simmons," Pickler says. She sneers at Grant and points a long, thin, tremulous finger toward the ward. "Back. To. Bed. Lieutenant." Nurse Pickler storms out of the room, her head high.

"You looked like you were about to unload on her," Grant says. "I mean, physically. Seen that plenty. I thought . . ."

"Thanks. I can handle myself."

"Not saying you can't. God, no. What's she have against you?"

"A bunch of things, I suppose. She's from Boston and worked at Mass General—I'm just a country bumpkin to her. She's a head nurse and I'm only an aide."

"For the moment, right?"

"Yeah. The funny thing is, I'm the one who went to a university nursing school. Not her. There were none when she trained. But I went to Minnesota. She probably can't find the state on a map."

"Respect problem."

"Both ways, I suppose. Look, thanks for the hand. I think you may have saved her a broken beak, but I'd better go."

A grin creeps across Grant's face. "Break many snouts?"

"One. Couple of weeks ago. A major. I damaged a captain, too. He's missing a front tooth."

Grant whistles. "If I do that? The stockade." Grant narrows his eyes. "How'd they tee you off?"

I take a deep breath. I don't want to deal with this now. What would he or the others think if they knew? Grant's eyes lose their hardness, and he tips his head to the left. Maybe he's a better cop than I imagined. "Attacked me. At night. In an alleyway."

"Are you all right?" A frown builds on his face like a thunderhead.

"Physically, yes. They were easy targets. Drunker than lumberjacks on a Saturday night."

"They under arrest?"

"So, let's suppose that two inebriated off-duty Chicago cops take advantage of a woman in a dark alleyway. There are no witnesses. What happens when she files a complaint?" My gut tightens as if a punch is coming. "It's their word against mine—two officers against a female journalist? They're trying to get *me* on criminal charges. They accuse me of leading a gang of German spies that assaulted them. The French have threatened a firing squad." The quivering finger on the pistol's trigger flashes past my eyes.

"They raped you?" His face colors, eyes hard again.

That snaps me back. "No. They didn't get that far. That was their obvious intent."

"Who are these two jokers?" His neck muscles are ropes.

"Lieutenant, I appreciate the concern. I'd better go. Thanks for the help."

The treatment room is in the next wing. I wipe a stray hair from my face and stretch a neck knotted with tension, not sure whether to be angry or thankful for Grant. Maybe he thinks I can't fight my own battles. On the other hand, he appears to be an ally, someone my gut tells me I can trust. I hope.

I push my glasses up while hurrying along the hallway.

In the heat of the moment, he was like the friendly cop down the block who had asked what was wrong and I'd just let it go. I hope I'm right in trusting him. Otherwise, my story will be all over the ward by the time I get back. Oh God, if I'm wrong about him . . .

And Henri—it looked like he'd been about to get in the middle of things again. I don't understand why he's taking risks for me. I pause outside the treatment room, relax my shoulders, focus, and then walk in.

Colonel Catlin sits on a treatment table, chest bare, a goose-neck procedure lamp aimed at his back. A wide muslin bandage wraps around his upper chest, keeping his front and back dressings in place— the bullet had gone straight through. Captain Jensen's new nurse steadies Catlin by his left shoulder. Walker's gloved hands shake as she lays equipment onto a sterile white towel topping the treatment stand. Captain Jensen gazes at Catlin's chest X-ray hanging from a lit view box behind the colonel. The room has light green painted walls, the proce-dure table in the center, and a set of cabinets with a counter behind, including a sink. There are no linens to fold or organize. Nurse Walker frowns at me.

Jensen yawns. "Welcome, Miss Simmons. You know Nurse Walker. And this is Nurse Finlay. Both trained in Chicago, but neither has assisted with a thoracentesis before. You said you had helped with a couple dozen? That's quite a few in such a short time."

"The TB ward was busy," I say.

"Well, let's get to it."

"What would you like me to do, Captain?" I ask.

He shrugs. "Just watch. If I need something, I'll tell you." Jensen slips a stethoscope into his ears. "Colonel, are you comfortable?"

"As much as a man facing a firing squad can be."

Jensen laughs. "Won't be that bad." He places the stethoscope on Catlin's chest. "Breathe in and out deeply." He listens and then uses a thumbnail to indent an *X* on the skin where he will insert his needle.

Jensen goes to the sink and washes his hands. After drying them, he dons rubber gloves and dredges them in a basin of alcohol.

Jensen hums while he works, suppressing yawns, blinking. He scrubs Catlin's chest with soap and water, paints it with alcohol and then iodine. He speaks quietly to Walker and Finlay, describing what he's doing. He injects Novocain into the skin with a small needle, then goes deeper with a larger one, pulling back on the plunger as he advances. "There we are," he says when a puff of bloody fluid appears in the barrel of the syringe.

He turns to the instruments Walker laid out. I move to his left side, next to Finlay. "Stay right where you are, Simmons," Jensen says. "You'll be able to see. I'll let you know if I need you."

Jensen screws a needle onto a three-way stopcock, then threads a two-ounce glass syringe on the other end. He connects a yellow rubber tube to the middle port of the stopcock and dangles it into the mouth of a glass jug on the floor. "Walker, when the needle is in position, hold it steady with your right hand and work the stopcock with your left. Understand?"

Walker nods, but an uncertain frown crosses her face.

Oh boy.

I edge a little closer in case something goes wrong.

"Okay, Colonel Catlin, I'll get this show on the road. Let me know if you feel any pain or lightheadedness." Jensen inserts the needle slowly while pulling back on the syringe plunger. Dark blood courses into the syringe when the needle is an inch and a half deep. "Okay, Miss Walker. Hold the needle in place, please." He fills the syringe with bloody fluid. "Now turn the stopcock."

Walker's hand shows a slight tremor as she turns the stopcock. Jensen pushes the plunger in, squirting the fluid into the collection jug. "Now turn the stopcock back." Walker's tremor worsens, and her eyes became distant. Beads of sweat form on her pale forehead. I've seen others do this the first time they watched the procedure.

"Nurse Walker, are you all right?" Jensen asks.

Walker doesn't answer. She shifts, unsteady. I move behind Jensen. A loud crash startles me.

"Damn it!" Jensen says.

"I don't like the sound of that," Catlin says.

Walker lies on the floor next to a pool of bloody fluid. Her fall disconnected the rubber tube from the stopcock and tipped over the collection jug.

"Get her out of the way. See if we have more sterile tubing."

"Doctor, perhaps I should take her place," Nurse Finlay says.

"Stay put. You and I need to keep the colonel and the needle stable. Miss Simmons, you got this?"

"Yes, Doctor." I right the jug, pull Walker to the side of the room, and drop two towels into the pool of bloody fluid. I rifle through the drawers and find a sterile pack of rubber tubing and plop it onto the treatment stand. There isn't enough time for a proper hand wash, but for what I need to do, it won't matter. I snap on a pair of gloves, dunk them in alcohol, and then grab the rubber tubing and attach it to the stopcock.

"What the Sam Hill is going on?" Catlin asks.

"We've got it under control, Colonel. Nurse Walker just resigned from my team. Miss Simmons is Johnny-on-the-spot again, and we'll continue in a moment."

The circuit looks good: stopcock in place, rubber tubing from it to the collection jar, no breech of sterility in the process. "Ready, sir."

Jensen sighs and gives me a thankful expression. I now hold the needle steady where it enters Catlin's chest and work the stopcock without prompting. Nurse Walker rustles, but I concentrate on my work in silence.

After withdrawing a quart and a half, Jensen says, "Colonel, there's probably some left, but I think we should stop here."

"Doctor, not to tell you your business, but I'm doing okay. I don't enjoy these procedures, so if you can get it all, go for it."

"Tell me if you get lightheaded." Jensen continues, though more slowly. After another four pulls of the syringe, Catlin begins to cough. "That's it for today. Miss Simmons, would you please get a Vaseline gauze?"

I put the gauze next to the needle. Jensen pulls out the needle, and I cover the spot with the dressing and rub. The colonel continues to cough. I keep the dressing tight so the colonel's coughing doesn't suck air in through the entry site.

"Needle's out, Colonel. Miss Simmons is massaging the tract to help close it."

Jensen sets the syringe and its attachments on the tray. He holds a long muslin roll bandage and puts a hand on mine. I feel the warmth of his touch through the gloves. His hand lingers for a moment, then he unrolls the bandage around the colonel's large chest, wrapping the bandage around four times. I hold the end of the bandage in place while Jensen secures it with two safety pins.

"We'll get you down for a chest X-ray, Colonel."

Walker stands in the corner of the room, adjusting her cap. The daggers are replaced by a sheepish expression. Finlay's face remains professionally neutral. I use my foot to swipe the bloody towels to the side and then disassemble the equipment and set the pieces in a tray for sterilization. Over two quarts of bloody fluid slosh in the jug when I set it on the counter. I clean up the rest of the mess and wash my hands while Finlay and Jensen ease the colonel down on the gurney. Walker seems back to herself. She mouths, *Thanks*.

I walk back to the ward, tired but pleased. Mary Sloan flags me down right when I'm thinking about a cup of coffee.

"Alice, I need another little favor."

Chapter Thirty-One
Alice Simmons

Mary Sloan and I pass a long line of ambulances heading toward the Annex as we head to the old American Hospital. What can be more important than admitting these patients? I glance back and see a policeman duck behind a tree. Will they ever give up?

"You'll recall the last favor you did for me," Mary says.

"Geneviève." The image of how my sister would have looked at thirteen floats through my mind like a fleeting shadow. "How is she doing?"

"I heard she's still in the respiratory isolation ward. No word beyond that."

A pang of guilt shoots through me—I think about her each night as I lie in bed, but the days are too busy to consider looking in on her.

"You remember Ab's letter said her brother and dog were on their way," Mary says.

"They arrived?"

"Yes, and I need your French skills again—Marcel doesn't speak English."

We enter the American Hospital by the back door and make our way to Mary's office. A robust dowager sits in her guest chair, a panting Bichon on her lap. "This is Madame Lucier," Mary says.

I speak in French. "Madame Lucier, I'm Alice Simmons, a nursing aide here. You brought Marcel Durand to us?"

"Yes." Madame Lucier narrows her eyes. "Are you Parisian?"

"No, American. But my family is French. I spent quite a bit of time in Paris in the past."

"You sound like a Parisian. In any case, I came upon young Marcel and his dog, Abby, a short time ago. He suggested I take care of this little one." Madame Lucier rubs the petite dog's head. "They call her Foofoo."

That makes me smile. That's what we called all the little dogs when I was a girl.

Madame Lucier stands. "I brought Marcel and Abby here. They are outside, since the guards won't let Abby into the hospital. Let me introduce you." She leads on.

A young man and a border collie stand outside the hospital gate. Marcel is a strapping youth about my height who looks as though he's fought a fire. Filthy, soot-stained clothes hang loose on him. A quizzical smile spreads on his gaunt face as he locks his brown eyes on me. He wears a large blue beret with a Chasseur Alpin pin, and I wonder what the story is behind this—he's too young to be in that elite French Army unit.

The dog's eyes follow me as I approach. I can't help but stare into them, and for a moment, we exchange something I've never experienced with a dog before. Border collies can have odd eye colors, but Abby's are almost like Justine's. I don't believe in reincarnation but sense a kindred spirit.

Madame Lucier breaks the spell. "Here is the young man, Marcel Durand."

"I am Mademoiselle Simmons, a nurse's aide. This is Nurse Sloan. We are both friends of Major Johnson. We are so sorry about your maman. We met your sister a few days ago. She's at an orphanage not far from here. Nurse Sloan has authorized me to take you there. Would you like to clean up first? You look as if you've been through a battle."

Marcel looks down at his clothes as if noticing them for the first time. "The bombing raid last night. The dogs and I helped search for the people trapped in a building a bomb hit while the fire brigade fought the fire. I was attacked by a gang of boys on the way here. They stole my pack and beret and ran. The dogs were faster and took them down. It's been a long journey."

"Dogs?" I ask, looking around but seeing no other dogs.

"Two others." Marcel gives me a crooked grin. "The rascals are probably busy raiding trash cans." He tells me about a harrowing trek from his home in the hamlet of Bouresches, many miles east of here, and the dogs that joined them along the way.

All the while I marvel at how much Marcel reminds me of two of my French cousins—ones I spent time with during summers of banishment from my parents' home when I was the same age as Geneviève. He brings back heartfelt memories of good times, warm summer afternoons, parks, playgrounds, friends. Memories that stand in stark contrast to the war-scarred young man telling us his story.

"One question?" Marcel asks.

"Yes," I say.

"Are you a relative of ours?"

"Not that I know of. Why?"

"Your eyes. They're like Maman's and Geneviève's. Your face reminds me of Maman." His eyes grow moist.

Memories of Justine stab me again. And I wonder. I don't know all my distant French cousins. "Let's get you a bath and clean clothes while Madame Sloan takes Abby for a walk."

Marcel takes a long bath, refilling the tub once, and dresses in used clothes left over from a former patient. We go to the cafeteria, where he wolfs down a huge meal and tells me his story between bites. His father, Pierre, was a Chasseur Alpin corporal—an elite soldier, killed in battle less than two weeks ago. Pierre had given Marcel the Chasseur beret when he was home on leave. Marcel's mother delayed evacuating until the last minute to give Geneviève the best chance on the trek. She died shielding Geneviève when a German aeroplane strafed them during their escape. American troops did what they could to help the kids evacuate. Ab Johnson found them and helped get them here.

"That's quite an adventure," I say. "I'm so sorry about your papa and maman. My position here is a little complicated. You see, I'm a journalist, but I also have a nursing degree. I came to report on the war, but they wouldn't let me, so now I work here. It's a long story. One that is far from done. May I use your story for one of my articles?"

"Articles?" Marcel's eyes narrow.

"Well, they won't be published right away—probably not until after the war. May I write about you?"

"I'm not sure."

"Your story must be told, along with those of all the other children. So many orphans. So many refugees. The newspapers at home only want articles about battles and soldiers right now, but I don't want people to forget stories like yours."

"Could you make up a different name for me? I don't want to get in trouble."

I narrow my eyes. "Did you commit a crime?"

"Well—you know I slept in someone else's house and ran away from a man who told me he was an agent for a mayor and that I owed him a toll."

"If it's after this war, none of that will matter. Besides, I won't include the address of the house you broke into."

"I don't know the address or even the town."

"So there you go. No problem."

"And Maman. Will you write about her? And Papa? And Geneviève?"

"I'd like to. I'll have to check with your sister."

"How is she?"

"I'm a bit embarrassed to say I haven't seen her since I took her to the orphanage. Things here have been too busy for me to visit her." My face warms in a flush. "Nurse Sloan told me she is in a ward for children with breathing problems."

"I suppose it will be all right for you to write about me. I'd like to see what you write before I see it in a newspaper, though."

Marcel cleans his plate with a slice of bread, and then we head to the front. I hail a cab and take Marcel and Abby to the orphanage. They order me to leave Abby at the front door—the orphanage won't take a dog. After a heated discussion with the matron, they allow Marcel inside. The matron tells me Geneviève is improving, though still in the respiratory isolation ward, and no, I can't see her. I return to the hospital with Abby, remembering our little dog, Fluffy, that led my sister into Lake Street so many years and miles ago.

The ward is busy upon my return, and I have no time to contemplate the Durand family and Abby, or my family and our dog. The busyness is good that way, since thoughts of Geneviève and Marcel leave me melancholy. I want to write about them, but their story is not complete. And I have a more personal one to work on first. My fingers itch for the keys of my typewriter.

I cut the evening short and leave the ward at ten. The basement corridor to my room is quiet. Bare light bulbs glow on white plastered walls and ceilings with black wooden doors on each side and a bare hand-troweled concrete floor. My mind wanders as I go. The pistol muzzle, shaking. The fingers. I rub my neck. The saliva dripping from the wet kiss followed by the bite. Martel's drunken drawl—his threats. I glance behind. Nobody.

Muggy air redolent with soap and chlorine becomes stifling near the laundry, mixed with the chatter of the workers through open double doors. The air cools and noise fades when I turn down a side hall, then another, and finally the dark passageway to my room. Today I think of it as my crypt. I unlock the door and flick on the light. No new bottle of wine tonight. A glass of the scotch that the police are probably enjoying would be nice. I move to the typewriter on the small table and touch it, then let down my hair and get in my nightclothes.

Would anyone care if the sergeant had pulled the trigger?

Martel would have won. Somehow, I don't think this was his first time. I need to do something to make sure it is his last.

I insert paper into the typewriter roller and feel the gears click as I wind the sheet into position. Time to tell my story. I'll give it to Howard Enright, with instructions to open it upon my death or disappearance. The next man to point a pistol between my eyes might not have a conscience.

They Murdered Me
Alice Simmons

I am dead. I can't name my murderer. The authorities will bury his name along with my corpse. I was murdered to silence me. To keep me from telling my story. This story. It all began in the Paris office of US Army Major Richard Martel . . .

.

Chapter Thirty-Two
Alice Simmons

Wednesday, June 12

A bell interrupts my one nice dream in the past month—playing with Fluffy and Justine at Lake of the Isles. Damn. I flick on my flashlight and whack the alarm clock. What to call this place: cell, cellar, dungeon, crypt? This morning it's a cell. The only things missing are chains and dripping water. The fourth-floor dorm rooms will be my alternative when my credentials come through if Pickler doesn't convince them to fire me in the meantime and the Paris police don't execute me. All the girls complain that the rooms are sweltering. The cell is cool. And safe. Merci, Henri.

Henri. So many unanswerable questions. I can't put my finger on it. Kind stranger? Guardian angel? French agent keeping an eye on me until they decide whether to hang or shoot me?

No, that's paranoid. People in cells get paranoid.

Henri seems to be up to something. He's had conversations with Floyd Gibbons and Colonel Catlin that seem hushed, all of them with sidelong glances toward me that I catch when they don't think I'm looking.

Then there's Ira. I don't know what he's up to.

I click the lights on, settle into the chair, and sponge off my face. So this is what my life boils down to. A cell. There's no other option but to take Pickle's abuse—for now. Going above her head to Emily would send the wrong message—that I can't handle adversity. No. Pickler's worst is nothing compared to Martel.

Pickler started this fight. Ira always said, *know your enemy*. But so far, nobody I've asked seems to know much, and it isn't like I can walk up and ask the woman about herself. One thing seems obvious: Nurse Pickler is fastidious and, at her last job, worked in the orderly environs of a Boston hospital urology ward. She had probably never dealt with the kind of filth that has fouled the ward since the sixth. But that doesn't help me figure out how to deal with the woman now.

The last four days are a blur. I go to the table and leaf through the six pages I typed before bedtime. Too long for a newspaper. It lays out the whole sordid story about Martel and the aftermath of the assault. I put them in the top drawer of the steamer trunk. I'll get them to Howard or Pete later, or Ira, if he ever shows up. That is an advantage of my cell—I can work late without raising suspicions. The police won't find me—Henri and Trudy are the only two who know where I sleep. Unless Henri is a French spy, of course. Paranoia. It doesn't mean they aren't out to get me.

It isn't too late to pack it in. Go back to the States. Beg to get my old job back. Write medical articles for the *Journal* with a reasonable expectation of my name on a byline. Meet a nice boy. Have a nice life. The image of Scooter hangs over me—killed by a preventable disease that had insinuated its way up his leg and overwhelmed his system. My heart skips a beat. Hiram. How is he this morning? Urgency pushes me on, and I rush into my uniform.

I can't lose him too.

Ten feet past my door I remember—*the book*. I unlock the cell and grab the tattered book I brought with me from home. Hiram is barely literate, and I want to work with him on his reading.

Hiram's right leg hangs from the traction trellis above his bed. His face is hidden behind the Paris edition of *The New York Times* sports section. I pull up a chair and clear my throat. "Financial page?"

Hiram's hands jump. "Oh, sorry, Miss Alice. Working on my letters.

Sports section is easier than the others. Can't make heads nor tails of the rest."

"Here." I hand him *The Wonderful Wizard of Oz*. "I think this'll be the ticket. Try it out."

Hiram opens the book and reads, slowly, aloud. After the first two pages, he says, "This is better. I can make out most of the words. Sounds like they have a pretty fine spread there in Kansas. Met a guy from those parts the other day."

I helped Hiram write a few words yesterday. His penmanship looked like he wrote with the toes of his left foot, and his spelling was atrocious. But I see innate intelligence that doesn't give itself credit. At his age, the penmanship is probably hopeless and his speech so idiomatic that it won't change. But he has ability. I just have to find the right angle. And there's more than that. Along with innocence is an underlying good-ness. "Did they tell you when the next operation is yet?"

"Late afternoon. 'Nother clean-out. Darn, those things hurt after-ward, them all diggin' around in there, puttin' more of them tubes in. The first flush-out hurts like the dickens, dontchaknow?"

"A lot of the men on my ward get those too."

"They treatin' you any better?"

"Pay attention to the Wicked Witch of the West in the book. I'll quiz you later about who she's like."

Hiram laughs. "Don't need to read no book to figger that one out."

"I'll see you after surgery." I shouldn't fear for Hiram with the surgery. It's routine. Most of the wounds like his go to surgery several times for clean-outs. Still, I worry.

I check my watch as I enter the linen room. Five minutes early. The French aides are chattering about boys again while I open the cupboards to check supplies. The night crew must have been busy—they didn't restock. I send Geneva and Marie to the laundry while Betty and I go into the ward.

"Place is full," Betty says. "Where should we start?"

"Let's split up and do a quick walk around."

Colonel Catlin and Grant are talking quietly when I approach. Grant looks up at me. "How's Hiram?"

"He's going to have another operation today. A clean-out."

"Think they'll save his leg, really?" Catlin asks.

"I'm not sure. Maybe, sir."

"Breaks my heart to see cases like his," Catlin says. "I mean, me? My own stupidity. Well, maybe not that. I had to stand in clear sight of my men to bolster their courage. Look what that got me—and them."

"When do you think I can make a trip over to visit Hiram?" Grant asks.

"He'll be groggy after today's surgery and sore tomorrow. Maybe day after tomorrow, if Dr. Jensen allows it."

"Can you take me? I know they won't let me go by myself."

"That's usually an orderly's work, Lieutenant."

Jensen walks in. Nurse Finlay pushes a clattering white enameled treatment cart with basins on top and dressings on the second shelf. Jensen motions me over. I steal a glance toward Pickler, standing about halfway across the ward, facing away.

"Miss Simmons will take Nurse Walker's place today. Glove up," Jensen says as he makes his way to the first patient.

Hurried clicks approach, and I look over at Jensen, whose jaw is set like a granite statue. "Now you've crossed the line," Pickler hisses. "You may be the ward surgeon, but I'm in charge of the nurses. This—this girl—isn't a nurse. I insist I be the one to choose your assistant from the pool of trained nurses under my command."

What's he thinking? My chest tightens. I don't want this. Not until my credentials are verified. Sure, I want to move forward, but this is the best way to ruin my effort.

Jensen's voice seethes. "Last one you foisted on me passed out during Colonel Catlin's thoracentesis. Simmons is the best nurse on the ward. And I need Cunningham on the ward when I'm not here to keep you from killing my patients."

Finlay's face is crimson. I hadn't liked her at first, but she's competent. She doesn't deserve this.

"Captain . . ." Nurse Pickler's mouth works, but no words come out for a change.

"Now, unless you have a better idea, I have work to do. Stay out of my way."

I pull on thick rubber gloves from the bottom of the cart and walk next to Finlay, who glances over, her face edged with contempt. I give her a sweet smile. Treat them with honey. We stop at Major Berry's bed. He is young for a major, a slender, handsome man with nut-brown hair.

"Major, how are you this morning?" Jensen asks.

"Not looking forward to this."

I dunk my gloved hands in the alcohol basin and shake them. When they're dry, I undo the safety pins holding the muslin bandage wrapped around Berry's arm and dump the bandage in a laundry container—they can sterilize and reuse it. I unwrap the gauze and drop it in the waste bucket. A bullet had entered at his elbow and tore through the forearm before stopping in his palm. The surgeons had to slit the palm open to remove the bullet and placed several irrigation tubes. The forearm is swollen and discolored with fading bruises. A dribble of pus oozes from the palm.

Finlay's eyes are drilling twin holes into head while I work. This little victory should feel better. True, Jensen is the one who made it possible. But in this case, Pickler's right—not her tone, but the substance. Discomfort grows as I concentrate on doing every step of the process with perfection while I devise a plan. I don't want to usurp Finlay. This is not the way to show her that I'm as good as any RN on the ward.

Jensen takes a four-inch gauze square soaked in Dakin's solution and dabs the palm. "I'll replace these two drainage tubes." Jensen points.

I pick up a sterile drainage tube from a tray and hold it ready.

"Why do you tolerate that useless bitch?" Berry asks Jensen, nodding toward Pickler, who glares at us from the nursing station.

Jensen speaks quietly. "Like you, I work with what I'm given, not what I'd like."

"Touché."

"This is going to hurt." Jensen twirls the first drainage tube between his thumb and forefinger and eases it out. Berry takes a sharp breath, and his face pales. "There. Miss Simmons?" I hand him the new tube. He nudges it into the wound. Berry exhales forcibly after the second tube is in. "Major, we'll do the irrigation in an hour or so. Miss Simmons, re-dress and wrap the arm."

Jensen goes to the next bed while I put gauze dressings on the wound, then wrap the arm with a roll of gauze. I don't apply a muslin bandage since the irrigation will soak it. When I finish, I say, "I'm sorry that hurt so much."

"That's okay. For what it's worth, I think you're tops. Rest of the men do too."

"Thanks. I'll see you for that irrigation in around an hour."

"Not the way to say *you're welcome*." Berry gives me a pained grin.

Captain Jensen stands at Lieutenant Grant's bedside when I catch up. "Captain, may I speak with you for a moment, in private?" I ask. Finlay shoots me a look almost as lacerating as the one Walker had given me in the dorm.

"Sure." He motions me to follow him.

In the hallway, I say, "Sir, I am honored that you chose me to be your lead assistant. I really am. But the Pickle's right. I'm just an aide. Finlay should be your first assistant with me lending *her* a hand."

"You're so good, though." Jensen stares at the floor as if in thought.

"Please? I'd feel more comfortable. Finlay is the RN with the credentials to do the work today, not me. Sure, I can do the work, but we really must follow protocol on this. I don't want this to cause you trouble. I'm skating on thin ice. I can't afford to lose this job."

"Okay. As long as you're with me. Keep your eye on Finlay. She's adequate, but she's not you."

"With due respect, sir, she's better than that. You just need to give her a chance. That's all I'm asking for, for myself."

Jensen shrugs. "Better get back to it."

At Grant's bedside, Jensen says, "Nurse Finlay, you'll take the lead. Simmons will assist. Please remove Lieutenant Grant's dressings."

Finlay narrows her eyes in a questioning expression when she glances at me. I give her a small smile in return.

The redness along the edges of Grant's leg wound looks normal, and there's no pus. The wound is healing on its own and hasn't required drainage tubes. The gunshot wounds in his side are reddened from healing, but no pus. Jensen pokes along the skin overlying the bullet track. Grant's jaw tenses several times, and his breathing becomes more rapid.

"I think you're coming along, Lieutenant." Jensen cleans the wounds with Dakin's solution while he speaks. "Miss Finlay will re-dress the wounds. I'll let the therapists start ambulation today. We'll get you back on your feet."

"Thanks, Doc. When can I visit Stoops?"

"I don't know his current status."

"Well, Nurse Simmons told us that he's going for surgery again today. He's still got infection. But I was thinking tomorrow or the day after."

"Long as you don't touch him. You don't want his infection."

"Thanks, Doc."

Jensen examines the colonel while I help Finlay dress Grant's wounds. "I've seen your X-ray from earlier this morning," Jensen says. "We'll have to remove some more fluid this afternoon, Colonel. It just keeps building up."

"Can't you put in a tube and leave it in there?" Catlin asks.

"We've been doing that with infected chests, but not with your type of injury. The thoracentesis procedure is standard care."

"Thought I'd ask. Nothing else to do around this joint."

Rounds continue for another hour. Then Finlay and I set up the irrigations, which take another hour. Finlay is the same age as me, probably went through nursing school about the same time, but then worked as a nurse while I pursued my journalism career. After setting up an irrigation, Finlay says, "Look, I'm not sure what you said to Captain Jensen, but thank you. I wanted a chance to show I'm not Walker. The rest of us—we know you're a nurse, and I hope this whole credential thing works out. But anyway, thanks."

I coach Finlay in the role of first assistant at Colonel Catlin's thoracentesis. Captain Jensen pulls about a quart of straw-colored fluid out. After the procedure, I roll Catlin's wheelchair down to radiology. We wait in a room by ourselves.

"So, you say that straw-colored pleural fluid is a good sign, Miss Simmons?" Catlin asks.

"Yes. I assume the fluid looked bloody at first."

"You assume correctly. They did the first tap before I got up to the ward. Right from the ambulance to the operating room. Our battalion surgeon came with me—pushed me to the head of the line."

"The fluid goes from blood to bloody to the straw color we saw today. The rate of accumulation usually goes down after that."

"Think I'm going to need another tap?"

"Time will tell. How are you feeling, sir?"

"Breathing better. Not as much pain."

"How are you doing otherwise?"

Catlin sighs. "Sometimes I feel like a failure. Now don't get me wrong. I'm so proud of my men. They're Spartans. Never a complaint, in my presence at least. I keep thinking of the things *I* could have done differently."

"How so?"

"Looking for a scoop?"

"Only if you want to give me one." I narrow my eyes. "I'm concerned as a nurse. Well, almost a nurse. I get the impression you have a lot on your mind but can't talk in front of your men. I'll be honest, though. I'm keeping a journal and writing some articles. To remember. People should know—*must* know—what you and your men did. We have to *know* to remember."

"How soon'll I see my name in *The New York Times*?"

"Talk with Floyd Gibbons if you want that. I'm not on the *Journal* staff anymore. I've been fired. Nothing I write will see the light of day until after the war. Maybe not even then—the old boys' club isn't open to women." Though Floyd Gibbons had offered to send some of my stuff out through his backchannel, and Mary Sloan had mentioned Pete's willingness to do the same.

"How come you were fired?"

My throat tightens. If I want him to open up, I have to. "Tell you what. Let's trade. I'll be honest, and what we say just stays between us until the time is right." Catlin nods. I tell my story and don't gloss over anything. Catlin's face registers no surprise, as if he already knows. But how?

"I won't repeat your story, but I reserve the right to re-break the man's nose if I ever meet him—once my right arm moves, that is. Fair's fair. We'll trade the father confessor hat. Our orders arrived an hour and fifteen minutes before the attack. A couple of officers risked their careers to warn us an offensive was imminent, but the details weren't available until the orders arrived. Our generals didn't include me in the planning."

"Is that normal?"

"No. The regimental commanders, Colonel Neville and I, should have been in on the planning from the start. I'm so angry I'm ready to burst. My men suffered as a direct result. Buck Neville and I are the only senior officers in the brigade with combat experience. It would have been different if we wore army collar pins. And there's no way we would have come up with such a hare-brained battle plan. I know the army looks down their collective noses at us. Sort of reminds me of the way the Pickle talks about anybody who trained west of Boston. The way they did this was incompetent."

"So how did you fail your men? I mean, what could you have done? Refused your orders?"

"No. Orders are orders when they come from the generals. I did the best I could. But rational thought doesn't kill a nagging feeling like that. I suppose I'm beating myself up over things outside my control. I'm glad you weren't there to see it. The Germans cut Berry's battalion to pieces. That should never have happened. The only brilliant leader of the day spoke German. The men who ordered our attack should be shot. Well, court-martialed at the least. I just wish I could have . . ." He straightens in his wheelchair. "But you're right, nothing else I could have done."

"I get the sense that there are others in our ward with the same sort of feelings. Maybe not the same specifics. They don't say anything, but I can tell." All the while, I think about Bill with growing concern. If Colonel Catlin thinks the division leadership is poor, what's in store for Bill? He's in the army half of the Second Division. Are the same generals going to send him into battle with poor planning?

"Maybe when you get them alone, they'll open up to you, Nurse Simmons. Thank you for listening."

The rest of the day drags on while I ruminate about the things I've heard from Gibbons, Berry, and Catlin. There is a great story here. But I have to respect the confidence in which some of the information has come to me. My fingers yearn for my typewriter, but there are irrigations to do, linens to Pickle-proof, and a head nurse to avoid. But Finlay and I are getting along well. One more ally.

I visit Hiram after my shift, catch a quick bite of more sawdust masquerading as food, and then return to my cell. I put on my nightgown and robe and sit at the typewriter.

```
UNTITLED, by ***
```

I want to put my name on the byline. But if someone finds it? Any good investigator would match the typewriter to what I write, but why make it easy?

```
When the dust settles, the smoke clears, and the
dead are buried, the fields to the west of
Belleau Wood will stand in silent tribute to the
courage of men who followed their orders and
fought valiantly against overwhelming odds.
Others may tell of the battle, but there is a
human dimension to the story found in the wards
of the hospitals caring for the wounded.

Casualties flooded a medical system that had no
time to prepare. Men languished on stretchers
from aid stations to hospitals in Paris. The
fifty-mile trip from Lucy-le-Bocage, the
epicenter of the battle, to American Red Cross
hospitals in Paris took more than a day in many
cases.

Consider the case of a young marine who called
himself Scooter. He should have survived.
Healthy, fit, strong. But a jagged shrapnel wound
```

festered during the two-day trip to Paris. By the
time he reached the American Red Cross hospital,
gas gangrene had begun its deadly mission. A high
leg amputation failed, and within a day of his
arrival this reporter had the sad duty of rolling
his remains to the morgue. The delay killed him.
How many others? We'll never know . . .

Chapter Thirty-Three
Alice Simmons

Thursday, June 13

Chit-chat while doing sponge baths gives me a chance to get to know my patients better. The journalist in me squirrels stories away—not for scoops that break the confidential nature of what I hear, but as background. Some are harrowing, others heartbreaking, and still others inspiring.

Many of my patients seem numb when they arrive. Taciturn, quiet. Others are like boys in a locker room—jovial, animated—but it seems like emotional cover. Some shout in their sleep—wake confused, gasping for air, sweating, shaking. Men vent feelings in a way they never would at home.

And although the source of the trauma is different, I still awaken gasping for air amid dreams of alleyways, a wet tongue on my neck, fingers . . . down there. The pistol muzzle. Nightmares are our common currency, a kinship shared with my patients, though I never share my story with them, other than the colonel and Grant.

Some of the single marines kid around, asking me out on dates—in jest, to pass the time. More like boys in school—"when I get out of here, I'll take you out on the town"—that sort of thing. Of course, they wouldn't. I joke back, keeping it light, wondering if I can ever trust any man. The thaw of my heart that began with Scooter continues when I visit Hiram. It offers a glimmer of hope—maybe my heart won't be in a deep freeze for the rest of my life.

We're all damaged goods.

I stop by the commissary during a break and buy a small pad of writing paper and envelopes and slip them into my purse. After the end of my shift, I head to the ortho ward. Hiram is asleep, so I write him a short note. I stay to jot letters for patients in adjacent beds. The last is for a farmer from Iowa who lost his right hand. He was right-handed. How will he ever farm again?

And what about the children like Geneviève and Marcel? How many have been kidnapped by Germany and brought to forced labor camps? How many have been killed? So many of their homes are destroyed, whole towns and villages leveled by artillery. Families wiped out. Who will take care of the orphans?

Tears well up in my eyes as I wander back to my basement room, thinking about the day—Hiram, Catlin, Scooter. The aftermath of the battle left all of them lost in different ways, unsure of the next step. We're all traumatized, but each is unique. I try to think of what else I can do but am too tired to come up with a solution. Too tired to write. Too tired to think after bolting the door and turning out the lights. Then, I smell beer breath and feel his warmth on my cheek. I flick on the flashlight.

Will those memories ever leave me alone?

Chapter Thirty-Four
Major Ira Cunningham

Friday, June 14

My mission to bring down Martel and Buck was put on hold until after I did all the processing into the main Intelligence section at AEF Headquarters. It's unbelievable how much paperwork is involved and how slow the typists are. We need to get female secretaries into this process. In the meantime, things have gone from bad to worse in the battle around Belleau Wood. Colonel Nolan sent me to eyeball the situation late yesterday, but I got here too late to do anything other than find a billet and sack out. Artillery thunder bothered me all night, punctuated by the staccato of distant machine gun bursts. Ab Johnson will be my best source for the inside scoop—gotta find him tomorrow.

Ab can wait, however. I roust my driver as dawn breaks, skip breakfast in favor of a thermos of coffee, and drive to the headquarters of the Army Twenty-Third Regiment, south of the main action. Ambulances chug past, and walking wounded are on the march back to the field hospitals. The faces I see are vacant, exhausted, with faraway eyes looking at a horizon only they can see.

A nearby artillery battery fires. I plug my ears with my index fingers. The reports kick air out of my chest, and I can't hear myself think. The smell of sulfur permeates the air along with the faint, nauseatingly sweet smell of rotting flesh. The road is a potholed mess. We keep the windows up despite the humidity to reduce the noise and smell. I put a handkerchief over my nose to try to keep my stomach in place. The coffee goes untouched.

I keep my eyes open for Bill. He won't be that hard to spot—at six-one, he'll be taller than most. When we reach their headquarters, a corporal tells me Bill's battalion is at a place called Triangle Farm and rustles me up a motorcycle ride, since the Germans use cars for target practice. After a cramped sidecar ride, I unfold my legs and walk toward the only two officers in sight—a marine lieutenant talking with an army major.

"Major, I'm sorry, but we haven't received orders," the marine lieutenant says.

"Well, I have, and mine are to relieve you and have your men move north."

"But where? I don't understand where my men are supposed to be. Major Shearer is in Bouresches and won't be back until evening."

"All right. I'll move my men forward to the south side of the ravine between these woods and Bouresches. I sent reconnaissance patrols out last night to probe the German dispositions to the east."

"Find much?"

"Lot of contact."

"That explains all the shooting I heard."

I approach the two and the major says, "Help you?"

"I'm Cunningham, Intelligence. Trying to find a soldier in A Company, First Battalion."

The major points. "They're over there."

The men he points to are a jumble, some lying on the ground, others cleaning rifles. Four privates sleep near the trunk of a large tree. A first sergeant stands, smoking a pipe, talking with two corporals.

"Sir?" the first sergeant asks.

"Looking for Private William Stevens. I believe he's with this company."

"Yes, sir." The first sergeant's eyes avoid mine. "Anything in partic-ular I can tell you, sir?"

"I'm trying to find him. He's my daughter's fiancé."

One corporal kicks a tree root. He glances up at the first sergeant. "Um, sir. I was just giving my report. He's missing."

"Missing?" My heart sinks. I narrow my eyes. "When?" I'm light-headed and lean against the tree for balance. My mind goes blank.

"Sir, are you all right?" the corporal holds my elbow.

"Not really, but go on," I whisper.

"Last night. Recon patrol. Six of us. We were probing the Heinie defenses. Trying to figure out what we'd be up against today. Got in a dustup. Musta been a whole platoon of the fucking Krauts. Lot of shooting. Stevens covered us when we beat ass back here. Haven't seen him since."

Bill. Missing. Damn it. "Has the report been sent up the chain yet?"

"Sir, I was just making my report now."

"Be a few days for that report to go through command, sir," the first sergeant says.

Where are you, Bill? My imagination grabs hold of me: dying in a ditch, wounded, hiding, lost, captured, being interrogated by a German intelligence officer schooled in the art of *persuasion*.

I shake my head.

How can I break the news to Trudy? Missing. So indeterminate. Purgatory. Thousands missing in this damned war. Many of them will never be seen or heard from again—nothing more than a bone fragment here, a boot there. Others *will* return—focus on that. The possibility that offers hope. That's how I have to portray it to Trudy.

Hope. The emptiest word in my vocabulary.

After catching a ride back to the Twenty-Third's headquarters, I find my driver, and we head back to the Fourth Brigade HQ at La Loge Farm. Each time I close my eyes, I see Bill and Trudy—stopping by my office at the newspaper, at our home, on campus, at graduation. Then I imagine Bill and his patrol shooting it out with the Germans—Bill motioning for the others to go ahead while he stands his ground, covering their retreat.

My mind is swirling. Each series of thoughts ends with Germans laughing over Bill's corpse.

Imagination is winning over reason.

Ab Johnson is talking with others in the staff room as I enter the farmhouse headquarters building. I mosey in to be a fly on the wall. "Gas last night," Ab whispers to me. "An area about one kilometer long by a half kilometer wide. Thousands of shells—gas and high explosives. Twenty-five hundred men in that area. Casualty stats are pending, but there are hundreds. Total disaster."

The brigade commander, General Harbord, motions Ab over. I pour myself a glass of water from a pitcher and slug the whole thing down. Thoughts about Bill run rampant in my head.

Ab catches my eye and says to Harbord, "We'll need gas suits if we go there, sir, but La Voie is in the clear. Everything east of there is toxic. Mind if my friend from Intelligence tags along, sir?"

"Could use some intelligent company." Harbord slips his gas mask pouch into the alert position, puts his helmet on—a French one—and walks out of the room. I follow Ab, adjusting my gas mask pouch to the front of my chest.

I hold Ab back. "Bill's missing."

"Where?" Ab asks, eyes wide.

"South of Bouresches. Recon patrol last night."

"Trudy know?"

"No. Nobody but us and his unit, so far." I choke the words out.

"Don't lose heart. Missing can mean many things. He's probably fine." Ab pats my shoulder as we follow Harbord to his car.

I ride in the front seat of the general's Cadillac staff car while Ab and General Harbord talk in the back. A yellow-brown mist hangs over the landscape ahead of us, and I hope we're not going there. The smell of rot seems stronger, and there's a mixture of odors I don't recognize, sweet grass and garlic. Ab and Harbord are going to meet with the Marine Fifth Regiment commander. Ab must want me near him, and I appreciate my friend's concern as what-ifs about Bill roil in my head.

The car turns left off the road to Lucy and heads into the hamlet Ab tells me is La Voie du Chatel. "I'll stay outside and have a look-'round, if you don't mind," I say. As a major, I know when to stay out of the way, and this is one of those times. Ab waves as he follows General Harbord into a large farmhouse. I need time to process Bill's situation, and there is nothing inside La Voie HQ that I need to know. I'm sure Ab brought me along to distract me.

The noise of the battle rattles my chest—the incessant thump and boom of artillery, the machine gun bursts, the random crackle of small arms. But La Voie is just far enough away to give me a momentary sense of safety. I look up at a buzzing noise and meld myself against a tall oak. Three Fokkers fly overhead. One drops to strafe a car scurrying along the road we just traveled over. The car dodges, leaves the road, puffs of dust in its wake, about to catch up. The driver veers to the right. The left-side wheels rise, spinning, and the plane flies by, the high note of its engine dropping an octave. It rises and joins the others veering off to the south.

I take a breath. That could have been us.

The headquarters door slams. General Harbord hustles to his car and hops in. Ab emerges and stops to light his pipe while Harbord's car peels out.

The Fifth Regimental surgeon comes out behind Ab and says a few words I can't hear. My heart is still in my ears from the strafing run and my stomach unsettled with Bill's news. Ab motions for me to follow. I jog to catch up as Ab and the surgeon enter the aid station across the compound from the headquarters. The surgeon sits down behind his field desk and sorts through a book of wound cards. His expression makes my heart sink.

"What's wrong?" Ab asks.

"Take a load off." The surgeon points to a campaign chair next to the desk while I stand.

"What?" Ab asks.

"Well . . ."

"What?" Ab's eyes narrow, and his brow furrows.

"The first letter of the first name is *J*, but the rest of the name and the serial number were unreadable on the identification tag." The surgeon hands Ab a slip. Ab's hand shakes as he reads the wound card. He hands it to me. *Johnson, J., 2nd Lt.*

I sit down in the chair next to Ab and put a hand on my old friend's shoulder. The world shrinks, the war far away. Questions flood my mind faster than I can ponder any one of them. Sadness rolls over me. First Bill, now this. The wound card states that Johnson, J., was shot in the face, awaiting evacuation. The image in my mind is too horrible to fathom.

Ab stares at the floor, eyes moist, breathing deeply, hands shaking.

I'm empty.

Finally, Ab asks, "Where is he?"

"The corpsman said he was still alive when he left him. Captain Williams's Fifty-First Company. They got cut to pieces trying to get into the woods yesterday."

"Did he make it to Lucy?"

The surgeon shakes his head. "Still in the field."

"But how do you have the wound card?" I ask.

"That corpsman wrote out a copy of the wound cards on each man he thought wouldn't make it. I don't know if you know him—Lyle McCormack. He does it after the dust has settled—not in the middle of the fight. Not standard procedure. Kid has a remarkable memory."

Ab and the surgeon talk. My eyes mist over. For Jack. For Ab. For Trudy and Bill. All those hopes and dreams, dashed by a bullet in a desolate field surrounded by so many others whose dreams also died there. How many fathers, mothers, sweethearts, will weep?

"I need some air. Thanks." Ab rises and leaves the tent.

Ab and I walk through La Voie in silence. When we approach the last tree in the lane, I stop and envelop Ab in my arms. We stand, sobs wracking Ab, tears flowing from my eyes. I remember the good times, when Trudy and I visited Ab's home in Montana, Jack and Trudy off for mountain hikes. I let go with a soft pat on my best friend's back, and we walk toward La Loge. Jack's death is not confirmed. *J.* Johnson, not necessarily Jack. Dream on.

It's as though a part of my soul has died. I gasp for a full breath, my chest empty, airless. Anything to fill the void. Oh, God—no. Not Jack and Bill.

"I can't believe it," I say as we walk. "I remember the times we had . . ." I decide to take a risk—anything to bolster my friend. "Thing is, Ab— might not be Jack."

"Sure." Ab's voice sounds distant, like his mind is elsewhere. "And Bill's probably fine too. Old friend, I've seen too much calamity in the last two weeks to be an optimist."

"No, I mean, how many Johnsons are in the service? And how many have a first initial of *J*? Jack's not the only one. I don't think we should rush to conclusions."

"Frustrating thing is, I don't know." Ab stares toward the east, where the distant crack of rifles and stutter of machine gun bursts echo. "I need to go out there—find out. You with me?"

"Ab, think about it. His body's in the field between Lucy and Belleau Wood." I point. "There's still a cloud of mustard gas over that whole place. What if we find the body? Is that the last memory you want of Jack? To see him like that? Shot in the face. You might not recognize him."

"I'd know."

"And if a sniper shoots you, then Helen loses both of you in that damned field. If they don't shoot me, what the hell do I tell her?" And if they put a round through my old head, Trudy's loss would be all the more.

Ab is silent, staring toward the east.

"What would Jack tell you to do?"

"Stay alive. Carry on. Make him proud."

"Yeah. Though I think he'd have said, 'Pops, keep your line in the water.'"

Ab huffs. "You're right."

"Then for all the Jacks still fighting this thing, we better keep our lines in the water and carry on in their honor."

I hope my words mean something to Ab.

They sure don't make me feel any better.

Like an uplifting hymn at a child's funeral.

Chapter Thirty-Five
Alice Simmons

Hiram has his breakfast tray when I visit before my morning shift. We share a few thoughts, but his nutrition is more important than anything I can say this morning. Back in the surgical ward, Finlay and I assist Captain Jensen on rounds, and Pickler again voices her objections. When we reach Lieutenant Grant, I ask, "Captain Jensen, would it be okay for me to take the lieutenant to see his friend down in ortho this afternoon? I'll use my lunch break so I won't miss any time here."

"Sure. Fine with me. You can do it after you and Finlay are done with the irrigations. I'm leaving Colonel Catlin's chest alone today. Your afternoon should be light unless something else happens." He yawns.

Colonel Catlin gives me a wink.

Following irrigation rounds, I grab a wheelchair and roll over to Lieutenant Grant's bed. "Want a ride, Marine?"

"Sure. Best offer I've had all year." Grant puts on a robe and stands. "I can walk."

"I know." I point to the seat of the chair. Grant shrugs and sits, and then we head toward the door. Nurse Pickler looks up from a chart as we pass the nursing desk.

Grant's tone is hostile. "Captain Jensen said I could visit a friend as long as Nurse Simmons takes me. His orders were specific. Didn't want me to suffer any complications along the way without her present. Ask him, I'm sure he'll confirm that."

"He's in surgery." Pickler's tone is neutral. She goes back to the chart.

I grin and wheel Grant to the ortho ward. Hiram is eating lunch when we arrive. He looks up and beams. "Ben—Lieutenant Grant, I mean. Sorry, sir. How are ya?"

"Starting to walk. I'll be getting out in a few weeks. How are you?"

"Well, not so good, you see. They operated yesterday and tell me they're going to do it again day after tomorrow. Probably need it every three or four days, 'n so. Hurts like the dickens right after they do it. And those washings they do? Oooheee. Send me through the roof, they do. But you're looking good, sir." A small grin grows on his face, and he says in a confidential tone, "Gotchyer gal with you today, too."

Grant's face flushes, and he gives me a glance that I can't decipher.

"Well, she's not my *gal*, Hiram." Grant shifts his gaze. "Not that that would be so bad. But who'd want a cuss like me? She'd do better with a dashing surgeon like Captain Jensen. He seems sweet on her."

And now it's my turn to blush. "Look, boys. Let me make something clear. I'm not a hen hanging from a hook at the meat market. Quit trying to fix me up, Hiram. Got it?"

"Yes, ma'am. Not meaning to be pushy. Just thought . . . What do you hear about the boys, sir? How's the fight?"

"Scuttlebutt's not good. Pulled our battalion out after they stalled halfway up the south side of the wood. Last I heard they were bathing the place with artillery."

Hiram's eyes are somewhere else, and Grant stares at the floor, both mute. As if they're replaying the events that brought them here, imagining what has happened since.

Hiram breaks the spell. "Let me show you some reading. Been working on it, you see. Miss Alice brought me a book." Hiram reads for ten minutes from *The Wonderful Wizard of Oz*. He stumbles over the bigger words. I'm amused to hear him speak without his central Minnesota idioms.

Grant's eyes sneak in my direction several times while we listen, the way Jensen's do on rounds. I push my glasses up. Why would anyone like Grant or Jensen be interested in me? Even friendship seems foolish. More than that? Insane. Grant is headed back to the front. More second lieutenants were wounded or died than made it through each battle so far. Grant's a hard case. He has that cop edge, a short, belligerent fuse—I wouldn't want to be on the receiving end when it blows. But then, in that way he's a lot like me.

I've always shied away when someone showed an interest. In fact, bolted for the door. Does that make me the Tin Woodman?

No.

I have a heart. A confused one. Maybe closed off. But it's in there. Somewhere. And since Scooter, and now with Hiram and the rest of this ratty bunch, I think I'm finding it fuller than I ever hoped. But shedding the armor that has surrounded my heart makes it vulnerable. Friendships are forming with men I'm supposed to keep a clinical distance from. The consequences scare me.

Chapter Thirty-Six
Alice Simmons

Grant is quiet as I guide his wheelchair back to our ward. I return the wheelchair to storage after helping Grant back into bed and go to the linen room. Betty looks up from her work with a worried expression. "Alice, they want you in Nurse Enright's office. They were looking all over for you."

"I told Pickle where we were going."

"She said you absconded with a patient and she had no idea where you were. She said she'd discipline you after your return."

The liar! I close my eyes and concentrate on breathing slowly. What does Mrs. Enright want with me? Pickler threatened to complain to the administration. Has she finally done it? Without this job, and without my crypt to sleep in, I'm out on the street at the mercy of the Paris police.

I leave the ward and make my way to the front door. My skirts and propriety keep me to a slow jog, but I break a sweat after three blocks. I slow down and fan myself during the last block, trying to let some of the perspiration evaporate before I go into the main hospital building.

The door to Emily Enright's office stands open. I knock on the doorframe. Mary Sloan sits in a guest chair, back to me, holding a cup of tea. Emily is behind her large oak desk with diplomas on the walls and a bookcase behind. A whiff of air through the open window is a relief, but a dribble of sweat trickles down my spine.

Emily frowns. "Nurse Pickler told us you were AWOL."

"I'm so sorry. I told her where I was going. I'd been requested to take a patient to visit one of his friends . . ."

"She made it sound like you'd skipped town." The corners of Mary's mouth turn down.

"But in spite of that, I have good news," Emily says. "Chicago confirmed your credentials." She stands and picks up a nursing cap, comes around the desk, and sets it on my head. Mary applies a hairpin to hold it in place. "Congratulations. You're now official, Nurse Simmons."

Finally. My chest swells with a sense of accomplishment I did not experience when I earned my RN in the first place. Back then it was just one of many stepping stones. Now it's . . . much more. I touch the cap. "What next?"

"Oh, go ahead and take a seat." Emily motions me to a chair. "Mary and I'll have a meeting with Marion Pickler. I know how she's been treating you and consider it a credit to you that you haven't come here crying about her. That tells me a lot about your character. And that matters as we take you through the next steps."

I don't know whether to be proud or angry. But I passed the test. Maybe that's all that counts.

"What is her problem?" I ask.

"Granted, that affects you and the other staff, but there are things here that I don't feel at liberty to share. What I ask is that you keep your heart generous, your mind open, and don't break her nose."

Wait a second. Did Ira tell them? I can't decide if he betrayed a confidence or simply took care of his accessory daughter.

"Next we get you into the Nurse Corps," Emily continues. "I'm trying to figure out how to do it without sending you back to the States."

"They'll want you to have additional training," Mary says. "Most of it has nothing to do with nursing, though. Army regulations, customs and courtesies, and some indoctrination. We can teach you all of that. Whether the powers that be will agree is uncertain. As long as you're healthy and morally upstanding—not a criminal or anything like that, you know—then it may be possible."

My neck hair tingles. Criminal. What did Ira tell them? How much trouble will I be in for not telling them the whole story from the start? Think quick. "So, I fill out an application? Then what?"

Emily slides a stack of papers across her desk. "I took the liberty of collecting these for you. Fill them out and return them to me. I'll arrange for you to have a physical examination. We'll have to convene a selection board to review your credentials and recommendations." Emily gives Mary what seems like a knowing wink.

Time to take the plunge.

"I . . . I have something I should talk with you both about." I go on to tell them about the events with Martel and Buck. The words rush out in a torrent, my throat tight, the voice not mine. Calm down. Deep breath. Ease it out. "I haven't been arrested or charged with anything. Paris police searched my room at the apartment. The landlady threw me out. Martel's latest accusation is that I'm a spy. It's just so maddening." My pulse quickens with the thought of Buck's breath in my face.

"Where are you staying?"

"A friend found me a room." I can't look either in the eye as I tell them this.

"Pete and Howard keep in touch with Ira Cunningham," Mary says. "He told both of them. We knew too. I . . . just didn't know how to talk with you about it. Howard feels guilty for not insisting he take you home that night. I get the feeling Ira is working behind the scenes on this, but—well, you know how he gets when his teeth are into an important story. It's like that."

"Have you heard anything from Ira? I know he was going to try to find Bill. No word since," I say.

"Howard told me that something's gotten under Ira's skin, but he clammed up when Howard tried to find out more," Emily says. "He seemed very upset about something. Look, we have a meeting to get to, but why don't you join us for drinks tonight, to celebrate. We're meeting our husbands at a little bar not far from here." She gives me the directions. "You can stay here and fill out the application."

"Do you have a nursing uniform?" Mary asks.

"Yes," I say.

"Nine o'clock, then."

I fill out the paperwork and leave it on Emily's desk, then take my time strolling back to the Annex, mulling over events. I stop and stare down the street where I had rented the room—no patrol car. Maybe my luck has turned. When I walk into the ward, Trudy is at the nursing station, talking with Finlay. "What was the command performance all about?" Trudy asks.

I point at my cap.

"'Bout time," Trudy says.

Finlay smiles. "Ditto."

The rest of the afternoon speeds by in a flurry of activity. I don't have time to go to the basement to change into my nurse's uniform, but I keep the cap on. Pickler is in meetings and doesn't return during my shift. Is that the meeting Emily mentioned? At the end of my shift, I stop to see Hiram and then go to my cell and change into street clothes. It won't do to have a nurse's uniform on if I have any drinks, even with my bosses. I walk out into the evening with a smile and a spring in my step. I stop and watch passing traffic. A policeman, a hundred feet behind, turns and gazes up into a tree as if looking for a runaway cat. Does he really think I don't notice? What a waste. On the other hand, Martel and Buck won't dare get close with a policeman near me. And there's a thought—are they tailing me, or are they protecting me?

It's nearing nine when I approach the bar. Nothing to eat since breakfast. I pinch my tummy—no fat left. I hope this joint has food. Otherwise, I'll be the type of drinker college boys dream about.

The bar is dark and smoky. My nose doesn't detect kitchen aromas, but when I reach the table, two meat and cheese trays lie in the center along with a crusty baguette.

"Nurse Simmons, so glad you could join us again," Howard Enright says. "Don't worry, I refuse to let you walk home this time. Emily and I have our car."

"Eat. You look gaunt." Pete Sloan motions to a chair.

A tumbler with amber liquid sits at my place. I pick it up, sniff it, and offer it up in a toast. "Ira must have told you my favorite. Thank you. For everything. The job, the support, and especially this." I take a sip, then let out a long breath. "The police *confiscated* my last bottle of Famous Grouse."

"I was just telling Pete, our old friend Ira Cunningham's been in touch," Howard says. He takes a sip of his drink. "No sooner got to the main headquarters in Chaumont than they sent him to the Second Division. They're the ones fighting in Belleau Wood. Met up with our other old friend Ab Johnson there. You know his son, Jack, don't you? He couldn't tell us much, other than it's a hell of a mess. Well, he used other words not suitable for polite company. He asked about you. Heard any more from Martel?"

My throat tightens. "I understand you all know the story." I feel naked.

"Yeah. Ira spilled the beans," Howard says. "Look, you're among friends. Ira asked me to tell you that he's working on an angle."

Ira would. He's full of angles. Trust him. He understands. I hope. No, that's unfair. He does.

"So now that you're legal, what next?" Pete asks.

I shrug and take a sip. The burn is wonderful. I follow it with a cracker dripping with warm brie.

"I can answer that," Mary says. "Captain Jensen wants you to be his primary assistant."

"Nurse Pickler is unhappy about me assisting him," I say.

Mary leans forward and whispers, "Pickle can kiss my posterior." She leans back and takes a sip of red wine. "Thorn in my side since day one."

"She seemed so . . . promising when we interviewed her," Emily says. "From a poor family in Boston, pulled herself up by her bootstraps, working at Massachusetts General, very bright, driven. Sort of person who would ordinarily not volunteer to come here—especially since she doesn't speak French. She said she needed a change—*fresh air* was how she put it. Her husband and daughter died last year in an accident. Apparently they made it to a hospital. She didn't share the details. I think all that had a profound effect on her."

"None of that excuses her," Mary says. "We're too short-staffed to let her go quite yet. Maybe when things calm down."

"Speaking of short-staffed—I submitted your army application,"

Emily says. "Physical's tomorrow at two. Then a review committee. They'll talk with Mary and me, then with you."

"How's Trudy doing?" Howard asks.

"I'm worried about her—we haven't heard from Bill."

Howard gives me a ride back. I make up a yarn about forgetting something at the hospital and tell him I'll be safe between there and my apartment.

The cool air of the basement feels good after the balmy night. I put a dab of perfume in a finger bowl and take a deep breath through my nose. I roll a clean sheet into the typewriter carriage.

UNTITLED

The aftermath of battle. Some seem hardly touched beyond the physical wounds. They joke, play cards to pass the time, make smart remarks to doctors and nurses. Others are edgy, jumping at loud noises. The physical effects of their wounds can be profound—men who will never walk again and others who will, but with crutches or prosthetic limbs. Still others horribly disfigured.

The physical wounds are obvious and the topic of much conversation. The unseen, unspoken wounds lurk in the shadows. Will they ever heal? Many are sad about the loss of comrades, gone in ways too horrific to imagine. Tasting air filled with the blood mist of their best friends and the chemicals of an industrial death creates indelible memories that a lifetime of nightmares cannot reconcile. To willingly experience this is amazing. Their courage is profound. To

consciously send boys and men into this cauldron
is testimony to the sheer madness of those who
rule this continent.

I yawn as I pull out the paper and slide it into a portfolio that I hide in the rafters at the far corner of my dungeon. After checking that the door is bolted, I flick on the flashlight and peer under my bed and in the corners. No rats or mice, so I douse the light and keep the flashlight at my side, hoping to not have the recurring nightmare about two shadowy men in an alleyway that visits my sleep every night.

Chapter Thirty-Seven
Alice Simmons

Saturday, June 15

It seems like I've just put my head down on the pillow when the alarm rings. The dungeon is timeless, silent except for my ticking clock, black. I flick on the flashlight. Six o'clock. I get up and blink when I whack the light switch. Pickle's reaction to me in the uniform and cap could be interesting. What new slander will the woman invent? Emily's comments about Pickle are puzzling. I find it hard to justify the effort to find a silver lining in my head nurse.

Should I move to the dorm? It would be great if I could room with Trudy. But there's no guarantee about roommates, and I don't want to end up with someone like Walker.

The rumor mill swirls with a story about two army officers found roaming the dorm. Henri and Luc confronted them and forced the officers to leave. A chill runs down my spine at the thought. What would have happened if I ran into Martel and Buck?

Perfume in the finger bowl freshens the cool room. The police will have a hard time finding me here. That is, unless Henri is somehow in league with them and this is a convenient place to stash me while they decide what to do. No. I don't think that's Henri's game. Just being paranoid again.

The dungeon feels more like a cocoon. A cave where I hide, safe, and sleep behind a locked metal door. It would be impossible to write, type, and hide my manuscripts in the dorm as long as I'm a suspected spy. What would they call me? Mata-Simmons or Alice-Hari? My neck hairs tingle. Time to get on with the day.

I stop to see Hiram first. He had a fever during the night, and small beads of sweat glisten on his forehead. Scooter. He was like that. No, this is different. Maybe. Please.

He has *Oz* open when I pull up a chair. He smiles. "Well, lookee here—Nurse Alice, all gussied up with her new cap."

"How's your reading?" My face warms.

Hiram reads two paragraphs, then looks up, beaming. "Think I'm getting the hang of it, Miss Alice. Still some words I can't figger, but I sort of sound 'em out. A couple puzzle me."

"Does the leg hurt much?"

"No, except when I move, or they move it, or someone bumps into my bed, or when they do those washing things. They're doing another operation later tomorrow. Worried about the fever, they are."

"That's pretty routine." Fevers like this can mean anything from a minor skin infection to a catastrophic bone infection—osteomyelitis. Will they have to amputate? That would destroy him. I try to keep things cheerful while we chat until it's time to head to the ward.

Betty, Marie, and Geneva are busy folding sheets and dishing up gossip in the linen room. Betty salutes me. "Nurse Simmons."

I wave my hand in front of my head in a mock salute.

"Will you be too important to talk to us?" Marie asks. "Perhaps we should work on a nickname for you? What can we make out of Simmons?"

"'The Rabbit.' My grandmother called me that."

"What about the Pickle? You'll help us with her?" Marie asks, frowning.

"I'll continue to come in early, and we'll do a quick walk around in the ward to help you organize your mornings."

I lead the three into the ward. We talk about which beds need new linens first and which men will need fresh pajamas. I speak with Henri, telling him where to start, and give him a pat on the back. "I'd like to talk with you later, when we have a chance." Henri nods and returns to his mop. As we go through our rounds, I realize that I do have friends in this world, people I can count on.

When we're done, I stand at the nursing station and look over the ward. Colonel Catlin says, "Congratulations, Nurse Simmons. I'd clap, but my right arm's still too gimpy, and I think it would kill Berry over there to do so." Those with two hands clap. And there is a glint in Lieutenant Grant's eyes. What does that mean? Trudy works on a marine at the far end of the ward. I go over and motion her aside.

"I'm in a pickle," I say.

"Being punny? Look what just waltzed in." Trudy nods toward the door.

"Trying to decide where to stay."

The clicking heels approach. "What is this, a theater performance? Nurse Simmons, get to work." Pickler goes past, chiding Henri in her slow. Deliberate. English.

I roll my eyes, then smile. "We'll talk later."

Wound rounds with Captain Jensen last three hours. I convince him to let Finlay continue in the lead assistant role. After we're done and the equipment put away, I return to the ward. Men who earlier had looked at me with a sense of resignation over the irrigations now smile, their spirits restored to a degree. Several ask when I'll replace Pickler.

I sit at the nurses' desk, sorting out the forms I now have to complete. Vital signs and short notes hang on clipboards at the end of each bed. We do the rest of the charting at the nursing station. I look up after completing Major Berry's irrigation note. Colonel Catlin and Lieutenant Grant are speaking with Berry, laughing at something. Catlin makes his own rounds, talking with his officers, spreading cheer. I can see why his men respect him—stern and demanding but supportive to a fault. He loves his men, whom he often calls his "lads."

Lieutenant Grant often accompanies Catlin. He has a limp but seems determined to get back to his unit. He'll transfer to the convalescent ward tomorrow. A week ago, I would have told Trudy that I wouldn't miss him, but I'm not so sure now. He does have that look in his eye—interest? Perhaps. As distant as he had seemed at first, he stands by his men—like Hiram. And the way he'd intervened with the Pickle left me with a debt of gratitude. Everyone respects the Chicago cop even though he is one of the most junior officers in the ward. His reading selections are curious. He has a stack of books from the library, including *Of Human Bondage* and *Pride and Prejudice*. Not your average Chicago cop.

I still eat lunch with the aides, feeling out of place with the nurses. As much as I'd wanted my credentials to come through, now that they have, I'm reticent about living the life of a staff nurse.

My physical exam is at two in the outpatient clinic. On the way, a thought occurs to me—will they do a virginity exam? No worries about passing that, but then a thought flashes through my mind—Martel's fingers. Damn it. How long will that vile memory linger? The doctor does a cursory exam, measuring chest expansion with deep breaths and my ability to do deep knee bends. No gynecologic exam. Thank God.

The rest of the afternoon and early evening are routine. At five to eight, I go to the cloakroom and gather my things. I could have left them in my room, but keeping my purse in the cloakroom prevents questions. I go to the front entry for fresh air and a break. Henri Barton is having a smoke with a French soldier, watching the ambulance traffic. He nods and field strips his cigarette, scatters the tobacco, and pockets the shred of paper. "Mademoiselle Alice, allow me to introduce my nephew Phillippe. He is an ambulance driver."

We talk about the wine industry, my family's cooperage business, the quality of recent vintages, and the difficulties the war has created. The evening is golden, and I feel a sense of unrushed camaraderie. It reminds me of what it means to be French—unlike my recent adventures.

Phillippe tells about the harrowing experiences of ambulance drivers transporting casualties from the front. He works with the French 167th, who are fighting to the north of the American Second Division. Phillippe bids us farewell a half hour later. Henri says, "You said you wanted to talk with me . . ."

"I have a decision to make." I go on to describe my debate about staying in the basement or moving to the dormitory, and about my writing. Henri lights a cigarette and seems to contemplate the sky while I speak.

"Well, mademoiselle, I do not pretend to make your decision. But the room you have is one we have never used, and I see no reason to believe we will need it. As you say, it is safe, cool, private. I hope you will continue to write stories. We, all of us, need these events recorded. Write me a story about Phillippe. Each time he goes out, I fear I will never see him again. Write in remembrance of his courage. I suspect many in your country don't view us French as having courage. They simply don't understand us or what we are going through. You should move to the dormitory in the fall. That part of the basement gets too cold in the winter."

"I heard you and Luc ran into some men roaming the halls of the dormitory."

Henri's face hardens. "It was nothing. They were lost."

"Did one have a damaged nose and the other a missing tooth?" My neck tingles.

"*Non*, mademoiselle. We did not, as you say, do anything of the sort."

"That's not what I asked, Henri. Did they show damage, from, say, a few weeks ago?"

Henri shrugs and walks away humming a Ravel tune—"Pavane for a Dead Princess."

I stop at Hiram's ward, where we read alternating parts of *The Wizard*. Others listen in—the only entertainment for most. Afterward, I sneak up to the dormitory to talk with Trudy and take a bath. I'm not sure what will happen if one of the residents finds me, but sponge baths in the basement have worn thin. Trudy sits with her back to the door of the lavatory while I soak in a warm tub, talking over the question about where to stay. Trudy talks about Bill. I chide myself silently for being too preoccupied with my own problems, and I listen to my friend without interrupting.

The question of what to call my room worms through my mind on the way to the basement. Cell? Cellar? I like the idea of being like a fine wine, ageing, maturing, mellowing. Cave? A cave where wine ages in my family's cooperage, going from raw to almost finished product. That's how I think of myself. A glass of Rhône would be nice. Or the sort of cave a monk lives in—apart, safe. Secret. I roll a sheet of paper into the typewriter carriage.

UNSUNG HEROES I

In this war raging across the world, unsung heroes are legion. Phillippe Barton was an assistant wine broker in Paris before the war. He volunteered and was assigned to an ambulance company.

When casualties became a flood, Phillippe Barton and his assistant driver, Jacques Dubois, made run after harrowing run between aid stations and field hospitals. German balloon observers called artillery strikes on the ambulances during daylight. This forced the men to drive at night. Even then, the use of headlights attracted sniper and artillery fire. Jacques walked with a hand on the front left bumper while Phillippe drove, creeping through the night. Jacques kept Phillippe on the road, guiding him around shell holes. The wounded had to wait in the aid stations from dawn to dusk. Phillippe and Jacques got no rest, though. They evacuated men from the field hospitals to Paris during the long June days. On and on they drove, night and day—hungry, thirsty, sleepless.

These are unsung heroes, their courage, forti-
tude, and commitment no less than those in the
front trenches. Remember them.

I pull the paper out and read. A corrected comma later, I set the paper down and stick the pencil behind my right ear. The theme of the piece is hardly original, but it's also timeless. My conversation with Trudy leads me to roll another piece of paper into the carriage.

UNSUNG HEROES II

Guns blaze, cannons fire, and troops charge into eternity. Heroes become the stuff of legend in the crucible of battle. But what about those who stay behind? They live under a constant cloud of fear. Imagine a young engaged couple on the eve of war. She is filled with dreams, hope, love. She tells him how handsome he looks in his uniform, filled with dread she cannot mention to him. She fears that speaking the words could make them come true.

He heads into the belly of the beast of war—but where? He cannot say for security reasons. She writes. At first the letters are answered. She holds each one close to her heart, reading them over and over until they are tattered rags.

She is a nurse who volunteers to be as close to the front as the army will allow—to be closer to him. The letters stop. Why? Perhaps his unit has moved and the mail hasn't caught up. That must be it, she tells her friends. She struggles to convince herself of her words. Fear frames every-thing. And her world shrinks each day down to one question—is he alive?

At night, before bed, she prays he is not dead. That he hasn't abandoned her for another. She

cries herself to sleep. Dreams become nightmares
of him in a desperate struggle. She wakes in
panic when he is shot—before she can know if he
survives. She can't fall back asleep for fear her
nightmare will return and show her his mangled
corpse.

Each morning, she paints on a smile and tries to
cheer her patients, treating them each as she
would have her man treated. Seeing him in her
patients, always wondering: is he among those who
didn't make it to the hospital that day? Perhaps
he is alive and far away from the fighting. And
that thought, that hope, however evanescent, is
the single thread tethering her spirit.

The articles can't see the light of day until after the war. But in my cave,
the monk can say, "Think and write whatever you please." I hide the
manuscript in the rafters like a secret scroll and turn out the light,
finding my bed with the flashlight. Perhaps Henri will be the subject for
Part III if I ever figure out his angle.

Chapter Thirty-Eight
Alice Simmons

Sunday, June 16

Sunday morning. No bible in this cave. So much for being a monk. Catholic guilt. Did it begin with baptism, when the priest used the holy water to make the sign of the cross on my forehead? Or is it more like a genetic trait? My mother would be upset that I don't attend Mass. My faith was not strong and never blind to begin with. Some say battle and war deepen faith, but this war is having the opposite effect on me. I can't see how a loving God could allow the horrors of this war to exist. I don my nursing uniform, lock the door behind myself, and head upstairs. Maybe I owe a few Our Fathers. If only that would help.

Chaplains circulate on the wards. Aides and orderlies roll wheelchairs and help ambulatory patients to the chapels. I carry on and cover for several nurses who want to attend services. I haven't had a day off since I joined the hospital staff, and today is no exception. But guilt is like a mosquito bite I don't want to scratch this morning.

Nurse Pickler enters the ward, her half-glasses exaggerating her already long nose, a sour expression crinkling her face. My neck tingles. Pickle writes on a clipboard when she talks with the other nurses and aides. She walks up as I adjust the stopcock on Major Berry's wound irrigation tubing. "Simmons. You and Cunningham have lunch from one thirty to two." The pencil slips off the clipboard and dangles by the string. She grabs the errant instrument, opens the clip, and snaps it down, nearly decapitating the pencil. I think, *How dare it!* and turn back to my work before Pickler sees my smile. The heels are quieter. Did Emily tell her to remove the thumbtacks or whatever made them click?

At half past one, I motion for Trudy to follow, and we head to the cafeteria. The food is edible but overcooked. American cooks in the kitchen now. Well-done meat loaf chews like boot leather today. The filler must include the sawdust they used in the bread. We all play a game —speculating on the species of the tree. I'm about halfway through when a hand pulls a chair away from the table. Ira Cunningham stands behind the chair, holding a cup of coffee.

"Dad." Trudy stands and hugs him, beaming.

"Hi, sweetie."

Ira's expression worries me—something's wrong.

"Hear anything about Bill? I'm dying to know," Trudy continues.

Ira's mouth twitches. "How are you, Alice?"

"Dad?" Trudy has an expectant expression.

Ira sips his coffee, his eyes not leaving mine. He's avoiding something. His expression is inscrutable—his editor's face.

"Sweetheart, I haven't seen or heard from him."

"What about Jack?"

"Saw Ab the day before last, and he hadn't heard from Jack."

"I've been writing Bill each day. I know he's too busy to write back. And the mail! Who knows where I should send mine? No wonder I haven't heard. I hope he's not too low about not getting my letters. I'm sure they're hung up somewhere."

Trudy's face beams as she speaks, barely able to contain herself, as if Bill is coming to lunch. My throat tightens at the thought of how she would react if anything happens to Bill. Ira's expression makes me think there is something else he has to tell us. And I'm afraid it's about Bill. But I work a smile onto my face, the way Ira taught me years ago. I need to talk with him alone.

"Everything safe and secure around here?" Ira's frown piques my curiosity.

I'd like to ask him about the story of the two *lost* American officers, but I don't want to alarm Trudy. Of course, she's probably heard it from others.

"Sure. Why?" Trudy asks.

"Oh, nothing. Just wondering. Writing any stories, Alice?" Ira asks.

"Late at night." I describe my cave. "At least nobody will hear my typewriter. At first, I felt like the cave was punishment for my sins. But it's a safe place where nobody can find me. I can write stories. They may never see the light of day, but they're mine. No censor will ever redact them. I guess what I put on paper is my sanity."

"How did you end up there?"

I tell him about the events at my former apartment. "You may have saved my life. I remembered what you told me once, staring into the barrel of a pistol."

Ira's eyes show alarm. "It's come to that?"

"Martel accuses me of being a spy. I really think they planned to just shoot me. I worry they might still, if they find me—but they won't do it here, I'm sure. I think."

Ira's face softens into a subtle grin. "That's my protégé. Remember, keep your eyes open."

It seems to me that Ira is saying that to himself.

He drops his tray at the bus window on the way out, and motions as if beckoning me. I excuse myself and follow Ira out the door. He leads the way down a back hall, peeking through open doors, and turns into an empty room. "I need advice only you can give."

Something is terribly wrong. It's written on his face.

Ira closes the door and paces. He tells me about his trip to the front and that Trudy's Bill is missing in action and Jack Johnson is presumed killed. I'm lightheaded and sit, staring at the wall while he talks. The room is airless. This will destroy my best friend—is destroying my mentor. I think about Scooter, Hiram, and the others on my ward while Ira talks, my mind muddled, overloaded with fractured memories and images. Jack and Bill were my friends. Are. Are my friends. Missing doesn't mean dead, and reports of deaths in this stupid war can be wrong. Tell that to my breaking heart.

And Jack. Oh my God, Jack. The memories rush in, filling my head.

The times we spent together with Bill and Trudy, studying in the Art Library to get away from the science and journalism students, to be alone. Friendship, but always the possibility of more, later. Now there is no later.

"So, the question tormenting me should be obvious. Do I tell my daughter or wait?"

Darkness envelops my heart. "I don't even know how to think about it, to come to grips with it."

"You see my dilemma."

"Trudy will jump to the conclusion that Bill is dead, like I just did. The news of Jack's death will cement that for her." I choke the last part out—I have to concentrate on my living friend, Trudy. Ira is in knots. "I'm not sure you and I will be able to pick up the pieces. Maybe there's a way to break it to her slowly." I take in a sharp breath. "That had to be the stupidest thing I've ever said."

"I think we should wait until there's confirmation one way or the other," Ira says. "Better to risk breaking her heart late and having her angry at us than to break it unnecessarily."

"Okay, we'll play it your way. If she ever finds out we knew and held back, and he is dead—I'm not sure she'll forgive us. But it's the right thing to do."

Ira's eyes seem lost, his face slack.

"Do you have agents here, in the hospital?" I ask. Now's my chance.

Ira squints. "What?"

"Two of our janitors found a pair of army officers wandering around the nursing dorm. I got the impression things became physical and the officers were forced to leave."

"Buck and Martel?"

I shrug. "I don't know. That said, I assume so. Have you heard anything?"

"Martel threatened to go after Trudy if I didn't back off." Ira's eyes narrow.

"Did you? Back off, I mean."

"No. I took the advice I gave you. I'm taking a different direction."

Chapter Thirty-Nine
Major Ira Cunningham

Monday, June 17

It rained overnight, freshening the air as I wend a circuitous route through the Tuileries Garden before heading to my old office building. Spring flowers grow in undisciplined beds. Trees that are normally trimmed with precision look ratty. The gardeners are either at the front or left with the civilian exodus when the German offensive threatened Paris. A few taxis putter by while I cross the Rue de Rivoli. The honking of a horn draws my eye to a near collision between two French Army supply trucks a block to my left. The drivers shout at each other in a language I can't make out, shaking fists from behind their wheels. They must be from the French colonies in Southeast Asia. I smile. Some actions transcend the barriers of the tongue.

Menacing gray clouds hang low; I forgot to bring my umbrella.

Guilt is my personal cloud, for which there is no protection.

What if Trudy discovers that I knew Bill was missing and didn't say anything? How far does filial forgiveness extend? And now I've put Alice in the middle. On the one hand, it was unfair to add to her burden —she's been through so much in the last month. On the other hand, I was at the bursting point and had to tell someone I trust.

My face tightens as I think about the incident at Alice's apartment. The policeman who pulled a gun on her. Memories rush in, staring down the barrel of a gun during the O'Connor investigation. The nightmares haunt me still. I always put a brave face on it, but it was terrifying. Alice now carries that memory like a scar and will have her own nightmares.

When I arrive at the Paris headquarters, I head to Lieutenant Joseph Green's office using back corridors, glancing around corners. I should get some spy training to learn how to skulk better—I feel clumsy. They must do that somewhere in my department. I knock on the doorframe, and Green looks up from his work.

Two beaten wooden desks face each other with swivel chairs next to two large filing cabinets and a window in bad need of a wash. The room smells of paper and old wood and coffee.

"Major. Didn't expect to see you back so soon. Come in."

I close the door and ease into the desk chair facing Green. "Look, I'll get right to the point, Joe. I'm dealing with three messes. One is in this office, and another came through it."

"Me?"

"No. No. You're doing a great job. Martel."

Green's eyes narrow, and the corners of his mouth edge up a millimeter. "Sir?"

"You remember our conversations about how he and Buck got their injuries?"

"Sure. Heard both sides of that. Sounds like they're trying their best to arrange a firing squad for Miss Simmons. Buck even told a few of us he issued a shoot-on-sight order if she comes back here. I don't think the guards are taking that seriously."

"I've been out of the loop for a few weeks. Catch me up. I need the unvarnished truth and your honest opinions."

"Martel and Buck went to the French to get her declared persona non grata. Rare thing for someone who's not a diplomat. Not unprecedented regarding the press, however. Their basis appeared to be that she was unemployed. Martel cabled her editor in Milwaukee and got her fired. Well, turns out she has a job—a nurse, no less. They went to what must have been plan B and told the French she's a German spy."

"They offer any evidence?" I keep my poker face. I know all that but don't want him to know I know.

"Nah. Friday, Buck upped the ante another notch and claimed they were doing counterintelligence work on Colonel Nolan's orders and had been assaulted by German operatives they claim Simmons controls."

I laugh. "You're joking, right?"

"No joke. They tossed her apartment, got her evicted. They've been stationing men outside the hospital to tail her—trying to figure out where she lives, who she sees. Got them in a muddle, I hear. They think it confirms her clandestine nature. Seems that she never leaves the hospital, but she isn't staying in the nursing dorm."

"Any substance to the spy theory?" I want to scream.

"Not a shred. Buck's desperate. The French have to take the accusation seriously since he's with Intelligence."

"Are the French complete morons?"

"Do I have to be honest?" Green rolls his eyes. "That's unfair. I have a few friends who have friends. I've told them this is a plate of hot, steaming horse manure. I'm hoping that will create enough doubt to keep them from accepting Buck's shoot-on-sight order. As of this point, I haven't seen that order in writing."

"Okay. Where is she working?" I continue to play dumb—I don't want to bias him.

"Military Hospital Number One in Neuilly. To the French perception, America is demanding her expulsion or arrest. At least that's the way Martel and Buck are painting the picture. But we're so short of nurses we wouldn't kick out Hindenburg's sister if she were one. Martel claims all his information is classified and he can't show it to the French. But she's second-generation French American, from a family with a stellar reputation. She must have friends. I've never seen French intelligence so . . . uninterested . . . in an accused spy. They seem content to just watch Simmons. Someone is holding them back."

I've done my part, talking with the Enrights and Sloans about Alice's problems, hoping Emily can do a few things to make Alice safer. But this business with French Intelligence is out of my league.

The facts spin through my mind like wildfire. In our first meeting,

Colonel Nolan had scribbled a note as I told him Alice's story. Alice had remarked about suspecting she had a *friend* out there. Ab has connections in the French government after his stint with the embassy years ago. A French intelligence officer is Jack's godfather—Ab never mentioned his name. Some pieces begin to fit together.

"I take an interest in this case since Miss Simmons is a friend of my daughter's," I say. "And before you ask, Colonel Nolan is aware of that. What else do you hear about Martel and Buck?"

Green frowns. "Two things. You'll love the first. They each put the other in for medals. Wound stripes and Citation Stars."

"When did rape become heroic?" My face warms.

"There's more. They apparently got *lost*—in the nurse's dorm at the hospital where your daughter and Simmons work. Two janitors *persuaded* them to leave and never come back. Martel's left ear looked like a boxer after a bad bout."

I drum my fingers on the arm of the chair. That answers the question Alice asked me. Who are the janitors who *persuaded* them to leave? I'd like to shake their hands. "Anything else?"

Green looks uncomfortable, his eyes moving side to side rapidly. "Um. Well." His face flushes. "I'm not sure how to describe this. Now, mind you, this is all hearsay."

"This conversation is just between us."

"There's no official report. I know an officer in the Sûreté."

"You seem to have many friends," I say. Green hesitates and swallows. What the hell is his problem? Why doesn't he just spit it out? He seems to fumble with his own embarrassment, turning in his chair, as if he's about to accuse the president of having an affair. That, or somehow the words he is about to utter will send him to hell.

"Off the record?"

"Just tell me. I'm a big boy."

"Last Saturday, the fifteenth, the two were out drinking."

"Martel and Buck?"

"Yes, sir. New York Bar . . ."

"Where they were when they assaulted Miss Simmons."

"Well, this time, after empties covered the table, they went to visit some ladies of the night. Apparently for a . . . foursome. Things got . . .

rough. Both women are in the hospital with severe injuries—faces, chests, and . . . well . . ." He points toward his groin.

"What are the French doing about it?"

"Sitting on their hands. They don't want to create an incident. Can't afford the sort of sordid publicity this could garner if our press friends found out—well, you understand."

This is it.

The newspaper editor in me clicks in. I know a scoop when I hear one.

Don't look excited. Don't overreact.

I have a pang of guilt that two women were injured. What would Martel and Buck have done to Alice if she hadn't fought back? A weight pushes in on my chest. I look Green in the eyes. "Provost marshal know about this?"

"No. The French are debating, so my contact tells me. After all, they're prostitutes. It's a risky profession. And these are American army officers. Buck is a West Pointer from a prominent family. If this happened in New York, where his father is an investment banker? Or with Martel—if he did this in New Orleans?"

"For all we know, they've done this before." I sit straight in my chair. "And that's why we need to stop them here and now. Nolan'll hit the roof when he hears two of his men have done this. I'll deal with the provost marshal."

Green jots a note, then sighs. "I'm afraid to ask about the other two messes. One wouldn't relate to medical, would it?"

"Tell me what you know," I say.

"Well, sir, a reporter sent us a news story to approve. It alleged multiple serious medical failures in the Belleau Wood engagement. I showed it to Colonel Wadhams, the head of the Paris Medical Group. He told me the story was accurate in some areas but incomplete. Made us look like clowns in a dogcart."

"The clowns in this case all speak French," I say.

"The reporting of which at this time would create an incident we can't afford. I killed the article and sent it to Wadhams and Nolan."

"I'm doing some of the lead work on this for the inspector general. Have a copy?"

"Sure. I'll get it for you. Anything else you need?"

"Call your French contact," I say. "I need to talk with him. I'm going there next."

"The third mess?"

"Does not affect you."

I leave Green's office. In the middle of the second-floor hallway, within earshot of several reporters, stands Martel. His handsome face is bruised, with a wide, swollen nose and left ear.

Martel sneers. "Thought I told you what would happen if I saw you in this building again."

"Nice to see you too, Major." I don't break pace, knowing that Martel expects a salute. I want to give one with my middle finger but refrain.

I have something better in mind.

Chapter Forty
Major Ira Cunningham

Armed with names of the women and where they are hospitalized, I tell my driver to drop me off at the provost marshal's office. Frustration swirls in me as I ride in the staff car. I tell the desk sergeant at the provost marshal's office that I need to speak to the man in charge. Now. Ten minutes later, a major walks through the swinging half-door that separates the waiting area from the office.

"I'm Burrows," the man says with irritation.

"Cunningham. I need to talk with you—in private."

Burrows leads the way to his office and closes the door after I enter and take a seat without being invited to do so.

"What is this all about?"

"Colonel Nolan ordered me to investigate allegations made by Major Richard Martel and Captain Ralph Buck. Both are men under his command. I understand your office is leading an inquiry that touches them."

"I'm familiar with the case." He goes on to describe the current accusations that I already understand better than he does. "We plan to force the French to arrest Simmons on Monday after I clear it with the judge advocate. We've been pushing them to arrest her, but they've been dragging their feet. Goddamned French. No wonder they need us to win their war."

I want to reach across the desk and slap the ignoramus. Okay, I'm better than that, except in my own mind. Take a deep breath. I pull a reporter's notebook from my inside coat pocket and make a show of reviewing my notes. "I understand that Miss Simmons came into your office and talked with a Lieutenant Malone with a rather different story."

"So she alleges. Malone filed no report to corroborate that."

"The lieutenant wouldn't be in today, would he?"

"Is it relevant to anything in particular?"

"Your career."

"Major . . ." Burrows's eyes narrow.

"Think of me as an extension of Colonel Nolan. Now, get the lieutenant in here."

Burrows picks up his phone and asks Malone to join us. A knock on the door a minute later makes me look up.

"Enter," Burrows says.

Malone opens the door and walks in. "Sir?"

"Close the door," I say. Burrows frowns and begins to say something, but I cut him off. I've had it with this clown. "Lieutenant, did a Miss Simmons meet with you on Sunday, May 26 to report that two officers had attempted to rape her the night before?"

Malone shifts on his feet and stands in an uneasy version of the at-ease position. His eyes show momentary shock and quickly swipe by mine, then to Burrows as though looking for support. His hands are restless. "Well . . . you see, sir. The broad came in with wild claims that could hardly be credible, and there are no witnesses or corroborating evidence. She was hysterical."

"I see. Describe what you mean by hysterical," I say.

"Well, sir, you know how dames can be. Distraught, agitated."

"Lying?" I ask.

"I'll stake my reputation on that." Malone squares his shoulders.

He is.

"Specifics." I have no more pity for this bastard than a spider for a fly.

"I don't recall all of them, sir. The matter didn't even rise to a level that justified keeping notes. But she is attractive enough, I suppose. No beauty, as I recall, but, well, you know." His hands fidget; there's a slight twitch in his right eye. "Besides, she's a reporter. You know how they are."

I stare into Malone's eyes. "Oh, and how are they, Lieutenant?"

Spider. Fly.

"If I may speak freely?"

"I expect no less."

"Well, I think most of 'em are as much the enemy as the Kaiser. Why, we have to tiptoe around them. Like walking on eggshells. We have a war to fight."

My throat tightens. It's struggle to keep my voice even. "So, her complaint cannot be credible since she is a member of a press that is conspiring day and night to fabricate false stories to undermine the war effort."

"Exactly, sir. Well put."

Burrows shifts in his chair, scowling. At least he's listening.

"Want to know why it's well put?" I ask. Malone nods. I fix my eyes on the lieutenant. "I learned writing precision when I worked as a reporter in Chicago. I honed it working as an assistant editor at the *Minneapolis Tribune*."

"Sorry, sir, I . . . didn't mean you."

"The hell you didn't—"

"So you didn't write up a report." Burrows's interruption keeps me in my seat. Good thing. I need to keep my composure.

"You know the effect such a report would have on these men."

"And the bag she brought in, with her ripped clothing?" I ask.

Malone's eyes widen with shock. "I figured she ripped it up herself. No chain of evidence. It wouldn't be admissible. How did you know—"

"What did you do with it?" Burrows asks, his face red. Maybe he's figuring it out.

"Um . . ." Malone shifts from foot to foot, gazing above Burrows's head. "Tossed it in the trash."

Burrows scowls. "I asked you about the report, remember? After I interrogated the young woman. You told me you'd never heard of her."

Malone's face pales. "Sir, Ralph Buck's a fine officer. Class ahead of me at the academy. Captain of the debate team. I—"

"Lied to me. That'll be all, Lieutenant. Dismissed." After Malone leaves, Burrows turns an embarrassed expression toward me. "Jeez, I really raked that girl over the coals. I supported Buck when the French asked about the matter."

"Let me add a layer to this mess. Miss Simmons *is* a reporter. She has elected to not pursue the matter in the press. So far. Probably too embarrassing for her. We both know how rape victims are treated. Hell, man, the way you and Malone treated Simmons. To make matters worse —for you and your office—she had been out for a drink with two American reporters and their wives that evening. New York Bar. Neither of them are lightweights. You probably aren't aware of that. I questioned them. They told me that, though she drank one glass of wine, she was not drunk; they heard Martel make lewd comments to her at the bar; they'll tell you that she dressed professionally—nothing provocative. Finally, Buck and Martel were inebriated and staggered out of the bar moments after her. These reporters witnessed no enticement at all, and they saw everything except the assault. I know for a fact that these correspondents have cowritten an exposé. Worse, contacts tell me that they have a way to get their stories back to the States without submitting them to our censors. Imagine how your department and career will look when that hits the newsstands in Washington. You and Malone are named in the article."

"Shit."

"It gets worse. Floyd Gibbons has caught wind of this. He was at the New York that night and saw Miss Simmons leave on steady feet while Buck and Martel staggered after her."

Burrows's face is pale. A fine sweat breaks out on his forehead.

"Know what the best way to make up for that is?" My pulse slows and my neck muscles relax. "One of my lieutenants told me a story . . ." I describe what Green's French friend said. "I don't mean to tell you your business . . ."

"Give me the name of that French officer. I'll get the rest from him."

Chapter Forty-One
Major Ira Cunningham

Tuesday, June 18

The reflection of my face in the glass shows desolation as I gaze out the window of my hotel room on the Paris morning. Bill haunts me along with the guilt of burdening Alice. I don't know how Ab will carry on after hearing about Jack. I'm like a man being drawn and quartered trying to reach out to all the people I love here—Trudy, Alice, Ab —while figuring out how to neutralize Martel. A juggler with too many objects in the air. Not balls. Knives. One pointed at my daughter's heart.

This is a subtle game, with critical moves around the corner. But someone else is playing an even more subtle hand. I have to be careful to not tangle my lines with that person, especially if it's Colonel Nolan.

Burrows seems adequately motivated to sort things out now that a sufficient threat hangs over him. To do more at this point might invite questions about my objectivity. I can always up the ante, but not now.

I head to Trudy's hospital after a light breakfast, pressure building, restlessness churning my gut. The parking lot in front of the Annex hums with activity. Do the ambulances ever stop coming and going? I walk into reception and ask for Emily Enright. The receptionist makes a call, and I take a seat along the wall to be out of the way. Older

Frenchmen lug stretchers with soldiers wearing soiled uniforms and bloody bandages. The amputees are depressing—moaning, crying out when jostled the wrong way. The place smells of earth, shit, and pus.

Emily winds her way between stretchers and smiles at me. I stand and shake her hand, wanting to hug my friend, but this is not the time or place. Emily raises an eyebrow.

"Fact-finding mission. Investigating a report that our medical folks haven't done their jobs well. So, I thought a good place to start would be to ask the men who came through that system."

"Good day for it. Quieter than most."

The lobby is crowded with boys Trudy's age on stretchers, the walking wounded. Litter-bearers rush by, shouting, carrying a soldier, his head engulfed in a blood-soaked bandage. I think about Jack and slide shaking hands into my trouser pockets.

The faces of the rest share a sameness in their filth. "This is quiet?"

"Where do you want to start?"

"Any colonels?"

"One."

Emily leads the way up the stairs and stops at the door of a ward. "This is where Trudy and Alice work. These are marine officers from Belleau Wood." She peers around the ward. "Oh, there's the man I want you to meet." She walks over to an imposing man stretched out in a chair, reading the Paris edition of the *Chicago Tribune*. "Colonel Catlin? Excuse me, this is Major Cunningham."

"Colonel Nolan sent me here to do some background research for a review of the medical preparedness of the Second Division. Do you mind talking with me?" I look Catlin in the eye.

Catlin gives me a hard look and folds his paper. "Little old to be just a major, Major."

I chuckle. "Same reception a friend of mine got when he reported to your division to be the medical liaison a few weeks ago."

Catlin seems to think for a moment. "Pops?"

"If you mean Ab Johnson, yes."

We talk for about ten minutes. Catlin had been too busy dealing with the operations of his regiment to notice the medical disaster until it engulfed him. My eyes rove around the ward at times, but I don't see

Trudy or Alice. "You familiar with Alice Simmons?" I ask. "I hear she's a nurse on this ward."

"Not *a* nurse. The best nurse." Catlin glances at Emily. "Note that in her record. She is outstanding. Exactly the right person. The opposite of the head nurse, who, if she were under my command, would have been relieved weeks ago." He bores stern eyes into Emily's. "Note that also, Mrs. Enright. I say that in the strongest terms. When Captain Jensen performed one of my several thoracentesis procedures . . ." He smiles. "See, I can pronounce it correctly. The primary assistant passed out. Nurse Simmons didn't miss a blink and grabbed the gear before the collapsing RN could rip a hole in my chest. I am mighty appreciative of that."

"My daughter, Trudy, is one of Alice's friends," I say.

"The other best nurse here," Catlin says, his expression earnest. He motions around the room with his left hand. "Talk to the other officers. I also suggest you speak with a young marine, Private Hiram Stoops. He's in the enlisted orthopedic ward. They'll fill you in, Major."

Emily and I talk with several of the officers on the ward, including Major Berry. I ask each if they've met Jack, but none remember him.

Emily leads the way toward the enlisted ortho ward.

"Mrs. Enright, a moment of your time," a shrill voice demands. A tall, thin woman with graying hair disciplined into a bun better suited for a German approaches us. "Simmons is AWOL again. Along with Cunningham."

The corner of Emily's mouth tightens, and she flashes a brief conspiratorial glance at me. "Nurse Pickler, this major is from Intelligence. Colonel Nolan sent him to investigate charges made against Nurse Simmons."

"I told you there was something suspicious about that young woman."

Emily's face betrays nothing. "I'll see you in my office at two o'clock. The conversation we need to have is inappropriate in a hallway."

I smile at Pickler while Emily walks away. "You seem very perceptive, Nurse Pickler. Perhaps you would consider sending a full written report to my office in Chaumont."

"I didn't catch your name, Major."

"Jones." I turn and jog to catch up with Emily.

Emily stops at the ortho ward nursing desk to ask where Private Stoops is, but I keep going. Alice and Trudy sit in chairs next to the bed of a man with his right leg in traction, their backs to me. Another man sits on the opposite side of the bed wearing pajamas and a robe—a big guy with broad shoulders, mid-twenties—someone you wouldn't mess with. I stop behind Alice and listen. The man in the bed reads from *The Wonderful Wizard of Oz*. My first moment of calm. A brief respite. I dread what lies ahead for me later today.

Chapter Forty-Two
Alice Simmons

Lieutenant Grant told Captain Jensen that he needs a wheelchair ride to visit Hiram due to leg soreness. That lie gives me a pretext to get away from the ward. Colonel Catlin insists that two nurses accompany his favorite lieutenant, so Trudy comes along as well. Grant and Hiram are an unlikely pair. Yet there seems to be more than Belleau Wood bonding them. Sort of like city and country cousins who become close friends despite their differences—one with electric lights in his house and a car in his garage, the other with a coal oil lantern and a swaybacked mule in his shed.

Grant's honesty has grown on me. I think of him as a rock—not the inanimate type, but in the sense of someone solid, dependable, predictable. Someone I can count on. Romantic as granite, too, which is all right with me. Certainly not handsome like Captain Jensen. I'm torn in a way I've never experienced. Jensen seems interested in me—I catch the sidelong looks, the momentary touch of his hand guiding mine during a procedure. But the handsome ones weren't created for me. I'm so gawky, awkward, owlish in my damned glasses. That's part of the reason I kept Jack's interest at the friendship level. Dalliances are short-lived, and I love him too much to lose him as a friend. Loved him. I wouldn't have admitted to that word before.

I was there to watch Trudy fall in love with Bill. It had not been infatuation; no fireworks, no sudden drama. More like my friendship with Jack. It snuck up on them. The kind of love that lasts a lifetime. My friend beams at Hiram. Grant averts his eyes a bit too quickly when I look across at him. That's the other way he's like a rock—doesn't say much.

"Um. So. Okay. It says: 'That is true, said the Scarecrow. You see, he continued' . . . um." Hiram's lips move, sounding out a word. "Okay. 'Con . . . fi . . . dentially, I don't mind my legs and arms and body being stuffed, because I cannot get hurt. If anyone . . . treads on my toes or sticks a pin into me, it doesn't . . . matter, for I can't feel it. But I do not want people to call me a fool, and if my head stays stuffed with straw instead of with . . . brains, as yours is, how am I ever to know anything?'"

Hiram stares at the page, lost in thought. He hands the book to me. "Your turn, eh?"

I clear my throat and make my voice small. "'I understand how you feel, said the little girl, who was truly sorry for him. If you will come with me, I'll ask Oz to do all he can for you.'"

Hiram says, "I get it, Miss Alice. You're my Dorothy."

"You betcha." I choke. Tears stream from my eyes. I want to smack myself. What's wrong with me? I've read the book with dry eyes before. Something lets loose. I can't control myself. It's like all the tears I haven't shed for all those years chose this moment to come out. Grant has his eyes on me, as though looking past my spectacles.

The sound of someone behind me makes me turn. "Major Cunningham . . ."

Ira wipes his own eyes, gazing across the ward. Trudy stands and hugs Ira. "Thanks for being here, Dad."

Emily enters the ward and approaches. She pats Ira on the back and whispers, "Alice and Trudy do this with my blessing."

"Your reading is coming along, Hiram," Grant says.

I stand and blink.

"We might as well dispense with pretense. Gentlemen—" Ira turns toward Grant. "Trudy is indeed my daughter. That out of the way, I'm curious about you both."

"This is Private Hiram Stoops," I say. "He is a litter-bearer with the Sixth Marine Regiment, from a farm near Osakis. Our literacy project and new friend. That surly looking fellow trying to decide whether to stand at attention or not is Lieutenant Ben Grant. He's a Chicago cop in his other life."

"Sir, Miss Alice is teaching me my letters," Hiram says. "Didn't get much of a chance first time 'round, 'n so."

"Lieutenant Grant and Private Stoops were both wounded on the sixth, at Belleau Wood," I say.

"Oh. That's the official reason I'm here. There've been charges that the medical care at the battle wasn't adequate. Your impressions matter to me, Private."

"Well, um. You see." Hiram has a perplexed look. "I'm pretty much at the bottom, dontchaknow."

"Then you're exactly who I need to ask. Was it organized? Did they give you the equipment you needed? Did you get clear orders?"

"No, sir. We tried, best we could, but the doctors and corpsmen didn't have much gear, 'n so. Not enough stretchers—well, not enough of nothing. Everything was mixed up, but the doctors didn't cause that."

"How were the corpsmen?"

"Heroes. Ran right into the machine guns like the riflemen. A lot died."

"The doctors?"

"Sir, bullets and artillery don't know the difference 'tween a marine and a doctor."

"I have others to talk to, so I better be going," Ira says. "Girls, can I buy you a late supper? We need to have a conversation."

Chapter Forty-Three
Major Ira Cunningham

My heart surges at the sight of Trudy when I mosey into her ward around eight. The courage drains out of me with her anxious smile. How will I pick up the pieces?

Nurse Pickler stands behind Trudy and Alice at the nursing station, looking over their shoulders like a first-grade teacher as they write in patient charts. "Nurse Pickler?"

"Major Jones."

Trudy looks up in surprise. "These two nurses and I have an appointment . . ." I look at my wristwatch with a flourish. "Now. Will you excuse us?"

Trudy narrows her eyes, and I hope she catches my Jones ruse.

"Colonel Nolan's investigation?" Pickler asks.

"Hush-hush, remember," I whisper to Pickler and catch up with Alice and Trudy. A quick look back at Nurse Pickler, and I nod to her like there's a secret between us before leaving the ward. In the hallway I say, "Looked like you'd never get out of there."

"She always finds a way," Alice says. "Who is Jones?"

"I'm in intelligence now, remember? That's my code name." I try to grin. "We're all either Smith or Jones."

"Where did Colonel Nolan order us to eat?" Trudy asks.

"That little brasserie two blocks north, I'm thinking."

"I have a lot to do here before my day is done," Alice says. "Could we do the cafeteria?"

"She's right, Dad. We write letters, usually till after ten," Trudy says.

"Rain check, then," I say. "Lead the way."

The large cafeteria is about half full of nurses and others eating at bench tables. I find an open table away from the crowd and dig into a plate of meat loaf, potatoes, and carrots, thinking about the slop the men at the front get on the rare occasions they have hot food. And I think about how to tell my daughter the terrible news. The girls join me and eat as though it's their first meal in a week.

"Any word about Bill?" Trudy blurts.

"I have looked but have not found anything, sweetie. I don't know where he is." I'm not sure I can tell her.

"But you're in intelligence; you should be able to find him . . ."

"Not as easy as all that. I really don't know anything for certain." I keep my eyes on my plate. Damn it, I can look politicians in the eye and spin yarns, but I could never do it with my daughter. The ugly truth hiding behind it this time pulls at my heart. It's like being a tightrope walker with no net and a case of vertigo.

"How about uncertain?" Trudy asks.

I look up, and the hope on her face stabs me. Oh, God.

"I wish Bill would write," Trudy says. "I've been feeling pretty blue. Maybe there's a French girl . . ." Her eyes are downcast.

"I'm sure it's nothing like that," I say. The weight of this is a straitjacket. I can't maintain the charade any longer. If Trudy finds out from anyone else, she may never forgive me. Who else would I *want* to tell her?

No. This buck stops with me.

Trudy waves her hand in front of my face, breaking my reverie. "Dad. What's wrong?"

"Trudy. I have something to tell you. I don't know how, though . . ."

Fear shoots across Trudy's face. "Bill?"

"Well, I don't know."

"What do you mean, Dad? You're scaring me."

"He's missing in action. Just heard."

Trudy's eyes widen, then she buries her face in her hands, breathing and weeping in giant gulps. I wrap my arm around her shoulders, and Alice moves her chair to sit on Trudy's other side.

Trudy weeps, and I hold her shoulder tight. Tears stream down my cheeks as I let go of the grief dammed up inside—for all the Bills and Trudys and Jacks in this godforsaken war. Alice's glasses are off, staring at the table. Here, in the middle of a cafeteria, as private as Times Square.

After several minutes, I dab my eyes with a napkin and speak in a quiet voice. "I have more bad news. Probably better get it all out. They think Jack Johnson might be dead. They haven't recovered him yet, so there's no confirmation."

"Bill *and* Jack," Trudy screams, tears streaming down puffy cheeks. "Do you know any more?"

"No, sweetie. I'm so sorry to tell you this. It breaks my heart. I held off a little, thinking he'd make his way back to his unit, but . . ." I blink and wipe tears from my eyes. So many dreams—gone. After what feels like an eternity, I listen to the clatter of plates and trays, quiet conversations, utensils clicking as others eat and converse. The aroma of food and nearby cigarettes fills my nose. Trudy's chest heaves with sobs. There was no good time to tell her this news, only the worst times.

Alice puts her right arm around Trudy's shoulders and pulls her close. Sobs wrack Trudy, her head buried in Alice's chest. "Thanks for telling us. I'll stay with Trudy."

This is the first time I've seen tears in Alice's eyes.

"Sorry," I say. "Heading back there tonight. I'll try to find out more. Ab's taking this hard. He's all alone. Well, you know what I mean. He has nobody to talk to about it. I need to go." I stand, my hand still on Trudy's shoulder.

"I'm here," Alice says. She looks at me. "Don't worry. Go help Mr. Johnson. Send him our love."

Trudy stands up and holds me in a bear hug while she weeps.

Chapter Forty-Four
Major Ira Cunningham

The sun fades in the west, gilding the treetops and sending crimson streaks though cumulus clouds. On another evening, it would be glorious. Here, it's ironic. I told my driver to pick me up at Howard's place in two hours. The walk will help me clear my head. An ambulance passes, rustling litter in the gutters. The street sweepers are probably all at the front, or dead. Like Jack. Or missing like Bill. Families grieving in either case.

The only glorious things about war are the words of politicians, historians, and saber-rattling articles like the ones Floyd Gibbons writes about the heroes and their derring-do. And the war stories told by those not at the front. My own feelings—and Ab's—had been patriotic when we rejoined the army. We were caught up in a sort of idealistic fervor, determined to make a difference. We were both old enough—cynical enough—to have known better.

American nurses are not near the front lines of this war—yet. It won't be long before the depleted medical department moves female nurses to the evacuation hospitals, or farther forward. I dread the thought of Trudy or Alice near the front.

All of this lurks over me like a thunderhead about to explode.

I pause at a market, almost at my destination. Damn, I know better than to arrive not bearing gifts . . .

So many depend on me—to be the father, the friend, the one they can lean on, the one to bring Martel to justice. Could use a stiff one. But only one. I fear my own emotions, and I'm barely conscious of buying the liquor, walking the rest of the way, and standing at the door of the apartment building.

Howard's apartment is on the first floor, facing the street. The door swings open before I can knock.

"Hope you brought booze," Howard says.

"Glad to know there are certain constants in an ever-changing world." I force a smile and hand Howard a bag with scotch, vodka, and two bottles of Rhône. "I haven't forgotten."

Howard clicks the door lock. "Meeting with an intelligence officer. Very clandestine. Emily—pull the drapes." He begins pouring drinks while Pete Sloan uncorks the first red wine. "My goal is to ply the secret agent with liquor until he spills the beans."

"Do I need to wear my fedora for this?" Pete asks. "Mary, go get that gooseneck lamp off Howard's desk. We may need to give him the third degree. Emily—bamboo sticks in case I need to do a manicure . . ."

I accept a tumbler of scotch from Howard, look at my friends, and slump into a chair. "Okay, okay, you beat it out of me. I lied."

"That all?" Pete says. "Hell, you're in intelligence. All you guys do is lie. My question is: what about?"

"I told a senior man in the provost marshal's office that you'd both written stories about Martel and Alice. That you had a way around the censors." I grin.

"Why do you think that's a lie?" Howard asks.

"Good point. I should have asked you before." The burn is good with my first sip, and I relax. "No. Actually, I don't want to know. Truth is, I need to hole up for an hour with friends I can trust. Heading back this evening, though." But even friends don't reveal everything. I contemplate that while staring into my scotch. I tell them about my meeting with Burrows while Pete jots a few notes and confirms the spelling of Burrows's and Lieutenant Malone's names. Then I tell them about meeting with the Sûreté officer. "Look. I'm not here to tell you what to do, but I do have a favor to ask."

"Now it comes out. I knew there was a hitch," Howard says.

Maybe I shouldn't have told them about the Sûreté information. But if I can't trust my friends . . . "If the provost marshal fails to follow through, talk with Alice before you publish. If this hits the papers, she'll always be known as 'that girl' or 'the one who was almost raped.' You know what that'll do to her career. Shit, to her life. You may not need to use her name. Give me a little space on this." I don't mention the report about the medical disaster. That has to stay under my hat. "I spent Friday with Ab. He's at Belleau Wood. Medical."

"*Medical?* Sounds safe enough," Pete says.

"Not really. He's been at the front. Worse, I was with him when the regimental surgeon showed him a wound card from a deceased lieutenant, J. Johnson." Emily gasps. "Ab's beside himself. He assumes it's Jack." The next words catch in my throat. I barely croak them out. "Bill, Trudy's fiancé, is listed as missing."

"Oh no," Emily says. "Oh my God."

"Know any details?" Howard asks.

"He was on a night reconnaissance patrol. Somewhere near Vaux, the army sector south of Belleau Wood. I spoke with his CO."

"Missing can mean many things, can't it?" Mary asks.

"Yeah. One of which is dead." I take a drink. "Patrols get lost, some captured. Missing could be one of those." Hope is the thread my soul hangs from. "Trudy'll need support. At least she's got Alice. I'm worried about how well she'll be able to deal with Pickler, though. Isn't there something you can do about that witch?"

Howard pours more scotch in my glass. "You need this more than me."

Okay, I promised myself to have only one. But two is sounding good.

"I'm working on Pickler," Emily says. "She has a difficult anniversary in a few days—it will have been a year since she lost her husband and daughter. I'm worried about how she'll react to anything stressful."

"Trudy's vulnerable." I pause and sip my scotch. "I'm sure she'll be searching every ward for Bill."

"She's resilient," Emily says. "And don't worry about that other business."

"Which one?"

"Martel. He and Buck tried to get in—I'm not sure what they thought they were going to accomplish."

"I heard about that."

"I don't think they'll be back. The French fellows who work in the hospital include some with interesting backgrounds. Too old to fight in this war, but carrying patients in litters up and down the stairs builds up a lot of strength."

"Is there something you're not telling me?" I ask.

Emily gives me an innocent smirk. "I'm sworn to secrecy."

"By whom?" The scotch is helping. "Remember, I'm in Intelligence."

"It wouldn't be a secret if I said. Besides, I'm not the one being interrogated. You are."

"I might have the final fix on the way if all goes well," I say.

"Anything else I can do?" Mary asks.

"Get Alice up in the dorm with Trudy."

"She is." Confusion clouds Emily's face.

Doesn't Emily know? "Well, um . . ."

"Out with it, or we'll get the bamboo, Buster," Emily says.

Shock grows on her face, along with an angry flush in Mary's, as I tell them about Alice's accommodations.

"I had no idea. I thought it was all set for them to room together," Emily says. "Things have been so busy. I lost track. I just assumed."

"Nothing we can do about it tonight," Mary says. "Emily, first thing in the morning we'll fix that." Emily nods and takes a drink, not meeting my eyes.

"Talk to Alice first," I say. She likes that room—refers to it as her cave. She can type without raising suspicion. She needs the solace of her writing. Now more than ever. Says she feels safer there, too. Wait until this Martel business is over. I have a plan."

I finish my scotch. Breaking Trudy's heart shattered mine.

Chapter Forty-Five
Alice Simmons

Trudy stands and stares at the door after Ira leaves. "I need some air, you?" I ask.

Trudy nods. I return our trays and lead the way to one of the back doors. Convalescent patients sit on benches and around tables, playing cards or checkers. Dozens sit in wheelchairs, blankets over legs—those who still have them. Many smoke. At least two men hide hip flasks. The Eiffel Tower stands in the distance. Trudy walks as though in a trance. We head out of the park and continue west to the Seine, where we head north along a sidewalk amid the noise of traffic and waves lapping the wall alongside the river. The dank aroma of the riverside is interrupted when the breeze wafts truck exhaust past. Church bells peal nine strokes. I try to think of what to say, lost in my own memories. Bill, Trudy, and Jack during college, walks along the Mississippi River, graduation—not so long ago. Trudy sniffles from time to time, wiping her nose with her handkerchief.

Life was simpler when I kept my heart locked in a box.

The world softens to a more pleasant Paris dusk after I slip off my glasses and pocket them. I like the ability to push reality back into a blur, if only for a moment. My thoughts whirl, between my friend's fractured heart, Bill missing, another friend dead, and an overwhelming sense of loss.

We re-enter through the same door and up to the dormitory after an hour walk. I help Trudy into her nightgown and hang up my friend's uniform. It's still clean enough to use another day. Her shoulders shudder with a sob. I tuck her in, sit on the side of the bed, and stay until my friend's breathing slows with sleep, then adjourn to the lavatory for a long soak in the tub.

I shake out my hair after drying—I've hardly looked at myself in the mirror with my hair down. I brush it out, then gaze at my reflection, glasses off. My skin is clear; my hair has a few new waves brought on by days of confinement in a regulation bun. I check on Trudy and stay a while in case a nightmare intrudes upon her.

An hour later, I descend the stairs, go back to my cave, and roll a sheet of paper in the typewriter.

HEARTBREAK

What do you say to your dearest friend when she
hears that the love of her life is missing in
action? The future they envisioned is in tatters.
How does a father tell his daughter the terrible
news? How did he feel, holding the knowledge
until it nearly burst out of his breast? The news
he knew would shatter her heart like a mirror
falling on a stone floor. The depth of despair;
hope torn asunder.

Do the dreams of three little people matter in
the tidal wave of world war? Not to generals. Not
to the politicians.

And what about the kings, kaisers, and czars?
Moving their minions with all the emotion of chess

players, bereft of human feeling, hardly a part of
humanity. Playing like the gods they think they
are. But this we know to be true: they are false
gods, the last vestiges of fossilized monarchies.
But what do we say to the young woman whose love
is now among the missing thousands?

I pull the paper out, read my work through tears, and touch my neck.
The locket is gone, its necklace broken. Like me.

Chapter Forty-Six
Alice Simmons

Friday, June 21

"Don't you dare talk back to *me*!" Rage contorts Nurse Pickler's face.

"But Nurse Pickler, I was just trying to translate your orders to Henri." Betty's eyes are wide with fright.

I roll the dressing cart, two steps behind Captain Jensen. Across the room, Nurse Pickler leans toward Betty like a gargoyle on a church parapet. Pickler's face is red, eyes hot with rage.

"When I need a translator, I'll call for one. And it won't be you, you miserable . . ." Pickler grabs Betty's ear and yanks her toward the linen room.

Jensen stops, his mouth agape. Finlay's face is red; her eyes flash at me, as if beseeching me to do something. Anger boils on Henri's face. The patients are silent, watching. Colonel Catlin rises from his bed.

"Ma'am, you're hurting me," Betty says.

"You'll learn your lesson today."

I jog toward the two and clamp my right hand on Pickler's.

"Unhand me!" Pickler's shout rings.

Blood drips from the earlobe as I use both hands to pry Pickler's fingers off Betty's ear.

"I'll terminate you," Pickler shouts. "You'll never work again."

I pull Pickler away from Betty. Grant scowls, but Berry smirks. Colonel Catlin winks and gives me a thumbs-up with his left hand. I take a breath and let go of Pickler's hand, keeping my voice even and deliberate. "Nurse Pickler, calm down." I drop to a whisper. "Let's go outside."

Pickler stands still, back rigid, head high, arms across her chest.

Jensen walks toward us, Henri at his side. "Please." I face Pickler. "For all our sakes. I know you hate me, but I don't hate you. Let's not make a scene that could end *your* career." Lieutenant Grant is at my side. "Captain Jensen, Nurse Pickler and I are going to sit down with Mrs. Enright. Finlay and Trudy can cover for us. Could you call Mrs. Enright and let her know we're coming?"

A dumbfounded expression crosses Jensen's face. He shakes his head, as if to clear his ears. "Sure you want to do this?"

"Never surer."

Two lieutenants begin to clap, followed by those who can as I usher Pickler out. She says nothing, but doesn't resist, head high but with great pain in her eyes. I lead her to the entry, across the parking lot, and north toward the main hospital and Emily's office. A policeman turns and appears to inspect the corrosion on the wrought-iron fence surrounding the hospital grounds when I peek behind us. Tears stream from Pickler's eyes. To lose husband and daughter? The porcupine has a heart—one that seems ready to burst.

Pickler stops and leans against a tree. Our police shadow does the same, a hundred feet back, and lights a cigarette. Pickler holds a handkerchief to her eyes. "She was just thirteen. So full of life. A car—the brakes supposedly failed. Hit them both. They were alive when they got to the hospital. She deteriorated that night. The aide didn't recognize the signs, didn't alert the nurse or doctor. Francine died. One year ago—today. My husband, Harold, two days later—I'm sure from heartbreak." She sobs, wiping her cheeks with the handkerchief. "He was inconsolable. Said it was all his fault. The excursion that day was his idea, a treat for Francine."

"To the degree that I can, I do understand, a little." I tell Pickler about Justine and this time get through it without tears.

After a few minutes, I lead on. Pickler's shoulders are slumped, eyes downcast. Emily Enright is in her office when we arrive. I close the door and sit in a chair next to Pickler.

"I understand there was an . . . event," Emily says.

Pickler nods, mute.

"If I may . . ." I go on to describe the outburst and my intervention.

Pickler talks about Francine and Harold in terms full of endearment that nobody would have suspected she was capable of.

Emily listens, fingers steepled under her chin.

"Mrs. Enright," Pickler says. "I had to leave Boston. Every place I went, I saw them. When the opportunity arose, I volunteered for overseas service, full of good intentions. Things were so clean, so . . . mannerly in the urology ward." She turns to me. "No traumatic pleural effusions, no gas gangrene. Every patient bathed and gowned before arrival. No mess. None of that prepared me for the chaos of the past two weeks. I can't cope with this and have taken it out on the staff." She blows her nose in her handkerchief. "My objection to aides is not new—we had quite the argument about them in Boston. Francine's death took me over the top on them. Miss Simmons, I apologize. You are much more than I imagined you to be. I'm so embarrassed. You, Cunningham, and Finlay are the backbone of my—our—ward. Mrs. Enright, please keep that team together. They're remarkable. They need a new head nurse—one who they can count on to do her job. I need to reassess my future, but I don't think I am suited to work at this hospital. I've burned too many bridges. Perhaps you might consider the Pickle for the new neuropsych hospital. On the staff, not as an inpatient." She gives a weak smile.

Emily lets out a deep breath. "Thank you, Marion. Take the next week off. Allow yourself to grieve. If I can be of help, please call. Check in with me in a week."

Pickler closes the door on her way out.

Emily lets out a long breath. "That ward needs leadership." She points at me.

Chapter Forty-Seven
Alice Simmons

The walk back to the Annex calms me—the morning air scented with the aroma of nearby gardens instead of engine exhaust. Ambulance traffic is light. My police shadow follows. Jensen's white coat billows as he walks briskly toward me about halfway back to the Annex. He stops as I approach.

"Thank you for doing that, Nurse Simmons."

"Someone had to."

"I imagine that meeting was . . . interesting."

"Not the way you imagine," I say. "She misjudged us, and we her. In the end, she apologized and resigned. There is a heart under all those quills. A very injured one."

"You're our best, you know. You've got my support to be head nurse."

"I've only been credentialed in this hospital a few days. I'm hardly the person for that position."

"But your qualities trump time in the saddle. For what it's worth, I really enjoy working with you."

"Thank you, Captain. I enjoy working with you." My mind spins, contemplating the words and their meaning.

"Well, I mean in other ways, too. When we get a break, I wonder if you would be willing to join me some evening for supper?"

Part of me wants to say yes. To shout it out. He's a catch—anyone can see that. Most of the other nurses, except Trudy, would swoon at the thought. Jensen is dapper, a handsome face, strong chin, straight nose. Every girl's dream.

But is he mine?

I push my glasses up on the bridge of my nose and look at my feet, which seem like a duck's. For a blink, I'm in high school again when a boy asked me to dance at the prom and I said no, only to regret it for the next month. Well, longer. I shake the memory out of my head. "Let's come back to that when things quiet down."

"Fair enough." He sounds disappointed.

Same old Alice. Turn down offers, run from them, bolt for the door. Sabotage myself. I've made it into an artform.

A dusty ambulance putters by, blood dripping down the back bumper. Another swerves around the first, engine screaming. More on the way. We pick up our pace. I'm out of words, but my mind spins over Jensen's interest. At least I didn't refuse outright. Count that as progress.

Rounds start with Colonel Catlin. Finlay removes the dressings while Jensen listens to the chest. "Colonel, the fluid has finally stopped accumulating," Jensen says. "I'm going to transfer you to a convalescent unit. There are several private rooms available."

"I don't need a private room."

"Protocol, sir. You'll be able to visit your men whenever you wish, between therapy sessions. We still have a way to go with your right arm."

"Can Miss Simmons accompany me on my rounds this afternoon?" Catlin asks.

"Sure."

"Thank you for your performance today," Catlin says. "That woman's a hazard. What do you think will happen?"

I describe the meeting. Catlin gives me an expression of gratitude, and in that I see the commanding officer he is.

Jensen casts sidelong glances toward me during rounds. Romance under these circumstances is ridiculous. My neck prickles at the thought of any attachment and the gossip it would create.

After rounds and lunch, I catch up with Colonel Catlin, talking with Major Berry next to an open window, the curtains billowing in the humid summer breeze. I listen while they discuss the latest news from the front, all the while thinking about Bill and Jack. Trudy has been struggling to hide tears when she looks at the wound cards hanging from each new admission's clothing. A war that seemed emotionally distant to a reporter is now so personal.

"Colonel," I say. "Time to move to your new room. Do you want me to pack your things?"

"Go right ahead. I guess I got spoiled by Carl, my orderly. Hiram's friend. I'll be along in a minute."

I place the colonel's things in a box. The Fourth Brigade staff sent his luggage to the hospital, cleaned and pressed.

Catlin walks over. "Shall we go?" I pick up the box and we walk out, Catlin saying his goodbyes. In the hallway, he says, "Bet that felt good, chewing the Pickle out."

"Part of me wanted to pop her one, before."

"My, oh my. So unladylike."

"Nobody ever accused me of being ladylike, sir."

"No?"

"No. Tomboy when I was a kid, before these things came along—" I hike my glasses up on my nose. "—and they started calling me *four-eyes*."

"Well, glad that's over. Looks like Captain Jensen's sweet on you. What do you think—Jensen or Grant?"

My blush must radiate all the way to the Atlantic. "I have too many irons in the fire, sir. Not men. Problems. They hang over me. I can't get them out of my mind. We just heard that Trudy's fiancé, Bill, is missing. She's practically a zombie—did you see her today?" We continue down the hall. "Truth is, I've never been any good with boys. Can't say the right things, can't do what I'm supposed to, I guess. I don't know why anyone would be sweet on the likes of me."

Catlin looks down at me. "Miss Simmons, I don't know how you would look with your hair out of that proper bun, but I can assure you that there are plenty of young men who could get quite lost in those eyes of yours. Don't sell yourself short. You'll know when the time is right."

We continue down the hall and around two corners in a comfortable silence. Catlin's words replay in my mind.

"Here we are," I say as we enter the new room. It must have been a teacher's office before the hospital took over. The room is light and airy, with cream-colored walls, a small desk between the open windows, and a neatly turned-down bed along the opposite wall. A dark wooden armoire stands against the far wall.

"I could still use some help with letters home, if you have time."

"I'll be by after my shift is done today, sir."

"Good."

I make my way back to the ward. Mary Sloan walks in behind me and says, "I'm in charge of the ward until we find a suitable replacement for Pickler. I'm relying on you to make my job so easy that I don't have to be here more than once a day."

"Finlay, Trudy, and I can keep it under control. We have some great aides. If it meets with your approval, I'll ask Betty Harrison to take the lead with the aides. They all love her."

"Good. Henri is already the leader of the custodial staff and will continue to be an asset."

"What about my application for the army? Have you heard anything? It's driving me nuts."

Mary smiles and pats my right shoulder. "They have to have a senior officer review your application. I haven't heard when that'll occur. On another matter, I'll ask Henri to move your things to Miss Cunningham's dorm room. Why didn't you tell me you were living in the basement?"

"I didn't want to be a bother." My face flushes. "And, in a way, it fit my banishment."

"What?"

"I was raised to be a very good Catholic. Well, I'm not so good now. Part of that must have been in the back of my mind. I was banished—first by the press corps and then the army. I felt the same with Pickler. Well, when you're banished, living in a cave makes sense. If you don't mind, I'd like to stay where I am for now."

"For heaven's sake, why?"

"Martel and Buck. Other than you, Trudy, Ira, and Henri, nobody knows where I sleep. I like it that way. What would the other nurses think if the police tear the dorm apart looking for my spy ring?"

Mary laughs. "You and Mata Hari?"

"They shot her last year." Just like they almost shot me.

Mary frowns. "I see your point."

"It's nice and cool," I say. "Sleeping in a cave is better than the dorm. As long as the rats don't find their way in and I can use the lavatory in the dorm, I'd like to stay put."

"Henri found you the room, didn't he?"

"How did you know?"

"He's a lot more important to this place than anyone realizes."

Colonel Catlin dictates a letter to his wife while I write. He signs it when we're finished, and I slip it in an envelope. Hiram next.

Major Berry sits next to Hiram's bed, his wounded arm in a bulky dressing. Ben Grant is next to Berry with the book open before him. "'Aren't they beautiful, the girl asked, as she breathed in the spicy scent of the flowers.'" Grant hands the book to Hiram.

Hiram reads: "'I suppose so, answered the Scarecrow. When I have brains, I shall probably like them better.'" He hands the book back to Grant.

"'If I only had a heart, I should love them, added the Tin Woodman.'"

I think about my heart, and those of the men with me, and feel warm with the camaraderie, the comfort of reading with friends. I take off my glasses and rub my eyes. Friends.

Berry takes the book with his good hand. "'I always did like flowers, said the Lion. They seem so helpless and frail. But there are none in the forest so bright as these.'" He hands the book to Hiram.

Grant's eyes hold mine while Hiram finds his spot. His eyes do not leave mine.

Hiram reads: "'Now they came upon more and more of the big

scarlet poppies, and fewer and fewer of the other flowers.'" He puts the book down.

Who we should ask to be the Wizard of Oz?

An idea pops into my head.

"I'll never look at a poppies the same way," Grant says.

"Why is that?" I ask.

"The field between Lucy-le-Bocage and Belleau Wood is full of poppies. Was. One was right in front of my face when I was cut down." Grant's eyes seem a thousand miles away. Then he looks back. "Heard you gave Pickle the boot."

"I did no such thing. She volunteered to leave."

"What's next?"

"I'm not sure. Let's read. I'm Dorothy."

I get back to the cave at half past ten and sit at my typewriter.

POPPIES

The humble poppy grows throughout French farm
fields. Like a dandelion, it is a weed. But it
has come to symbolize this war. It represents the
sacrificial blood of the infantrymen on all sides
—ordered over the top through poppy-dotted
fields, as if blood has already been shed. They
are the last thing dying soldiers see, lying on
the ground, their lives leaking out among the
poppies and wheat. Some even manage to grow in
no-man's-land, where all other plants are too
weak or wise to sprout.

Children love to pick poppies and give them to
their mothers. A gift of love and innocence. When
this terrible conflict is over, fatherless chil-

dren will pick them, bringing tears to the eyes
of mothers bearing the sad memory of loves lost.
The orphaned children of France may look at them
and weep for their lost parents, lost families.
So many tears.

Chapter Forty-Eight
Alice Simmons

Monday, June 24

Hiram underwent surgery again this evening and is asleep when I look in on him after my shift. I grab my purse from the cloakroom, head out the back entry of the Annex, and stand by the door for a moment. My shoulders and neck are stiff. I haven't gotten much exercise other than the physical work of a nurse. The walk to my apartment, before moving to the cave, was about it. And now all I have to do is descend a couple of flights and down a hallway. I work my jaw open and closed, then rock my head from side to side to loosen up. The smiles I offer my patients have locked my facial muscles like a fashion model. I push up my glasses—some model. I reach up to the back of my head and pull out the pins holding my hair in the prescribed proper bun, then run my fingers through to detangle it as I start to wander the grounds.

The Eiffel Tower stands in stark contrast to the misery surrounding me. I slip off my glasses, drop them in my purse, and wander among the tents and past a pavilion where men smoke, play cards. Some stare at the evening sky. A few wear uniforms—they could be visitors, staff, or patients tired of pajamas. Maybe there's an open restaurant around here. Cafeteria food is not on my agenda this evening. A solo supper seems like a good idea—a break from Trudy's grief. I have my own to work out.

"Any chance an officer and possible gentleman could buy the lady a drink?"

Lieutenant Grant stands with his overseas cap at a jaunty angle, eyebrows raised, wearing a uniform that looks like he pulled it out of a crushed duffel bag. "Looks like you could use one. I sure could," Grant says.

"What?" I squint and shake my head.

"Oh, sorry. I thought you were Nurse Simmons, and that perchance I could purchase you the libation of your choice."

"I'm sorry, Lieutenant, it's been a long day. Heavens, a long month." I continue walking. Grant falls into step beside me. We reach the corner of the building and stop. Grant stands, staring at me. I shake my head and continue to the parking lot. "Are you up for a walk on that leg of yours?"

"Depends how far we're going."

"I don't remember inviting you, Lieutenant." I struggle to keep a serious face. Grant isn't the worst company. And he doesn't leave, despite a statement I hope he took as a joke. After going through the front gate and walking half a block, I pause and stare behind us.

"Whatcha looking at?" Grant asks.

"The Paris police have had me under surveillance the past couple of weeks. Either they've become subtler or they quit. Do you see any policemen? My glasses . . ."

"Nah. Got a nose for cops. Nobody's on our tail."

He gazes into my eyes. Here it comes again. But this time I don't mind.

"I've been trying to figure out what color your peepers are. Easier to see with the grannies off." His eyes move back and forth between mine, his forehead knitted in concentration. "At the moment I want to say they're green, I think they could be hazel. What do you call them?"

"My identity papers say they're green. I'm thinking of saying hazel for my arrest reports."

"I saw a tiger in the Lincoln Park Zoo with eyes like yours."

"There's a thought. I wish I felt like a tigress."

"They haven't arrested you, have they?"

"Not yet. I've been told it's only a matter of time before they do, though."

"I can't believe the shit they've put you through."

"You don't know the half of it. Keep an eye out and let me know if you spot anyone following us." I walk at a good clip, and Grant keeps up despite his limp. "You're under doctor's orders to not drink, you know that, right?"

"I have been so ordered," Grant says.

"Nurses—" I make my voice sound like a high school hygiene teacher. "—are never to let their moral guard down and are forbidden from any unsuitable behavior. Demon rum must never touch their lips. Did you know that?"

"Wasn't aware, but I'll keep my eyes open, in case I see any nurses cavorting in immodest ways. By the way, you look stunning tonight. I've wondered what you'd look like with your hair down and the glasses off. No wonder they make you all wear your hair in buns."

Like saltpeter for the eyes, I'd like to say. But I let that one slide—too risqué. "There's a place I've been to—once, with older, responsible adults, mind you. I'd like a scotch, neat. That should get me around the rum prohibition. A plate of anything edible would be a nice touch." At the next corner, I stop and look back.

"What brand?" Grant asks.

"Brie."

I don't see anyone following us and continue down the sidewalk, Grant limping along.

"No—" Grant starts.

"Famous Grouse."

Grant's eyes show confusion.

"It's a type of scotch. I suppose you're a beer and shot guy."

"Really know how to peg 'em."

"Well?" I ask.

"Just beer. Beat cops don't make much. I couldn't name one scotch. Out of my league altogether."

"Hmm. A beat cop who reads Somerset Maugham. Oh, and why the uniform?"

"Only way to get off the grounds. They see you going into a bar in pajamas? Figure you're an escaped nutcase and send you to the psych hospital. Getting antsy, I guess. Had to do something different."

I take a left after four blocks and walk into the bar where I celebrated with the Sloans and Enrights. We take a booth in the back. Cigarette smoke tickles my nose, and I nearly cough. An ancient waiter trudges over.

Grant looks embarrassed. "Um, I'm not so good with French . . ."

I order a loaf of bread, a plate of cheese and meats, and two glasses of scotch.

"So . . ." Grant begins.

"What's a nice girl like me doin' in a gin joint like this?"

Grant blushes. "No." He sighs. "I'm sure you get come-ons all the time. I'm not too good with that stuff." He pauses. "Well, I guess the word is incompetent. So, no, not that. I was going to say—so, thanks for showing me the watering trough. How's the beer here?"

"I don't drink it. You'll like the food, though. It sure beats the cafeteria. I'm interested to see what you think of the scotch."

"Always willing to learn new vices."

"Hmmm. Well, the Grouse isn't anything fancy. It's way below the Vanderbilts. My mentor drinks it and corrupted me. It's a good, solid blended scotch, slightly sweet, not too much peat or smoke." I smile. The drinks arrive, and Grant holds up his glass and clink the rim with mine.

Grant takes a sniff and a small sip. He rolls it around in his mouth. "I can live with this."

The waiter brings bread. I break off a piece and hand it to Grant, then take one for myself. I make an act of tasting it, using expressions I saw a sommelier in a restaurant make once. "Hmm. Less oak than usual. A hint of elm stump on the back of my tongue. Oh, and watch for splinters."

"I was going to say . . . maple. Scotch threw my taste buds off."

I chuckle and dig into the cheese and meat tray when it arrives.

"Any news about that army job?" Grant asks.

"No. I don't know what's going on. Do you think they're just trying to jerk me around?"

"Seen it done. Wish there were something I could do to help."

"Really? Why?"

"I can tell it really matters to you."

"Thanks. For the thought. Colonel Catlin keeps telling me to be patient. But that's not one of my virtues."

Grant raises an empty glass.

The waiter swings by and I order another round. "Not to make small talk, but I don't know much about you, Lieutenant."

"Not all in my chart?"

"No."

"Born and raised in Evanston, Illinois. Dad's a cop—lieutenant with Evanston PD. Cop's in the blood—Gramps too. After high school, I went to Northwestern and graduated in '14 with a business degree. Joined Chicago PD."

"Lot of schooling to walk a beat." Maybe that explains the books on his bedside stand. I doubt many beat cops read English literature.

"Yeah. Dad insisted. He joined the force right after high school. Hit a ceiling. Got a degree through night school. Hardly saw him during that time. Told me the business degree would help later. Don't plan to be a beat cop my whole life."

"Chicago's a pretty tough nut."

"I was in the precinct that covered an area by the river on the Near North Side called Little Hell. Fact that I'm here to talk to you proves I'm a fast learner."

"Don't take this personally, but I heard a lot of Chicago cops are crooked. How do I know you're on the up-and-up?"

"Guess you'll have to trust me." He chuckles. "'Course, those are the felon's famous first words. I worked with plenty of good cops and the other kind too. Like to clean some of it up if I get through this."

"That sounds like an uphill battle."

"Yeah. But not a lost cause. I'm not alone. Your turn."

I tell him my story, all the way up to the present, while we enjoy a third round. I ask for the check when the waiter returns, grab it, and lay down bills.

"I brought money," Grant says.

"My treat. Support the war effort and all that. That little trust fund I told you about pays for this one."

We walk out into the darkening night. The streetlamps are unlit, but the full moon casts enough light to see. An ambulance passes as we head back toward the hospital.

"Fact that Martel's still out there bothers me," Grant says.

We walk in silence. And the funny thing is how comfortable I am, not needing to fill the silence with jabber, the way so many girls I know do. The mention of Martel's name brings back that memory flash again. Will I ever get over it? Will Grant or any of the men I've taken care of get over their memories?

Grant and I face each other when we reach the front gate. "We'd better act like we didn't leave here together, and make sure you don't stagger." I cup a hand over my mouth, exhale, and smell the scotch. I pull a breath mint tin from my purse and give three to Grant. He takes the mints and holds my hand. "Thanks for the evening. Maybe you'll turn me into a Grouse drinker."

"Yeah. I enjoyed it too." I look at an ambulance unloading stretcher cases across the parking lot. "Look. You're a nice fellow, and I do like you. Know what I need right now?"

Grant shakes his head.

"A friend. An ally. Someone I can talk with, maybe have a safe drink with. Like tonight."

"This was nice. I'd like to do it again, if you're willing." His gaze fixes on mine.

"There's always tomorrow."

Chapter Forty-Nine
Alice Simmons

Tuesday, June 25

Casualties from a new offensive flood our ward. Many are replacement officers like Jack was. They fought yesterday and are just arriving when our shift comes on. Trudy's eyes brighten when she looks at some of them, as if hoping one will be Bill, that he's still alive somehow. But these are marine officers. Army enlisted men like Bill go to a different ward—thank God. Imagine Trudy admitting a horribly mangled Bill. My friend would never get over the trauma. I take no solace that Jack won't be among these men.

The patients are different from the ones I saw on my first day. Trudy fiddles with an irrigation on a leg wound three beds away, working like an automaton now. Betty and the French aides scurry about their chores, cheering up the new arrivals with smiles and banter. Betty and I have taught the French girls enough English to get by, but smiles cross the language divide more effectively than words. And some of the patients seem to like the French accents they hear. A gentle, humid breeze wafts away the odors of the newly arrived lieutenants and one captain. I go to the nursing station to work up the duty roster for the next week when Emily Enright walks in and motions me over.

"You passed your physical. Not much notice, but I've managed to get an officer to hear your application."

"When?"

"Now."

My heart jumps.

My breath feels short as I follow Emily. I check my hair as we pass a window and pat my apron flat. Emily knocks on a doorframe, and we enter a small meeting room. A table with eight chairs makes it feel cramped. The room is paneled, with two wall sconces on each side and a portrait of Louis Pasteur at the end of the room. A colonel sitting at the head of the table stands. I've met him—I search for his name. He and I were the first to care for the woman with the arm injury from the Paris Gun attack—the moment I saw my career path change.

The colonel smiles.

"Colonel Wadhams," Emily says, "this is the young nurse I told you about." She turns to me. "Colonel Wadhams is the head of the Paris Medical Group."

"I'm glad to see you took my advice, Nurse Simmons," Wadhams says.

"Thank you, sir," I say.

"Mrs. Enright tells me she wants you in the Nurse Corps. I've reviewed your application, credentials file, and physical exam."

"Thank you, sir. I hope everything is in order."

His face turns grim. "Intelligence put a red flag on you. Accusations of possible espionage . . ."

"Martel and Buck." My voice strains at the names.

Wadhams nods. "Before we get into that, tell me about your nursing training."

I give him a quick outline.

"Why join the Army Nurse Corps? Your original reason for coming here was journalistic. You're already in the Red Cross. What about army nursing draws you?"

I think of Scooter. "This hospital is not like anything the army planned. At times it's like three hospitals rolled into one—field, evacuation, and base hospital. Many of our early patients came directly from the battlefield. We were their first contact other than triage. They waited many hours, even days, after their wounds. Some died of gangrene and infections that could have been prevented with better nursing care closer to the battlefield. I thrive on being the first nurse a marine or soldier sees. That's what I'm meant to do."

"Given the battle losses within the medical corps, I suspect we'll be moving army nurses to the evac hospitals, maybe even field hospitals," Wadhams says. "Living conditions in those are primitive. Are you prepared for that?"

"I'll do what it takes."

"Life in a tent, sleeping on an uncomfortable fold-out cot, dirt, mud when it rains, latrines instead of toilets, no bathtubs. Are you ready for that?"

Am I? I haven't thought that through. "If our boys can do it, so can I. Besides, I'm an expert at sponge baths."

"You won't be able to file stories while doing the sort of work we're talking about. Can the journalist inside you live with that?"

It's as though he read my mind. I'm not sure. "The urgency of the medical situation outweighs my itch to report about it in real time. None of the other journalists—all of whom are men who don't know what peritonitis is or how to spell it—will ever see the things I will. I'm content to take notes and handwrite rough drafts, if I may, and report about it after the war. I want to tell the stories I hear—the ones from the men themselves." It's best not to mention I'm already doing that.

Colonel Wadhams breaks eye contact and stares into open space as if mulling something over. "The medical department could use good writers to keep a record of our work—for internal purposes and, perhaps, later publication. You could be part of that. We may need reporting on some of the actions taken by the department in the care of our troops. The press corps doesn't seem interested in these sorts of things right now. Battlefield heroism isn't limited to the men with guns."

"I'd be happy to explore any or all of those," I say. "But my interest right now is taking care of the wounded. The writing comes at the end of the day, if I still have the energy."

"Good. Well . . . the path that brought you here is unconventional," Wadhams says. "Applications to join the Nurse Corps ordinarily take place in the States. This is the first time I've been asked to sign off on one. I hope you understand that I can't approve a nurse whom our intelligence section has identified as a security risk."

Damn Martel. Anger pulses with each beat of my heart. I take off my glasses and polish the lenses on my apron. I twist my mouth to the right slightly, then put the glasses back on.

Okay, I've got to take the plunge.

I tell the whole story about Martel and Buck, not sure if it's the right thing to do or if I'm torpedoing my career. At the end, Emily gives me a pat on the shoulder, and I look up. Wadhams's face is tight—but is it anger or disgust?

Wadhams stands. "I'm glad you took my first piece of advice and focused on nursing. Now, here's a second piece: please continue your excellent work as a Red Cross nurse and be patient with us. There's a lot going on in the background that involves you but which I am not free to discuss. I'm sorry. However, I look forward to meeting with you again soon."

Emily walks back to the ward with me. She stops at the door.

"Martel," I say.

"Indeed. This a bump in the road, not a derailment. I get the feeling that Colonel Wadhams is an ally waiting to pull a trigger, or for someone else to. Ab and Ira are mixed up in this."

The rest of the afternoon is a blur, struggling to keep my focus while the interview replays in my head like a tune that won't go away. The *Wizard of Oz* reading group in the ortho ward is a respite, and Hiram seems in good spirits, buoying mine for the moment. At the end of the day, Grant seems tired and asks for a rain check on a trip to the bar. I'm not in the mood for a drink either.

Back in my cave, I roll a fresh sheet into my typewriter.

```
HOPE
Hope is all that keeps us going at times like
these.
```

Missing in action. The words pull at our heart-
strings. Emotions bounce like a bullet rico-
cheting in a prison cell.

Despair. Many will never be found—vaporized by an
artillery shell, or blown into unidentifiable
bits. A finger bone found by a farmer plowing his
wheat field a hundred years from now. Coffins
with a few bones that may or may not be from the
same person, perhaps not even from the same army,
will lie buried under tombstones emblazoned with
"Known Only to God."

Fear. Fear that he is in a prisoner of war camp.
Will he be forced into slave labor in a mine or
one of the Krupp ironworks? Will he become ill
and die from typhus, typhoid, starvation,
torture?

Finally, hope. Hope he's alive. Perhaps lost. Or
maybe he got turned around and ended up with the
wrong unit. Perhaps he is wounded, suffering from
amnesia. But then hope fades into a fog of worry:
perhaps he's horribly wounded and unable to
speak, his identity disk lost. His name unknown.

Hope is the only thing that keeps us going.

Chapter Fifty
Alice Simmons

Friday, June 28

Rapping on the metal door startles me. My neck hairs tingle. I hurry toward the table and grasp my flashlight—the only thing I can use for a weapon in the cave. The rapping comes again, a notch louder. I move to the door and listen.

"It's me, Emily. Don't shoot."

I let out my breath and open the door.

Emily Enright stands in the dark corridor wearing her uniform. I let her in and lock the door, trying to slow my pulse. Emily takes a seat at my table, scanning the room. "This really is much more comfortable than I imagined. Where'd you get the furniture?"

"Henri Barton found it."

"I wonder where?" Emily inspects the table. "This may not be a reproduction."

"I'd offer you something, but all I have is a water pitcher and one glass."

"You can set down the flashlight. I'm safe." Emily gives me a conspiratorial smile. "I have a proposal. Mind you, this must absolutely stay between us. Howard said that if Ira finds out, he'll have a fit . . ."

Chapter Fifty-One
Major Ira Cunningham

My driver pulls up to the curb outside Paris headquarters. I slide out and stretch my aching back, then bend to touch my toes to loosen up my legs. At least I can still touch my toes. A lot of my stateside colleagues can't see theirs. It was a long ride from Chaumont, made worse by the truck-clogged roads. I send my driver to deliver my luggage to the hotel where I'll be staying until the third of July.

The rubble of the building that collapsed on Ab and me has been cleared from the street. Skeletal walls remind me of how close I came to dying that morning not so long ago. The sidewalk is scarred, the little café boarded up. Workers on the first floor toss wreckage into a truck parked on the sidewalk.

"Anyone ever tell you to look busy when you're doing nothing?" a familiar voice says behind me.

"I'm supervising those men over there," I say. "See that one? His name's Jacques. Goldbricker. I'll deal with him later." Howard Enright stands next to me. "Remember, we don't know each other."

"I don't believe I've had the pleasure . . ."

I smile. "Pete and the others here?"

"On their way. Showtime still at eleven?"

"Yep. Be in the hallway by the benches. Have a photographer?"

"We're ready for your little drama."

"Of course, the censors won't let any of this out," I say.

"I'll give that a solid *no comment.*"

"I don't want to know. Just don't want our lines crossed."

"Are we in one of Ab's Montana fishing stories?" Howard laughs.

"No, nothing so pleasant or fanciful." I pat Howard's shoulder and head around to the back entrance. Ab was a wreck the last time I saw him, both from his grief and the medical logistics mess he was trying to untangle. I try to envision a happier time when he, Jack, Trudy, and I went fishing in Montana's Pintler Range, west of Butte, upwind from the smelters and pollution. But it fades into my inescapable web of worries.

Deal with the things I can do something about.

I make my way to Lieutenant Green's office through back hallways. No skulking, though, just the most direct route. The young censor sits back in his chair and puts his pen down. "Everything set?" I ask.

"I thought about doing it during the press briefing for maximal drama. They would both be there. But the brass hats in Chaumont wouldn't want bad publicity. All those reporters in the room at once? So, we'll do it when they usually go to lunch."

"Good idea. Second thoughts?"

The lieutenant shakes his head.

Got a few myself. Maybe I should warn Green—I don't want to blindside him. But the ambush is for Martel. My gut seems hollow. "Let's go." I lead the way, avoiding the hall where Howard and his colleagues are stationed. We reach the corridor to Martel's office. Major Burrows, trailed by two NCOs armed with holstered pistols, comes from the other direction. We converge at Martel's waiting room door. Then, it occurs to me—damn it, I should have asked Alice to be here. She deserves closure. My choice not to include her was as paternalistic as the decision to not tell Trudy about Bill right away.

Martel's clerk looks up when I enter. "May I help you, Major Cunningham?"

"Martel in?"

"Yes, sir, but he's in conference."

"What conference?"

"Well, he and Captain Buck are meeting. He told me it's top secret and that he can't be disturbed."

"Dandy. Major Burrows, please proceed." Green stands next to me, out of the way, and then we follow the entourage down the hallway to Martel's office.

Burrows opens Martel's door. A baritone voice growls, "Didn't I tell you to knock?"

"Keep your hands where I can see them and stand," Burrows says.

Green and I stay outside Martel's office, shifting to see.

"What's this all about?" Martel yowls.

"Major Richard Martel and Captain Ralph Buck, you're both under arrest."

"What for? Do you know who I am?"

"Yes, and you make me sick. Actions unbecoming of an officer. Assault, rape, attempted rape, multiple counts. False accusations of espionage against your victim. Hands behind your backs. Men?" The corporal with Burrows pulls out two pairs of handcuffs.

Martel's sour face seethes at me with a mixture of red-eyed hangover and rage.

Buck's voice is calm, as though he's done this before. "Major, I remind you, we're officers and gentlemen. Please dispense with the cuffs while we're in this building. We are, after all, presumed innocent. As you can see, we're unarmed."

Buck seems amused. I imagine the man's heart rate has not risen by one beat. As a reporter, I've seen criminals like this. Confident they'll beat the rap. Or simply so coldblooded that they take arrest as just another part of a bigger game. My heart rages. A trickle of sweat dribbles down my spine, my arms tense. Then the rage passes. I see the gap in Buck's smug smile and wish I had the other half of that tooth.

"The major and I have nothing to say other than to demand representation and to be treated at all times in a manner commensurate with our ranks and stations in life."

Burrows does a quick search of Martel's office, opening drawers as if looking for something specific. He grabs a small silver object from the middle desk drawer and slips it in his pocket after showing it to one of his men.

"I don't think your father will get you off this time." Burrows leads the way out of the office. The enlisted men follow Buck and Martel. "Men, if these officers make one wrong move, cuff 'em."

Martel stops and leans so his face is a few inches from mine. "You'll regret this."

I poke Martel's chest with a finger to push him away. "Not on your life. And once the court martial hears the case, that's probably what they'll give you. Unless they hang you. The one you worked over with a beer bottle died."

"You're a goddamn liar."

My blood surges with each rapid beat of my heart. That scum. And Buck, unruffled as a mirrored lake. A pang of guilt strikes me. I should have told Alice about this.

Burrows leads the procession, Green and I at the rear. I motion Green to stop at the end of the corridor next to me. The main hallway is at least ten feet wide with a terrazzo floor, wainscoting, and a tall ceiling with bright lights. I round the corner and stop. Burrows leads the procession, his men sandwiching Buck and Martel on the sides. A throng of reporters clogs the hallway.

"So much for lunch hour," Green says with a wide grin. He seems unsurprised.

Camera flashes pop like machine guns from ten photographers and at least three times as many reporters jostling for position.

Did Howard play me? Green? Sure, there are supposed to be reporters and a few photographers, but this is a mob. This could spin out of control. Buck squares his shoulders and waltzes like a peacock. Martel's fists look ready to pounce.

"Jesus, there's Gibbons. Where'd they all come from?" I ask.

"Must have been a leak." Green shrugs, his smile wider.

Howard looks at me and smiles.

Then, my neat little plan falls apart.

Chapter Fifty-Two
Alice Simmons

Emily and I walk into Paris AEF headquarters, past a surprised reception clerk who stands as if to say something, and up the stairs to the hallway where I spent so much time until last month. My arms and legs feel electric, pulsing, pushing, tense. I try to think of what to say and stop at the top of the stairs and close my eyes. Nothing calms me. I've rehearsed what I'd say if I ever ended up face to face with the two of them. So many variations, so many words. But now, when I need them, I can't remember a single one of my well-practiced phrases, those words I'd labored over while lying awake all those nights.

Improvise. Be calm and collected. Don't come off as a smartass or a whiner. No shouting, screaming, or anything that could be attributed to "just another hysterical dame."

I open my eyes and stride down the hallway, thoughts crowding my mind. The reporters who come into view block the hallway ahead like fans at a boxing match.

We stand next to Howard.

"Ira's going to be steamed when he finds out," Howard says. "You sure you want to do this?"

"Yes." I try to sound more certain than I feel. I take a deep breath and let it out as I roll my head to get a kink out of my neck.

"Stay behind me until Martel reaches us." Howard flashes me a worried expression, then pushes his way through the crowd, which parts when reporters see me. One catches my eye and murmurs to the man next to him. Others turn and jot notes. A familiar figure, now wearing a black eye patch, moves next to Howard. Floyd Gibbons stands front and center—where else would he be?—flanked by two photographers. He says something to one of them. When did he get out of the hospital? Gibbons's arm is still in a sling. He wears his army war correspondent uniform—an officer's uniform without rank insignia, a well-used Sam Browne belt, and a correspondent's armband—the brassard accredited correspondents are required to wear. One I will never wear.

Gibbons turns to me. "I told you, your nursing work is a fabulous angle. I hope you're up to this."

Major Burrows rounds the corner from the corridor leading to Martel's office before I can answer. A sergeant follows, then Martel—his face purple with rage, saying something I can't make out over the rising noise from the reporters. Buck is next, followed by a corporal. Ira and Lieutenant Green are last to appear, stopping at the corridor intersection like happy spectators.

Buck smirks, his mouth closed.

All of a sudden, this doesn't seem like such a good idea. His confident expression makes me think he has a plan of his own.

"Wait until they reach us," Howard says. "Keep your head down—I'll tell you."

The alleyway plays in my mind. The hot beer breath, the sloppy kiss, saliva dribbling, the pinch of Buck's bite. Martel's hands, his rapid breathing as he tore off my clothes.

My heart races.

They can smile all they want.

This is my moment.

"Now." Howard stands aside.

Ira's grin melts when we lock eyes.

Burrows scowls.

Buck's smile widens, showing me his missing top incisor.

I touch my neck at the memory and move into the open corridor to block the procession. Reporters murmur behind me. A flash pops. This will either make my career or destroy it. "Major Burrows, are you still planning to have the French arrest me?"

"No, Miss Simmons."

"You weren't very nice the last time we met."

"No, and I'm sorry, Miss Simmons. I misunderstood . . ."

"You believed them, not me."

"Do I have to listen to this hogwash?" Martel's eyes bore into me, then a lascivious grin grows from the corners of his mouth, revealing teeth as white as a Klan hood. "Think you're something, don't you, sugar?"

"I'm not your *sugar*." I stand two feet from Martel. Sweat dribbles from his forehead, his cologne strong enough to gag me. "You attacked me."

Martel licks his lips as if savoring the memory.

I turn to the press. "These two men assaulted me. I'm not the only one they did this to. When I reported it to the authorities, they swept it under the carpet, like so much insignificant dust."

"Captain Buck and I were tasked with a mission to seek out spies," Martel rolls with his bayou accent. "And guess who we caught." He points at me with a flourish. "She makes Mata Hari look like a choirgirl. A choirgirl. Make sure you quote me on that."

"You'll never get away with this," Buck whispers. "My family will destroy you. You'll never work again." He grins for the photographers. Flashes pop.

"In case you couldn't hear him," I say, "Captain Buck just told me his family would make sure I never work again. His father might be rich and powerful enough to pull it off. If *you* let him. Secret mission? Your table at the New York Bar was covered with empties. You were so drunk you could barely walk."

How far can I go with this? What gives Buck so much confidence?

A hand pats my right buttock.

I spin around to face them.

Flashes pop. Martel squints in the glare.

Buck's hate-filled stare bores into me.

"You're a cute little piece, honey," Martel whispers. "Save some for me. I'll be waiting for you."

I want to smack him with everything I have.

The sergeant at Martel's side steps in front, his eyes sympathetic. He says quietly, "Please don't, miss. That's how they win."

Burrows stands next to me. "It's an open and shut case, Miss Simmons. Don't muddy the waters."

He's right. Get back on task.

Burrows faces the press and reaches into his coat pocket. "Is this yours?"

My locket. Tarnished and dented. I open it and look at the photo inside. I take a deep breath, remembering the night in the alleyway. The pistol in my face. And something Ira told me, years ago: Fight on your terms, not your enemy's.

"Where did you find this?"

"Major Martel's desk drawer."

I hold the locket in front of me. "If Major Burrows needed proof of my claims, here is part of it. Martel ripped this off my neck in the alleyway."

Flashes blind me for a moment. The murmurs grow louder.

"Boys, don't forget to get a photo of Captain Buck's right hand." Words flow now. "He gagged me with it. The thumb still looks a little odd where I bit it. I don't think your father, Mr. Evander Harrington Buck, will be able to buy your way out of this one. He still does his investment work in New York, doesn't he?" I reach into my purse and pull out the fragment of Buck's tooth. "Oh, Captain Buck, here's the missing part of that broken tooth." I hold it out for the photographers. "Major Burrows, I assume you'll keep the locket for evidence, but please give it back when you are done. Here's the rest of that broken front tooth—I don't want it. See if it fits like Cinderella's slipper on that gap in his Broadway smile."

"Miss Simmons," Floyd Gibbons says, "please come closer, over here so we can hear you better. You're telling us that Evander Buck's son, the scion of the Buck family and Harrington Investments, and Major Martel attacked you in an alleyway and attempted to rape you?"

I swallow.

That word stops me.

Rape.

The air goes out of my chest.

That word.

I will be branded for life. By the act for me, by the word for everyone else. By Buck and Martel. Not my own actions. This is not my fault. I keep telling myself that.

But Gibbons is on my side. He knows what has to be said, what has to be in print. Ira once said: *There is nothing more powerful than the brutal truth.*

"Yes." I choke. Gibbons holds my eyes with a steady gaze, as if willing courage to me. "Yes," I say loud enough to be heard over the murmurs.

"And then accused you of leading a gang of ruffians, unable to admit that one girl beat them both up whilst defending herself."

"Yes."

Gibbons is on a roll. Thank you. Another friend. "Then they accused her of being a spy. Pure balderdash!"

"I faced that accusation down the barrel of a pistol pointed between my eyes," I say.

Apprehension clouds Ira's eyes when I look over at him.

"Miss Simmons, would you mind standing two feet in front of me, so my men can get a photo of you, with Major Richard Tremont Martel of New Orleans and Captain Ralph Evander Buck of Fifth Avenue, New York, New York, in the background?"

Howard clears his throat. "Miss Simmons, may I ask a question?"

Two flashes blind me as I nod.

"Miss Simmons, do you have a few words to say to our colleagues?"

The reporters hush.

This will make or break me. I hold my hands behind my back to hide the shake. "How many of you knew what paper I worked for?" An uneasy silence. "How many knew Martel got me fired? How many felt relieved? Like I got what I deserved?" I bore my eyes into a reporter known to be a strident misogynist. His angry expression makes me think about the men wearing white robes in a lynch mob. "Don't respond, please. I don't want to put any of you on the spot."

Footsteps come up behind me. Ira takes my side.

"Do you remember me?" I ask. "Sitting on that bench over there?

Most of you probably knew my name, but never spoke to me. You smoked your cigarettes and conferred with your colleagues, but I wasn't one. If you had a press club here, I would have been barred from admission.

"I came here to be a reporter. Not the story. To report about the biggest war in human history. Not to distract anyone from the heroic victory at Belleau Wood, or the incredible sacrifices by our men, fighting under horrific conditions. I don't want my story to overshadow theirs. I want you to write about Major Benjamin Berry and the courageous men he led from the Third Battalion of the Fifth Marines on June sixth. Most of his command fell in their attack, Mr. Gibbons among them. Major Berry and twenty of his thousand men made it to the edge of Belleau Wood. Berry led despite a horribly painful wound. Write about Colonel Albertus Catlin, who stood tall to steel the courage of his men and was shot down for the effort. Write about the little guys, like Private Stoops, a litter-bearer whose leg was ruined by a bullet while carrying a wounded lieutenant from the field. Write about the doctors and medical people who have done an extraordinary job under circumstances you cannot imagine." I want to go on, to name all the men I've taken care of. Scooter. Grant. Countless others. "Those are the people you should write about. Only write about Martel and Buck when you get to the dregs. In the end, they won't deserve a footnote."

I take a quick breath. "I'm a reporter. Sure, I may be a woman, but that doesn't make me inferior to any of you. In my work as a nurse, I've witnessed more suffering, more blood, more mud and manure than most of you will see during your entire time here. This war has changed everything. Get used to it or get out of the way."

A hand pats my shoulder—Floyd Gibbons.

"Hear, hear!" exclaims Gibbons. "By Jove, that's telling them." Voices around us gather steam, and more flashes pop. In a quieter voice he says, "I know the army and Red Cross won't let you publish your stories while you work with them. However, keep in touch. I'll make sure they're published after the war."

"And if Floyd forgets, I won't," Pete Sloan says.

I paint a sweet smile on my face.

The misogynist from the bar walks away, alone. Several shuffle out, eyes averted in the awkward silence.

Howard Enright claps. Pete Sloan joins him. Floyd can't, his arm still in a sling. He pats me on the shoulder and has one of his men take a photograph of us, shaking hands. Applause swells among the ranks of the press crowding the hallway.

Ira smiles and says, "I'm heading to your hospital. Can I give my protégé a lift?"

Burrows motions for his entourage to move forward, wading into a crowd that does not part to let them pass.

Chapter Fifty-Three
Major Ira Cunningham

My thoughts storm as Alice and I head down the front stairs. We took a huge risk and may have won. I felt bad about fooling Green, but I think he fooled me in return. And Gibbons—what a showman. An unexpected ally. He and Alice seemed to play off the same script. This did not turn out like I had envisioned it—my ambush was hijacked. The end result is better than I could have hoped for.

The Packard stands at the curb, and my driver scurries around the sedan and opens the back door. Alice and Emily slide into the back while I hop in the front. I'm out of words for the moment. The same seems true for Alice and Emily. So much has happened, so much has changed since I arrived. This war has set the world on its head, and there is no telling how things will turn out in the end. The ramifications may echo for a hundred years to come.

The next challenge is Alice's application for the Nurse Corps. If I can pull this off . . .

My driver heads south and skirts the Louvre and the Tuileries Garden, through the Place de la Concorde, and onto the Champs-Élysées. The tree-lined boulevard is busier than the last time I saw it—more cars and taxis along with horse-drawn carriages. One woman wears a bright green scarf, and another a red bonnet—Paris easing out of its latest nightmare. Crews of men unload trucks while others hammer bleachers together for the upcoming parade.

"Penny for your thoughts?" Alice breaks my spell.

"Other than witnessing the performance of a lifetime?"

"It felt good to confront them. To do it in front of everyone."

"That took a lot of courage, Alice. I'm proud of you. I . . ."

"What?" Alice's face turns serious.

"I'm just worried that you'll forever be 'that girl.' Some will be scared off, and others will resent you. It was a big risk."

"I remember a very wise person saying to me, 'winning requires risk.'"

"Touché. I hope you still think I'm wise by sunset. We have a lot to do before then."

"What next?" Emily asks.

"Surgeon General Ireland is visiting your hospital today. He and a few others are in town for hearings that have bound me in knots."

"What about?"

"The following is between us, okay?" I look into Alice's eyes, then Emily's. Alice nods. I know I can trust them both with my deepest secrets. Alice points at the driver.

"Corporal Locke has heard this all before," I say. "A reporter submitted an article accusing Army Medical of incompetence in their handling of the medical support for the battle at Belleau Wood. General Ireland is here to testify. He and Colonel Wadhams want to talk with some of our patients to prepare for the hearings."

"He told me there is a hold on my application—accusing me of being an intelligence risk," Alice says.

"Colonel Wadhams couldn't have approved Wilson's daughter for the position at that moment. You're in the clear now—Burrows ripped up the charges against you. I spoke with General Ireland about it."

The car circles the Arc de Triomphe while I think about that Montana stream. Ab showed Trudy how to tie a fly onto a line: *Five twists. Thread the end through this little loop. Pull it tight, and voila!* Then an image of Bill flashes in my mind, and my spirits sink. And Jack.

Alice asks, "Is there any news about Bill?"

"None. But I haven't talked with the men in his unit since they told me he went missing—they've been busy mopping up after a fight. There's a lot of chaos in their sector. They're finding men who got lost or hid to evade capture, that sort of thing." Hope can be cruel. How do I mend Trudy's broken heart if Bill doesn't show up? I think of Jack's body rotting in a field, if he's even intact, and take a hard swallow.

"Is there any substance to the report? The one critical of the army?" Alice asks.

"How long did it take the first arrivals to get here?" I glance at Alice and regret asking. She's white, eyes half a world away. Damn it, I hit a nerve.

"Scooter," Alice says with a weak voice.

"Who?" I ask, not sure I want to open another can of worms.

"He was just a boy. He died of gangrene. It took more than a day for him to get to us. He languished under the hot sun in a place he called Julie. He would have lived if he'd had surgery sooner."

"When was he wounded?"

"The third or fourth, I don't remember exactly."

"This is the stuff you can't report on. Not now. The army won't let this see the light of day—not that they did anything wrong, but news of this at home will be very damaging to our friendship with the French." I take a deep breath. "When the Germans broke through the French fortifications at Chemin des Dames a month ago, the French had nothing left between here and there. They begged Pershing to transfer the Second and Third Divisions to them. In return they promised—*promised*—to provide medical care for our wounded. They lied. They'd lost all their medical facilities in that sector to the Germans. When the Second Division went into battle, they did so with twenty-four Ford ambulances and no hospitals. That's one ambulance for every eleven hundred men. The French refused to let them set up hospitals in Meaux, where it would have made sense, or field hospitals farther forward. Wadhams and our friend Ab Johnson finagled by hook and crook—and I mean it about the crook part, from a French perspective— an evacuation hospital in the town of Juilly. The problems were a lack of ambulances and the fact that Juilly was fifty kilometers from the front lines and almost that far from here. Further, the French denied us railroad access from Juilly. That led to the problems evacuating men like

Scooter. Surgical teams worked twenty-hour days, but it wasn't enough when the shooting started. Twenty-four ambulances and three surgical teams confronting nearly two thousand casualties around the time Scooter was wounded. That more men didn't die is amazing."

"None of the men talked about that—just the long waits," Alice says.

"Wadhams and Ab, and some others I don't need to name, performed miracles to get your patients here. And, like you, they risked everything to do so. They may have bent too many fingers, and rules, to get the job done."

"How is Jack's father?" Alice asks.

"Not good. To have worked so hard. To have done his all. The news about Jack was devastating. I don't know how he carries on." Or how Trudy will unless Bill shows up. "Corporal, stop at the main entrance of the Annex." I check my watch. Barely enough time.

"General Ireland and Colonel Wadhams will be here in about fifteen minutes. Alice, I need you to get your ward spick and span. We'll tour it in a half hour. Can you do that?"

"The *Oz* reading group in ortho begins then. I'll have to cancel it."

"Don't. I have an idea . . ." I say as Alice scurries off.

Chapter Fifty-Four
Alice Simmons

Trudy and I organize the ward staff in preparation for the inspection, then hurry down to ortho for the *Oz* reading group. I pop into the officers' rec room first. The sweet aroma of pipe tobacco fills the room, adding a whiff of elegance. Colonel Catlin is talking with two others I don't recognize. He stands as I approach. "Nurse Simmons, you look lovely, all pressed and polished . . ."

"It's time for our group, Colonel. I'm told General Ireland may stop by."

Catlin straightens his robe and cinches the belt. "No time to get into my uniform, I suppose. If it's an inspection, that is."

I brush his shoulders and do a walk around, smoothing the fabric along his back. "You're in the uniform of the day, sir."

"Lead away." Catlin squares his shoulders, towering over me.

Hiram's right leg still hangs from the traction framework. A semi-circle of men are seated around his bed. His dark eyes sparkle when he looks up at me. Grant and Berry sit on Hiram's right side, backs toward the nursing station. I take the empty seat next to Grant. The rest of the group is made up of officers and enlisted men I imagine would ordinarily never mix together other than in battle. Illness and injury have leveled the playing field for a short time. Catlin settles into a chair next to me.

"Our session may be interrupted today, gentlemen," Catlin says.

"General Ireland is touring the hospital, so belay the salty language," I say. "We'll continue where we left off."

"Yes, ma'am," Catlin says with mock reverence and a wave of his left hand near his forehead.

I pat Hiram's right arm. He has a worried expression, mouth drawn, eyes showing that deer-like look. "Be yourself. You'll be fine. You're not the one on the spot today." Grant's eyes are fixed on me. "Very well." I pick up *The Wonderful Wizard of Oz*, open it to the bookmark, and look over my shoulder as I hear footfalls behind us. I hand the open book to Hiram. "You know what to do."

Hiram reads: "'They all went into the . . . throne room of the Great Oz. Of course, each one of them . . . expected to see the Wizard in the . . . . sh . . . ape he had taken before, and all were greatly . . . sur . . . prised when they looked about and saw no one at all in the room. They kept close to the door and closer to one another, for the . . . stillness of the empty room was more . . . dreadful than any of the forms they had seen Oz take. Presently they heard a voice, seeming to come from somewhere near the top of the great dome, and it said solemnly . . .'"

Hiram hands the book to Colonel Catlin, who speaks in a deep baritone. "'I am Oz, the Great and Terrible. Why do you seek me?'" He hands the book to me.

"'They looked again in every part of the room, and then, seeing no one, Dorothy asked, where are you?'"

Several of the men stand and snap to attention. I replace the bookmark, stand, and turn along with Grant and Catlin.

Ira is speaking to General Ireland and Colonel Wadhams as they approach. "These men were wounded in the initial attack on Belleau Wood. Some will be discharged next month, others will not. This young nurse, Miss Alice Simmons, brought in her copy of *The Wonderful Wizard of Oz* to help Private Stoops here improve his reading skills. It has turned into a daily performance."

"Not sure if there is a hidden meaning in my being cast as the Wizard," Catlin says.

"I read that to my son, Paul, when he was young," General Ireland says.

"Happy to see you again, General," Catlin says. He extends his left hand to Ireland. "Right one's still gimpy, sir. I'm afraid my men and I are not quite prepared for a surprise inspection."

"Colonel, this isn't an inspection. I need to talk with you and a few others."

"General Ireland," Catlin says. "I want to introduce you to the best Red Cross nurse in this hospital, Miss Simmons." I extend a hand to Ireland. "I only say that knowing that Mrs. Enright, Mrs. Sloan, and Miss Cunningham are in the army." He pauses, as though winding up. "Miss Simmons applied to join the Army Nurse Corps. Seems her application is hung up . . ."

This smells like one of Ira's setups. I shift on my feet, and a trickle of sweat runs down my back. What are they up to?

Ireland aims angry eyes at Ira. "Let's do this somewhere private. Miss Simmons, please join us?" He faces the men in the room and says, "I need to borrow the Wizard and Dorothy. You can carry on after a short intermission."

Chapter Fifty-Five
Major Ira Cunningham

Emily leads the way to a conference room. I take a deep breath. Been bushwhacked once already today. Ireland's anger surprises me. We've always gotten on well. He may think he smells a rat. Catlin and I may have pushed it too far. But there's no choice but to play our hand and hope for the best. Catlin's face betrays nothing. Colonel Wadhams's eyes seem to be somewhere else.

"Alice, wait out here for a moment." Emily shuts the door. The others seat themselves around a long table.

Catlin tells Ireland about Alice, her work on the ward, and the morale boost she has created by writing letters and organizing the *Oz* performances. "General, I assure you, I won't rest until Miss Simmons is accepted into the Nurse Corps. If the army doesn't take her, I'll contact the navy. I know a few people there."

Ireland nods. "Mrs. Enright, your thoughts?"

"I'm the one who encouraged Alice to apply. She's top-notch. The army can't do better."

"And you think the only holdup has been these bogus espionage charges?"

"Yes," Colonel Wadhams says. "I examined her credentials. We want her. I like to think I recruited her after we took care of a wounded civilian when the Paris Gun blew up the building next to ours. Martel's charges forced us to defer acceptance. That man is a disgrace to the uniform."

"Nobody has ever had the audacity to put me in the position of approving a nursing post." Ireland sighs and adjusts his tie. "Colonel Nolan already filled me in about Martel and Captain . . ." Ireland raises his eyebrows while looking at me.

I'm trying to keep my breathing even and not show the stress raging in me. "Buck. Ralph Buck, sir."

"Bring Miss Simmons in, please," General Ireland says.

Emily goes to the door and motions Alice in. Alice's nursing uniform is crisp and flawless. She stands tall and looks at Colonel Catlin, then me, eyes narrow as if asking a question.

"I think Colonel Wadhams has something to say to you, Miss Simmons," Ireland says.

"Colonel Nolan asked me to convey his apologies to Miss Simmons," Wadhams says. "He assured us that the allegations of spying were false. In fact, the general strongly recommends we get her in as soon as possible. I concur."

Ireland motions Alice to a seat. "Nurse Simmons, please. You're making me nervous. They really did that to you?" Alice nods, her eyes seeming to recede behind the reflection of the ceiling lights off her glasses. "This business is deeply embarrassing." He turns to Wadhams. "To have this happen when we desperately need nurses is absurd, don't you think?"

"Sir, I agree," Wadhams says.

"Nurse Simmons," General Ireland says. "On behalf of the AEF and my army, I apologize. The way you've been treated is reprehensible. We have a few more things to go over with Colonel Catlin and Major Cunningham. I'd like to see you in an Army Nurse Corps uniform when we rejoin you in the ortho ward. I want to hear more of Catlin's Wizard."

Chapter Fifty-Six
Alice Simmons

Thursday, July 4

Grand-Mère Elise wouldn't have been caught dead in my wire-frame glasses. I've finally found an optician who can put my old lenses in some new tortoiseshell frames, but they won't be ready for a few days. These ones migrate down my nose as I edit last night's installment.

```
The salvation of Paris shook the ennui from the
weary French, depleted and fatigued by a war that
laid waste to the northern part of their land.
The mood in May was one of defeat. In June,
anxiety morphed into abject panic. In July—jubi-
lation. And when Paris is jubilant, there's
nothing like a massive parade down the
Champs-Élysées. And plenty of wine. And kisses.
They would probably have a good bash for Bastille
Day, but the Fourth of July was hard upon them,
and what better time to show their appreciation
```

of Les Americains, who were responsible for
Paris's second salvation? American flags materi-
alized from storerooms throughout the city.

Nurse Emily Enright arranged for buses to transport those able to a section the Red Cross
reserved along the parade route for their
patients. The wounded would not march in the
parade. Many couldn't have if they wanted to.
Seeing wounded men hobble by would be too vivid a
reminder of the costs of this war to people who
had borne that burden far too long. The nurses in
charge of each ward were instructed to choose
patients who could safely make the trip and had
presentable uniforms. The recent arrivals were
out of the picture, since their luggage was somewhere between Meaux and Paris. The patients
unable to attend would be there in spirit. But
the strongest spirits—felt by all—were those of
the fallen. The selfless, the courageous, the
departed.

I take a deep sigh as I read it over. It seems unlikely the army will keep
me at this hospital. The wounded here are already filtering to the new
army base hospitals, and others back to the States. The battlefront is
moving forward for the first time in years. That will mean that the evacuation and field hospitals will move. They'll need nurses. Base hospital
construction is at fever pitch, and they'll need nurses too. The tempo of
the work is exhausting and leaves little time for writing. My typewriter
will raise questions I don't want to answer. Pen and paper? That will be
the key. Whether I call it a diary or field notes, I can tell everyone I'm
writing home and keep it for after the war. Articles or a book? Time will
tell. Colonel Wadhams left an opening for me to write a diary and even
type up some notes for army records.

A knock on the door startles me. I leave the manuscript on the table. No fears of discovery for this one, and besides, Martel and Buck are in the stockade. Trudy's hair is in the regulation bun, her uniform crisp and tidy. She fusses over my Army Nurse Corps uniform. It is blue serge with a calf-length pleated skirt and a shirtwaist with a high collar under my tunic, cinched at the waist with a belt. My black lace-up boots shine with a high polish. The only insignia are my Nurse Corps collar pins. No rank. I stand at attention, filled with pride, when Trudy is done. She offers a mock salute.

Henri has added a dresser, a nightstand, two chairs that look like Louis XIV restorations, and a full-length mirror to my cave. A small print of Georges Seurat's *A Sunday Afternoon on the Island of La Grande Jatte* stands in a frame on the dresser. Thank you, Henri. The cave has turned into a decent living space, cooler than the dorm by twenty degrees. For a Minnesotan—heavenly.

"Not a perfect fit, but it'll do." Trudy picks off a couple of loose threads, then steps back. "Goes pretty well with your hair and eyes, though."

Trudy pulls out a handkerchief and polishes my Nurse Corps pins. "There. Let your hair down, lose the glasses, and I bet Captain Jensen'll gape."

I frown. "That's the last thing I want right now. The way they went through doctors at the front, it won't be long before he moves up. Look what you've been going through. I don't think I could handle it."

Trudy turns serious. "Love isn't something you handle, Alice. It just . . . happens. You're so darned brainy. You think you can reason your way in love. My heart chose."

"I don't know . . ."

"Don't think—feel. Captain Jensen's a catch."

"He is, for the right girl." I shake my head. "But . . . how can I put it? My heart doesn't say so?"

"Okay. Just a suggestion . . ." Trudy smooths her skirt. "But then, Lieutenant Grant has a sparkle in his eye too." She laughs. "Not sure I see you as a copper's missus."

"He and I go out for drinks and all the sudden you have us married and living in a broken-down Chicago tenement?"

"I love that look in your face. False shock. My dear, you'll never live in a tenement, even if you marry a copper. But really, what do you think of Grant?"

"His defects and mine fit together . . ."

Trudy laughs in a way I haven't seen since her arrival in Paris. "That sounds awful! 'His defects and mine'? Like you're a bankrupt farmer describing the only sway-backed mule he can afford . . ." She deepens her voice and speaks with a lilt like Hiram. "Guess dat one'll have to make do. Haul my wagon, but won't be winning no races, dontchaknow?" She chortles and wipes her right eye. "You are so strange. It's like you feel awkward being a human." She pauses. "Come to think of it, that's what you have in common with Hiram—and Grant."

"A mule with a limp, pulling a wagon with a crooked wheel, and a skittish driver who don't read so good?" My cheeks warm like a wallflower at the school dance. It is good to hear her laugh, finally, even at my expense.

"No. Dorothy, the Scarecrow, and the Tin Woodman."

That about hit the nail on the head. I take off my glasses and polish them on my skirt. Trudy *is* Ira's daughter. "Just . . . don't marry me off yet. Let's get through this first."

"Through what?"

"This stupid war."

Trudy's face pales. She takes a deep breath, nods, and extends her hand. "Deal." We shake, and Trudy says, "Let's go."

I think about the changes over the past few days as I follow Trudy up to our ward. The populace of Paris is starting to return. Children play in the streets and parks for the first time in six weeks, many wearing rags and sullen faces. Refugees are staying wherever they can find shelter, their villages a toxic wasteland, still subject to German shelling. I helped Marcel and Geneviève, who turned out to be distant cousins of Henri, to an orphanage. They are living with him now. Their experience was harrowing, orphaned by the war. Herding them was the most delightful dog, Abby. But that's another tale.

French Army General Degoutte's order from June 30 circulated among the patients. I've read it out loud so often to the men that I memorized it. *In view of the brilliant conduct of the Fourth Brigade of the*

Second US Division, which in a spirited fight took BOURESCHES and the important strong point of BOIS DE BELLEAU, stubbornly defended by a large enemy force, the general commanding the VI Army orders that henceforth, in all official papers, the BOIS DE BELLEAU shall be named BOIS DE LA BRIGADE DE MARINE.

The French love dash and gallantry. The dramatic salvation of Paris in 1914, when taxicabs had carried troops to the front during the First Battle of the Marne, was a good example. And now, in the Second Battle of the Marne, the marines stepped into the spotlight—in the right place at the last desperate hour. Victory after a fight against overwhelming forces—as though the Light Brigade or Leonidas's Spartans had won. I hear it whenever I'm out of the hospital. Perception became reality, and the press stoked the fires with glee. But the medical story is lost in the clamor. I want to report that one. Pete Sloan has offered to keep my drafts safe if I'm shipped out of Paris, and Floyd Gibbons is in my corner.

Captain Jensen and I choose which of our patients are fit to make the trip and sit on the sidelines. Major Berry insists on going, though we tried to talk him out of it—he's still getting hand irrigations. In the end, we bandage his arm and say, "Yes, sir."

Lieutenant Grant rolls an officer in a wheelchair into the ward. They both wear army class A officer uniforms. Neither wears any ribbons, but Grant wears a shooting badge above his left breast pocket and marine pins on his collars. Grant helps one of the men into his coat and buttons it for him.

"Is there an army nurse available to give me a hand?" Major Berry says.

The bulky dressing wrapped around his left forearm and hand will never get through the tunic sleeve. "I'm afraid I'll have to take the hem out of the sleeve, Major."

"Well, I don't want to miss this little show, so let's hop to it. I assume you keep scissors around here somewhere."

I take out the seam and help Berry. With the ward under control, I go to find Colonel Catlin. He'll need help with his weak right arm. I find him in his room polishing the medals on his dress uniform with his left hand. "I was wondering when you were coming." His shoes and slacks are on, but he only wears an undershirt on top.

"Sorry, Major Berry's uniform took a bit of modification."

"That's all right. 'Long as we get there in time." He glances up from his medals. "Look at you, army nurse. The uniform is becoming."

I help him into his shirt and button it. Then his double-breasted tunic with a high collar and gold epaulets. After the buttons, I help him with his belt.

"Going to skip the sword," Catlin says. "Afraid I'll cause casualties getting on and off the bus. Wish Martha could be here. She'd be proud to see me on my feet again, to see my lads, what's left of them, in the parade. She'd love you."

"Thank you for the recommendation the other day."

"I have a confession to make."

"Sir?" I squint.

"I appreciate and respect your candor. And the fact that, like my marines, you're no whiner. You took on the army. Seemed like the whole damned army, at times. One person against the army? Any army? That's a losing proposition." Catlin pauses. "But you won."

It's humbling to know that people like him have faith in me. I'm glad I didn't let him down and smile at the colonel. "Thank you." The words seem inadequate. I button Catlin's tunic. "I've never seen the Medal of Honor before."

"Battle of Veracruz, in '14. Cakewalk compared to what we've been through. There aren't enough medals to go around for all the heroes in our company today." He pauses. "And those who didn't make it."

I close my eyes and take a deep breath in remembrance. Then, I blink them open. "I think that just about does it. Let's make sure you'll pass inspection." Catlin stands at attention. "You'll stand out in the crowd."

"Well, I'm a foot taller than most of them."

"It's more than that, sir. More than that."

After picking a few bits of lint off, I'm satisfied.

When we walk into the ward, I follow Catlin over to Grant, who is talking with Berry. Catlin pats Grant on the shoulder. "Lieutenant, you're looking fit."

"Discharging me any day now, sir. I'll be heading back to the regiment if I can hitch a ride."

"I imagine Nurse Simmons will miss you," Berry says with wry grin.

"Well . . . I'll miss the company. Yes." Am I that transparent? Grant's expression is impossible to interpret. My rock.

Henri walks in and tells me the motorbuses are ready. Those leaving the ward line up in order of rank. Grant rolls another man in a wheelchair. When they reach the stairs, two orderlies hoist the wheelchair and carry the officer down to the first floor. I supervise the others and finally sit in the front of the bus next to Catlin, across the aisle from Grant and Berry. Henri waves from the entry steps and disappears through the front doors. Why isn't he coming?

We ride through the streets to the parade route, quiet, watching the gathering crowd, many waving tiny French and American flags. Large ones hang from windows. Blue, white, and red, in any order, serve the day.

The bus pulls up behind a large gap in the crowd lining the Avenue des Champs-Élysées. We're at the end of a row of buses that must have come from the other Paris American Red Cross hospitals, doughboys walking, hobbling, or being carried off to wheelchairs by nurses and orderlies. A contingent of policemen keep a space clear for us. I help several off the bus. As they move to their seats, Colonel Catlin insists that I sit on his right and Berry on his left, Grant next to him. Behind us are rows of officers, and behind them the enlisted men, with at least one nurse at the end of each row. I adjust my hat and feel my hair, the bun tidy and in place. I scan the men from the other hospitals, a glimmer of hope rising—could Bill be there? Trudy's doing the same, eyes focused like an eagle.

Henri's nephew, Gaston, walks up and salutes. I'm not sure if I should salute, curtsy, or run for cover. The last time I saw him he was ready to shoot me. He speaks in French. "Mademoiselle Simmons, I trust all is in order. My men will watch the perimeter. And my apologies. My men and I treated you shamefully. I hope you will find it in your heart to forgive us. We were misled about you by men not worthy of their uniforms."

I'm taken aback, not sure what to say, remembering the revolver muzzle, and take a deep breath. "Thank you."

Distant trumpets fill the air to our left. I squint against the bright afternoon sun and tug at my high collar—it's going to be a hot one, especially in uniform. Most of the men remain seated, but a few stand and lean forward from time to time to look down the avenue. The clatter of horseshoes and marching hobnail boots approaches. A French cavalry unit in full regalia leads the parade. Their feathered, crested dragoon helmets shine like beacons in the sunlight—now relegated to ceremonial use. The men wear dark red trousers and light blue tunics. Their color guard holds French and American flags aloft, followed by mounted trumpeters. An equine aroma fills the air amid whinnies and snorts. Their leathers creak as the horses pass. Colonel Catlin calls the men to attention. Those who can stand do so.

The cavalry unit passes. Next, French officers mounted on horses lead ranks of their soldiers. These officers wear the usual dull-metal Adrian helmets of the French Army. Polished steel and brass glint in the sun. Bayonets bristle from rifles at shoulder arms. They are a sea of light blue—veterans, by the look of them. The rifles are clean but well-used. The trumpeters fade to our right, replaced by the crunch of boots and shouted commands. Two ranks of French Colonial troops pass. The American axiom that Africans won't fight is so stupid. These Senegalese, with their long fighting knives, black skin, and fierce reputation, terrify the Germans.

Someone sidles in on my right. Henri. Wearing a French colonel's uniform. Five rows of decorations glint on his chest. His face is somber, but he gives me a wink. He's wearing a dark blue beret so large it flops over his left ear. The same sort of beret I saw on Marcel Durand. It has a brass insignia clasp with a hunting horn within a circle, the Chasseur Alpin pin.

I want to say something, ask him about the uniform, his service, but a French unit approaches, all wearing the same berets as Henri. The unit stops. A sergeant orders them to salute a family across the street from us. And I see Marcel, Geneviève, and a slender gray-haired woman standing, Marcel saluting. Their border collie, Abby, sits, eyes scanning the soldiers as if inspecting them. The sergeant then orders the unit to turn and salute Colonel Barton. They then resume their march. The little family across the street waves, Marcel wide-eyed. Abby locks eyes with mine like the first time we met.

Henri points to them. "That is my wife, Sophie, with my cousins and our dog."

Confusion swirls in my mind at the sight of the man I had thought was a wine broker. A thousand questions flood my mind, but then a tune floats in the air from our left. It's hard to make out over the noise of thousands of marching boots and the departing trumpeters. Then above the clatter: "Over There." The American units near, and the music fills my ears.

The American Color Guard approaches, and Colonel Catlin says, "Alice, would you be kind enough to help me with my right arm?"

I gently raise Catlin's right elbow enough for him to complete a salute. The other men follow the colonel's lead. Four officers on horseback lead a formation of US Army troops, all wearing soft fore-and-aft overseas hats. Not a combat unit—too clean, too healthy. After they pass, Catlin asks me to lower his arm. Another color guard goes by, followed by a line of officers, and then soldiers wearing steel helmets. These must be the veterans. The units wearing helmets are all smaller. Trudy's eyes seem to examine each row in desperation as I look over at her.

"Here they come," Catlin says. The smallest unit yet approaches. They're led by officers on foot—no brass band, no horses. Their uniforms hang loose, tattered and worn. But their boots strike the cobblestones in perfect unison, and sunlight flickers off battered bayonets swaying in rhythm. Faces are hard, weary.

"Glad you could make it, Colonel Barton. Please help me again, Miss Simmons," Catlin says. I raise his elbow and stand taller, holding his arm for a crisp salute. "The men passing are part of my unit."

As the outfit approaches, one of the officers at the front of the small column shouts, "Colonel on deck! Eyes right!" The marines march by. The faces are gaunt, but their eyes are intent, undefeated. The crowd seems to know *la différence* between the army soldiers and the marines. Shouts rise: "*Vive la Marines!*" Girls rush into the avenue as if a floodgate has opened. They hand those not shouldering rifles—the NCOs and officers—flowers and kiss cheeks of marines who struggle to maintain unit cohesion and straight faces.

Catlin asks me to let his arm down as we watch the backs of his marines.

"Monsieur Barton, I didn't know . . ." I say.

Henri shrugs. "I retired fifteen years ago. And my wife had to let the uniform out a bit. It seems like the right time to put it back on."

"But . . ."

"I was a Chasseur Alpin first and then moved to intelligence. The men I trained run it now. They owe me a few favors. I really am a wine broker since I retired. Too old to go back in. Being a janitor is a great cover, no? When Colonel Nolan and another old friend told me what was going on with Martel, I, how you say, boxed two sets of ears."

"Another old friend?"

"Monsieur Ab. A contact of mine in the old days, when his son, Jacques, was a baby. Well, I called him that. Jack. My godson."

"Have you heard about Jack?"

"Yes. Ab contacted me. He's alive and well, with his father and Monsieur Cunningham, searching for Mademoiselle Trudy's betrothed."

Jack's alive!

Henri puts his arm around my shoulders. "I just heard."

Another US Army unit marches toward us—fatigue-etched faces, battered helmets, bayonets not as shiny as the marines, boots in step. Catlin stands. I help him salute. "Men from the Third Brigade, our army counterpart in the division. Just finished a battle. Must have rushed them here overnight. Nurse Cunningham's beau is in that unit, the Twenty-Third Infantry."

I blink.

My eyes find a familiar face.

Fourth one, third row.

Can it be?

"Trudy!" I point when my friend looks over.

Bill's head turns at my shout, relief flooding his face as Trudy sprints toward him. She falls in line with his row and walks alongside, like the French flower girls did with the marines. A sergeant moves as though to block her. "Sergeant," Catlin shouts, "if you know what's good for you, you'll let the young nurse accompany your men."

Applause breaks out among the officers from our ward, started by Grant, then spreads along the stands.

One dream restored, hope not lost, if only for a moment. And moments are all we have now.

Trudy waves at us, beaming.

"Is that Miss Cunningham's betrothed?" Henri asks.

"*Oui.*" And despite being surrounded by the human wreckage of war, my world seems almost right for the first time since I arrived in France.

A thought stops me. Ira. He went back to search for Bill. And now, word that Jack's alive. It's as though I can breathe again.

More units pass, and the men who are able salute the colors. Others with arm and shoulder wounds, like Catlin, let it go. The crowd grows restless as the parade peters out. A small contingent of blue-uniformed American Red Cross nurses march toward us. They have none of the military precision of the preceding units. There are no flowers or shouts. As the nurses approach, Catlin calls the men to attention and doesn't need to say a word as I help him salute. I don't know any of the nurses in the group. They could be from elsewhere in my hospital or any of the other four American Red Cross Military Hospitals in Paris. My vision blurs.

The crowd on both sides of the avenue begins to mix after the nurses pass.

I sit for a moment while Henri and Colonel Catlin chat. Henri introduces his wife and the children with her, the ones I helped—Marcel and Geneviève. Their dog, Abby, puts her head on my lap and gazes into my eyes with more wisdom than a dog is supposed to have. Warmth flows through me as I rub Abby's head. It is more than the effect of a sunny summer day—a glow radiates from her heart to mine.

A step on my journey seems complete. This was the right place to come. My original plan to report on the war went off the tracks only to lead me on a journey I never expected—one where I can contribute and get better stories than I could have hoped for as a reporter. Nobody—not the press corps, not the army, not the French—thought a woman had any business reporting on the war. But we nurses showed the men that war is not just a *man's job*. This war involves, and affects, everyone.

My next chapter remains unwritten. Will I stay in Paris or move to a hospital farther forward? I've talked with Pete Sloan about using the stories I've written over the past month with both our names on the bylines if I can get clearance. I'll be hard-pressed to write any more if I move closer to the fighting, but that is another day's concern.

Chapter Fifty-Seven
Alice Simmons

The buses ferry us back to the hospital following the parade. While ambulatory patients like Grant can now leave the hospital on passes for hours at a time, the medical staff forbids them from the carousing and drinking that will follow the parade. I help get the men on crutches and in wheelchairs off the bus. And I explain Trudy's absence for the rest of the day to Emily. I stand outside watching the other buses unload, then Henri and I accompany Colonel Catlin to his room. His lung injury still plagues him, and his progress up the stairs is slow. Will he get back to active duty with his limited endurance? Time will tell, I suppose. He's a great leader, and it will be a shame if this is the way his career ends. I help Catlin out of his top garments while Henri regales us, in his accented English, with a story from his service with the Chasseurs in the Franco-Prussian War.

The colonels reminisce and I head down to the ward. Betty and the aides are helping the men back into their pajamas. I'm off duty for the rest of the day and stop to visit Hiram.

Ben Grant, still in his class A's, sits at Hiram's bedside when I enter the ortho ward. I give Hiram a kiss on the forehead and say, "Too bad you couldn't come. It was a good show."

"And you're one nurse down today," Grant says.

"Trudy's fiancé was in the parade, though I wonder how?" I say.

"There are stories of men who went missing for days, some lost, some captured while on patrols probing German defenses. I bet that's what happened," Grant says.

"Betcha the party tonight'll be fun, 'n so," Hiram chortles.

"Just planning to take a stroll," I say. "I've been getting out so late I've forgotten what Paris looks like in the sun."

"Care for company? Got a pass, so I'm legal today," Grant says.

"Hooey! Finally, a date." Hiram smirks.

"Not a date," Grant and I say in unison.

"Yah sure, youbetcha, b'gosh," Hiram laughs.

Grant gives Hiram a dirty look. "You heard, I didn't ask for a date . . . I need to loosen up my legs and go for a walk, with or without her. Part of my therapy."

"I'll be happy to have the company, Lieutenant," I say.

"Don't do anything I wouldn't," Hiram says with a grin.

That makes me chuckle, since Hiram has never gone out with a girl. I go down to the cave to retrieve my purse and pause in front of the mirror. *Four-eyes.* I put my glasses in my purse, take down my hair, and brush it out. Why not?

Grant stares at me with a sheepish grin when I emerge from the stairs. "Where were you?"

"My room. Its location is my secret. As far as you know, I live in the dorm."

Grant shakes his head. "Tell me about it someday." He huffs when we reach the hospital's front door. "Hiram the matchmaker."

"You can't say he hasn't tried. I'm thinking of going to the Isle of the Grande Jatte. It's a few blocks west and over a bridge. Georges Seurat's painting of a Sunday afternoon there is my favorite."

"Never heard of him, but I'm game."

We walk side by side in silence until we reach the Seine, then stand on the bridge for a few minutes, watching the water, moored barges rocking along the banks. A carriage creaks by, the shod horse clattering amid the comforting thumps of barge bumpers.

"Why aren't you wearing your glasses?" Grant asks.

"I didn't feel like it. Sometimes the world looks better without them."

"Why don't you put them back on? The world is beautiful today. And you are too, wearing them."

I fumble in my purse as if I have two left hands, unsure of myself. I polish the lenses on my skirt, wind the frame wires behind my ears, then run my hands through my hair to get it back in place. Grant watches me, and I suppose I can learn to live with that intrusive cop stare.

After crossing the bridge, we head north. The few boys I've dated have filled silence with small talk. Grant seems to not need that. That suits me. I'm comfortable walking beside him in a way that's new to me. Maybe this is what it would be like walking next to a brother, if I had one. But not quite that, either. I test the limits of his quiet and say nothing as we pass rows of stone buildings and residences. Even here, the street-level windows are taped in geometrical patterns.

The aroma of fresh bread from a café tempts me, but I keep on. Bunting and a profusion of flags flutter in a northerly breeze down the Seine, which carries a faint fishy river odor. Flowers in small gardens and window baskets add sweeter notes that make me breathe deeply. We pass older men in bowler hats, bow ties, one in striped trousers and a long-sleeved shirt wearing sleeve garters. Women wear long skirts and snug shirtwaists, and there are children at play. The men tip their hats to Grant, and the children stare, talking about the brave American soldier. I don't stop to correct them—to tell them he is a marine, not a soldier. But to the public, and to the men themselves, they're all doughboys now.

We find a bench and we sit, watching the river flow by. "Do you have a dream?"

Grant seems startled by the words. He leans back and crosses his legs. "I dream at night, if that's what you mean, Miss Simmons."

"Better call me Alice. We're not at the hospital."

"Okay. Ben makes it square."

"But no, Ben. I mean the aspirational kind."

"Like, what do I want to be when I grow up?" Ben asks.

"That sort of thing." A rowboat glides by, a teenaged boy and a girl laughing.

"I didn't dream of being a cop—I considered it preordained. Well, that wasn't the word I would have used then, but the idea. A given. Gramps, then Dad, me next."

A gull dives into the water and emerges with a small fish in its beak.

"Before all this? I dreamed of being the chief of police somewhere. Not Chicago. Maybe Evanston, Oak Park, someplace like that. Where corruption isn't a way of life, but the job would be busy enough to be interesting."

A lady with a bustle and a parasol and a man in a boater hat stroll by. The woman says in French, "Thank you."

Ben gives the man a two-fingered salute.

"At least, I did until I came here," Ben continues. "Out there? At Belleau Wood? The dream died. When I started across the field, my men falling beside me, me shot down, staring at the poppies. I was a dead man. Our dreams died on that field. Now all I want, all any of us want, is to survive it."

"France is the land of lost dreams." I take a sharp breath. "Millions of them. Mine was to become the first woman war correspondent." I huff. "A pipe dream that died in a Paris alleyway. Now I just want to carry on the best I can."

We sit, silent for a time. Then Ben says, "I understand why you don't want a boyfriend. When you're a dead man walking, you don't want any hearts broken when yours stops. A lot of guys have gals back home. They talk about 'em, brag about 'em, show pictures they carry in their helmets. Pictures that now lie in wheat fields amid the poppies and dreams. I wouldn't do that to anyone. Not to you."

"I was there when Trudy heard that Bill had been reported as missing. I don't know. Everything we just said makes sense. It's rational. But I know the anatomy of the heart. It doesn't have a brain. It's not rational. Just . . ."

"What?" He gazes into my eyes.

"Just . . . try to not get killed. I don't think my heart could take it."

A tear trickles down my cheek, and I blink. A child throws a stick to his dog, laughing, cavorting on the lawn, his mother nearby, chatting with another young woman with a girl hugging her skirts. I get up and go to the riverbank. Two birds across the water dive, wheeling, then flutter up to perch on a tree branch. Ben stands on my left. A hand caresses my right shoulder. I lean into him an inch. This is not so bad. Not at all.

Afterword

This second edition is different from the first in ways that don't change the story fundamentals. It includes two new chapters that I think add richness to the story and it also simplifies some of the named minor characters.

The historical details in this novel are as accurate as I can make them. I take full responsibility for any errors. Some are deliberate for the sake of the story. This is my chance to provide some historical context and confess my sins of fictional license.

The American Expeditionary Forces (AEF) had an uneasy relationship with the press. It attempted to control the messages going home with briefings to 'guide' reporters, mixing facts with overt misinformation meant to confuse the enemy. All dispatches were censored. Journalists, on the other hand, wanted the real story. Conflict and tension between the two were as constant then as they are today. Many reporters created backchannels to get uncensored stories out, Floyd Gibbons chief among them.

One point of agreement between the press corps and AEF was that women didn't belong. Journalist Henrietta "Peggy" Hull from the *El Paso Morning Times* was the only American woman journalist to file stories from France. She had become acquainted with General Pershing during his actions against Pancho Villa some years earlier. She managed to get a few stories out before General Pershing sent her packing back to the US after other (male) American reporters howled their protest to her presence. I used her story as the basis of Alice's frosty reception by the AEF and press corps. However, the story of Alice's sexual assault is fictional as are Major Martel and Captain Buck. I am not aware of any AEF officers accused or convicted of sexual assault.

Floyd Gibbons was a flamboyant journalist prone to hyperbole in his writing. I used his memoir of the war as the basis for the creation of his character. I made up Ira's comment about "Front-page Floyd", though the characterization is true. The description of his wounds is accurate, but I do not know which Red Cross Military Hospital treated him. I used the exact text of his "last dispatch" in his discussion about the battle with Alice.

Some real people are fictionalized characters in this novel for two reasons. The first is to remember them. Now you know their names. The second is authenticity. The thoughts, feelings, conversations, and the events in the hospital are fictionalized. General Ireland was the AEF Surgeon General. Colonel Nolan was the head of the AEF Intelligence Section. Brigadier General Harbord commanded the 4th Brigade of Marines; Colonel Wadhams was in charge of the AEF Paris Medical Group; Colonel Catlin commanded the 6th Marine Regiment and Colonel Neville commanded the 5th Marine Regiment; Commander Paul Dessez was the 5th Regiment Medical Officer; Major Richard Derby was the 4th Brigade Medical Officer; Major Benjamin Berry commanded the 3rd Battalion of the 5th Marine Regiment; and Captain Holland Smith was on the 4th Brigade intelligence staff. I relied on memoirs and other material written by Harbord, Catlin, and Derby to help form their characters. A full list of the historical sources used is contained in the bibliography on my website.

<h1 style="text-align:center">Afterword</h1>

The German "Paris Gun" didn't hit the building next to the AEF Paris press office. However, it did hit buildings in Paris on Thursday, May 30th. One round barely missed the Church of Sainte-Marie-Madeleine, where many senior AEF and French officers had gathered for a Memorial Day service. Fifteen minutes earlier and about fifty feet farther and it would have been a famous moment of the war. German Gotha bombers carried out night raids over Paris during the spring of 1918, but not on the exact day I portray in the novel as far as I can tell. The records regarding the dates of the bombings were hard to find.

Wounded officers and enlisted men were treated in separate wards in most hospitals, and colonels would have been given private rooms most of the time. I chose to mix things up a bit for the sake of the story. I like to think Colonel Catlin would approve.

The other characters and events are fictional. My description of the wards and rooms within the ARCMC Number One Annex are the best I could conger from the few photos I could find. The Lycée Pasteur still stands. It reverted to its original purpose as a school after the war.

Alice's copy of *The Wonderful Wizard of Oz* was the 1900 edition by L. Frank Baum, with pictures by W. W. Denslow published by Geo. M. Hill Co. This work is in the public domain. The electronic book version of this can be obtained through Project Gutenberg or the Library of Congress. The illustrations are delightful and worth a look. I chose this book to show Alice's whimsical side.

Alice is based on nurses and physicians I have known, admired, and respected over a forty-plus-year career as a physician. I will not name names other than the fact my wife, Susan M. Piechowski, M.D. approved Alice. I would be remiss to not thank the nurses I worked with at Beaumont Hospital in Royal Oak, Michigan, Virginia Regional Medical Center in Virginia, Minnesota, and St. Vincent Hospital, St. Mary's Hospital, and Bellin Hospital, all in Green Bay, Wisconsin. My Wordpardner critique group associate, Marilee Aufdenkamp, RN, MSN, kept me on the straight and narrow.

Afterword

Medical readers might wonder about some of the medical care I describe. World War I was early in what might be described as the modern or scientific era of medicine. The Thomas traction leg splint was used routinely in the field to stabilize femoral and tibial fractures in WWI. It led to a dramatic reduction in femoral fracture-related deaths during the war. We now only use traction splints on femoral fractures in the pre-hospital setting. The Carrel-Dakin method of wound irrigation was the state-of-the-art at the time. Intravenous therapy was rarely used and very cumbersome, as were transfusions. Thoracic surgery was rare, though it can trace its modern birth to that era. Colonel Catlin's case did not require full thoracic surgery. Chest tubes were used only to treat pleural space infections and would not have been used in the Colonel's case. Repeated thoracentesis was the standard of care for hemothorax treatment at the time. I could not identify the American Red Cross Military Hospital where Catlin received his care, though I suspect it was ARCMH-2 on the east side of Paris. I invoked my writer's prerogative and transferred him.

My website: https://johnfrederickandrews.com includes a bibliography, additional background material, biographies of several of the real people included in this novel, as well as many vintage and recent photographs of the battlefield. Please catch my Facebook page for updates: https://www.facebook.com/JohnAndrewsFiction or look for me on Instagram @johnandrews63. Please consider signing up for my email list at: https://46-north-publications-llc.kit.com/743a603dd0. I promise to keep the emails infrequent, to the point, and non-political.

Acknowledgments

My thanks to you, my reader. I hope you found the story rewarding and enjoyable. Please give the novel a "star rating" or a short review to the source you used to find this novel. These, and word of mouth recommendations, play a huge part in letting other readers discover novels.

Please consider reading other books in my Novels of the Great War series. You met Geneviève, Marcel, and Abby in this novel. Their full story is in *Dogs Don't Cry*. You met Major Ab Johnson, and Lieutenant Junior Grade Arthur Beck. Their stories take center stage in *Our Desperate Hour*.

I offer thanks to the many who helped me create this novel. My first reader, Susan Piechowski, MD, tolerated my many hours of research (including two WWI battlefield tours), writing, and revision of this and my other novels. Thank you, Sue!

My critique group, Wordpardners, played a large role in helping me write this story and mastering my writing craft. They include Marilee Aufdenkamp, RN, MSN, Rex Griffin, Scott Hibbard, Margaret Rodenberg, and Mike Torreano. Marilee's nursing expertise and our shared research into World War One nursing were very helpful.

Thanks to my beta readers including Spencer and Jessica Millimen, Diana Davis, RN, Richard Davis, MD, Patti Draude, Gloria Zimmerman, Ray Rigel, Tom Mack, DDS, and Chuck de Maille. My thanks to the Gallatin River Ranch Book Club and its members: Patti Draude, Sue Piechowski, Maria Fraser, Vanessa McMurray, Amy de Maille, Christina Braggiotti, Liza Hughes, Alicia Ochs, Rhonda Eide, and Kelly Brief.

Jenny Quinlan from Historical Editorial provided great advice with a developmental edit, a copyedit, and other feedback and encouragement over the years. Her colleague, Aaron Redfern, did the final three copyedits. I thank them for correcting my always-deficient grammar and recommend them without reservation. Thanks also to Kelsey Klosterman of Klosterman Literary for her creative consultation for this second edition. More Visual did the cover art. The background photo for the front page was used with permission from the United States Marine Corps Historical Division. I took the back cover photo near the battlefield in late May of 2018.

A special note of thanks to my agent, Laurie Blum-Guest of the Renaissance Agency for reaching out to me and representing this novel. She has provided me with advice and encouragement to publish this second edition.

This novel could not have been written without heavy reliance on historical source material and years of research. A number of people helped me with review and advice. These include George Clark, Col. William White, USMC (RET), SSGT Steven Girard USA (RET), André Sobocinski, and Col. William Anderson, USMC (RET).

I took two WWI battlefield tours with Military Historical Tours, the first led by William White and Gary Andrejak, and the second led by White's son, James, and Steven Girard. Historian Gilles Lagin led our tours of Belleau Wood and provided a great depth of understanding of the battle and the people who fought it. The opportunity to have my boots on the ground in the battlefield with these historians was moving and critical to an understanding of the terrain. I recommend Military Historical Tours as an excellent provider of battlefield tours.

Discussion Questions

- Who was your favorite character and why?
- Did the novel affect your emotions? Did it make you smile, laugh, angry. Did it bring a tear to your eye? What scenes affected you the most?
- How well did the author weave history and fiction together? Did the fabric of the narrative feel natural? Did any parts feel contrived?
- Did the historical setting feel real to you? Did you learn anything new about the era and events surrounding the novel?
- Was the novel thought-provoking?
- In what ways did World War I change the role of women in society?
- How do you think Alice's childhood formed the person you met in the novel?
- How did Alice change or grow during the story?
- What effect did Alice's preferred drink (scotch, neat) have on your view of her?
- Did your view of Ben Grant change when you read that he had a copy of *Pride and Prejudice* at his bedside?

Discussion Questions

- Alice faces an ethical problem when Dr. Jensen appoints her to be his "lead nurse". How well do you think she handled this?
- What do you think of Ira's decision to not tell Trudy about Bill being missing in action? About his decision to tell Alice before Trudy? How does this compare to the way Ab Johnson learned about "Lt. Johnson, J.'s" death?
- In an overall sense, did you enjoy reading this novel? Would you read any more novels by this author?

About the Author

John F. Andrews is an award-winning author who began writing fiction in 2012. His novels leverage his fascination with history along with his knowledge and experience as a physician and a Marine Corps father. The latter has given him an intimate understanding of what it is like to be a service family member. It led to an intense interest in the history of the United States Marine Corps and the US Navy medical personnel who provide the medical care for Marines.

Andrews was born in Chicago and raised in Wisconsin and Minnesota. After earning a BA in psychology, he completed medical school at the University of Minnesota. He trained in internal medicine at Beaumont Hospital in Royal Oak, Michigan, and then completed a pulmonary medicine fellowship at the University of Chicago. He earned board certifications in Internal, Pulmonary, Critical Care, and Sleep Medicine. After a successful practice in Green Bay, Wisconsin, he and his wife, Sue, moved to Manhattan, Montana. He joined his local volunteer fire department and trained as an EMT and basic wildland firefighter, became its medical officer, and served on the department for seven years. John and Sue moved to Arvada, Colorado, in 2024 where they enjoy family and the magnificent Rocky Mountains.

Also by John F Andrews

OUR DESPERATE HOUR – NOVELS OF THE GREAT WAR

A father's search for his estranged son plunges US Army Major Ab Johnson into a pivotal battle, the outcome of which could determine the fate of Paris and the outcome of the Great War. This is a story about honor, courage, commitment, a father's love for his son, and the bonds of combat. This is the "other side of the story" to the one you read in *An American Nurse in Paris*.

DOGS DON'T CRY – NOVELS OF THE GREAT WAR

June, 1918 . . .

A dog's devotion, courage, and intelligence stand between two French teens and despair. Love and determination sustain the threesome as they flee the tidal wave of war. A story of hardship, peril, resilience, and hope. This is a dog novel wrapped inside a coming of age story about two orphaned French teens and their dog. You met Marcel, Geneviève, and Abby in this novel. *Dogs Don't Cry* shows their story.

Our Desperate Hour: Chapter 1

Major Albert "Ab" Johnson, US Army Reserve

Paris, France. Thursday, May 30, 1918

The army lied to me. And I think it's about to get worse.

My old friend Ira Cunningham—now Major Cunningham, US Army Reserve—charges toward me with a scowl that tells me my arrival is unwelcome. His fists are clenched. I overpay the cabbie who brought me from the train station to get him out of my hair.

Ira stops two feet from me. I face him and narrow my eyes. Do I extend a hand or duck?

"We've gotta to talk." Ira glances back at the building behind him. "Now. Not here."

I snatch my luggage and double-time it to keep up as he leads me into a café two doors down. Empty sidewalk tables and paper tape criss-crossing the windows to prevent them from becoming shrapnel flash a warning. The war is near.

Wary faces glare at us when we enter. The waiter frowns as he takes an order. The chef, wearing an immaculate white double-breasted chef's coat, apron and striped trousers hustles us to a window table away from the other patrons. I order two coffees, black, since Ira's French is embarrassing.

Ira's eyes don't stop moving. He's winding up.

Before Ira can say anything, the waiter sets two china cups of strong-smelling coffee in front of us.

My hearing goes haywire.

A thunderous explosion blasts the air from my chest.

Then—nothing.

Chapter 2

Major Ab Johnson

Pain pounds like a spear stuck between my nose and the back of my skull. Blood floods my throat. I'm choking and cough out a mouthful. The only smell is blood. Muffled shouts and screams barely make it through my ringing ears. The world is black. I try to open my eyes but they're caked with something—sand, dust?

Where am I?

How did I get here?

What's all the yelling? I can't make out the words.

My head is trapped. I can't move. Something solid pushes my face into a flat, hard surface.

My arms and legs pulse with an electric current.

Each beat of my heart sends a new jolt through my head. Each shot of pain stops coherent thought.

It means I'm alive. But where?

The weight pushing my head down disappears. Hands grab under my arms and yank me up. I hazard a blink. No luck. I reach up to rub the dirt from my eyes. One touch to my nose launches another lance through my skull. I try blinking but the world's a blur.

"Ab, can you stand? We gotta get out!" That's Ira's voice, as though he's shouting through a pillow.

I reach up and try to brush off my eyes without touching my nose. I blink. The blur is less, but none of this makes sense.

We're in a room. Ceiling collapsed. My face was pinned to a table in a pool of blood, coffee, and plaster dust. There are chairs, fractured coffee cups. I glance to my side and see two unmoving legs wearing striped trousers protruding from beneath a collapsed ceiling beam. The chef.

The café. Having coffee. With Ira.

"Get out!" Ira shouts.

A woman moans, holding a screaming child. A man limps away from his table holding a napkin to his bleeding head.

I grab a napkin and wipe the dust off my eyes and then hold it ever so gingerly beneath my nose. A gob of blood chokes me, and I spit it out. Ira pulls me through the shattered doorway toward an intact building stoop.

"We should go back, help the others," I shout above the ringing in my ears.

"All you'll do is bleed on them. Come on."

"What was that?" My hearing is returning, but my ears still ring.

Ira leads, picking our way over debris and shattered glass. My brain's never felt this way—thoughts dull, slow, uncertain. Ira pulls a chair over to the stoop leading into an intact building and guides me into it. It looks like a Parisian café chair. I glance back and see toppled chairs and tables in front of the former café now buried in debris. How the hell did we get out of there?

Things are making a little more sense. I'm in Paris. I blink and take in the surroundings. The buildings along the street—Paris. To my right, where we were, is a rubble pile with the remnants of walls around a smoldering crater in the center. Stones, bricks, plaster, and glass extend onto the street. A chunk of blasted wall crushed the roof of a cab. The cabbie's beret sits on a head turned at an unsurvivable angle.

I tip my head back, but everything spins.

Bile mixes with the blood in my throat, my brain too numb to be anything more than a bystander. I spit out another mouthful of blood. It's as if I'm watching through a dusty looking glass.

"Close your eyes. Let me clean up your face," Ira shouts, his voice now clearer.

I hold the napkin under my nose while Ira wipes off my face. I try squeezing the nose to staunch the bleeding. A shot of pain stops me.

Ira's face is in front of me, inspecting me with a frown. I've seen that expression before. Where? Chicago. When one of our friends, a fellow reporter, was tortured by the Mob and dumped, barely alive, in front of the Tribune Tower.

Okay. I'm Ab Johnson and this is Ira Cunningham, and we're in Paris. Got that much. The way he's looking at me tells me I look like hell.

I can see better now. I'm hurt, a building has blown up, Ira's in an army uniform—a major. I blink.

Uniformed army soldiers and officers erupt from the building to my left like bats from a cave. One small man in a navy uniform shoots past into the rubble to stand by a man cradling a young girl in his arms. I know that officer but can't remember his name. A scarlet stain surrounding a void on the center of the girl's pink-and-white-striped pinafore brings bile into my throat. A little girl torn apart by shrapnel, held by a man who must be her father.

"Trudy, here!" Ira shouts.

What's she doing here? Ira's daughter, Trudy, cute as ever, petite, porcelain skin and black hair in an Army Nursing Corps uniform and cap. She inspects my face and takes over holding the napkin to my nose.

The navy officer stoops down and touches the child's neck while saying something to the distraught father, shakes his head, and shouts, "She's dead." His name's Arthur. A navy surgeon. Where did I meet him? The man holding the girl pleads in French and grabs Arthur's left leg. Arthur jerks his leg free. "She's dead—there's nothing I can do," he shouts. The father continues to beg for help as Arthur rushes away.

A woman I recognize—Alice Simmons—picks her way through the rubble with an army captain. Taller than most of the men around her, slender, with auburn hair in a loose bun, Alice is Trudy's best friend, from Minneapolis. A journalist with an RN. My son Jack's friend from college. They kneel next to a woman whose right arm is a mangled mess, blood spurting. An older man, a colonel, joins them and squeezes the woman's arm with both hands.

Arthur rushes over, shoves the colonel away, and grabs the arm above the elbow. The colonel nearly trips as he staggers back, his face red with rage. The captain gives Alice his belt. Alice encircles the arm with it and pulls it tight, speaking with Arthur, nodding. The captain uses a short board to support the shattered wrist.

There's a little less fuzz in my ringing ears. I blink. I must look terrible—I see it in Trudy's eyes. She's been Jack's chum since childhood.

Jack. *Jack.* That's who I need to find. That's who I came to find. But he's not here. With the goddamned Marines—somewhere. This isn't the place I'll find him. But how do I know that?

I lean back in the chair, Trudy holding the napkin to my nose. Ira steadies me with a hand on each shoulder. I'm a bystander. One of the wounded. A casualty before I can even report for duty. Useless.

My fog is clearing a little.

Bells clang, engines roar, and hoofbeats echo as emergency vehicles approach. A horse-drawn fire engine pulls to a stop. The crew wades toward the smoking center of the ruin, pulling a hose. A motor ambulance screeches to a halt, followed by two more. One crew takes away the man still holding the child, pleading, crying. Another crew loads the woman onto a stretcher and hurries her away, followed by Alice. Arthur—what the devil is his last name?—and a captain approach. It seems to take Arthur a moment before recognition dawns on his face. "Let me look at you, Major Johnson."

Trudy eases the napkin away from my nose. Arthur and the captain inspect my face, telling me to blink, move my eyes, open and close my mouth. "Nose is broken," Arthur says. "You'll have to get to a hospital."

I once watched a doctor *fix* the broken nose of a union leader who had been roughed up by mine goons back home in Butte, Montana. I want no part of that. "I'm sure I'll be okay. Just need a washcloth and some aspirin." I try to pop my ears—sound is still muffled.

"No. It has to be fixed. That's an order," Arthur says.

Chapter 2

"Lieutenant, I'm not sure you can order a major anything other than a drink at the officers' club," I say.

"But I can," a voice next to us says—the colonel Arthur shoved away from the woman. "Local hospitals'll be jammed." The colonel turns to the captain. "Take him to the American Hospital in Neuilly." The colonel glares at Arthur. "Lieutenant, Junior Grade, do you make a habit of interfering with fellow physicians in the middle of life-threatening events? *Never* do that again." Arthur's face is red, I'm guessing more in anger than embarrassment.

The captain returns. Ira and Trudy help me to an idling Dodge staff car. I keep the napkin to my face to catch the blood. My head feels full as I bend down to get into the rear seat.

Ira slides in next to me. "What would Helen say if she could see you now?"

www.ingramcontent.com/pod-product-compliance
Lightning Source LLC
Chambersburg PA
CBHW032011310726
48972CB00002B/367